The Mad Raven's Tale

Andrew Walbrown

Say hi to Andrew on Twitter
@AWalbrown

First Edition
First Published 2020

Cover Design by Cristina Tănase
silverleaf30g@gmail.com

Library of Congress Control Number:
2020900814

ISBN:
978-0-578-63646-7

For CC

The Ulam to my Amantius

Prologue

My name is Rasmus. I am an apprentice mage at the Academy of Echona, where I have studied the field of restorative magic for most of my life. Currently, I am tasked with filtering through many long-forgotten texts that have been buried in the archives of our prestigious institution. My chief function, as far as I have discerned, is to determine the importance of these works and ultimately decide their fate. Many crinkled pages have been incinerated under my watch, old court proceedings about land markers that disappeared generations ago being chief among them. Parchment regarding taxes and other financial information from more fiscally-minded archmages have joined them in the embers of the furnace. All in all, it is a monotonous affair, but I must pay my dues if I wish to ever advance in rank.

Among the border disputes, tax information, and incoherent ramblings of a bygone era, there were a few books that stood out to me like a beacon in the dark. Books, not scrolls, written by someone with a superior handwriting skill many ages ago. These volumes are not decorated in any fashion; they are simply leather-bound books filled with parchment stained yellow from age. Upon picking up the first volume, entitled *The Mad Raven's Tale,* I discovered a story of two friends from different races, raised by the same woman, in a place known as Accaria. I have never heard of this place, and I cannot seem to find anything in our modern records indicating it ever existed. But if I am to believe the date inscribed on the first page to be accurate, then this story is at least as old as the Academy itself. The Academy is over one thousand years old, and this Accaria may have existed long before her.

I have thumbed through the first two volumes of the series, and have found the fifth book, but not books three and four. This gives me great exhilaration and anxiety, the former due to the excitement of recovering a relic lost in time, the latter because I am afraid I will never find the complete set. But while I search, I will take care to copy the words from the books I possess by using this newly invented device known as a "typewriter." By using this machine, as well as our superior paper, perhaps I can cement this saga's legacy forever.

The names of the protagonists are Amantius Jeranus, a naïve youth from an island kingdom known as Accaria. His foster-brother, an Orc known simply as Ulam, was raised by Amantius' mother Pelecia from an early age. In the first volume, the duo embarks on a voyage across the sea to the City of Silverwater. I know this name, for that city remains at the bottom of our continent to this very day. Perhaps if the third volume remains missing, I shall board a train southward and try my luck in Silverwater's library. Assuming, of course, my superiors approve of my absence.

Until that time, I give you the first volume of what I have labeled as *The Accarian Chronicles*. Titled by its original author as *The Mad Raven's Tale*.

Chapter 1
Amantius

A lad of eighteen years stood at the edge of a cliff, halfway up a mountain named Meganthus by the first human settlers of the island. He was taller than average, with straight, midnight black hair tied into a small ponytail at the nape of his neck. His skin was sunkissed, darkened by his love of the outdoors. A fine layer of stubble decorated his face and upper neck, a result of his indifference for shaving. He leaned on a branch he found while passing through the nearby forest, having fashioned it as a sort of walking stick. From a cliff, he stared across the ocean, the water as blue as his eyes, a serene look across his face. He breathed in the salted air, the sensation tickling his nose.

"Beautiful as always, isn't it, Ulam?" He asked the traveler beside him, who made the trek through the forest and up the slopes of Mount Meganthus with him daily.

Ulam grunted, his typical response. He found a flattened rock and sat down, pulling a book from his bag. Within moments he was reading, oblivious to the world around him.

"I have never met an Orc that reads so much," the lad said, watching as his green-skinned friend made himself comfortable on his stone sofa. "Especially with such beauty around him."

Ulam looked up, his stone gray eyes fixed on his raven-haired friend. He was large, easily stronger than any man on the island. He had two tusks jutting out of his bottom row of teeth, as white as pearl and as sharp as any knife. His charcoal-colored hair reached his shoulders, unbound, with a braid on each side. His face was a perpetual scowl, regardless of his mood. Though his eyes were deep-set, there was a softness in them.

"Amantius," Ulam began, his voice rough, yet strangely proper, "You have never met another Orc. As far as I know, I am the only one in the world."

Amantius smirked. "You have a point. And to think, if it wasn't for Mother, I might not have ever met you. And we definitely wouldn't be brothers."

Ulam grunted. It was the truth, Amantius' mother had adopted the Orc from an early age, though she refused to let anyone know how she came across the infant. Though they were from different races, she raised both children as brothers. They were met with ignorance and closed-mindedness from time to time, but those experiences made them a stronger family unit. Now, months removed from Amantius' eighteenth birthday, the two of them were practically inseparable.

Ulam returned to his book, his big, moss-colored Orcish hands engulfing the leather-bound pages. Amantius watched a few chipmunks chase one another into a patch of overgrowth, before using a blanket he brought as a pillow. Over the years his body had grown accustomed to the cold, stone ground, though his neck and skull never had. He closed his eyes, seeing the red tint of sunlight color the insides of his eyelids. Although there was a natural awning above him, the waning hours of the day slanted golden beams into their little alcove.

He never truly fell asleep, though his body had entered a meditative state on more than one occasion. Unknowingly a smile pursed his lips, as though the solar presence nourished his soul. He did not know how long he remained on the stone ground, but he knew he would need to stand soon, for his back was beginning to ache.

Ulam flipped a page nearby and grunted, louder than normal. "Interesting."

Amantius almost did not want to ask, because usually when Ulam read a book and muttered to himself it led to a conversation. And of course, the topic was never anything which interested him. Amantius had never been much of a reader, though he had learned how to do so at an early age. His mother had taught both Ulam and him how to read, but reading had never developed into a hobby as it had for his Orcish foster-brother. If anything the only use Amantius had ever found for reading was to record and memorize ballads that he would later recite to swooning maidens.

He sat up, thinking maybe if he could at least see the title of the book, he could pretend to care more. Unfortunately he could not; Ulam's large hands obscured the font. He sighed and braced himself for some dull discourse that he could not possibly avoid. Amantius had ignored the mutterings before, but he was still unable to dodge a conversation. If gone unchecked, Ulam would eventually launch into a monologue, and that was much worse than having a quick discussion.

"What is?" Amantius replied.

"What is what?" Ulam mumbled without looking up from the pages.

Amantius sighed again. "What is interesting? In your book."

"Oh," Ulam cleared his throat and looked up for a moment, "This book is about vampires, written by a huntress who swore her life to avenge her slain husband. Anyway, she wrote if someone afflicted with the disease does not convert another, then the two red marks on their body will never disappear. However, if a vampire does turn someone else, then the puncture marks will vanish."

Ulam continued, but Amantius quickly lost interest. Somehow, Ulam made something as exciting as vampire hunting boring and scholarly.

Time passed slowly as they enjoyed the evening at their usual scenic overlook. Practically every day they would adventure into the wilderness that surrounded Accaria, exploring their island home for hidden paradises. Amantius often wondered how many people knew of this spot, this little cliff that jutted out of the side of the mountain with a panorama worth dying for. He oftentimes could not believe that Accaria had once been home to many ancient beasts, having been driven out by his ancestors thousands of years ago. There was a part of him that secretly hoped that he and Ulam would stumble across a secret lair someday, untouched by time. He knew the likelihood of such a discovery was next to impossible, but that did not prevent him from hoping to find a petrified dragon or griffin's egg.

Amantius shielded his eyes from the warm beams of twilight as the sun began to sink into the ocean. His stomach growled; aside from a few wild apples and berries, he had not eaten much since breakfast.

"We should be on our way," Amantius said, "the sun will be gone soon, plus it's about time for dinner."

"We should have been on our way an hour ago," Ulam muttered, then tossed a stone off the cliff. "We are going to be late again, and Mother will not be pleased."

Amantius cackled. "We wouldn't always be late if you could run faster. I would think with legs as wide as an oak that you would have some serious sprinting power in those. But I guess not."

Ulam grunted, turning away from the cliff. He started back down the path towards the base of the mountain, disappearing behind a row of trees. Amantius gazed across the island once more, taking in the different sights and sounds coming from across the landscape. A flock of birds launched themselves from the forest, their feathers creating a rainbow of colors. Monkeys babbled to one another nearby, lemurs adding to the choir. Nearby he heard the gentle flow of a brook cascading over a formation of rocks. Amantius smiled; there was no place he would rather be than here. Even though he had never left this island, he knew in his heart this was the place where he wanted to spend his entire life. He could not imagine a place with a more beautiful, diverse landscape than Accaria, where even the air was sweet and refreshing. From what Ulam had shared in his books, it seemed Accaria was the very definition of paradise, and to have been born on the island was a blessing from the Gods.

"Until tomorrow," he whispered, then darted into the forest.

Chapter 2
Ulam

"Someday, my child," Pelecia said as they approached the house, "you are going to be so late for dinner that breakfast will be served on time."

Ulam snickered at the jab as Amantius rushed inside. Unlike his foster-brother, he had the courtesy to remove his dirty sandals before going too far into the home. On the floor, he saw Amantius' footsteps, all the way to the long, oak table where dinner had been served. He shook his head in annoyance; not only were they grossly late for dinner again, but they were also bringing the mud from Mount Meganthus into Pelecia's clean home.

Ulam hated the fact that they were late more times than not, and he knew with time their tardiness would continue to grow. He hated seeing the look of disappointment in Pelecia's eyes, one that she almost entirely reserved for Amantius. Though sometimes, Ulam was the target of her frustration. Often she had implored him to abandon Amantius to the wilderness and to stay home, telling him to detach himself from the shenanigans. More times than not he agreed with her, though he did not believe he could separate himself so willingly. In some ways, he needed Amantius as much as Amantius needed him. Without him, Ulam felt he would be trapped within the four walls of their home for eternity. Not that he was not grateful that Pelecia had raised him and put food in his stomach and a roof over his head, but his heart ached for exploration, and Amantius was his guide.

Sometimes he felt as though he should simply hoist Amantius in the air and carry him to the house, so they could not possibly be late for dinner again. However, such a sight would be a circus, and he did not want the prying eyes of his neighbors on him any more than they already were. Being the only Orc, and the only non-human, in Accaria already came with that perk. Everywhere he went people gawked at him, sometimes out of curiosity and sometimes out of fear. Children often ran away screaming from him, although occasionally some bold child would assault him with a barrage of questions. He only met hostility when sailors from foreign ports would dock in the Whaleport, bringing prejudice along with their merchandise. Countless times he had been attacked by drunken, ignorant sailors, and many times he had to knock them unconscious.

They took their places at the table, Pelecia at the head, Ulam and Amantius across from one another. To Ulam's never-ending lack of surprise, he found the meal lukewarm. Of course, he knew it was no fault of Pelecia's; Ulam guessed the food was ready to be served around an hour prior. As a result, his annoyance with Amantius increased tenfold, causing him to grind his teeth out of frustration. But as he filled his stomach with food and good wine, his anger started to completely disappear. At one point he became so relaxed he was surprised to find that he was enjoying the taste of the cold fish in front of him.

As usual, there was little conversation during dinner. Of all aspects of life, Amantius and Ulam both agreed that eating was an almost spiritual experience, one that should not be sullied with pointless banter. Ulam welcomed this moment of quiet in his life, for he did not get much of it. The only sounds in the house were the scraping of forks on plates, the perpetual chomping of food, and the occasional belching. The latter usually coming from Ulam's side of the table.

After their plates had been ravaged, Amantius retired to his room to rest while Ulam stayed behind to help Pelecia clean. Though he said nothing, he could not help but be annoyed by Amantius' laziness. *Not only does he bring mud into the house Mother has spent all day cleaning, but he also skips on chores. Why is he so ungrateful?*

"It is okay, Ulam," Pelecia said. He looked up from the pile of plates to see her smiling. "You can go read if you wish. I can clean this by myself."

"There will always be time to read," Ulam replied, his voice betraying his annoyance.

"It is fine, I assure you. I know you boys had a long day. I am guessing you went to Mount Meganthus again? There is only one place on the island where that kind of reddish soil is, and that is at its base."

Ulam quickly glanced at his sandals in the next room, covered in the blood-red mud that resides at the base of the mountain. He sighed, put the pile of dishes aside, and grabbed an iron brush. "Sorry, Mother. I will clean our sandals…and the floor."

"Oh Ulam," Pelecia said as he walked into the adjacent room, the brush appearing minuscule in his huge, Orcish hand. "You need to learn to relax. You will not live a very long life otherwise."

Ulam grunted. He tossed both sandals into the yard and exited the house, grabbing an overturned bucket and an unlit torch. He went to a nearby well for the water, using the lit torches aligning Accaria's dark streets to set his own ablaze. The clouds were thick in the sky, blocking out the moonlight that would have illuminated the city. Ulam was thankful he remembered to bring the torch, otherwise he might have found himself at the bottom of the well.

He set his torch in a sconce near the front of the house, using the light to scrub the soil from both pairs of sandals. He felt the iron bristles warping beyond return and knew he was ruining the brush with each stroke. But it felt good because he was taking out his frustration on the mud clinging to the soles of his sandals. Frustration at the mud, frustration at Amantius, frustration at his life in general.

He stopped to rest, listening to the sounds coming from outside their courtyard walls. He heard hammers hitting nails, the smooth slicing of saw teeth on lumber, and the occasional bout of laughter. The past few days Accaria had been in a light mood, as commoner and noble alike prepared for the Monarch's Festival, an event filled with contests and tournaments held yearly to celebrate the reigning King or Queen's birthday. This year was King Roderic's fifty-third and most likely last birthday. He had been gravely ill for over a year, having contracted an incurable disease not long after the previous year's festival. The royal physicians, as well as those brought from the mainland, had no answers; they were only able to use medicinal herbs to prolong his life a little longer while easing his pain.

Ulam turned his attention to the shadow dancing in the flame-light along the inner wall of the courtyard. The darkened outline of his body was massive, encompassing a large swath of the yellow and orange light on the stone surface of the wall. He became lost in thought, as he was apt to do, speculating about Accaria's future. He had already heard rumors of political maneuvers being made within the palace, oaths made by different families to support the individual princes if the next king's ascension was to be challenged. Fear and uncertainty settled in his gut as he daydreamed about the future, imagining the various landmarks of the city transformed into smoking ruins in the aftermath of a civil war. But deep within Ulam's heart, there was another feeling, one which brought him a small degree of shame: excitement. He could not quite understand why, but there was something exciting to him about the prospect of internal strife, about the monotony of their lives being capsized by war. *Have I grown tired of peace?*

After Ulam finished cleaning he dumped the bucket of brick red sludge into a ditch that ran parallel to their home, relying on the next solid rain shower to carry it to sea. He then collected the torch and returned inside to find a quiet house, both Pelecia and Amantius presumably having turned in for the night. He thought about joining his foster-brother in the room they shared, but he knew Amantius had always been a light sleeper, and his big Orcish footsteps would undoubtedly awaken him. As an alternative, he decided to sleep on the sofa in the foyer, an old but comfortable piece of furniture. He crashed into the cushion and stretched as far as he could, allowing the lower half of his legs to dangle off the very end. He stared at the ceiling, successfully pushing out all external thoughts, and simply allowed himself to relax. He felt the aches in his muscles, listened to the sound of his breathing, and melted away. Within moments his eyes grew heavy, and before he was aware Ulam had slipped into the realm of dreams...

Sunlight touched Ulam's face, a warm kiss announcing morning's arrival. The smell of cooked eggs drifted to his nose, rousing a hunger in his stomach that had grown overnight. He sat up on the sofa and discovered a sharp pain in his neck, the result of having slept awkwardly. Ulam yawned as he stood, careful not to cut himself on the tusks jutting out of his bottom row of teeth. He peered at the table in the dining room and saw Pelecia sitting alone by an open window, allowing a warm salt-breeze from the ocean to fill the house. The sounds of cheering crowds and musical instruments filtered inside as well, the occasional sudden roar of applause echoing within the walls of the small home. *I am surprised Amantius is sleeping through this.*

At that moment Amantius appeared in the doorway to the bedroom, dressed in the finest tunic and breeches he owned. He wore an incredulous expression on his face, as though he were confused by what he saw. As he looked from Pelecia to Ulam, the smells of breakfast wafted to his nose, causing him to pull a sour face. He instinctively clasped a hand to his mouth while shaking his head.

"Ugh, eggs!" Amantius muttered as he quickly brushed past Felecia and Ulam, heading for the main door. "Really, I don't know how you two can eat those things; they make me want to vomit!"

"Practically everyone in the world eats eggs, Amantius," Pelecia replied before she took a bite. It was a statement she made practically every morning, a daily ritual Ulam found rather comedic and endearing. "Someday you very well may have to choose between eggs or starvation."

"Then I'll choose starvation," Amantius' mumbled voice said from behind his hand as he pushed open the door and into the courtyard. He gasped for fresh air, which Ulam assumed was for the sake of drama. Amantius then turned and waved to the Orc, beckoning him to join.

"Come on, Ulam," Amantius yelled from the safety of the courtyard, "the festival has already started! We're going to miss out on all the best food and ale!"

What you mean is we will miss out on the contests; there will always be plenty of food and ale. Ulam had no desire to attend the Monarch's Festival; the thought of dealing with large drunken crowds annoyed him. He never knew what to expect, sometimes revelers would leave him alone, while sometimes the biggest drunkards would try brawling with him. Regardless, he knew Amantius would either pressure him into contests or simply enroll him in tournaments without his permission, which he hated more than anything. There was no one on the island stronger than he was, so contests such as arm wrestling and tug-of-war were empty challenges that brought him no joy or pride. The only part of the Monarch's Festival Ulam appreciated was when he melted down the trophies afterward and sold the materials to local smiths or merchants because then he could provide some income for their family. It was his way of giving back to the woman who brought him into her household and raised him as though he were her own.

Ulam grunted and went to the table, swallowing the contents of both his and Amantius' plates in a matter of minutes. He then proceeded to his room where he changed clothes, for he still had been wearing the tunic soiled with the dark red mud from Mount Meganthus. After he finished he returned to the dining room and kissed Pelecia on the forehead, and then walked outside, following Amantius into the city streets.

They headed for the King's Gardens, where the majority of the day's festivities would occur. The Gardens were a patch of land near the center of the city refashioned

18

from the ruins of the old palace, which had been built by the original settlers of Accaria centuries before. The beautification of Accaria had been one of the cornerstones of King Roderic's reign, aside from the increase in trade and prosperity the city had enjoyed over the past two decades. Twenty years prior Accaria was a poor, fetid cesspit wracked with plague and infighting, but under Roderic's guidance, it transformed into a land filled with personality and beautiful scenery, with a vibrant culture as well.

As they neared the King's Gardens the throngs of people grew thicker, as the aromas of roasting meats and vegetables began tickling Ulam's nose. Crowds cheered, dozens of musicians strummed their instruments while bards attempted to impress maidens with their soothing voices. Banners and flags of all colors and designs waved in the wind, with cobalt blue and white, the colors of the royal family of Accaria, being the most predominant. Soon the smell of ale reached Ulam as well, awakening a thirst deep within the Orc. His throat felt like a desert, completely devoid of all moisture, with his only salvation being a river of beer coursing through his body.

Amantius was a few steps ahead of him, flirting with a young woman in the shade of a large palm tree. Ulam overheard his foster-brother reciting a poem, one he had heard a dozen times over to mixed success. Though they were raised by the same woman Ulam could not help but marvel at how different they were; he could not imagine imitating Amantius' actions in a thousand lifetimes. While Amantius used words like "beauty" and "love" to describe women, Ulam used those same words to describe books.

He could not see the maiden's reaction, though ultimately it did not matter to Ulam whether or not Amantius was successful in his pursuit. Regardless of the outcome, Ulam knew he had a few moments to partake in the one aspect of this day he enjoyed the most: draining mugs of frothy delight. After all, if he was going to be pressed into participating in many of the day's events, a little liquid reinforcement would make him more tolerant of the stares he knew he could not avoid.

Though no one was outwardly hostile towards him, the crowd still shared a collective consciousness of where he was at all times. Ulam may have not looked at any individual directly, but he could still feel the hundreds of eyes following his every step. He still heard the whispers, and even outright conversations, of those who had never seen an Orc before. They were mostly denizens of the outlying villages, mountain folk and fishermen who came to the city only for festivals. No matter where Ulam roamed, there was a collective awe that always followed him. Even amongst neighbors and acquaintances, at times Ulam felt as though he had become nothing more than another exhibit in a sea of attractions. He had become equivalent to an exotic animal hailing from a distant land, paraded around for the amusement of the masses. *At least I am not in a cage. Or rather, I am not in one I can see or touch.*

After gathering a mug full of copper-colored beer, Ulam sat on a nearby stone bench shaded by an ancient tree. The spot was away from the main cluster of people, yet still close enough that he could observe the festivities. He put the mug to his lips and drank, the bitter taste of strong ale a perfect medicine for what was ailing him. Within moments he could feel the ale's effects; his muscles began to loosen, his humor improved, he even found himself laughing at a nearby jester's antics. As he watched he mindlessly imbibed the first mug of beer, bought two more and started sucking those down too.

"Slow down, Ulam, save some for the rest of us," Amantius said as he approached, a mug filled to the brim in each hand. "Besides, you need to be sober if you're going to win all those tournaments today."

Ulam grunted. What little joy he had obtained from the moment quickly diminished, a cold apathy supplanting it.

I guess it was only a matter of time.

Chapter 3
Amantius

An alabaster tower stood at the center of the King's Gardens, known as Kevea's Spear. It was named after the Goddess who slew the Mountain Witch, allowing the first Accarians to settle the island. Over the centuries The Spear had many uses; first as a lookout post, later as a beacon, and then finally as a hallmark of a bygone era. The archway leading into the tower collapsed generations ago, instantly condemning the building and causing every king and queen ever since to forbid anyone from attempting to climb to the top. King Roderic changed course, though, allowing anyone willing to attempt scaling the massive battlement to do so, but only during the Monarch's Festival. If they tried at any other time of the year they would be arrested on the spot, assuming they did not fall to their death. Many people had attempted over the years to reach the top, to touch the blue skies high above the city, but no one ever succeeded.

Amantius stood in the massive shadow of Kevea's Spear, the light of the afternoon sun glowing on the fringes of the white stone. He stared at the top, wondering whether he was brave, stupid, or sober enough to try scaling the side of the building. He felt nothing in his heart as he craned his neck back and looked at the pointed tip of The Spear. There was no fear, no excitement, nor any confidence brewing within him. Yet, despite the complete absence of thoughts or emotions, there was a voice in his head telling him to attempt the climb, a strange desire in his gut compelling him to do so. Amantius could not explain why, nor was he sure if even he knew the real reason, but deep within himself, he knew he must try.

I really wish Ulam was here, Amantius thought as he looked around at the crowd surrounding him and the other contestants. *He's probably halfway through winning the arm wrestling tournament now. Oh well, looks like I'll have to get the extra encouragement from the ladies watching. That shouldn't be a problem.*

Amantius looked around, noticing only a few women were in attendance, none of which were contestants. He shrugged. *So much for that. I guess women don't care about a bunch of guys trying to climb to the top of a tower to prove their manliness. But, now that I think about it, of course they don't care. Why would they! We're all going to fail anyway.*

"Remember lads," the man in charge of the event shouted, "if you think you're going to fall, or you wish to come back down, signal for help. Priestess Issa will bring you down safely with her abilities."

Oh good, the palace mage is here. So at least if I fall her magic will catch me. Probably. How effective can her spells be? She's about a hundred years old.

A horn sounded and the other nine climbers began racing for Kevea's Spear, battling for footing as they started to ascend the tower. Amantius remained still, though, watching as his opponents jostled for positioning. He traced paths up the side of the building, calculating his route in his mind. He saw the first person slip and fall, Priestess Issa quick to catch him with some form of magic Amantius had never seen outside of this yearly contest. If not for her annual appearance at this event, he would have thought magic, witches, and wizards to be nothing more than a myth. He watched the second person fall, then the third, fourth, fifth, and sixth. The seventh and eighth bumped into each other and tumbled at the same time, causing an exchange of insults as the crowd roared in laughter. Only two contestants remained, a masked man halfway up the tower and Amantius, who still had not yet begun.

"Are you going to even try?" Ulam's deep voice grumbled from behind. Amantius turned to see his foster-brother wearing three champion's medals around his neck, the gold from each glittering in the sunlight.

Amantius smiled and felt a swell of pride grow inside him. Though the Orc won the medals, Ulam was his brother, and his victories brought honor to the Jeranus household. "Of course. I can't let an ugly Orc like you have all the glory, now can I?"

Ulam grunted.

Amantius approached The Spear, got a firm grip on a stone jutting out slightly further from the rest, and began to climb. He followed the same path the others had taken, stopping to rest when he reached the halfway mark, where the fifth man had fallen. His muscles began to contract, his joints started to ache, while sweat dripped from his hairline and into his eyes. There he waited for them to stop stinging, hoping his vision would soon return. From above he heard grunting as the person ahead of him struggled to climb any higher, while below only a murmur of the crowd reached his ears. There was a part of him that wanted to give up now, to fall backward off Kevea's Spear, and allow Priestess Issa to gently guide him back to the ground. But seeing Ulam with all those medals around his neck inspired him to keep climbing, not out of envy, but because he wanted to share the fraternal pride with his foster-brother and go home as a family of champions.

Amantius reopened his eyes, focusing them on each stone brick of The Spear. He was forming a new path in his mind, determining which blocks would provide the most support. He decided not to follow the masked competitor above him, noticing the man's progress had completely stalled. Amantius looked to his left and saw the sunlight creeping along the surface of the tower, highlighting a set of bricks that had been previously camouflaged by the backdrop of the city. A smirk spread across his face as he followed them upwards, allowing himself to believe he found his way to the top of Kevea's Spear, the first to ever do so.

Heat radiated from the bricks directly exposed to the Accarian sun; they were hot, but not enough to burn his skin. Amantius cursed loudly, preparing himself mentally for the challenge that lay ahead. He knew by leaving the shadow he would no longer only have to fight gravity, but the sun as well. *Two forces that are undefeated all-time. I like my chances.*

Amantius took a deep breath, steeled his heart, and swung around the face of Kevea's Spear. His fingers tingled as they wrapped around the first block, a wave of heat spreading into his hands and down his arms. Suddenly he felt the suffocating oppression of humidity, the invisible adversary draining his limbs of all energy. Amantius began to suck in great gasps of air, his throat burning with each sun-roasted breath, while a fountain of sweat poured down his face and back. His clothes started sticking to his skin, forcing him to instantly regret his decision to leave the comfort of the dark side of Kevea's Spear.

Though he felt like he was melting into the surface of the tower, Amantius did recognize three major advantages to being on the sunlit side of The Spear. First, he could see his path to the top much more clearly, each progressive brick waiting to be climbed. Secondly, there was no one else on this side of The Spear, which prevented someone above him from falling and taking him with them. Lastly, and most importantly of all, the surface of the sunny side of The Spear was beginning to become so hot it served as extra motivation for Amantius to climb faster.

With lightning speed Amantius scaled the side of Kevea's Spear, hardly stopping to think of his next move. Within moments he passed his last remaining competitor, who stared at him quietly between the two holes cut into his emotionless mask. As Amantius continued to climb he spiraled around The Spear even more, until eventually he was on the exact opposite side from where he started. There he found an old window to jump through, falling to his knees as soon as he was inside. He scrambled out of the sunlight immediately, joy quickly filling his heart as he avoided the sun's tyrannical rays. But that joy was short-lived, for as he rested he looked around the room, spotting thousands and thousands of cobwebs decorating every corner. A cold shiver went down his spine, for although he was not afraid of spiders, the thought of thousands of them swarming his sweat covered body was enough to give him goosebumps.

I can't catch a break. Amantius stood up and hobbled to the window, groaning as the sunlight hit his flesh again. Though he had only been resting for a quick moment, he could already feel his muscles stiffening from inactivity.

Amantius climbed into the window sill and immediately looked down, curious as to how far he had climbed at that point. As he took in just how far he was from the ground, the strength in his legs vanished, forcing him to sit down once again. From there the people were the size of mice, their little faces all staring up at him. Ulam was the only person he recognized from such a great height, the Orc's large green head the easiest to see. Amantius searched for others in the crowd, specifically Priestess Issa, but he was unable to find her. Panic infiltrated his spirit as he kept looking because without her to safely lower him to the ground, the smallest miscalculation would mean certain death.

"Where the hell is she?" Amantius yelled towards the ground, but he was too high up for anyone to hear. "How the hell am I supposed to get back down?" *Aside from jumping.*

Though his complexion was dark from years of running through fields and beaches, he could feel the sun piercing through the shield and begin roasting his skin. More out of desperation than determination, Amantius jumped to his feet and continued his climb, hoping there would be a staircase at the top that would allow him to safely descend to the bottom of Kevea's Spear. *This thing was part of the palace once; there have to be stairs inside. Right?*

Amantius had spent so much time worrying about falling, he did not realize he was almost to the point of The Spear. He was so close he could even see the ledge at the very top, as well as his path there. The excitement began to build in his stomach, victory and a sense of accomplishment were starting to overwhelm his other senses. The pain in his limbs disappeared, a second-wind filled his lungs, even the sun did not seem so bright; Amantius had become drunk on the notion that he was about to become the first person in history to conquer Kevea's Spear. There was only one more brick to go before he could hoist himself over the top, undoubtedly to the cheers of the entire city. *My name will be remembered for eons. Mother and Ulam will be so proud of me…*

And then he fell.

Chapter 4
Ulam

Time lurched in slow motion as Ulam watched Amantius fall from Kevea's Spear, every heartbeat feeling like a hundred lifetimes. Only seconds before, the crowd shrieked on the other side of The Spear, where the other climber had fallen too. Ulam's blood ran ice-cold as he saw Priestess Issa casting a spell on the other man, completely oblivious to Amantius' tumble. He tried yelling but no words came out, the silence of his voice somehow deafening. Running out of time and with no other options, Ulam ran to the base of the tower and held out his arms as though he was going to catch his foster-brother. Deep inside he knew it was a fool's hope, but it was the only plan he had.

Ulam watched Amantius flail his arms in the wind, still desperately reaching for the top of Kevea's Spear though it was comfortably out his grasp. A chorus of screams grew behind him as people began to recognize the same thing he did: that Priestess Issa was engaged in lowering the other contestant. Ulam sealed his eyes shut, no longer able to watch, dread filling his soul as he expected to feel Amantius' body go crashing through his arms at any second. Though he was not very spiritual he even muttered a few prayers to Kevea, hoping She would save his foster-brother. *Please, I beg of you! Spare him!*

Suddenly a crystalline sound came from Ulam's right, followed by a blast of cool, rejuvenating air. The big Orc opened his eyes while turning around, following the lingering trail of bluish-white light to the source. In the distance behind him was Priestess Issa, her long white staff with a beryl stone pointed directly at Amantius. There was no panic on her wrinkled face, only poised confidence as she held her staff firm. Behind her was the other competitor, who was being attended to by a dozen guards. Though Priestess Issa had initially lowered him, the mystery climber had fallen unaided the last quarter of the building as the priestess turned her attention towards Amantius. At a glance, Ulam could tell the other person had sustained some injuries, none of which were serious, aside from hurt pride.

Amantius hit the ground with a thump, catapulting grass and dirt skyward. He let out a sigh, one hand still reaching for the top of Kevea's Spear, the other clutching an ancient stone brick. Ulam ran to him instantly, kneeling in the grass beside his foster-brother. Though his face would never betray his emotions, inside Ulam was overwhelmed with joy and relief. *I must visit the Temple and give thanks to Kevea, as well as Priestess Issa.* When he turned to thank the mage he could not locate her, though, frowning as he searched every face in the crowd. *Where has she gone?*

Ulam climbed to his feet to see above the crowd, using his height to instantly locate her. She was surrounded by the troupe of guards tending to the masked man on the ground, watching with cold indifference. The other competitor was now upright, throwing a tantrum of sorts, his petulant shouts loud enough for all to hear. Eventually, he stormed away, the guards following shortly behind. Reluctantly Priestess Issa followed as well, but before she walked away she turned and made eye contact with Ulam. Slowly she bowed her head towards him, the gesture a complete surprise to the Orc because she was a complete stranger to him. Out of politeness, he returned the salute, which brought a smile to the old woman's face, and then watched as Priestess Issa disappeared into the festival's crowd. *She acts as though she knows me, but do I know her?*

"I was so close," Amantius said as he stood up, brushing blades of grass off his clothes, "And all I have as proof is this brick. No trophy, no medals, only an old chunk of stone." He showed Ulam the brick that served as his demise, its surface grooved and eroded from centuries of tropical storms.

Ulam grunted.

They decided to take one last lap around the various contests, solely for the purpose of spectating. Ulam had no interest in participating in any other events, although Amantius would have attempted everything if his muscles did not hurt so much. They elected to enjoy the food and sights, and in Amantius' case, some fame. Rumor had spread quite quickly that he had almost reached the top of Kevea's Spear, causing no shortage of free drinks or companions, which the duo enjoyed immensely.

They eventually wandered to the archery range, where dozens of circular straw targets were constructed for a javelin throwing contest, the last competition of the Monarch's Festival. It was the most prestigious of all the sports; not only was finesse and skill required, but King Roderic himself used to participate as well. For years the winner would not only receive a gold trophy but also be the guest of honor at a royal banquet, but since King Roderic's illness had grown worse the palatial feasts were canceled altogether. Regardless, great wealth and fame were still bestowed upon the champion, which provided ample incentive for many of Accaria's denizens.

Ulam watched the rounds unfold with his fingers firmly wrapped around a mug of beer that never seemed to empty, while Amantius' hands were firmly wrapped around whichever buxom maiden fought off the others for his attention. His foster-brother's fame had spread like wildfire, but no matter how many people came to shower Amantius with drinks or kisses, his iron grip on the brick in his hand never loosened. It was as though the stone had melded to his palm, becoming a single entity with his body. It was proof of his accomplishment, like the head of a legendary monster he had heroically vanquished.

Within an hour the field had been narrowed down to the last three contestants: two male palace guards and a hooded woman. Ulam kept his eyes on her, quietly rooting for the only woman who entered the contest. She was not very tall, the javelin's point easily surpassing her height. She was slender, with midnight black hair flowing out of the bottom of her hood and down the center of her back. Though she wore a fisherwoman's clothes, there was a certain grace to her which Ulam found familiar, almost too familiar.

With only one target remaining each contestant was given one last throw, with the strike closest to the center deemed the winner. The first man threw his javelin high, the tip piercing the very top of the target. In order not to repeat the initial man's mistake, the second threw his lower, the point thumping near the center, mere inches away from a bullseye. The crowd erupted in applause as he danced around, so sure that he would win. Though there was still one person left to throw, the man began receiving congratulations from many of the spectators nearby. Though Ulam thought the celebrations were a bit premature, in fairness the throw had been so close to the center he could not foresee anyone getting closer. And from the crowd's reaction, they certainly shared this belief.

31

The hooded woman approached the line and set her feet, lifting the javelin above her right shoulder. The crowd grew quiet again, aside from a small group of people supporting the previous man's attempt. The woman took a few deep breaths and then went into motion, grunting as she hurled the javelin. The sleek projectile sliced through the air, creating a loud thud as iron bit into the tightly packed straw. As the target rocked back and forth the head judge and two others rushed to its side, preventing anyone from seeing where the woman's javelin had landed. Restlessness grew within the crowd as the judges examined the strike, the spectators shouting for them to declare a winner.

Right as the crowd was about to reach a fever pitch the head judge pulled away from the pack and raised his arms, the gesture silencing all those watching. Behind him the other two presented the target to the mass of spectators, their faces fixed in surprise. Ulam felt his heart race when his eyes focused on the much smaller javelin in the center of the target, hoping the woman's throw had triumphed. He respected her for challenging the men in a contest of martial skill, just as he was always the only non-Human in every contest. In this way, he found the woman's role as the outsider relatable, though he did not know who she was.

The head judge walked over to the woman and grabbed her by the wrist, pulling her arm into the air in victory. "I am proud to announce the winner of this year's javelin contest is Pelecia Jeranus."

The women in the crowd went berserk, their shrieks of joy drowning out any dissenting opinion. Amantius spit out a mouthful of ale while Ulam froze, confused by what he just heard. *Mother? Surely not!*

The woman then removed her hood, revealing her identity for all to see. She was, indeed, Pelecia Jeranus.

Ulam hopped the fence he was behind and rushed to her, lifting her high in the air. He was so proud of her at that moment, not just because she had won the contest, but because in doing so she had beaten so many prideful men. Pelecia laughed as he did so, imploring him to put her down, but Ulam did not care. His mother had just won the most prestigious event in the Monarch's Festival and he wanted everyone to know.

"For the last time, Ulam put me down!" Pelecia said as he lowered her to the ground. "You are too drunk to be lifting old ladies into the air."

Ulam chuckled and then turned towards Amantius, who was still motionless behind the fence. He had not moved at all; one hand clutching the stone brick, the other wrapped around the waist of a brunette. *I am not too drunk, but perhaps he is.*

"Come, child, let's go home," Pelecia said as she collected her javelin-shaped trophy, "And let's save Amantius from his stupor too."

As they crossed the range people came to congratulate Pelecia, even the two men she had just defeated. The majority of the crowd then began filtering away, returning to their homes as the sun dipped behind the city walls towards the sea. Those who remained were mostly workers paid to clear the city's streets of litter and vomit, as well as those revelers who had too much to drink.

"Come, Amantius," Pelecia said as they approached him, her eyes drifting to the woman beside him. "It is time we retire for the evening. You do not want to stay out too late, you might catch fleas."

Ulam chuckled.

After they returned home Ulam set about cleaning everyone's clothes, washing the dirt and sweat that had accumulated on them during the day. He was tired, but he knew he needed to rinse the fabric now before the grime permanently settled. As he did so Amantius sat in the corner of the courtyard, pouring buckets of water over his head. He did this not only to clean himself but also in hopes of sobering up too.

"That was a fun day," Amantius said as water fell from his chin. "I love festivals. But by the Gods, I'm going to have a headache tomorrow. I can already feel it starting. But at least all three of us brought home trophies, right? Your medals, Mother's javelin, and my brick!"

Ulam grunted as his foster-brother cackled. *It was an entertaining day at least. Who knew Mother was so skillful with a javelin?*

Suddenly a bell rang, but in a solemn, low tone. Ulam thought it strange that a bell was ringing at such a late hour, for there could not have been a wedding or spiritual function at that time of night. Powder blue flames suddenly appeared on top of the two towers flanking the palace, the fires burning with such ferocity they basked the city in an azure glow. Within moments Ulam heard wailing coming from the homes of his neighbors, followed by the sounds of people running in the streets.

"The King is dead!" He heard someone say. "The King is dead!"

Ulam knitted his brow and pushed open the courtyard door, exiting into the main street. He saw messengers bearing the insignia of the royal family, a white sun on a cobalt background, shouting the news. A youth

34

wearing a tunic with the same crest ran near Ulam, who only needed one arm to grab the boy and pull him into the courtyard. As he did so Pelecia appeared, instantly demanding Ulam to release the terrified lad.

"What has happened?" Ulam grumbled as he let go of the messenger, who immediately ran to Pelecia's side.

"King Roderic has passed." The boy said, tears in his eyes. "His illness has finally claimed his life."

Pelecia let out a sudden shriek, though it was quickly muffled as she buried her face in her hands. Amantius himself looked saddened, though visibly much less distressed than Pelecia. Ulam's expression remained unchanged, he was not even surprised. Because the King had been sick for a very long time with no signs of ever recovering, Ulam had expected this news at any moment. If anything he felt some relief, for he questioned the effectiveness of a bedridden King, no matter how beloved.

"Is there any other news from the castle?" Amantius shouted over the growing noise in the city. "What of the three princes? Or the Queen?"

"The Queen is in mourning, obviously," the boy replied, "Prince Zeno has gone missing, as has Prince Balian. There are rumors though," he stopped, shaking his head. "No, I should not say anything, rumors are seldom the truth."

"What rumors?" Ulam asked, focusing his intense eyes on the messenger. The boy squirmed before his gaze, but was able to keep most of his composure.

"Well, there are, I mean, there is, someone has been," the boy stuttered.

"On with it!" Amantius shouted.

The boy took a deep breath. "Prince Varian is already sitting on the throne, issuing commands. Prince Zeno left the

35

city with a warband an hour or two ago, heading towards Mount Meganthus. I don't know what any of this means, but...I must be going. I've said too much."

Suddenly the messenger sprinted past Ulam and back into the street, disappearing into the chaos and darkness of the night. Ulam remained stoic, though his mind was racing. *Prince Zeno left the city? Prince Varian is on the throne? Nobody knows where Prince Balian is? How has such madness happened so quickly, especially when the day was so peaceful?*

"Come, back into the house," Pelecia said after gathering herself. "Tonight is not a night to be outside."

They filed back into their home, Ulam locking the main gate as well as the main door for the first time since he could remember. He was not sure if he had ever locked both in the same night. Crime was unheard of in this part of the city, so much so that he had never truly entertained the idea of a break-in. But the uncertainty of the night inspired him to do so, though he could not say he felt any more secure.

"What do you think is happening?" Amantius asked as the lock clicked shut. "What do you make of the rumors?"

Ulam grunted. "Regardless of whether or not they are true, the city will be torn apart. A kingdom with three princes never has a smooth succession."

"Let's say they are true," Amantius continued, "What do you think would happen?"

Ulam thought for a moment; he was not sure if he wanted to answer truthfully. He knew Amantius was the type of person who forever wanted to see the good in things, and never the bad. In some ways Ulam envied him, wondering how different life with a childlike naivety was from the one he lived. It annoyed him that he could never speak his mind, or what he thought was the truth. He had always told himself he would be more honest someday, though he was smart enough to realize this would be the wrong day to begin. One look at Amantius told him that his foster-brother's intoxication had made him far too irritable, and any negative statements would not be received well.

"Maybe Zeno was overcome with grief and took a warband for protection," Ulam said, his voice gruff enough to sell the lie.

"Perhaps," Amantius replied, more optimistic than Ulam had wished. "Where do you think Balian is?"

Dead, or in a dungeon, Ulam thought but did not dare say. "Perhaps he is with his brother, or he is overcome with grief as well. How am I to know?"

"I'm sure of it," Amantius replied, "If my father died, assuming I had known the man, I would be paralyzed with grief as well."

Pelecia groaned from the couch, where she had been resting. Her eyes were bloodshot from the tears she had shed, though she had been so quiet that Ulam forgot she was in the same room. Beside her on a table were the three trophies of the day, all of which Ulam feared would now be synonymous with the King's death. He found the reversal of symbolism to be quite fascinating, if not a little saddening as well.

Ulam slowly walked to the window and watched the blue flames dance high above the palace, the leaping flames shaped like spears piercing the darkness of the night's sky. As he drew in a deep breath a foreign feeling penetrated his stomach, one unlike any other he had ever felt. He could not tell if it was fear, excitement, or a combination of both, but whatever it was, it made Ulam feel alive.

Everything will change. Everything has changed.

Chapter 5
Amantius

Amantius thought the last few days were the longest in his entire life. Spending every day locked inside his home was nothing short of torture to him, especially since he could see Mount Meganthus from a window in the living room. He yearned to climb the mountain again, to watch the gulls dive into the sparkling sea, but ever since the news of Prince Zeno's disappearance the city had been under martial law. Townspeople were allowed to be out of their homes, but they were under the constant scrutiny of Prince Varian's most loyal soldiers. A curfew had been enacted as well, and every night the screams of some unfortunate soul were proof of the rule's enforcement. Because of this, Pelecia forbade both Amantius and Ulam to leave their home, unless an emergency were to arise.

Amantius was worried about his mother; she had been deeply affected by the news of King Roderic's passing. She had become distant, spending many hours of the day staring endlessly into space. Initially, Amantius did not understand her reaction, because to the best of his knowledge the two had never interacted, but as the days passed he began to sympathize with her. After all, under King Roderic's reign, the economy had stabilized, war had never touched the land, and the populace was generally content. There were some problems on the island, such as issues with mudslides after heavy rains or the occasional meager harvest, but overall Roderic had left Accaria in a superb state. But with his passing the future suddenly became uncertain, leading Amantius to believe this was why his mother was so distraught. *I suppose every good era must end eventually. But maybe the next won't be so bad; it could even be better.*

Amantius was staring out the window in the dining room when the main door opened, and a tall man entered the house without an invitation. He wore a priest's robes, but to Amantius nothing seemed priestly about the man. He was older, a few years his mother's senior, with a bald head. A large scar ran down the right side of his face, stretching from his temple to the corner of his mouth. His eyes were cold and calculating, his lips curled in a perpetual scowl.

Amantius immediately stepped in front of his mother, who was still lounging on the sofa in the living room. Ulam joined him, folding his arms and exposing his tusks a little more than normal. It was clear to him that Ulam had the same impression of the newcomer, and without a word spoken they agreed to defend their mother first and foremost if need be.

"What is the meaning of this?" Amantius croaked, unsettled by the man's sudden appearance. He had hoped his voice would be more authoritative, but the pitch betrayed him. "Who are you? Why have you barged into our home?"

"Lady Felecia." The stranger said, his voice as harsh as his appearance. "Forgive my intrusion." He then went to one knee and bowed his head, the glint of iron showing under his robe. The man was wearing chainmail, with a sword dangling at his hip.

Amantius instinctively retreated a step once he realized the man was armed. Uncertainty and fear spiked through his heart; he had nothing to defend himself with other than his fists, and he had never been much of a pugilist. But this man did not appear to be their enemy, for he called his mother by her first name as though they were old acquaintances, and even referred to her as "Lady Pelecia." While Amantius was recovering from his confusion and gathering some semblance of courage, he heard his mother lean forward on the sofa and let out a defeated sigh. When he finally opened his mouth to speak, Pelecia stopped him by raising her hand.

"Master Marinius," she said softly. "No need for apologies, these are troubling times. You may stand, at our age kneeling is not our friend. Take a seat, too, if you wish." She gestured towards a chair on the opposite side of the room.

You may stand. Amantius thought those words sounded surprisingly regal, as though his mother was the Queen. To Amantius' recollection, she had never spoken with such authority; even when scolding him during his childhood she still adopted a more balanced tone. He looked to Ulam, to see if his foster-brother had noticed the change in disposition. But Ulam's face was as hard as stone, his expression utterly indiscernible. In his gray eyes there was an unspoken threat lingering, the gravity of his glare a warning to the newcomer to proceed with caution.

As Marinius sat down Pelecia asked Amantius to grab their guest a drink, which he did reluctantly. As he poured the glass of wine in the adjacent room he heard some of Pelecia and Marinius' conversation, though he thought they were speaking in a secret language. He could make out full sentences at times, none of which made sense to him, however. When he returned he offered Marinius the wine, retreating to Ulam's side immediately afterward.

"So that's the lad, eh?" Marinius said as his calculating eyes sized up Amantius. For the first time in his life, he felt as though someone could peer directly into his very soul.

"Yes, Marinius, that is my son," Pelecia replied with a glow in her eyes, though there was sadness too. Amantius attributed that to the King's death, though he was beginning to wonder if more was happening without his knowledge. A sickening feeling hit his stomach as his thoughts ran amuck within the confines of his imagination.

"Does he know his weapons?" Marinius asked.

"Who would have taught him?" Pelecia replied, rather sternly. "Do you think the palace would have been the best place for him to be?"

What are they talking about? Palace? Weapons? Amantius thought. Now he was really confused and anxious. He knew something important was happening, or about to happen, but there were still too many pieces of the puzzle missing.

"Who are you?" Amantius blurted out. "And why are you incognito, armed, in our house, talking about my knowledge of weapons? I feel since I am the subject of this discussion then I am entitled to know!"

Marinius gave Pelecia a quick, searching look, as though nonverbally asking permission to continue. When she nodded, he stood and approached Amantius, the leather sheath of his sword thudding on his thigh.

"You really don't know, do you?" Marinius said before turning to Pelecia again. "I am impressed that you were able to keep it a secret for…how many years? How old is he?"

"I turned eighteen last month," Amantius stuttered, his voice failing him. If he had been asked by anyone else, he might have sounded more of a man, but in front of Marinius, he felt he was still a child.

"For eighteen, almost nineteen years then." Marinius continued, rubbing the stubble on his chin. "That's impressive." He returned to his chair but did not sit down.

What is impressive? I'm utterly confused.

"I am afraid I have kept a great secret from you, my child," Pelecia said, sitting up, "about your father."

"My father?" Amantius said. "What about him? He was a sailor from a faraway land who promised you the world and then disappeared. You have told me this many times."

Pelecia took a deep breath, her mouth a tight line. "I am sorry, Amantius, but that was all a lie."

"A lie?" Amantius felt a twinge of betrayal in his gut, taken aback by his mother's revelation. While he figured this was not the first time she had lied to him, he was still a little shocked she had hidden the truth about his father for his whole life. *Why would she lie to me about who my father is?*

Pelecia sighed and looked out a nearby window, a worried expression written on her face. She remained like that for a few minutes, appearing as though she was unearthing memories like ancient artifacts buried deep underground. Amantius thought the moment would last forever, every second causing his impatience to grow tenfold. He had always wanted to know more about the man who had sired him, and now it seemed as though he was about to have some questions answered.

"I do not like talking about my past, about my roots," Pelecia said, "but now I feel I must, because, for you to understand, you will need some background."

"I was born in a fishing village outside of Accaria, on the other side of Mount Meganthus, named Toron." Pelecia started, still looking out the window, "It was small, five hundred people at the most. I lived in a hut with my mother, my father having died in stormy seas before my ninth birthday. Without him, my mother and I were forced to learn his trade. Every day we went to the docks and fished, hoping to catch enough for the both of us. Most of the time we had enough, but there were days when we went to bed hungry. Sometimes weeks."

"We had four walls, a roof with holes, and one bed. We slept in the same bed most nights, using each other's warmth in place of blankets. Eventually, we had scraped together enough money to afford a blanket." Pelecia smiled. "I felt like a queen; no more cold nights. I cannot tell you how exciting it was."

I never knew any of this. Amantius looked at Ulam, who was sitting on the floor, his entire attention directed towards their mother. *Apparently, he didn't know either.*

"But the feeling was short-lived," Pelecia continued, her expression darkening. "My mother had contracted some foul illness, a plague of sorts that had swept the island. I witnessed as, one by one, our neighbors died; their bodies withering away until they could no longer function. My mother was no different. I watched as this proud woman who spent every day hauling monstrous fish out of the ocean became so feeble she could not even get out of the bed. From then on all the responsibilities of the house fell on my shoulders: cleaning, cooking, fishing, trading, and so on."

"That year was a particularly good year for fishing, or perhaps because there were fewer people fishing I was able to catch more. Day after day I caught more fish than I needed, selling the excess to local merchants who smoked and salted the meat before taking it to the city. I had collected quite a bit of coin during that time; I planned to move to the city after my mother recovered because even during the darkest of times I still had hope for her. Unfortunately, she died months later, leaving me alone in the world."

Pelecia muttered something under her breath, a tear slipped down her face. "After she died I packed all I could carry and moved, unaware the city was infected with the same plague as well. I moved into a house near the docks, slightly bigger than the home I had shared with my mother. I then went to work fishing, since it was all I knew how to do. Day after day I toiled in the sun, hoping to catch dinner. I constantly reeked of fish guts, sweat, and sea salt, but after some time I no longer noticed the odor. It was not the only smell that no longer registered in my mind; the plague had claimed so many lives that I no longer smelled death. I accepted that death was coming for me too; it was nothing short of miraculous that I avoided it for as long as I did."

"Then one evening, on my way home from the docks, a man offered to carry my day's catch home for me. I refused, mostly because I did not need the help, but also because I did not know his motives. He politely accepted my refusal and disappeared, only to offer again the next evening. I refused again, and again the next day as well. I cannot recall how many days in a row this man offered to help me before I finally conceded. I made some stew for him, like my mother had made, as a way of thanking him." Pelecia chuckled. "The stew was awful, but he was very polite. To this day I do not know how he ate so many bowls."

"We spent the night talking about everything. History, philosophy, the different types of fishing nets, different types of metals. He told me about what was happening in the city, rumors and the like. He knew a lot about the palace, telling me he had family that worked within the palace and they routinely passed along gossip. Among his stories was one about one of the princes, who was looking for a wife now that he was of age. All the most beautiful maidens of the kingdom had been brought before him, but the prince was not interested in any of them. I asked him why, and he replied, 'because the Prince wants a woman with intelligence, one that can hold a conversation with him.' It made sense to me; if I had been searching for a husband I would have wanted someone like that as well."

"He visited me many times over the next few weeks, each time I tried to cook something different for him, each time he ate two helpings regardless of how detestable the food was. Everything was going great, but then one day we got into a fight " Pelecia looked annoyed, as though the fight had happened only hours ago. "It was a stupid quarrel; I do not even remember what it was about. But it was bad, really bad. A day went by, then two, then three. Then a week. Then a second week. He was gone."

Pelecia frowned. "A huge hole opened in my life. He was a lone sliver of light in my otherwise dark world. Without his visits, everything slipped back into the same, monotonous routine. Fish, cook, clean, repeat. I had not truly realized how important he had become or how much our friendship mattered to me. But just when I thought things could not get any worse, they did."

"I got sick." A dark cloud passed over Pelecia's face. "Really sick. At first, I thought it was just a cold I got from being on the water too long. But then a few days went by and I realized it was much worse. I lost my appetite, and then my strength. Within a week I could not even get out of bed. My whole body ached; I coughed up blood. At first, I was in denial, but deep inside I knew it was the same plague that killed my mother. Of course it was, the symptoms were exactly the same; I had the same rashes, the same sores. I thought I was going to die. And honestly, I was in so much pain I was ready to die." Pelecia shivered at the memory.

Amantius was shocked; he never knew his mother had come so near to death. He thought it was almost unbelievable since Pelecia had always been so healthy, so strong. Whenever he or Ulam would contract some sort of illness she would be spared of its wrath, her health seemingly impenetrable. *What is even more remarkable is that she doesn't have any scars, at least I don't think she does. Everyone I have ever met that survived that plague has some kind of blemishes.*

"I will never forget those dark moments when my life was hanging in the balance." Though Pelecia was staring at a small maroon and gold rug in the center of the floor, her mind was decades in the past. "I will never forget the thousands of knives stabbing my lungs and throat when I coughed. Or the feeling of my skin burning from the rashes on my arms, legs, back, everywhere. The cold sweat that soaked my face, the shivering, the chattering of my teeth. Childbirth may be the single most painful event of my life, but at least it did not last for weeks on end."

Pelecia then looked at Marinius, then Ulam, and lastly Amantius. A smile slowly replaced the grave expression on her face, her eyes began to sparkle again. She cleared her throat and then checked her hand, a strange habit Amantius had always noticed but dismissed as nothing more than one of his mother's quirks. But now that he knew she was a plague survivor, the ritual made complete sense to him. *So that's why she does that; she has been looking for blood, even after all this time. I guess she wears her scars on the inside.*

"Just when I thought my life was over, he came back," Pelecia continued, "At first I thought he was a spirit,

46

coming to take my soul to the Otherworld. But then when my eyes focused, I saw it was him. I tried to warn him not to come near; I was mortified that I would pass that wretched disease to him. But I could not gather the strength to form whole sentences, the pain in my throat was too overwhelming."

"He did everything for me. He fed me and brought fresh water every day. He fished, he cooked, and he cleaned my little home. He stitched up the holes in the blanket, he fixed my leaking ceiling. He changed my bedsheets and washed my clothes. He even spread herbs he bought from local healers, hoping they would help in some way." Pelecia was beaming now. It was so infectious even Ulam and Amantius were smiling as well.

"But what I appreciated more than anything," Pelecia continued, "was he never spent a night elsewhere. He was with me every night while I was sick, remaining ever vigilant by my bedside. And every night he would pull out a book of fairy tales and read them to me, stories of knights and dames, kings and queens, dragons and giants. When I had recovered enough he even taught me how to read, and we spent countless nights reading to one another."

"I probably do not have to tell you," Pelecia blushed a little, a sly smirk gracing her face, "but I was in love, and thankfully he was too. I cannot believe I did not see it at the time, because it is so obvious now. What man risks catching the plague for a woman he does not love?" Pelecia chuckled.

"So this man is my father?" Amantius said, "Does he still live?" He looked at Marinius, a sudden thought passing through his mind. *Is he my father? He does have scars on his body…*

Pelecia held up a hand. "Patience, my child. He asked my hand in marriage shortly after I had recovered, and I accepted without hesitation. I had no doubt in my mind this was the man I wanted to live with the rest of my life, to raise children with…" she stopped and looked at Amantius. "But that was not our fate."

"Why not? Did he catch the same plague as you?" Amantius immediately regretted asking, not only because his mother had begged for patience, but also because he realized he may have stumbled onto a raw wound.

Pelecia sighed. "It was much more difficult than simply saying yes or no. When he told his parents they outright objected to our union."

"Why?"

Pelecia squeezed her hands together, releasing years of pent up frustration. "Because I was a fisherman's daughter. I had no advantage, financially or politically. I was a plague survivor who lived in a shanty down by the docks, who was far more likely to smell of fish guts than rose petals. I would have been an embarrassment to his family."

"So you gave up?" Amantius asked in disappointment. *That doesn't sound like my mother.*

"We almost ran away. We were going to pay for passage to the mainland and start our lives together, wherever we thought we would not be followed. But it never happened. On the night we were supposed to sail away together, his father and two brothers perished. The plague had touched their home too, killing his whole family and only sparing him."

"So if his whole family had died then what was there to stop him from marrying you?"

Pelecia straightened her back, her posture radiating pride.

"Because Amantius," she began, "the man I had fallen in love with, the man I promised to marry, was no ordinary commoner. His name was Roderic, third son of Demos, King of Accaria."

"The King!" Amantius and Ulam yelled in unison. "You can't be serious!"

"Yes, the King," Pelecia repeated. Amantius could not believe what he was hearing, that the man who had nursed her back to health was the late King. He suddenly became amused, breaking out into a fit of laughter, thinking the story a well thought out joke. But as he looked around the room he noticed no one else was laughing.

"By the Gods," Amantius whispered, feeling the air being sucked from his lungs. "The King?"

"When I had met him he was a prince, the third in line for the throne." Pelecia continued, staring at her child. "Growing tired of the maidens being paraded in front of him he ran away from the palace and found me. When he asked for my hand I did not know who he was, I only knew he had a gentle soul, a kind heart. I also knew I loved him, and he loved me too, and that was all that mattered to me."

"But unfortunately, the world is not always so black and white. As King, he had new responsibilities, ones he rejected at first. We continued our romance for quite some time after his coronation, but deep inside we both knew it was not going to last forever. He needed a wife and children for the good of the kingdom, because if he suddenly died without an heir, Accaria would be engulfed in chaos. I did not like it, and to this day I still have not entirely accepted his decision, but I understand its merit. Roderic then married Verona of House Cassia, who you simply know as Queen Verona. At first, I held onto a lover's hope thinking that he would eventually leave her, and he and I would sail away as we had planned, but over time I realized how foolish that was. So I faded away, to live here. Before our relationship ended, though, there was one last gift Roderic gave me. You."

Amantius gripped the arms of his chair, digging his fingernails into the wood. He had trouble breathing; he could hear his heart pounded in his ears. "Me? Are you sure?"

Now it was Pelecia's turn to laugh. "Yes, my child, I am sure. You are Roderic's son."

"And the rightful king," Marinius added, his gruff voice drawing everyone's attention.

"But how?" Amantius managed to say, "How can I be? Even if what you say is true, I'm just a bastard. How could I have a claim to the throne when there are three legitimate children?"

"It doesn't matter," Marinius replied, "you are the oldest of King Roderic's children. His blood, the royal blood, flows in your veins."

"Who else knows?" Ulam asked. He had been customarily quiet, a large Orcish hand thoughtfully rubbing his chin. "Who in the palace, or the entire city, knows this story?"

"There are a few people like me who know," Marinius replied.

"That reminds me, who are you, exactly?" Amantius said. "How are you involved in all of this?

"I was King Roderic's warchief and closest companion. He was like a brother to me," Marinius replied with a hint of emotion. "I even stood guard outside the chambers when your mother gave birth to you. And to answer your question further," Marinius turned to Ulam, "aside from me, a couple of nurses and Priestess Issa were present. They would be the only ones to know, assuming everyone has kept the secret."

"Priestess Issa, eh?" Ulam mumbled.

Amantius heard his foster-brother's comment but was too overwhelmed with life-altering revelations to care. "So what now? Am I the King, even if I don't want to be? I can't even manage to be on time for dinner, how could I possibly rule a kingdom?"

Marinius looked to Pelecia, who had looked away. She began to sob as tears formed in her eyes.

"Around a year ago, when King Roderic's illness began to best him, he had me contact your mother and devise a plan for when this day would come." Marinius began as he paced the room. "He was no fool; he knew that his death would tear the kingdom apart. There are no peaceful transitions when three princes want the same throne. Though I do not think he knew exactly how much conflict there would have been."

"Roderic ordered arrangements to be made. And since the rumors are true about Prince Varian seizing power and murdering his older brother, as are the stories about Prince Zeno rallying loyal followers to Mount Meganthus, it is time these arrangements be put into action."

"He murdered his older brother!" Pelecia yelled. When Marinius nodded she looked to Amantius and shuddered.

Arrangements? What kind of arrangements? Amantius thought, the ice-cold hand of fear gripping his heart. *Is there a secret army waiting to rise up and place me on the throne?*

"The King had paid for passage to the mainland for two," Marinius continued, "He purchased the fastest ship in the harbor and hired one of the best smugglers money could buy to captain the vessel. The man and his crew have been paid a generous wage for the past year to remain ever vigilant in the docks, waiting for the day their services would be needed." Marinius turned and stared at Amantius. "And that time has come."

"So Mother and I are supposed to sail away from Accaria?" Amantius managed to say, his voice heavy with disbelief.

Marinius nodded. "In two days there will be a knock on the door, like this," he beat out a rhythm on the arm of a chair, "I personally will take you to the docks."

"Surely there must be another way," Pelecia managed through the sobs. "We can go to the mountain, live as shepherds. Or we could ask for clemency."

Ulam grunted. "The new king has murdered his own brother and is about to go to war with the other. I do not believe he will be so accommodating."

Marinius nodded. "He speaks the truth. Even I have to fear for my life, and my family's. They have already left the city and headed to Mount Meganthus. As soon as I tend to a few more affairs I will be joining them."

"Why can we not go with you, then?" Amantius asked. He could not wrap his head around the concept of crossing the ocean just to protect a secret that may never be discovered. "Would Prince Zeno be more tolerant?

"Who is to say?" Marinius replied with a shrug of the shoulders. "Any political rival is in danger in this upcoming war. Not just blood relatives, but anyone with power, and the war will not end until one side is completely annihilated."

A horn sounded from the direction of the palace, long an ominous. Marinius looked out the window towards the keep. "I must be going."

"Thank you, Marinius," Pelecia replied. "For your secrecy. I could never repay you."

Marinius bowed once more to Pelecia. "Roderic was like a brother to me, and you were the only woman he ever truly loved. It has been my privilege. One last thing," Marinius reached into his robes and pulled out a book, old and worn. "His last request was for me to give you this."

Pelecia opened the book and read a few lines, immediately bursting into tears. "I know these stories. They are the ones he read to me when I was ill."

Marinius nodded. "It was his most prized possession. Farewell Lady Pelecia, I will return in a few days."

Amantius was unsure how to react as he watched his mother press the book tightly to her chest. There was too much happening for him to process, too many thoughts flying through his mind to remain still. *Am I supposed to be the king? Why has Mother kept this from me for so long? Are we in any real danger?*

"Before you go." Ulam said as Marinius strode towards the door. "Do you know about me? Do you know of my origin, how I came to be here?"

Marinius shook his head. "You were by Pelecia's side when Amantius was born, though you were nothing more than an infant. We asked no questions. My apologies, but I must go."

Marinius exited the house, quietly disappearing into the streets. Accaria was still chaotic, more so than at any festival or parade. People ran to and fro, some shouting in anger, others in mourning. After sunset, the noise began to slowly drift away, until only the ocean breeze drifted through the windows.

"What am I to do when you leave?" Ulam said, breaking the silence. Of all his thoughts, Amantius did not even consider the idea of leaving Ulam behind. *It will be strange without him beside me. I will miss him.*

"You will not be. You are going with him," Pelecia said, her voice sad but firm.

"Master Marinius said nothing about my passage having been paid." Though Ulam showed no emotion, Amantius knew the Orc was worried.

Pelecia bit her bottom lip as she looked at them both. She forced a smile, though tears were still pouring down her reddened face. "I will not be making the voyage across the sea."

"What do you mean!?" Amantius yelled. "We are a family; we must stick together!"

Pelecia sighed and shook her head. "No, Amantius. Even if all three of us could go, I am an old woman now. I am not made for a life of adventuring. But," she said as she ran her hand through his midnight black hair, "you two are young and have your whole lives ahead of you."

Amantius jumped up; he could not believe what he was hearing. First, he was being forced out of his home, off the island that he loved. Now he was losing his mother as well. It was preposterous, as though none of this was real and he was living a nightmare.

"No! I will not leave you behind!" He declared as he took her hand in his. Despite his best attempts, he could not keep his voice from trembling. "Nor will I leave Ulam behind. Either the three of us go together or none of us go."

"Do not be foolish," Pelecia snapped, "You must go. If Varian discovers your lineage then…"

"How will he?" Amantius said, interrupting his mother. "How could he know? Even I did not know who my father was until now!"

"Torture," Ulam replied, his voice flat, the emotion in the room crashing on his words like a waves on a seaside cliff. A chill went down Amantius' spine. "No one willingly said anything all these years, but that does not mean a little torture will not help people remember. If what Master Marinius said was true, then there are potentially scores who know of their romance before his marriage to the Queen."

Though Amantius was aware of the truth in Ulam's words, he did not want to recognize it. He tried argument after argument, but Ulam crushed each attempt with articulate, sound logic.

"Very well," he acquiesced after his last effort had been soundly defeated, "Ulam and I will go together."

My beautiful life is over.

Chapter 6
Ulam

"It is today, right?" Amantius asked as Ulam stood by the window, playing the part of a sentry. "Today is the day we leave?"

Ulam said nothing, not even his customary grunt. In truth, he knew this was the day they would board a ship and sail to the mainland. Ever since Marinius spoke of the exodus from Accaria, Ulam had become progressively more excited about leaving.

Even though he knew this was the day, and the hour was near, he could not bring himself to tell Amantius. He knew the poor lad was hoping against hope, falsely misled by youthful optimism and denial. But he also knew he had to speak, otherwise, Amantius would know he was hiding something.

Ulam eventually grunted. "I assume. But, I have been wrong before." He turned from the window and took a seat on the nearby sofa, studying his foster-brother's face all the while. He could see the sweat and frustration building on Amantius' brow and took a strange satisfaction in that. Knowing he could not tell the truth, and that a lie would ultimately be more harmful, he was comfortable leaving Amantius in the dark. Ultimately it did not matter to him, he had been prepared for Marinius' arrival for days.

"What was it that Marinius said, exactly?" Amantius continued as he paced across the room. "That on the second day there would be a knock at the door, similar to this." He balled up his hand and smacked his knuckles on the wood of a nearby desk. For a brief moment, Ulam saw that Amantius' worries had disappeared, but now that silence was setting in again, doubt had returned to his face.

"There is nothing else," Ulam replied, "as soon as we hear the knock, we need…"

With uncanny timing, a faint knock came at the door.

A hooded figure entered the room, dark robes obscuring any discernible feature. Though Ulam could not tell exactly who was under the clothing, he assumed it was Marinius. A flicker of nervousness and excitement suddenly filled his belly, for it was the dawn of the next chapter of his life.

"Everyone ready?" Marinius said as he removed his hood. "Lady Pelecia, forgive me, but you need to hurry packing."

Pelecia frowned. "I am not going, Marinius. Ulam will take my place on the ship."

Marinius started to say something but stopped before the words could fully form in his mouth. He nodded instead. "Very well. Both of you have twenty minutes to prepare. I will wait outside. Also, don't pack metal, the clinks and clanks will echo across the city, and we don't want them to hear us."

"We do not want who to hear us?" Pelecia asked.

"The patrols searching for curfew breakers," Marinius replied, "Two bells will ring. The first is curfew, the second will close the harbor and gates. If you haven't boarded the ship and left the harbor by the second bell, then you will be trapped in the city."

"Why are they closing the harbor?" Ulam asked. "Will that not hurt the city more?"

Marinius sighed, "I believe so, but Prince Varian, or rather King Varian, wants to keep everything internal. No outside influences."

"But how do we know when the first bell rings?" Amantius asked. "Surely there is a set time."

"No one knows. It is whenever he decides. The second is sunset, so I assume the first bell will ring soon. The first one does not matter, we will be out past curfew regardless, but the second?" His words faded away.

"Must they go?" Pelecia spoke for the first time. She was in a rare form, one Ulam had never seen before. She looked as though she had not slept in days, the restlessness adding at least ten years to her appearance. For the first time, Ulam thought she looked old, the youthfulness and glow of her skin drained.

"I still don't understand why I have to go," Amantius said, "I don't want to go! We can make up some story about who my father was."

"To stay is not only to put your life in jeopardy but your mother's as well." Marinius turned his attention to Pelecia, his features softening. "No, I am afraid they must leave for the mainland. Roderic would come back from the dead to personally flay me if something were to happen."

"But he is my only child, Marinius," Pelecia pleaded, her voice cracking. She then turned to Ulam and frowned a non-verbal apology. Ulam winked; he knew she meant no offense. No matter how much of a mother she had been to him, and as much as she owned the role and all of its responsibilities, Amantius would always be her only natural child.

"He's not a child anymore," Marinius replied. It was apparent to Ulam that the man was trying to be sympathetic, but his gruff voice did not allow for much empathy. "He is, by all right, the true king, and that is why he is in great danger."

"I know." Her words were faint and full of pain. Ulam could hear her heart breaking even more, something he did not think was possible. Though he was excited about embarking on their journey, it was tempered by the pity he felt for Pelecia. After all, she had raised them both by herself, through good times and bad. And now, she was losing her entire family. In a way, Ulam felt a great remorse building inside him, shamed by the optimism growing in his heart. *How can I be eager for what tomorrow holds when I am surrounded by the agony of the only two people in this world who truly accept me? What kind of ungrateful monster am I?*

"Go now and pack," Marinius ordered, "I will be standing guard outside."

Amantius looked dazed and confused, but he obeyed and disappeared. Ulam already had his travel bags packed; he had done so hours ago because he wanted to be ready on a moment's notice.

He walked to a nearby window and stared at the palace as the sun began to set, its reddish-orange rays illuminating the white walls of the city. He had never truly appreciated the architecture of the building, or any other building for that matter, until that moment. A sweet, summery breeze rustled the leaves of the palms that adorned the nearby alleyways. Brine tingled his nostrils, a feeling he knew he would become accustomed to as they sailed across the sea. Dogs barked, seagulls squawked, and horses neighed as they dragged carts down the road. He was trying to capture one last mental image of Accaria, one that would live on in his memories forever. He was not a fool; he knew the impending civil war would leave wounds that would never heal. He knew if he ever returned the city would be different, both in appearance and spirit.

The first bell began ringing, low and foreboding. Each brass repetition was even more ominous than the last. After an initial shout of panic and desperation, the noise in the streets began to taper off, until nothing could be heard other than the iron boots of guard patrols up and down the cobblestone streets. The seagulls grew quiet as well; even they seemed too afraid to speak.

Ulam had accepted this to be their fate, although he was not entirely sure why he also needed to leave Accaria. He was not the bastard son of the late king; he would not pose any danger to the legitimacy of Varian or Zeno's claim. He understood Pelecia's logic to an extent, that she was not fit emotionally or physically to traverse the open sea, nor to live the life of a refugee. What he could not understand was what had driven Pelecia to insist on his accompanying Amantius. *Would she not want me here with her? She would be safer if I was around.*

"Oh, Ulam," Pelecia said, interrupting his thoughts. She walked over and hugged him tightly, her small arms not long enough to wrap completely around his body. "I regret sweeping you into this mess."

"It is not your fault," Ulam replied, laying a huge palm on her back gently, "You did not murder anyone, or cause a civil war. Besides, there is a huge world out there. I might even find another Orc."

Pelecia smiled. It was a warm display, though grief remained in her eyes. "You want to find other Orcs, do you not?" She let go and took a seat on a long sofa. She sighed, her expression now completely ruled by sadness. "I knew no matter how hard I tried, I would never be your mother. I always knew that someday you would want to leave, to find others like you. I just did not expect that day to come so soon."

"You are right, I want to find others like me." He walked over to her and kneeled, putting his eyes at the same height as hers. He took her hands in his; two delicate, caramel hands engulfed in his sea of dark green. "You did not give birth to me; you had no obligation to care for me. I cannot imagine how difficult it must have been raising an Orc, especially while you carried the secret of Amantius' lineage inside. There is no way I could ever repay you for the kindness and love you have shown me throughout the years. No matter what happens, for as long as I live, I will always consider you my one, true mother."

Pelecia smiled. "And you, Ulam, will always be my son." Her expression changed, the smile faded away. She turned her attention towards Amantius' chambers and tensed, Ulam feeling the difference like a cold breeze on a warm day.

"Watch him, Ulam. Take care of him. Make sure he doesn't do anything too reckless. Amantius is naïve, and in a lot of ways, he is still a child. I was too soft on him; I made him too dependent on others." She turned her ocean blue eyes towards him, the same color and shape as Amantius'. "Promise me, Ulam, promise me you will protect him."

"Of course I will," Ulam said as he hugged her.

"Promise me," Pelecia said, her voice muffled by his shoulder. "Say the words."

Ulam hesitated. A moment ago he was excited to see the entire world. He wanted to hunt dragons, drink the finest wines and beers, lay eyes on ancient cities, and experience many other things he had read in adventure novels. But now that excitement had vanished, and was replaced with the same sense of entrapment that he felt living in Accaria. He was torn. He felt selfish for wanting all these things for himself, and Pelecia's wailing did nothing more than intensify the guilt growing within him. What she said was true, Amantius could not survive in the world by himself. Even here on the island, where every vicious monster had been slain generations ago, Amantius still found trouble in the most foolish of places.

Ulam knew what he had to do, and knew there could be no other way. The wind in his sails had disappeared, stolen away by a sense of duty and responsibility. In a way, he even felt embarrassed for allowing himself to dream.

"I promise."

Pelecia's crying subsided, his oath having an instant effect on her. As Ulam stared at the wall behind her, he felt the weight of a new burden slowly piling onto his massive, Orcish shoulders.

Chapter 7
Amantius

"Amantius, it is time," Ulam said as he stood in the doorway, his expression as grave as always. "We must go now."

"Why?" Amantius yelled. "Why must we leave? No one knows the truth, no one will suspect Mother or me!"

"We have been over this," Ulam grunted, "It may seem as though no one knows, but there are those who remain. Nursemaids that were present during your birth, who have remained silent throughout the years." Ulam sighed deeply, "Humans are ambitious creatures. Whoever wins this war will look to eliminate any potential threats, any other claims to the throne…"

"But I don't want the throne!" Amantius interrupted. He had no ambition to be a leader of any kind, let alone to be a king. The idea was absurd to him; he was as much of a monarch as he was a pelican. "Why do you not understand that? Surely both Varian and Zeno can understand, if either of them were to discover my heritage. And even if they came to arrest me, I would just flee to Mount Meganthus! They would never find me there! I could live with the shepherds until all this ends."

"And you would condemn them all to death," Ulam retorted. "Innocent men, women, and children would be slaughtered on the slopes of Meganthus. Amantius, the only way to survive this is to leave the island completely. Maybe in a handful of years, we could return…"

"Years!?" Amantius shouted in disbelief. He could not imagine being away from Accaria for longer than a week, let alone multiple years. As he waited for Ulam to reply Pelecia slipped into the room.

"Come Amantius," she said warmly, though the authority in her voice could not be mistaken. "Enough talk, it is time to leave."

Amantius reluctantly grabbed his travel bag and hoisted it over his shoulder. He tried having heavy feet to slow down their progress, but Ulam had gripped him by the forearm and was dragging him like a ragdoll. The Orc's grip was so strong Amantius thought the bones in his arm were snapping; he had always forgotten exactly how powerful Ulam was. The pain convinced him to walk faster, as he had no intention of experiencing dismemberment.

After carefully navigating the back alleyways of the city, taking extra precautions to avoid the roaming patrols, they finally arrived in the Whaleport. Amantius' heart sank when he saw the last ship in the harbor, for he had hoped the captain would have become too anxious and fled the city already. He still could not believe what was happening; his whole life had been turned upside down. Only a week ago everything was perfect and serene. Now, it was confusing and chaotic.

"That's their ship," Marinius said, pointing to the lonely vessel floating in the harbor, "We need to get you onboard right now, the harbor will be closing any minute now."

As they approached the second of the two bells began to ring, followed by the blaring of horns. Men on both sides of the harbor began working in tandem to close the Seawall, a large iron-barred gate spanning the entrance of the harbor. Amantius grew excited as he watched, his desperation allowing him to believe they were too late. The feeling quickly gave way to a sense of triumph, as though he had just won a bout against time and fate.

"I guess that means I have to stay," he said as he quickly turned towards home, but before he could take any more steps, a pair of hands yanked him from the dock. Suddenly, he found himself on the deck of a merchant's vessel.

"Set sail, you worthless lot!" A gruff voice yelled over the noise. "We'll all be swingin' by our necks if we're not out of here within the next fifteen minutes!"

Amantius tried jumping to his feet, but the rocking of the ship caused him to stumble. The excitement and sense of victory were gone, replaced by confusion and terror. "The harbor is closed! Why are we still going!?"

"Ya think this is the first blockade I've ever snuck past, lad?" The captain said with a sneer, "Ya don't make a good smuggler if ya follow the rules."

"Mother!" Amantius yelled, ignoring the explanation. He tried to climb out of the ship, but as he stepped forward Ulam jumped onto the deck, the Orc's massive body too huge of an obstacle for him to surpass. "Mother!"

Pelecia practically jumped into the harbor after them both, and would have too if Marinius had not grabbed her at the last second. She was screaming, her words an incoherent mess, as the moonlight highlighted the tears on her cheeks.

Amantius continued to yell for her as he struggled to get around Ulam, but the Orc was not allowing him to escape. No matter how hard he pushed, punched, or kicked, Ulam was as immovable as a mountain. Eventually, Amantius crashed to the deck, emotionally and physically exhausted.

"Can we not take her with us?" Amantius' voice was raspy from his shouting, "Why can't we, Ulam? Why?"

Ulam said nothing. Instead, he quietly sat down beside Amantius and wrapped a big, green arm around him, squeezing tightly. Around them, the sailors scrambled to their rowing benches as the captain barked orders at them. Within moments the ship pushed away from the dock and was heading for the edge of the harbor, the Seawall still not completely closed. The night's wind blew hard into the sail, propelling them forward, as the sailors strained to get them through the gap.

Amantius sat in the middle of the ship and watched with a cold numbness as his mother grew smaller and smaller. By the time they blasted through the blockade and into the open sea, Pelecia and Marinius were nothing more than a pair of silhouettes on the docks, statues at the base of a city in shadows.

"I didn't even get to say goodbye!" Amantius broke down into tears, shaking uncontrollably. Ulam embraced him tightly, pressing Amantius' head against his shoulders. "I didn't even get to say goodbye, Ulam. Or tell her that I love her."

Ulam patted him on the back. "She knows you love her, Little Brother, she knows."

Chapter 8
Ulam

The ship swayed to and fro, a sensation Ulam had never felt before. Though his legs were as strong as oak, he felt as weak as a newborn babe as waves crashed into the hull. He had been mentally prepared to retch over one of the sides, but to his surprise, his stomach had been remarkably calm. He thanked the Gods for this because nothing could have been worse than spending every waking moment vomiting over the side of the ship.

The sting of saltwater pierced Ulam's nostrils, a sensation he had never experienced. As they sailed further and further, the call of seagulls faded, and their snow-white bodies no longer dove into the sea for dinner. The only noises he heard now were those of sailors yelling to one another about riggings, the wind pounding into the woolen sails, and the creaking of wood beneath his feet.

Ulam daydreamed about his future for so long that when he returned to reality they were a great distance away from Accaria. He could not tell how far they had sailed, though he knew they could not have been close. Kevea's Spear had long disappeared over the horizon, as had any semblance of the city. The only part of the island still visible to the naked eye was Mount Meganthus, and even it was no more than a speckle of green and brown.

Ulam was surprised by the way he felt; after watching Pelecia and Amantius fall to pieces before his eyes he somewhat expected to join them. After all, he too had left everything he had ever known behind in Accaria. Instead, he only felt emptiness, a void taking over what he thought should have been sadness or even regret. The only part of his situation that brought him emotion of any kind was knowing he would most likely never see Pelecia again. Though she was not his real mother, he was eternally grateful for the life she had given him. He could not help but think there was something they could have done for her, some way they could have smuggled her out of Accaria as well. But as she said that night in the house, there would be no sense in doing so. She was an old woman, and she would have been too much of a burden.

Ulam spent much of the voyage speculating what would become of Accaria, playing out every scenario in his mind. He was not a fool, he knew the war that was about to engulf the island would kill many people, most of which he feared would be innocent. He had to push away any thoughts regarding Pelecia's fate if King Varian discovered Amantius' parentage, because in such an event he knew she would be murdered, and probably tortured first. *Please be safe, Mother.*

He shifted his thoughts to his future with Amantius; it was all he could do to keep from falling into a spiral of despair. He learned that within a month they would make landfall, and figured they should have a plan before they reached the mainland. Ulam was not entirely worried about finding work or living off the land, his large frame and immense strength would always afford him easy employment, he was more concerned about his dynamic with Amantius. To an extent they had been raised as brothers, although there had always been an unspoken separation between the two. He could not fault Pelecia for this, considering he was an orphaned Orc and Amantius was her only trueborn child. Nevertheless, they had always been family, and now that they were out of the confines of their home and away from Accarian society, the notion that they were brothers became increasingly foreign to him. *Maybe we are not family after all.*

As these thoughts swirled in his head, Ulam glanced at Amantius and watched as his distraught foster-brother mourned their collective fate. The poor lad was fixated on the small lump of tropical green in the vast blue ocean, the occasional tear escaping his bloodshot eyes. Ulam felt a sickening twist in his stomach as he saw the despair in Amantius' face, unable to imagine what he was experiencing. Because while Pelecia was not Ulam's real mother and Accaria was not his true homeland, both of which were to Amantius.

"Get one last look before it's too late," the captain shouted from the prow. "you may never see that rock again. Or if you do, it won't look the same."

Ulam almost peeked at the vanishing island, his home of the past twenty years, but in the end he chose not to do so. Accaria was his past, and the world was his future.

Chapter 9
Amantius

Amantius stared across the rippling blue waves of the ocean. Though they were many miles away from the shores of Accaria, he felt as though he could still see the city's alabaster white walls ascending to the heavens above. In his mind, he saw Mount Meganthus, a pang shooting through his heart as he remembered how the morning mist would gently kiss his face. But now he was an ocean away from everything he had ever known or loved, in a completely alien land.

"Where am I?" Amantius muttered to himself, his voice just above a whisper.

"You're in the southernmost reaches of the Emberi Empire, lad. Go a day's walk north of here and you will see the City of Silverwater," the sailor said as he pushed the small raft from the shore. "We would have taken you there, but the Empire has not been good to smugglers recently. Gods be with you, lads."

"Gods be with you," Amantius repeated, meaning the words for the first time. He had spoken the words so many times in his life that the reply was automatic, much like "thank you" and "you're welcome." But now he believed he would need all the blessings he could get.

Amantius and Ulam watched as the landing craft rowed away, becoming smaller and smaller until it was hoisted onto the much larger vessel anchored in the harbor. The men onboard unfurled the sails, and soon the whistling wind guided the ship back to sea. When there was nothing more than a white square in the far distance, Ulam gathered his things and proceeded towards an old stone road.

"Where are you going?" Amantius asked.

"North. To Silverwater."

"What will you do when you get there?"

"I do not know, Amantius," Ulam replied, his voice gruff, but sad as well.

Although Amantius had known Ulam his whole life, he had never seen such a look of uncertainty in the Orc's gray eyes. But of course, Amantius himself had never been as bewildered as he was at this moment. Only a month ago he was dining on crab legs in his mother's home without a worry in the world, and now he was unsure of what his next meal was going to be, or when it would occur.

Ulam dropped his bags on the road and trounced through the rocky sand towards where Amantius was standing. When the Orc was within arm's length he grabbed Amantius by the shoulders and squeezed firmly, staring directly into his eyes.

"Let it go, Amantius," Ulam grumbled, "there is no going back now."

Amantius did not want to believe him; he was already concocting methods of returning to Accaria. He thought that perhaps he could gain employment in Silverwater and make enough coin to pay for passage back to Accaria despite the closure of the Seawall. There were still plenty of points on the island where a ship could land, he argued, believing no blockade could successfully stop every smuggler from landing ashore. If that turned out to not be a viable option, he thought perhaps he could plead with the local lords, hoping they would sympathize and consent to return a man of royal blood back to his kingdom, regardless of the fact that he was a bastard.

As Amantius conceived scheme after scheme he began to realize perhaps Ulam was correct, that there was no going back. Each successive blueprint was slightly more absurd than the previous, until eventually his plans were completely senseless. It did not matter that his father was once the king because no one would care about the illegitimate son of a dead king. Sneaking onto a ship could work, but most likely he would be discovered and tossed overboard. There was still the possibility of paying for passage, but he did not see the point in doing so. Even if the ship found a receptive landing, to return to Accaria now would be a death sentence for him.

"You're right," Amantius muttered finally, "I guess we should head to Silverwater."

Ulam grunted and slapped his foster-brother on the shoulder before returning to his sand-covered bags. Amantius followed, his legs as heavy as lead, leaving a trail of ankle-deep gashes along the beach. With every step, he was one step further away from Accaria, not just in body, but in his heart as well.

They began their journey northward, along a twisting cobbled road. It was a path made of thousands of stones, gray and chipped from centuries of usage. It followed the coastline on the right, with the edge of an ancient forest to the left. From time to time Amantius and Ulam would peer deep into the malachite green canopy and spot wildlife that neither had ever seen before. There was a four-legged animal with horns sticking out of its head that Amantius was particularly fascinated with, which Ulam identified as a deer.

He was not sure if the Orc was right or not, but regardless he found the animal subtly majestic.

They traveled for hours, taking in as many new sights and sounds as they could. Over time the colossal brown trunks gave way to a clearing, where farmland dominated the landscape for as far as they could see. On the horizon was a walled city, the outline of a castle looming on a hill high above. As they drew nearer the farmlands gave way to vineyards, with supple fruits dangling from every vine.

"I've never seen grapes like these before," Amantius said as he marveled at the size and speculated about the juiciness of the fruit. "They must make the best wine here. I wonder how they taste…"

He reached out to pluck the fattest grape he could see, but before his fingers could make contact with the fruit's succulent magenta skin, he felt a heavy Orcish hand crash down on the back his palm. He pulled back immediately and scowled, incredulous with Ulam.

"What the hell was that for?" Amantius yelled as he rubbed his reddening hand. He stretched his fingers time and again, hoping to ease the stinging sensation.

"You do not know what kind of fruits these are," Ulam said in complete severity, "they may be poisonous. Besides, I will not tolerate thievery, especially in a land where we are both strangers."

Amantius sneered at the first comment, but he knew the merits of the second. It was true, they were foreigners in this land, and there could have been grave repercussions if he had been caught stealing grapes from the vine. *Still doesn't mean he had to hit me.*

"Fine," Amantius said, "I'll just buy some at the market then, when we have some coin."

Ulam grunted.

Not much longer they arrived at the front gate of Silverwater, where high above a flag of crimson and white danced beside one of purple and silver. A dozen men equipped with basic polearms meandered at ground level, while Amantius caught a glimpse of archers patrolling from the towers above the gatehouse. Getting into Silverwater was no difficult task; scores of men and women traveled through the south gate on this day. Amantius saw the usual riffraff, merchants and farmers going to market, but there was a mass of people very different from the rest entering as well. They sold a different kind of ware than the others.

"Ulam, is it me, or are there a lot of whores here?" Amantius said as he watched scantily-clad women practically throw themselves at anyone who displayed any kind of wealth. Accaria had plenty of ladies, and a few men, who practiced the "art of pleasure," but he had never seen so many gathered in one spot in his life.

Ulam shrugged. "It did not occur to me until you pointed it out."

"Far more than Accaria," Amantius replied as he ogled one of the women, though she would not return the attention. *It looks like she can smell my empty pockets.*

"A man wrote a book once, long ago," Ulam began as they squeezed their way through the crowd, "where he stated that a mass of such women only happens on two occasions: when there is a festival and when there is an army."

Amantius' heart began to beat quickly as thoughts of a grand feast shot through his mind. "Of course! There must be a festival soon, and that is why the grapevines remain full! By the Gods, Ulam, what luck we have!"

Ulam planted his feet, his legs reminiscent of the massive oaks in the ancient forest they passed earlier. "Yes, Amantius," he began with a grunt, "what luck we have."

A sudden crashing noise caught their attention, where nearby a group of drunken men were wrestling near stockpiles of weapons and armor. Instead of being greeted by the joviality of a grand feast, Amantius found himself in the company of soldiers and mercenaries. The feeling of defeat washed over him as he watched the men pummel one another, for he had hoped at the end of their long voyage from Accaria there would be some cause for joy. But instead of a never empty goblet of wine and a bed filled with women, Amantius was met with more gloom and despair.

"Now what do we do?" Amantius asked, his voice searching.

Ulam grunted. "Look for employment."

They headed to the nearest tavern, but finding it filled to the doors with people they decided to look elsewhere. Everywhere they went people stared at them, though not in the same manner as they had become accustomed to in Accaria. There was something different, something even sinister, about the hundreds of eyeballs following their every movement. Crowds made way for them as they perused the city, splitting to each side as frightened fish do when chased by a shark. Children hid behind their mothers' skirts, while the women themselves stood guard like frightened beasts protecting their young. *This is strange, so strange. Nobody should know who we are here.*

"Why do they stare, Ulam? What is so interesting about us?" Amantius said under his breath.

"Perhaps they have never seen someone as ugly as you?" Ulam retorted with a snort.

Amantius laughed, perhaps harder than he should have. He did not realize how much the stone gazes of the crowd had unnerved him.

They stopped in a square where three separate roads led to different parts of the city. A crowd of people blocked each way, the hustle and bustle of a city preventing Amantius and Ulam from walking any further. As they debated which way to go, a little girl with golden hair, who was no older than five years, ran up to them. Her clothing suggested she was not poor, but also not rich; she most likely was one of the merchants' children. In her hand she held a flower with lavender petals, the stalk bent from her tight grasp. Despite missing a few teeth she had the brightest of smiles, and she possessed the kind of youthful vigor only children enjoy.

"Hallo!" She said as she looked up at Ulam. "You're so tall! I wish I was tall like you!"

Amantius was shocked, especially considering how ice cold the residents of Silverwater had been thus far. He was doubly surprised by the fact that she approached Ulam and not him, for it was quite rare that anyone would approach his foster-brother. Being an Orc, Ulam was naturally inclined to wear a permanent grimace on his face. His eyes were intense, his tusks were sharp and protruding, his height and muscle mass alone often was enough to intimidate everyone else. Because of this he was always treated with suspicion and paranoia, for his appearance was one that terrified all but the dumbest. But for whatever reason, the little girl was not the least bit afraid.

Ulam slowly dropped to one knee, his expression unchanged. Even kneeling he still towered over the child, whose golden hair swayed in the wind. "Well good day to you," he began, his voice softer than usual, yet still gruff. "That is a pretty flower you have."

The little girl giggled in delight, "Do you think I can be tall like you someday?"

Ulam began to chuckle; the little girl's laughter so contagious even he could not resist. "If you eat right and take care of yourself, you can be anything you want. You can be twice as tall as me even!"

"Really!?" The girl said with a twinkle in her eyes.

"Of course," Ulam replied with a smile.

Before they could continue their conversation a panicked shriek came from somewhere in the crowd, drawing Amantius' attention. Suddenly a woman burst forth from the mass of bodies and rushed to the little girl, grabbing her by the forearm and dragging her away.

"Get away from him!" She screamed as she pulled. "You can't get too close to them!"

"Why!?" The child squealed as she began to cry. "He's my friend!"

"He's a Greenskin!" The woman replied, "They're savages that eat children!"

"What did she say?" Amantius said as he took a step forward. "Did she say you eat children?" His confusion turned to anger, an emotion he did not experience often. "What kind of nonsense is this!?"

"Easy, be calm," Ulam said as he grabbed Amantius by the leg. There was a great sadness in his voice, one Amantius had rarely heard before.

"Come back here! Come back here right now!" Amantius continued to yell as he tried to shake Ulam's grip on his calf, "Let go of me, Ulam, that woman is atrocious and spreading lies!"

"Amantius, let it be," Ulam replied again, this time tightening his hold.

"Protect the children! The Orc will eat them!" Someone shouted from the mob, followed by laughter.

"Child eater!" Someone else yelled, followed by similar insults and chants.

Amantius' fury made him want to fight every person in the crowd, but all he could do from his position was shout, and those words fell on deaf ears. Meanwhile, Ulam remained kneeling, staring at the cracks between two slabs of stone.

As the jeering became louder the crowd also became bolder, until someone threw a tomato at them. It splattered on the ground nearby, which did nothing but encourage others to try. Barrage after barrage of fruits and vegetables rained down on Amantius and Ulam until the situation reached a fever pitch, and someone from the crowd chucked a jagged stone.

"Kill the Orc!" A woman's shrill voice yelled over the crowd. "Cut off his head!"

Men from every part of the crowd stepped forward to do the job, liquor and bloodthirst equal parts in their eyes. Only one of which carried a blade, and unfortunately he looked the soberest of the bunch. Amantius stood petrified to the spot, not sure what to do. He looked down only to see Ulam remaining passive on the ground.

"Get up!" Amantius urged as he took a defensive stance. "Get up!"

Ulam did not reply. He remained still, absorbing countless blows from chunks of stone that continued to pelt him. He grunted as one hit him the ribs, and grimaced when the next gashed open his arm.

"Get up, dammit!" Amantius yelled as the men drew in nearer.

One of the attackers, a rugged man of average height, was the first to approach. He walked confidently, and the rock his fingers gripped gave him even more confidence. He wore a wicked smile on his face, one full of malice.

"Ready to die, you green bastard?" He said as he grabbed Ulam's tunic at the shoulder.

As soon as the goon's fingers wrapped around the fabric, Ulam sprouted to his feet and grabbed the man by the neck. He executed the movement with such speed and accuracy that the man did not have time to react, dropping the rock in his hand as Ulam lifted upward. He then squeezed with his big Orcish hands, so strong were they that he could crush the man's throat if he so desired. There was a fire of unbridled rage in Ulam's eyes Amantius had never seen before, the sight so terrifying even he began to fear for the attacker's life. Desperately Amantius kicked Ulam, hoping the blows would force the Orc to drop the ruffian, but his attempts were only met with failure.

Meanwhile, the other members of the mob watched in terror as Ulam stood statuesque with a death-grip on the squirming thug, no one daring to rush to the man's aid. The surrounding crowd collectively held their breath, each member understanding the man would suffocate if Ulam did not release him soon. While some urged the other attackers onward, most remained silent, alarmed the rage-filled Orc would unleash his wrath on them next.

Amantius was shocked by the sudden display of force. He had seen Ulam mad many times before, but he had never seen him this incensed. Ulam's tusks dripped with saliva as he growled like a wolf, his eyes fixated on the man at the end of his arm. Meanwhile, Amantius did nothing, his uncertainty paralyzing his legs and his decision-making capabilities. Not only was he unsure whether or not he could resolve the situation, but he also did not know how he wanted this incident to end. *This bastard should be punished for attacking Ulam, but does he deserve death? And if Ulam kills him, what happens to us after that?*

"Ulam," Amantius said as he placed a hand on his foster-brother's massive shoulder, "put him down."

Ulam grunted, though more like a scoff than anything else. He did not take his eye off the man, who started frantically kicking at the Orc's ribs in an effort to escape.

"Let him go," Amantius continued, his voice now as dire as it was loud. He realized if Ulam killed the man, then they would be labeled murderers. "You have to let him go!"

"If I let him go, what is there to stop them from killing us?" Ulam muttered through gritted teeth.

"If you kill him, what is there to stop them from killing us?" Amantius quickly retorted. "If you want them to respect you and Orcs everywhere, then show them you're not a killer."

With a snarl, Ulam effortlessly tossed his attacker aside. The man flew across the square, desperately gasping for air after he crashed onto the ground. A small group of people then surrounded the man, rushing him into a nearby house while the crowd began filtering away. Within minutes Amantius and Ulam were the only people left in the square, both of whom were still on the lookout for more assailants.

"Well, at least now we know why people are staring at us," Amantius said with a smirk, hoping to break the tension.

"We cannot stay here," Ulam replied unamused, "if everyone in this city thinks I am going to eat their children."

"So where do we go?" Amantius asked as a seed of anxiety was planted in his gut, "We have little coin and even less food, and we do not know where any other cities are."

"I do not know, Amantius, I do not know."

Chapter 10
Ulam

They sat in a well-lit tavern, one located in the shadows of Silverwater's city walls. Amantius had asked earlier if they had enough coin to drink their troubles away, Ulam responding with only a grunt. In truth, they had plenty of money to do so, but the Orc wanted to be more careful with their funds considering he did not know what the future held for them. He figured finding work in the city, especially after the display in the market earlier, would be next to impossible. The dumbest thing to do at this moment, Ulam reasoned, was to drink themselves unconscious.

He looked around the tavern and found nothing particularly special about it. It was somewhat refreshing, as every alehouse and pub in the city possessed some gimmick to beat out the competition. Most had straw mattresses or "female companionship," while other taverns had knife throwing and other similar competitions. They had even visited a saloon with a dragon's skull mounted above the bar, an attraction for people who had never seen one before. In the back of his mind, he wondered if there was a pub for dragons that had human skulls dangling from the ceiling. He chuckled at the idea.

This place was different, though, as if it took pride in just being ordinary. The ale was decent and fairly cheap, both of which he gave thanks. No one stared at him, they mostly kept to themselves, which Ulam found relieving. Most astonishing of all, the patrons in this bar were overwhelmingly female. Aside from himself, Amantius, the barkeep, and a few others, everyone else was a woman. It was surprising, though Ulam did not think it should have been. After all, the name of the establishment was "The Bride's Oasis." He thought it was a strange name for a tavern, so naturally his curious mind needed to know the etymology.

"So, you wish to know why I called this place The Bride's Oasis." The barkeep said with a chuckle. He was a balding older man with eyes that sparkled with humor, the kind of man that people instantly liked and trusted. "When I came to this city many years ago I opened this place but didn't give it a name. Why should I? Do you really care about the name of the place you drink in? Of course not! Anyway, over time I noticed that a good portion of my business came from women, specifically recent brides who were hiding from their husbands, or their husbands-to-be, or their families. I guessed being in the far corner of the city, shadowed by the walls, made this place attractive to people looking to get away from something or someone. But then one day I did some digging around and discovered I have the only tavern in Silverwater that allows female customers, that aren't whores of course. Imagine that! After that neat little discovery, the name just seemed appropriate."

Ulam nodded, satisfied. "How come there are so few men in here, though? It is hard for me to imagine the men of this city leaving these women unmolested."

"Oh, they try, friend, they certainly try," the barkeep continued with a smile. "I have my own personal guards, paid handsomely by me to ensure the women-folk aren't disturbed. The head of the castle's guards, a man by the name of Jalkett Karraman comes here from time to time, he and I go way back. On first offense, depending on the offense of course, you get thrown out."

"What about the second offense?" Ulam asked.

The barkeep smiled, a gold tooth reflecting the flame from a nearby lamp. "There's never been a second offense. I'm guessing my employees handle it how they best see fit. Also, that reminds me," he nodded towards Amantius, "you might want to watch your friend. He seems harmless enough, but I'd really hate to have to throw you two out. Especially since I don't figure either of you have anywhere to go."

Ulam turned and saw Amantius talking to a few women at a table, though thankfully neither lady seemed to be offended. For a few seconds, he watched them chat, feeling relief when smiles appeared. He was not surprised, for Amantius had always been quite the charmer when he wanted to be. Still, he thought it was best to keep an eye on him. Even though his foster-brother still had not finished his first drink, there was always the possibility he would make a fool of himself anyhow, and Ulam did not want to be thrown out of the only friendly tavern in all of Silverwater.

"I do not think you will need to worry about him," Ulam replied as he finished the last drops in his bottle. He put a few coins on the counter, "Another one, please."

The barkeep smiled as he swiped the coins from the bar and placed another bottle of ale in front of him. "I thought you only had enough for one drink each? Are you going to let him know that?"

Ulam smiled. "What he does not know will not hurt him."

The barkeep laughed and continued cleaning the bar as Ulam drank, enjoying this moment to himself. Since they left Accaria he and Amantius had been nearly inseparable, a moment of peace an incredibly rare gift. Because he always had to be on the lookout for trouble, he had not had the opportunity to let his guard down and relax. However, in that moment, he was able to finally find some sense of inner harmony.

As Ulam finished his second beer a man approached and sat down next to him at the bar. He ordered two beers, placing the second in front of Ulam. He was roughly two decades older than the Orc, with soft, brown hair that touched his shoulders and sandpaper stubble across his face. Though he was well-built, from the corner of his eye Ulam saw the man had a limp, no doubt an injury he had sustained years ago.

"My thanks," Ulam said as he grabbed the bottle.

"Don't mention it," the man replied. His voice was strong, full of authority. "What's your name, Orc?"

"Ulam."

"Ulam, what?"

"Just Ulam."

The man did not appear satisfied with the answer. "You're not from a Sanctuary are you?"

"No," Ulam replied. He had read about Orc Sanctuaries before, little societies Orcs built after their kingdom was destroyed, usually far in the wilderness where no one else could not find them. He always assumed he was born in one, though how he came to Accaria as an infant was still a mystery.

The man adjusted himself in the seat and took a swig of beer. "I guess it doesn't matter, you're still an Orc regardless of where you were born. Anyway, word spreads fast around here. Someone mentioned something to me about seeing an Orc in Silverwater, and then told me this story about how the Orc picked a man up by the throat and held him there without breaking a sweat."

85

Ulam tried to grunt, but no noise came from his throat. He was ashamed, even a little scared. The anger he felt inside, the fury, felt so natural to him. Even worse, a part of him even liked the sensation, and that was what truly terrified him.

"Some would call you a monster, a child-eater even," the man continued, "I don't care what they call you, or what you are." Ulam shot him a quick look, the rage building inside once again.

The man held up his calloused hands, "I'm not here to judge. I've met plenty of Orcs in my life and have never seen such a thing. Hell, most Orcs are better than the Humans I've met. Have you been trained in combat?"

"No," Ulam replied, the anger subsiding. He took comfort in knowing this stranger was not here to start another brawl.

During this time Amantius approached and looked at the empty bottles in front of Ulam, punching the Orc in the shoulder. "We can only have one bottle each, Amantius," he said, mimicking Ulam's voice the best he could. "Either you lied or you simply don't know how to count. Who is your friend?"

"Forgive me," the man said as he extended his hand, "I guess I forgot to introduce myself. My name is Jalkett Karraman, I'm the Captain of the Castle Guard. I am oath-bound to protect Aldamar III, Count of Silverwater County. And you are?"

"Amantius Jeranus," Amantius replied, shaking Captain Karraman's hand. "What business do you have with us?"

"Your friend is strong, very strong indeed, and Silverwater's guard ranks are bare. Especially now, what with the Mad Raven terrorizing local farms and villages."

"Mad Raven?" Amantius asked as he quickly glanced at Ulam.

"Haven't heard of her, yet?" Karraman said as he swallowed some ale, "Well, you lads haven't been in the city for long. I'm sure you've at least noticed the rabble that is flooding our streets and taverns? Yes? Well, the Count has promised a hefty reward for anyone who brings her head to him. So naturally, every jackass with a blade is going to offer his services."

Ulam grunted in amusement, he could feel Captain Karraman's disdain for the quality of "soldier" that had taken up the sword. "So tell me, why have you chosen to recruit us and none of the others?"

Captain Karraman thought for a minute as he washed down the rest of his drink. Using the sleeve of his tunic he wiped the foam from his mouth and then turned towards Ulam again. The burning embers from one of the nearby lanterns brought light to the other side of his face for the first time, illuminating a deep gash that ran the length of his jawline. The way the flames flickered his irises appeared almost bright yellow for a second, before becoming dark again.

"I was there, in the market," he said, his voice quiet yet firm, "I watched the mob try to take your heads."

Amantius laughed. "Yes, they definitely tried. They didn't do a very good job, though."

"No, they didn't." Captain Karraman replied, his voice much more hoarse than before. "I saw two things during that charade. First, neither of you begged for your lives, nor did you try to run away. You both held your ground, determined to either win or die fighting. That riffraff you see on the streets? They're farmers with pitchforks and bounty-hunters; they'll run at the first sight of true danger. And trust me, lads, if we are sent to find the Mad Raven, we will look into the eyes of true danger."

Although the tavern's walls were still filled with laughter and merrymaking, Ulam felt as though the entire building had become deathly silent. He was not one that scared easily, nor was he scared at that moment, but something unsettling was behind Captain Karraman's eyes when he mentioned the Mad Raven.

"And what is the second thing you saw?" Amantius asked.

"You two have a brotherhood about you; a sacred bond that compels you to face all obstacles together. That is something we have been missing in the castle for quite some time, unfortunately, and it is something I'd like to reestablish, if possible."

"What does joining entail, exactly?" Ulam asked. Even though their food and coin reserves would be drained within the week, he was cautious.

"You train in the yard with some of the other men, learn your weapons if you haven't already. You protect the Count if you see him, though I am usually by his side. You will patrol the castle grounds, and you follow orders if given any. In exchange you get some coin, equipment, a place to sleep, food, and drink."

"Doesn't sound too bad," Amantius commented with a smile. "You have yourself a deal, then. We, or rather I, will join your ranks. I'm sure Ulam will too."

Ulam grunted, but it was so quiet that it was practically inaudible. He was a little irritated that Amantius volunteered without discussing the proposition with him first. However, he knew he was not going to get a better opportunity elsewhere, especially if the rest of the continent was as hostile towards Orcs as Silverwater had been so far.

"Very well, I welcome you to the Castle Guards then." Captain Karraman shook Amantius' hand before turning to Ulam. "I can see you're more cautious than he is. If you choose to join the Castle Guards as well, report at sunrise with your friend here."

Captain Karraman shook their hands once again and then exited the building, disappearing into the night. An hour later the barkeep evicted everyone who had not paid for lodging, leaving only Ulam, Amantius, and a few other travelers in the building. Ulam was thankful that neither of the strangers seemed interested in him, although he would still sleep with one eye open tonight. He did not want to wake up with a knife in his throat.

The loft had many rooms, far more than either Amantius or Ulam expected. Though the straw mattresses in their room were not of the best quality, they were much more preferable than the swaying cots in the hull of the smuggler's vessel. After the longest day in recent memory, the moment Ulam's body made contact with the mattress his muscles ached in joy. He would have been fast asleep if not for Amantius, who would not stop talking.

"See, Ulam, all our problems are solved!" He began with excitement beaming in his eyes. "And you were worried about our future!"

Ulam grunted. He had been thinking of Captain Karraman's offer since it had been given. He could not deny the positives of guaranteed food, shelter, and drink, but he also felt as though he was about to be trapped. He wanted to come to the mainland to explore, to find other Orcs and possibly even his biological family. By joining the Castle Guards he felt as though those things would never happen, that he would be stuck in this city for many years to come.

"Everything is still not settled," Ulam muttered.

"Oh, come now," Amantius replied. "At the very least, it's far better than walking this unknown world with no direction. Besides, if we are close to Count Aldamar then there is a chance we will be able to overhear any news of Accaria. Maybe if we are lucky we will be able to return home soon."

The last comment saddened Ulam, not because he was homesick, but because he believed Amantius was delusional. There was no returning to Accaria, at least not as long as King Varian reigned. To set foot in Accaria would mean to forfeit not only their lives, but their mother's as well, and that thought was too much to bear. Perhaps someday, if the King died or one of his brothers usurped the throne, they would be able to return. But who knew when, or if, that would ever happen.

"You are such a bore sometimes, Ulam," Amantius said as he finally laid his head on the pillow, "here we are, presented with a golden opportunity to make something of ourselves, and you need time to think. What is there to think about? We need employment. We need food. We need shelter. Captain Karraman and the Castle Guards offer all these things, even if…"

"You must always be cautious, Amantius," Ulam interrupted, his voice stern, "Because even if the water is still, there may be serpents that lurk beneath."

Chapter 11
Amantius

Amantius was not going to admit it, but Ulam had been right. The food Captain Karraman had promised was basic and unappealing; slices of stale bread and a bowl of bland soup every day to keep from starving. The pay was meager, and the beds were stiff and covered in the thinnest of blankets. With time and no small amount of rationing, Amantius had saved enough money to buy a wool blanket for his bed, Ulam having done the same.

He and Ulam were often assigned to stand guard in abandoned areas of the castle, where over the duration of a day only a few people would meander by. Since Ulam was not one for a long conversation, these types of assignments wore on Amantius' spirit. He did everything he could to pass the time, but nothing seemed to work. No matter how many times he counted the stones or cracks in the floor, there never were going to be any more or any less. On occasion Captain Karraman rewarded their patience with a stint outdoors, ordering them to patrol the gardens or the castle walls. These were the days Amantius came to appreciate because even the heaviest rain was still preferable to the stagnant air within the castle.

Of everything, Amantius enjoyed their training sessions with the veteran guards the most. The sparring matches happened every day, during which he watched Ulam use brute strength to defeat the other newcomers. Whenever the Orc faced one of the more seasoned men he would lose, because they honed a gracefulness and skill that Ulam did not quite possess. Amantius, on the other hand, was quick and agile, but oftentimes would let his arrogance control him. But no matter how many bruises and verbal lashings he sustained daily, he always looked forward to the next day's training session.

Within a month Amantius and Ulam were no longer viewed as green recruits, but full-fledged members of the Castle Guards. Amantius was issued a light set of chainmail as well as a short sword, both tempered by the castle's quartermaster. The first time he wore the armor he learned he did not like the extra weight, the muscles in his shoulders and back grew tired quickly and ached for days. He was supposed to wear a helmet too but he refused; there was no way he was going to let a giant piece of metal cover up his beautiful, midnight black hair.

Meanwhile, Ulam carried a one-handed axe and wore a giant piece of chainmail, which had been created and promptly forgotten long ago by a different blacksmith. It was clunky and heavy, almost too heavy for Amantius to even lift from the ground, with rust in many of the chain links. Ulam religiously polished the metal for days, scrubbing hard, hoping to remove as much rust and grime as he could. When he had finished the piece of armor shined bright, like a shimmering lake.

One day Amantius and Ulam found themselves on top of the battlements surrounding the castle, serving as nothing more than decorations. A breeze blew across the dark gray stones, chilling their arms and legs. Amantius had been talking about nonsensical things for hours, failing to find a conversation Ulam would want to have. He had tried everything; he spoke of Pelecia, Accaria, the architecture of the castle, his favorite breeds of dogs, he even proposed theories as to why there were no Orcs to be found anywhere.

Yet no matter what he tried, nothing seemed to capture Ulam's interest.

"Sometimes I wonder if Count Aldamar even exists," Amantius said. Much to his surprise, Ulam grunted. *About time, I've only been talking for half this shift.*

"Do you ever wonder why we never see Count Aldamar?" Ulam said in a low voice, hoping no one overheard him. Although, Amantius was not sure if anyone could overhear them from their spot on top of the wall.

"Every day," Amantius admitted. "Why do you think that is?"

Ulam shrugged his massive shoulders, the chainmail clinking as he did so. "I am sure he is a busy man, what with all that is happening within his city and county. Mercenaries and ruffians rule the streets, and the Mad Raven is lurking out there somewhere."

"Ah, yes, the Mad Raven," Amantius said. Ulam's words had sparked a memory, something he had intended to tell him earlier. "I overheard Captain Karraman and others speaking the other day; it seems those mercenaries and ruffians are being sent out there soon to hunt down the Mad Raven and her Flock. The Captain will be personally leading them, though I do not believe we will be leaving Silverwater."

Ulam grunted. "And what of the Castle Guards?"

Amantius shrugged. "I don't know; we'll probably be stuck here guarding the damned pantries again."

Amantius had longed for some sort of adventure, anything to break up the monotony of guarding empty corners of the castle. Even though Ulam had not said anything since they joined, Amantius believed his foster-brother craved the same thing. After all, Ulam was the one who wanted to initially decline Karraman's invitation to join the Guards and keep journeying.

After they were relieved of their patrol they retired for the night, thankful that yet another long, uneventful shift had come to a close. As they entered the barracks they saw Captain Karraman standing in the center of the room with a strange man neither had seen before, addressing the rest of their fellow Guards. When Captain Karraman saw the two enter the room he stopped his lecture and turned to Amantius and Ulam, beckoning to join his conference.

"Come join us, this is important," Karraman waved as Amantius and Ulam moved nearby. "As I was saying, on the morrow I will be leading an expedition to find and capture the Mad Raven. A few of you will accompany me, but the majority will remain here to defend the castle. In my absence, Emmon will handle the assigning of patrols and other daily tasks, and he will do so until I return." He then turned to the stranger standing beside him, "My lord, Count, do you have anything you wish to add?"

Amantius flinched involuntarily. He had suspected the unknown man was the Count, though a part of him had hoped otherwise. In his mind, the Count would be much more buoyant and adorned in the finest clothes and jewelry, as many of the noblemen and noblewomen of Accaria were. Instead, the man that stood before him appeared sickly, deathly even, wearing a purple robe so dark the fabric appeared black.

"There are quite a many things I would wish to add, though, I fear time is not our ally." Count Aldamar replied, speaking with the eloquence that begat a well-bred man. Both his hair and skin were as white as milk, as though he had never stepped foot outside his castle.

"I feared this day would come; the day in which you brave men would engage in hostilities with the dreadful Mad Raven." Aldamar's voice indicated that he felt deeply troubled by recent events; his gestures and expressions matching. "But alas, the day has arrived. For those of you about to depart for the wilderness, I bid thee good luck. I shall pray to the Gods for your victory and safe return. And upon your return, we shall have a great feast honoring your feats!"

Some men cheered while others encouraged their brethren, already making plans for the prospective feast. While this happened Count Aldamar turned to leave, but he stopped by the exit to glance at Ulam. He stared at the Orc for a few moments with surprise and curiosity melted together across his face. He muttered something under his breath, words so quiet they were virtually inaudible, and then shifted his gaze to Amantius.

As the Count stared, Amantius realized his initial observation of the man had been rather flawed. There was something fraudulent about the Count, some specific idiosyncrasy that Amantius could not quite resolve. Though he at first believed Count Aldamar was an old man with few precious years left to his life, he now saw hidden robustness within him. Where he had at first appeared old and fragile, he now appeared fierce and strong. As he stared into the Count's eyes, he felt as though Count Aldamar was staring into his soul, reading his thoughts. In response Amantius immediately began thinking of some completely unrelated topic, hoping his silly precaution would prevent having his true feelings exposed.

The corner of Count Aldamar's mouth curved so slightly that it was virtually non-existent, but Amantius saw the change. He felt a chill go down his spine; the hair stood erect on the nape of his neck. His blood turned to ice, spear-shaped glaciers knifing through his veins. He tried to remain stoic with what little resolve he still possessed, but he knew even his best efforts were trivial.

Suddenly Amantius felt a heavy blow to his ribs, the jab courtesy of Ulam's elbow. He turned to the Orc and was about to say something, but Ulam's expression stopped him. His foster-brother held a stern, even worried, demeanor, one that nonverbally begged him to keep his mouth shut.

"Welcome," Count Aldamar said, the sinister smirk affixed to his face. He then turned towards the doorway and left the room, his footsteps silent on the cobblestone floors.

"Something isn't right about him," Amantius said just above a whisper. "Do you feel it too, Ulam?"

Ulam grunted. "Perhaps, but he is a man of power, and we would be smart to not interfere with him." He grabbed Amantius by the bicep, "What I mean is *you* would be smart not to interfere with his affairs."

Amantius pulled away, rubbing his arm where the Orc's powerful hand had squeezed.

At least if the Count read my mind he only learned that I've never liked blondes.

Chapter 12
Ulam

Ulam could not quite understand Amantius' opinion of Count Aldamar. For days after their encounter that was all he spoke of; as if he had become obsessed with the man. He began to loathe the moments they spent alone atop the castle walls, or in a tavern, or anywhere else. Amantius would not shut his mouth about the subject, and Ulam increasingly became more paranoid someone would overhear his ranting.

Ulam believed the Count was an eccentric man, much unlike any other he had met before. He believed that behind the Count's dark, brooding eyes was a gold mine of wisdom and knowledge, a level of which that far exceeded even the most intelligent of beings. Ulam respected that, and his respect for such brilliance unexpectedly bred a fiber of loyalty to the man. For all his quirks, Ulam did not suspect anything sinister about the Count. If anything, he thought Count Aldamar was a misunderstood introvert, much like himself.

Ulam was patrolling above the castle's gatehouse, watching as Captain Karraman's battalion departed from Silverwater. A strong wind blew across the city, causing the banners of the departing soldiers to dance in the breeze. The warband marching to battle was quite a spectacle, far more impressive than anything Ulam had read in any of his books. He stood in silence as the entire army poured through the northwest gate and into the farmland surrounding the city, as stray dogs and supply wagons followed closely behind.

"They're marching to their deaths," Amantius' voice suddenly came from behind.

Ulam grunted. Although he recognized the possibility of his foster-brother's statement, he still could not come to agree. "Captain Karraman has too many able-bodied men, strong men who have seen lots of combat. They will return victorious; I have no doubt."

"And how are you so certain of that?" Amantius asked as he joined Ulam on the rampart, "The Mad Raven, whatever she is, has her Flock. And if the stories are true, each has the strength of ten men and…"

"Stories are rarely true, Amantius," Ulam interrupted, quickly dismissed such fears, "If stories are to be taken as truth, then my favorite meal is the raw flesh of Human children." He cracked a smile at the lunacy of such an idea.

Amantius snickered, though Ulam sensed he was not entirely convinced. He was not too surprised, though, his foster-brother had always been more apt to believe rumors and legends. *After all, this is the same Amantius who believed fairies lived inside lava and would give him magical powers if he caught one. Damn fool almost got himself killed.*

"Fear not," Ulam continued as he kept his eyes fixed on the horizon, "Count Aldamar would not send members of his own personal guard to their deaths intentionally."

"And how do you know that?" Amantius exclaimed. "I know you do not believe me, but there is something malevolent about the man, Ulam. I can't prove it now, but I will in due time."

Ulam slammed his fist down on the stone parapet, loosening a rogue pebble that fell to the ground. "Again with this nonsense. I understand we have differing opinions of the man, but you need to move on. You have been trying to prove your theories ever since we were first acquainted with the Count, and each time you have uncovered nothing. Abandon this fruitless pursuit, Amantius, before you get us both thrown into a dungeon!"

Ulam returned his gaze to a spot on the horizon, where a single cluster of trees stood. He had been harsher than intended, but his words carried much weight with them. He did not think Amantius quite comprehended that they were foreigners in a foreign land, a land where no one would come to their rescue in a moment of crisis. This was painfully obvious to Ulam, perhaps because he was an Orc and knew his punishment would be far worse than that of his Human counterpart.

Amantius did not speak during the rest of their patrol, which Ulam believed to be a godsend. He welcomed the silence, the consistent hum of civilization filling the space between them. Ulam watched as storm clouds darkened the sky, flinching when the first droplets of cold rain hit his skin. He felt bad for the army marching in the direction of the blackest clouds; he could not imagine how frustrating marching in such conditions must be.

After their patrol ended they retired to the barracks for the night, the building left virtually empty from all the men who had marched off to war. Ulam found the rows of vacant beds pleasing because for the first time since coming to Silverwater he would be able to read a book by candlelight. Practically every time he had tried prior, he was interrupted by rowdy, drunken guards or men returning from their patrols. He smiled, because on this night he knew there would be no interruptions.

A few days earlier Ulam had visited a bookshop in one of the wealthier areas of the city, a place where he knew he would be able to find books. While there he used his wages to purchase a specific book, a narrative about Orcish history. It was a subject that he knew little about, which embarrassed him to no small degree. In a way, he half-believed if he read this book he would better understand his heritage, and quite possibly learn how he came to Accaria as an infant.

Ulam waited a few extra minutes until he heard Amantius snoring; he wanted to make sure before he delved too deeply in his book that his foster-brother would not start some meaningless conversation again. As soon as he heard the first few snorts, he opened the book to the first page and began reading.

Dawn arrived far sooner than Ulam expected. The first few beams of gold poured into his eyes from the windows, their presence prevented him from going back to sleep. As he sat up in his bed he heard swords cutting into wooden decoys, their clangs echoing off the walls of the nearby courtyard. Beside him, Amantius kept snoring, until the main door swung open and the overnight patrol returned to the bunkroom.

"Quiet night?" One of the guards asked the returning men.

"Quiet and wet," the other guard groaned, "And of course the damn sun decided to come out right before our shift ended."

"Lucky us," Amantius said as he jumped out of bed, slapping Ulam on the shoulder as he stretched. "Come on, Beautiful, it's our turn."

Ulam put away his book, disappointed that he had fallen asleep during the night and was unable to read more.

Not only that, but he also did not retain much of what he read before closing his eyes. *Such a waste of time. Oh well, perhaps I will be able to read tonight.*

Before long he found himself atop the ramparts with Amantius again, wondering if he had ever left. His previous shift seemingly blended into the current one, as though there had been no time in between. Perhaps in the past he would have cared about the lack of free time, but ultimately it did not matter. There was nothing he wanted to do in this city other than eat, drink, sleep, and read, and most of the time he was able to do at least three of those things.

"Weather isn't so bad today," Amantius said as they reached their posts. "How long do you think we'll be up here? You know, until the Captain's warband returns?"

Ulam grunted, then shrugged. "Who knows? I do not even know where the Mad Raven's…" his words trailed off as his nose picked up some smell. Silverwater had as many odors as any city, some pleasant, some not so, but there was one that Ulam had not smelled here before. He paced around the wall, following the wafting aroma as it grew stronger and stronger. "Do you smell that?"

"Smell what?" Amantius asked.

"It smells like…" Ulam crinkled his nose, his eyes expanding as soon as he saw a plume of black smoke spiraling towards the sky. "Fire!"

A couple of houses near the northern wall were on fire, a raging inferno of red and orange engulfing both structures entirely. Without any hesitation Ulam found the nearest staircase and ran, abandoning his post. The screams and ringing of bells giving his legs a boost of adrenaline as he sprinted through the courtyard and into the city proper.

"Ulam!" Amantius called from the top of the archway. "Ulam! Wait!"

There was no time to wait. He cast off his heavy armor, dumping the chainmail at the base of the castle's wall, and darted through the streets. Men, women, and children ran in the opposite direction, their shrieks of terror joining the symphony of crackling wood. In the distance behind him, Ulam heard Amantius' voice calling him, but the words were lost in the turbulence.

Ulam turned the last corner and saw the bedlam awaiting him. The first home had already imploded, the second undoubtedly following shortly. Whatever emotion that compelled him to rush to the fire now left, leaving only a sense of futility. There was nothing he could do except watch.

"Ulam!" Amantius yelled as he crashed into the Orc, panting. "The river is the other way! Come on, let's get…"

"Help! Someone help me!" Amantius' words were interrupted by the screams of a teenage girl standing near them, her face matted with ash. "Someone help, please!"

Ulam dashed towards her, nearly crushing the girl with his heavy arms. "I am here, child. Tell me what you need."

"My mother and sister!" The girl continued to wail through her sobs. "My mother and sister are in there!"

She pointed at the second home, the structure still somehow standing amidst the chaos. Flames leaped high on all sides, almost as high as the castle walls. Ulam looked at the house, bit his lip, and started to run for the burning building.

"Ulam, what are you doing!?" Amantius shouted, "You will die if you go in there! We should wait for the others, they will be bringing water!"

Ulam did not hesitate, he jumped through the flames and into the house.

Chapter 13
Amantius

Amantius watched as Ulam's hulking shape hurdled a fallen beam and disappeared into the leaping clutches of the blaze. Unlike the Orc, who charged in without a second thought, Amantius was frozen to the spot. His legs were as heavy as stone, his knees weak. A sickening feeling churned in his gut as he watched and waited, hoping Ulam would see the folly of his decision and come back before it was too late.

Why did I let him go in? Amantius thought, although he was not sure he could have stopped Ulam even if he had sincerely tried. *What if he dies? What if I am left here, alone, in this city?*

He stared wide-eyed at the house, its walls now blackened entirely. All that remained of the adjacent home was the thick logs used for the frame, and even those were not going to last much longer. The heat from the inferno was unbearable, so much so that Amantius had to remove his armor. The metal had heated to such an extreme that his flesh began to bake like a roast in an oven, though the smell was much less appealing.

Beside him the teenage girl was inconsolable, having collapsed on the ground in misery. She no longer looked at her home, instead keeping her eyes closed tight. She tried to scream from time to time, but her voice was so hoarse that she could no longer force words from her mouth. Amantius kneeled beside her and cradled her head against his chest, stroking what remained of her singed hair. Deep inside he was crying with her, but for some reason, no tears would leave his eyes. He was too numb, too paralyzed by fear, to feel emotion.

"He's gone," Amantius whispered. For the first time, he heard the brass bells ringing from the towers, as well as the shouts of the townsfolk. Much like the girl he closed his eyes, hoping to shut out the noise.

Suddenly the main beam over the entrance to the second home collapsed, shooting a squall of embers into the sky. Amantius' heart turned to solid ice as he watched, realizing Ulam's escape was now barred by certain death. Renewed shrieks filled the area, causing the teenage girl in his arms to begin moaning once more. Amantius hugged her tighter, hoping his embrace would bring her some comfort, though in his heart he was the one seeking comfort.

"Amantius!" A voice suddenly roared from within the house. It was deep, guttural, and filled with urgency. "Where are you!?"

Amantius sprang to his feet, his eyes locked on the entranceway. He searched every inch of the collapsing house for the voice, knowing in his heart of hearts whose voice was calling to him.

"Ulam!" He yelled, his heart feeling as though it would explode. "Ulam, where are you!?"

"Side window!" Ulam yelled back.

Amantius rushed to the other side of the house, where Ulam's face appeared in a broken out window. A thin layer of smoke poured out of the puncture Ulam's fist had made in the glass, and together the two of them worked to remove the rest of the shards.

"I thought you were dead," Amantius blurted out, the tears no longer holding back.

"I will be if we do not hurry," Ulam replied, his voice grave. Amantius noticed that his foster-brother's face was darker than usual, covered in soot. "I have both the mother and daughter, but they are not conscious, if they are even still alive. I am going to pass them through the window, I need you to grab them and take them away from this building."

Just then a part of the roof snapped off and flaming boards fell all around Amantius, reminded him that time was precious. Ulam passed the child through the window first, a little girl no older than five. She was small, frail, and easy to hold. Her clothes had been burned off, her skin covered in soot; Amantius could not tell if she was breathing or not.

He ran away from the burning home, cradling the little girl in his arms. When he reached the crowd a priestess showed herself, accepting the child into her care. Without hesitation Amantius ran back to the house, his chest burning from the black smoke swirling inside his lungs. Under normal circumstances, he may have taken a break and allowed himself to recover, but knowing Ulam's life hung in the balance was the ultimate motivation to fight through the pain.

When he reached the inferno he saw the city guard had arrived with buckets of water from the river, dousing the flames nearest the crowd. He realized they had condemned the burning homes to a smoking ruin, concluding they were a lost cause, and set about preventing the fire from spreading. Amantius cursed, but there was no time to argue, he needed to get Ulam and the other person out of the house.

"Ready?" Ulam said as he arrived, a thick trail of smoke flowing out of the broken window. He lifted the woman to the opening and gently passed her to Amantius, who grabbed her under the arms and pulled her out of the house.

She was not a heavy-set woman by any means, but Amantius' energy was fading. His muscles ached from a mixture of overuse and dehydration, while the shortage of clean air left him panting like a dog. He felt like he was on the verge of suffocation.

"Let me carry her," a guard said as Amantius dragged the woman to safety. The man threw a blanket over her body to protect her decency, because much like her daughter, the mother's clothing had been eaten by hungry flames as well.

"No, I have her," Amantius replied, "save my brother."

"Your brother? Is he in there?" The guard said, his voice turning to shock.

"By the window," Amantius said and nodded towards the side of the house. He left the guard, continuing to take the woman to the priestess. When he was within sight a few men ran from the crowd and took her from Amantius' arms, leaving him to collapse from utter exhaustion. He stared upwards into the cloudless, blue sky, his eyes following a lone gull. While lying there he heard footsteps near him and watched as a cloud of street dust floated above his face. He coughed violently, not because of the dirt, but from the smoke he had inhaled. He then turned on his side and vomited, the convulsions far more painful than anything else.

"Are you alright?" A woman said suddenly. "Hey! I think he needs help!"

Amantius tried focusing on the person above him, but his vision had become blurred. His whole world began spinning, causing him to vomit until there was nothing left inside him other than black smoke. When he finished he felt someone place a cup of cold water against his lips, the much needed liquid disappearing within seconds. Amantius drank

107

three more cups of water before he stood up again, using a fifth to wash the smoke, grime, and sweat from his face. Though his head pounded louder than a brass bell, and his eyes burned hotter than the sun, the water had given him enough energy to continue.

When Amantius returned he saw a few guards hopelessly fighting the flames near the window, Ulam nowhere to be seen. Amantius' heart sank as he searched for his foster-brother, his desperation driving him to grab a nearby hatchet and start hacking at the side of the house. In his panic, he hoped to create a big enough hole for Ulam to crawl through, though in the back of his mind he knew he was also weakening the house's structural integrity. But Amantius did not have time to debate the logic of his plan, he only had enough time to hack away. Each consecutive strike was more desperate than the previous until at last the blade had become so dull it was virtually useless to him.

Amantius tossed the hatchet aside, his frustration and fear so severe he started punching and kicking the hatchet-scarred boards in front of him. As he bloodied his knuckles on the blackened wood he heard a series of crackling noises emanate from within the house, and watched as the whole house started to sway back and forth. Amantius stepped back, certain the building was about to collapse under its own weight. His thoughts immediately turned to Ulam, and if he had not been so exhausted, tears may have flooded his ash-covered cheeks. But all he could do was slump to the ground and stare in horror.

The guards who fought the flames alongside Amantius had retreated as well, collectively agreeing they had done all they could. Many were slumped over, each desperately trying to quench their thirsts by sucking dry any container with liquid inside. Some had minor cuts and wounds that were dressed, while others orchestrated the removal of any bystanders. A few people were shouting nearby, though Amantius could not hear their words. His mind was solely focused on the house and his failure to rescue Ulam, all other sights and sounds would have to wait.

Then suddenly he heard a howl, one unlike he had ever heard before, followed by an ear-shattering boom. A barrage of warped wood shot through the air, eliciting a cacophony of shrieks from the nearby crowd. Amantius turned his head to protect himself from the thousands of embers riding the debris, wincing as a few pieces landed on his forearms. When he turned back around to observe the destruction he was greeted with a very different sight, one he thought he would never see again. Instead of a burning pile of rubble, Amantius saw Ulam, blackened from head to toe, a grimace on his face and a crazed look in his eyes. The Orc took a few steps before falling to the ground near a battalion of city guards, all of whom jumped to their feet to remove him from the chaos.

"Ulam!" Amantus tried to yell, but his dry throat produced no sound. He grasped a nearby discarded canteen, but there was not even a single drop to aid him. He attempted to stand, but his legs buckled like a newborn calf's. All he wanted was to be at Ulam's side, but his arms and legs were too heavy, as though they had turned to stone. He watched helplessly from a distance, praying his foster-brother would survive.

"No major burns," Amantius overheard someone say, followed by murmuring. Slowly people crept out of the alleyways to fill the area around, staring and speaking in hushed voices. Amantius' initial reaction was anger; he did

109

not want Ulam's pain and potential death to be a public scene. Though the longer he listened, the more he realized the people surrounding the plaza were not gawking at Ulam, but praying for him. Some helped bring more water for those that had fought the flames, one person even brought some cool refreshments for Amantius.

As he was drinking there was a sudden gasp, followed by men and women giving thanks to the Gods. Amantius immediately tossed the water aside, now finding the strength not to only stand, but jolt over to Ulam. He saw the Orc sitting up now, a pearl white smile spreading across his face, his tusks gleaming in the afternoon sunlight. Ulam stood as well, batted the ash off his mossy skin, and stepped towards his foster-brother.

Amantius wrapped his arms around Ulam, no longer holding back his tears. He felt his heartbeat in his ears and thought the organ would tear straight from his chest. Instead, he felt the massive arms of Ulam crush his torso, popping his spine as the Orc embraced him. They stood together in the plaza, both smothered in black ash, holding one another as they would never let go.

Both houses had become smoldering ruins, no more than a few thick beams that would burn for hours. As time went on the guards and townspeople started working together to extinguish the last of the flames, not wanting to take any chances. The sizzling of water hitting the burned wood replaced the sounds of burning thatch, the smell a little more bitter than before. Slowly Amantius became aware that the crowd surrounding them was clapping, even cheering. He thought it unusual because only a few hours ago the townsfolk would have happily murdered Ulam if they believed they would not be punished for the crime. But now, they were shouting his name like he was a hero of old.

"I thought you were dead," he said, wiping away the streaks his tears had made on his soiled face.

"Why would you think that?" Ulam replied, genuinely confused.

Amantius grinned, "You're such a slow runner, those big legs..."

Ulam jabbed him the ribs. It hurt, but the pain was worth the joke. They both started laughing, the pent-up emotion flooding out from the dams they had built. Though Ulam bellowed on, Amantius' laughter was cut short when a flash of yellow on top of the castle caught his eye. There, in the shadows of the tallest tower of the keep, stood an ominous figure.

"Aldamar," Amantius whispered. He had no proof, he just knew. The same cold shiver he always felt near the Count once again shot down his spine.

"What about him?" Ulam replied, a hint of surprise in his voice.

"He's watching us," Amantius said, still whispering. *Why is he watching us, though?*

But before Ulam could look, the silhouette had disappeared.

Chapter 14
Ulam

Though none of his injuries were major, Ulam still spent a few days recovering. He had only suffered minor burns and a cut across his arm where he punched out the window, nothing that some rest could not heal. Initially, he thought he was fit enough to return to his patrols, but his coughing episodes still happened from time to time, and they were quite violent. Often times a black liquid would ooze from his lungs, burning his throat and leaving him utterly exhausted. And since his post was frequently at the top of the castle walls, he figured a few more days of rest was a sound decision. *To survive an inferno only to fall to my death would be quite unfortunate, not to mention embarrassing as well.*

Ulam saw little of Amantius during this time, which was both a blessing and a curse. In one way he was happy with the silence and the alone time, finally finding the opportunity to read the book he had been dying to read. On the other, he was afraid Amantius would get himself into trouble, especially after his foster-brother thought he spotted Count Aldamar watching from afar. Ulam became deeply worried about the obsession with the Count, believing the newfound fame and celebrity would further embolden Amantius to act upon his suspicions. And since Ulam was not by his side to watch over him, to prevent him from doing anything irrational, anxiety constantly hovered over him like a black cloud.

Ulam decided to push those thoughts from his mind, realizing if he continued to worry he would only drive himself mad. Instead, he picked up his book and continued reading, getting lost in a different time and place. Over the last few days, he had learned a lot about Orcish history, how they had warred with both Humans and Elves until their sudden, mysterious demise. He felt a keen sadness while reading the text, believing had he lived during that time he would have been able to mend the distrust between the different races. But he was born too late, and as a result, the relations gap between Orc and Human had never been wider.

He burned through the pages, consuming every word until there were none left to read. Upon finishing he wondered about his own origin once again, dying to know the beginning chapters of his lost story. But more importantly, he still questioned how he came to Accaria as an infant, and why Pelecia raised him as her own child. He felt a great emptiness inside as he realized he would most likely never find the answers to those questions, especially now that he was exiled from his homeland.

Homeland was an interesting concept to Ulam. To some degree he thought of Accaria as his home, though in the back of his mind he knew this was not true. The people there had treated him well enough, but there had always been an obvious difference between Accarian and non-Accarian. In some ways, he thought Wrothvar, the fallen kingdom of the Orcs, to be a homeland of some sort. But Wrothvar had been destroyed long ago, with its people scattered to the four winds. *I have no home.*

Ulam decided he needed to get out of the barracks, to escape the cabin fever slowly taking over. He thought perhaps fresh air would do his spirit some good, even if he had to endure the vitriolic glares he would inevitably receive walking across Silverwater. But on the other side of that walk would be The Bride's Oasis, his reward a couple of beers and a lively conversation with the barkeep.

He stepped outside the barracks, the sunlight warming his face. Children's laughter filled the air, dogs barked, while bards sang for a small donation. As he crossed the city he noticed something different, something quite remarkable. No longer did the townspeople stare at him, shouting insults and openly scheming their plans for murder. Instead, they cheered for him, some even approached to shake his big, Orcish hand.

This is weird, Ulam thought as he continued his stroll towards The Bride's Oasis. *Everyone is being nice to me.*

He continued walking, even returning a wave from time to time. Although he had always been a more private individual and constantly warned Amantius of the perils of egotism, he began to understand why the feeling was so intoxicating. It felt good to be loved and respected by the masses, a foreign concept to Ulam and something he did not think he ever would experience.

He turned a corner and saw a child, who waved at him with a radiant smile on her face. Ulam waved back, even allowing himself to return the smile, feeling awkward at first. But as the little girl began to giggle, Ulam felt a warmth inside that he had never felt before. There was something about making a child laugh that brought him great joy.

"What are you doing!?" A woman's panicked voice shouted as she ran to the little girl, scooping her up before running away. "Stay away from him!"

The woman and the child disappeared into a house, leaving Ulam standing alone in the street, his smile quickly fading. He felt embarrassed, leaving himself unguarded for a brief moment. *Ulam, you damn fool! You should have known it would not last forever. To some people, you will always be a monster.*

The barkeep at the Bride's Oasis welcomed Ulam like an old friend, sliding a beer across the countertop before he had even ordered. Ulam snatched the mug with one of his big Orcish hands and then proceeded to empty its contents, the frothy delight the perfect remedy to his troubles. He was more than halfway through the second mug before he even stopped to breathe. *Gods, I needed this.*

"Tell me," the barkeep said as he cleaned a bucket of used tankards, "what made you run into that burning house? I would think you wouldn't be so quick to risk your life for a bunch of people who hate you."

It was a valid question, one which Ulam had no valid answer. He had engaged in an internal debate about that for days, wondering just exactly what drove him into the roaring flames. Did he really care about the people inside? Did he want the glory? Did he hope that somehow if he did enough good deeds, eventually the locals would accept him as more than a vicious demon on a mission to eat all their children?

"I do not know," Ulam grunted before gulping down more ale. "I just did."

The barkeep paused, and Ulam could feel the stare. He was used to it, the look people gave him when they were trying to figure him out, as though he was an ancient puzzle waiting to be solved. He remained motionless, staring at the copper liquid rippling in his mug.

"I believe you," the barkeep finally said and went back to scrubbing. "I can see you're confused. Still, that was a hell of a thing you did without a cause. Seems to me like you have a death-wish of sorts, which is not unusual for an Orc I suppose."

A thought shot into Ulam's mind, something he should have remembered earlier but did not. *The barkeep has traveled a lot, he probably has known other Orcs.*

"What do you mean by that?" Ulam asked, trying to stay calm. His heart began to beat quickly, hope overtaking his soul.

"Oh you know, it seems like your race is born with some kind of drive that compels them to do dangerous things," the barkeep replied, his eyes focused on a stain on one of the mugs, "It is like they seek out Death and challenged Him to a duel. Captain Karraman has told me many stories of Orcs he has known, like the story of the caravan guard in the far north who tried slitting a sleeping giant's throat. Do you know how big a giant's throat is?" The barkeep formed as large of a circle as he could with his arms, "About that big, maybe more."

"Did he succeed?" Ulam asked, knowing what the answer to his question was. He did not care though, he was happy to hear a story about another Orc. Happy to know there were still Orcs living somewhere, that he was not the last living member of his race.

"Yes, actually," the barkeep replied, surprising Ulam, though his lips quickly curled into a frown. "He did slice open the giant's throat, about as deep as I would slice open my hand on a splinter. Then the sleeping bastard grabbed the Orc, lifted him high in the air, and smashed his head against a stone." The barkeep shivered.

Before Ulam could ask any more questions or even change the subject, the barkeep offered up another story of a different Orc's ill-conceived idea that led to his death. And then another. And then another. At some point, Ulam began to wonder if what the barkeep said was true, that there was some natural temperament that caused Orcs to seek out their deaths. *Will I die a horrible death like the others?*

"Drink up, lad, I'm sure it was the line of work," the barkeep said as he passed another mug filled with ale to Ulam. "Don't worry about these things. You seem like you got a good head on your shoulders, best to put my ramblings out of your mind."

Ulam sat in silence for the rest of his stay, mulling over the barkeep's stories. He refused to believe all Orcs were suicidal, reasoning that if it were true the entire race would have been extinct long ago. But despite his logic, Ulam felt slightly unsettled, because he remembered the moment he ran into the burning house to save the mother and daughter, and how he felt no fear. Instead, where fear should have been, there had only been a rush of excitement.

It was dusk by the time he reached the barracks, his return walk far more pleasant. Of course, he was more relaxed now that his body was filled with a keg's worth of beer. He cursed when he passed the book shop, forgetting he had intended to pick up a new book before returning to duty. The mere thought of patrolling the walls again made him scowl; Ulam thought the whole ordeal was a colossal waste of time.

He entered the barracks, seeing Amantius' face first. His foster-brother was entertaining some of the other guards with tales of their childhood, specifically the time he smoked a grapevine hoping he would impress an older girl by appearing more mature. Ulam smiled, remembering that day fondly.

"So I put the stalk to my mouth, right," Amantius said, holding an invisible grapevine like he would a pipe, "and I inhale and suddenly," he started laughing, "I started coughing. And not the kind of coughing you do when you have a cold, but the worst kind of coughing you possibly could have. It felt like my lungs were on fire and I was going to suffocate. And the taste? It was so bitter I thought my tongue would rot out of my mouth! Anyway, I start rolling around, crying my eyes out, screaming at Ulam to give me water. But just when I thought things couldn't get worse…"

"What?" A few of the guards asked, their voices indicating they were ready to join in the laughter.

Amantius was laughing too hard to speak. He beckoned Ulam to finish the story.

"He began vomiting, not only on himself but on the girl as well," Ulam said, unable to hide his own amusement. He saw the scene vividly in his mind; an infant Amantius trying to impress the scarlet-haired daughter of a visiting diplomat. He could still see the shock and disgust on her face, while little Amantius' twisted in pain and horror. Instead of winning a kiss on the cheek, he instead got a slap across the face.

Everyone in the barracks was laughing now, none harder than Amantius. Although surely traumatizing at the time, Ulam was happy to see his foster-brother now saw the humor in the unfortunate event. Most importantly, though, Ulam was happy Amantius was mingling with the others, becoming more social with each passing day. He was able to talk of good times in Accaria without being overcome with a sense of homesickness, and that pleased Ulam greatly.

"So turns out you can't smoke grapevines, or if you do, be prepared to want to die," Amantius concluded, tears rolling down his cheeks from his laughter. "But of course, I probably don't have to tell you guys that. I've seen the grapevines outside the city, I'm sure you knew that long before I did."

"Aye," many of the men agreed with a chuckle.

For the better part of the night they continued telling stories, most of boyhood shenanigans but some of lost love. One by one the men fell asleep, creating a symphony of snoring that sounded more like a barn full of pigs. Eventually, only Ulam and Amantius were still awake, sitting quietly at a nearby table while sharing a jug of wine. They were playing a local card game one of the men had taught Amantius, though Ulam was not sure they were playing correctly. The wine may have had a part in that.

"So are you ready to go on patrols again?" Amantius asked as he played a card.

Ulam grunted. The injuries he suffered were fully healed, he just did not have the desire to go back. He enjoyed being the master of his own time, doing what he wanted to do. The thought of having to stand on a wall all day listening to Amantius lobby accusations at Count Aldamar was enough to sour his mood.

"There's been whispers," Amantius continued, "that you're milking this, that you're just being lazy. Just thought you should know before the others begin to resent you since you're likely not going to make many friends in this city. Hero or not." Amantius stood, stretched, and began walking to his bed. "By the way, I won."

"Looks like you did," Ulam said with a shrug, tossing his hand on top of the rest of the cards. He retired to his bed as well, stretching his limbs as he pulled the blanket over his body. He decided to return to duty on the morrow, the guilt of taking extended time off creeping into his gut once again.

He closed his eyes, and within moments he added his snores to the rest.

The morning was half over before Ulam had fully awakened, having arrived quicker than he had hoped. He was not excited about returning to duty, and even less so about having to retrain his body to rise earlier than he had been. He cursed when he realized he would have to skip breakfast, knowing by the time he joined Amantius he would be starving.

The sun was high overhead as he climbed the battlements, the rays unforgiving to the headache left behind by the copious amounts of ale and wine he consumed the day prior. Every sound was magnified a thousand times over, his ears making him aware of noises he had never noticed before. A bell on the other side of Silverwater rang for what Ulam believed was the first time ever, each chime thundering in his head. A flock of birds chattered on a house somewhere in the city, their squawks feeling like a thousand arrows shooting into his brain. *Of all the days I could have returned to duty, why did I choose this one?*

"You don't look so well," Amantius said with a snicker, "seems like your little vacation has made you soft."

Ulam grunted, not wanting to use the energy to form a reply. Amantius goaded him a little longer before changing the subject, continuously speaking for over an hour until he finally stopped midsentence. *Ah, silence.*

"Do you see that?" Amantius eventually said, using his spear tip to point across the city.

"Please not be another fire," Ulam replied, his voice grim. Even if a dragon set the entire world ablaze, Ulam decided he was not going to budge from that wall.

120

"No, coming down the road towards us," Amantius said, his voice serious. "It looks like…"

Horns blared from the northwest gate, spurring a dozen men on horseback to ride from the city. They headed along the road in the direction of Silverwood Forest, towards a series of blurred figures far enough away to be indiscernible. Within moments the two groups met, then with the same urgency a rider was hastening back to Silverwater. Ulam watched as the horseman rode through the gate, across the city, and into the castle's courtyard. Together Ulam and Amantius descended the stairs to find the horseman out of breath, his sleek mount glistening with sweat. Before they could speak to the rider the castle doors opened and outstepped a few guards flanking Count Aldamar, who stopped at the edge of the shadows cast by the stone towers.

The man stumbled off his horse and kneeled before Aldamar. "My Lord Count," he began, his voice full of panic, "dire news."

Aldamar's expression was cold, emotionless. "Take a breath, and then continue."

"It's about Karraman's warband," the man said, "they have returned."

That was Captain Karraman's warband? Ulam thought, *There was no more than…*

"Only six men have returned. The rest," the horseman paused, his voice trembling, "the Mad Raven, she has killed them all. Captain Karraman himself is gravely wounded, the survivors are unsure if he will survive."

Everyone in the courtyard gasped except for Count Aldamar, who flashed a pained look before recapturing his stoic countenance. Ulam studied Aldamar's face, not surprised to see that the Count maintained the same

121

indifferent demeanor which defined him. The man had a constant calmness about him, the kind of self-control that Ulam hoped to attain for himself one day. He admired the way the Count was handling the new information, even though a dozen voices had erupted in a panic-fueled conversation. Ulam thought Aldamar looked like a stone in the middle of a river, ever strong and constant while the rapids broke before him.

"Give this man refreshments, and send a host of healers and others to assist those returning." Count Aldamar said to a few guards who had just arrived, his voice strong and unwavering, "When they have been fed and rested, bring them to me; I must know everything before we decide upon our next course of action."

A new course of action? Ulam thought, a grimace unknowingly forming on his lips. He turned to Amantius, who was lost in conversation with a nearby comrade. *Are we next?*

Chapter 15
Amantius

Dead, they're all dead. Well, not all, but close enough.

Days had passed since the survivors of Captain
Karraman's warband returned to Silverwater. Only six
remained, the Captain amongst them. His health had not
improved much, but it was an encouraging sign that he had
not died yet. Their return cast a permanent gloom over
Silverwater, as the townsfolk and guards alike exchanged
worried looks and paranoid whispers. Even within the ranks
of the Castle Guards an uneasiness grew, the men fearful of
the future. While most believed there would be no more
forays into the wilderness, they knew if another attempt was
made they would be the ones dying.

Amantius sat alone in the castle's courtyard in front
of a garden of flowers, watching a bee happily jumping
between petals of blue and yellow. To some degree he envied
that bee, completely unaware of the panic spreading through
Silverwater. Unlike many in the city, the fuzzy little creature
did not have to worry about potentially fighting the Mad
Raven; its only purpose in life was to visit as many flowers as
possible. *You have no idea how good you have it, Little Bee. Enjoy it
while it still lasts.*

Amantius worried about the future, about what plans
Aldamar and his advisors were concocting at that very
moment. He feared he would be sent, along with the rest of
the Castle Guards, to hunt down the Mad Raven and her
Flock. But he questioned the logic behind such a decision,
because if Captain Karraman could not bring her to justice

then every other attempt would surely fail as well. *Hopefully the Count is smart enough to realize that. But even if he is, will he care?*

"Heard anything?" Ulam said as he approached, his voice gruff as always.

"Nothing other than whispers. Any word on Captain Karraman?"

"He woke up today," Ulam replied, "he has been in counsel with Count Aldamar for half the day. No one seems to know what happened out there. I have heard all kinds of rumors, but I am not sure if any are true."

"What have people been saying?" Amantius asked. He found it kind of odd that Ulam knew more of the local gossip than he did. The Orc had never been one to tell tales or spread stories.

Ulam grunted. "Nonsense mostly. Dark magic, monsters, the usual. I am sure those are all not true; they were probably ambushed in the forest somewhere. If I were the Mad Raven, that is what I would have done. You have seen how thick the brush grows here; you can hide a whole army in it and still have room for the horses. We will have to keep an eye out for traps like those when we go looking for her."

Amantius felt a sudden tremor shoot through his whole body. He knew it was a possibility, but he did not want to think about hunting down someone, or something, that had so easily killed an entire warband. "When? How do you..."

An uncomfortable look flashed on Ulam's face for the briefest of moments, but the Orc quickly settled back into his natural countenance. "I might have overheard a conversation..."

Amantius started laughing, the raucousness interrupting Ulam's words. "You were eavesdropping? You, the one who told me to keep my nose out of the Count's business, spying on…"

Ulam shot a fatal glare as he began to growl. "Be quiet you nitwit! Are you trying to get both of us killed?"

Amantius shook his head, still smiling. He did not care who heard him, he simply found too much humor in Ulam admitting to spying. His joy was short-lived, however, as the reality of their situation started to take hold. *What am I going to do? I've never fought in a battle before!*

Amantius heard the sounds of a metal boot on gravel approaching from behind, the familiar clinking of iron on rock indicating one of his comrades was approaching. He turned and saw Emmon, the man left in charge of the Castle Guards in Karraman's absence. Amantius did not know much about the man, other than what he could see on the surface. Unlike Captain Karraman, Emmon was shorter, with an average build and a calm, collected way of speaking. He was a man of few, but important words.

"I have been looking for the both of you," Emmon said as he approached, the same indifferent look on his grizzled face, "I have called a meeting inside the barracks; it is mandatory."

Amantius did not like the sound of that, but he figured he was not going to like the sound of anything soon. "Is this about Captain Karraman's return?"

Emmon gave away nothing, instead rolling his eyes in annoyance in lieu of a reply. Quietly he returned to the castle, leaving Ulam and Amantius alone once again. After giving Emmon enough of a head start, the pair followed, heading for the barracks as soon as they were indoors. As they entered the barracks they were met by a large number of their comrades, none of which looked excited by the emergency meeting. Though no one openly spoke about Captain Karraman and his failed expedition, everyone knew precisely why they had been assembled.

"Everyone here? Good." Emmon said as he surveyed the room. He then ceded the floor to Count Aldamar, who had been lurking a few steps behind him.

"Captain Karraman is conscious once again," Aldamar said, starting a chorus of whispers, "food and rest have brought him back to life, Gods be praised."

Some of the men repeated the phrase, Amantius arched an eyebrow. *How can a man so inherently malevolent praise the Gods?* He shuddered at the thought.

"Though most of his warband has been...lost...they succeeded in other ways." Aldamar began pacing the room, a faint smile on his lips, or so Amantius believed. "The Mad Raven's lair has been located; we now know where she and her Flock have been hiding. According to Captain Karraman, their numbers are not so great anymore. If they had not been ambushed, he believes his warband would have prevailed."

"So they were ambushed." Someone said towards the back of the room. It was not a question, more of a statement.

"Yes." Count Aldamar fixed his gaze upon the man in the crowd, cold and fatal. Amantius shivered and thought he could feel a collective ripple as the Count's dark eyes shot a hole through their ranks.

"No doubt people have heard rumors; it is only natural that these things happen in a time such as this." Aldamar began to pace once again, not focusing on anything as he walked. "I am sure you have heard rumors about the Mad Raven herself. Supposedly she is three times the size of a man, can use dark magic, and cannot be killed with iron. Her

Flock are monsters themselves that eat human flesh and use claws instead of swords and spears." He looked at the crowd once again, a playful smirk on his face. "Come now, this is absurd."

A few of the guards in the room laughed, their level of discomfort obvious in the intensity of it. Amantius was more unsettled by the strange expression on the Count's face. Somehow, he thought the man was telling the truth, and that was far more terrifying.

"Now that we know where she lives, and that her numbers are diminished." Count Aldamar continued as the laughter stopped, "another warband will be sent to strike her lair." He turned to Emmon, "I am naming you warchief for this expedition. Take as many of these men as you wish. Your warband will be bolstered by local warriors and militia loyal to Silverwater, unlike that mercenary rabble I wasted money on. Your numbers will almost double those of Captain Karraman's warband, which should be more than sufficient to defeat her. I wish for you to leave at the first opportunity, no longer than three days from now."

Emmon bowed, "I thank you, my Count. When we find the Mad Raven, do you wish her alive or dead?"

A bloodthirsty grin stretched across Count Aldamar's face. "Dead, of course."

Chapter 16
Ulam

They had been marching for days, pushing further into the dark depths of Silverwood Forest. Ulam and Amantius had been among those chosen to attack the Mad Raven's lair, the two of them marching beside a wagon train filled with provisions. A few days prior they had come across the abandoned wagons of the first expedition, the foodstuffs and supplies having been picked clean by the victors. A day later they found the site of the first ambush, the scene so grisly even the most hardened warriors debated turning back. There was no shortage of vomit from the ranks of the warband as the smell of rotting corpses reached their noses, the chests of the victims torn apart with the feral tenacity of a ravenous bear. A murder of crows dined on the dead, so drunk from their feast they did not bother to move as the new warband passed through. If anything they watched with gluttonous excitement, for those little scavengers knew the second course would soon be served.

Almost all the remaining Castle Guards had been selected for this expedition, with only a few remaining behind to protect the castle and Count Aldamar. Ulam was not surprised that he had been among those chosen to fight, his size and strength practically cementing his place in the warband. He was not upset by the selection; he actually had been quite excited initially. He was able to escape the castle and see parts of the world he never knew existed, as well as trees and flowers he had never seen before. But as they continued marching into the mysterious depths of the

Silverwood, he began to feel a little uneasy about their foray into the forest. Though his spirits were still high, the scores of dead men littered across the ambush site did nothing to soothe the quiet paranoia growing in his heart.

Amantius was beside him, the aroma of a brothel lingering on him, sweet yet repulsive. Ulam had spent the days before their departure sparring with some of the veteran warriors in their warband, believing that would be the best use of his time. Amantius, on the other hand, had spent the same amount of time practicing a more carnal technique. Ulam did not fault him; the prospect of excruciating pain and death was what provided most of the business for brothels. But he still felt disappointment that Amantius had chosen to practice the wrong kind of swordplay before leaving Silverwater.

Ever since Amantius' drunken debauchery came to an end his mood was one of perpetual gloom, the harsh reality of marching to battle heavy like fog covering a valley. During the first couple days Amantius did not cease complaining, his chattering only stopping when the fear inside grew to such an extreme that he could no longer hide it. Ulam felt pity for his foster-brother; Amantius had never wanted to come, instead wanting to be among those chosen for guard duty at the castle. The Orc did not quite understand the reasoning behind the stance, considering how much Amantius detested and feared Count Aldamar. *Better the devil you know, I suppose.*

The whole warband was restless, which Ulam thought was a positive thing, because that anxiety would keep them alive. There had only been one death so far, a man had fallen into the Silver River on the second night and drowned. Since then they kept a safe distance from the river, ever wary of the loose soil near its banks. Ulam thought it interesting that most of the men of Silverwater did not know how to swim, considering almost every Accarian could before their tenth birthday. *Different cultures, I guess.*

Accaria. He did not think of the island much, wanting to focus on the present and future. He could not help but wonder, though, what was happening there. He worried about Pelecia, praying that she was safe. As the sun began to set, homesickness stabbed him in the heart as he thought about a warm meal at the dinner table with her and Amantius, one he was sure they would be late for as well. An image of Pelecia floated in his mind, her arms crossed, scowling at them as they crossed the courtyard to the house. He chuckled quietly.

"How can you possibly laugh in a place like this?" Amantius said, his nerves getting the best of him.

Ulam hesitated. Amantius had not mentioned Accaria recently, which he hoped was a sign that his foster-brother was moving on. The Orc debated whether or not he should tell Amantius the truth, but he feared he would break open a dam of pent up emotion if he did. *No, now is not the time. He is already on edge.*

"Alright, don't tell me, I don't care anyway," Amantius continued, twitching at every snap of a branch, every call of a bird or beast he did not recognize. "There's more important things to care about right now."

Ulam was surprised by the fear that consumed Amantius, if not a little disappointed. He understood they were in a foreign land, in an alien forest, hunting a mysterious enemy that had massacred a warband already, but he simply could not feel the dread. He only felt excitement, which seemed utterly absurd to him. *How can I possibly be excited?*

Surely I am marching into danger, and most likely death. Perhaps the barkeep was right, maybe I am naturally drawn to combat and killing.

"We make camp here for the night," Emmon shouted from ahead. The warband had marched into a small opening in the forest, where a creek weaved its way through tall stalks of grass. Within minutes the men began to spread out, transforming the quiet meadow into a city of canvas tents. Though the glade was small, it was still large enough to fit the warband's numbers while also providing plenty of visibility in the event of an attack. Within an hour scouts were sent in every direction to collect reconnaissance, while small teams of men collected firewood and other resources from nearby.

As evening gave way to night, Amantius and a few others built a bonfire, the light and warmth provided by the flames welcomed by all except Ulam. As they sat around the fire smoke began drifting into the Orc's face, the bitter smell almost causing him to gag. He felt as though he was inside another burning house, trapped within smoke-filled walls as a raging inferno devoured everything around him. Suddenly Ulam became lightheaded, forcing him to escape to a clearing where he sucked in the sweet, fresh air of the forest. As he calmed down and his heart rate returned to normal, the fear which had overwhelmed him slowly disappeared, only to be replaced with shame. *What is wrong with me? Why am I so weak?*

"Are you alright?" Amantius said as he approached from behind.

Ulam grunted while straightening his shoulders. Though he could feel the cold sweat dripping down his forehead, he hoped the collective light from the camp was too faint for Amantius to see it. "Yes, I just needed some air. And to relieve myself."

Amantius frowned, clearly not convinced. "Was it the fire?"

Ulam grunted again. *If you are waiting for me to say yes, then you will wait until the end of time.*

"I understand," Amantius said as he stood beside Ulam, staring out into the darkness with his foster-brother, "it's the same reason Mother was afraid of dogs. One bit the back of her leg when she was a child, and the memory never went away." He began to giggle. "I was so angry when she wouldn't let us have a puppy, remember?"

Ulam smiled. He appreciated Amantius changing the subject and hoped the conversation would not return to his sudden aversion to smoke and fire. "I never knew she was afraid of dogs."

"Oh yes," Amantius replied, laughing still, "I was so angry at her at the time. I think I was, ten? Maybe eleven years old? I did not learn until a few summers ago, when I caught her standing on the table because a stray had wandered into the courtyard and curled up for a nap at the front door."

They laughed together for a few minutes, a story of home the perfect blanket on a chilly night. They both stared into the darkness, listening to the crickets and other creatures of the night sing their songs, as they had many nights in Accaria. Coming from the camp were the raucous sounds of men drinking, shooting dice, and singing songs. A cool breeze blew across the clearing, rustling the small piles of leaves resting on the ground. Nearby a flock of birds flew from the trees in front of them, the symphony of chirping adding to the ambiance. Ulam watched as they flew over the camp and across the moon, joined by even more of their kind from the other side of the forest. He thought it strange that two separate groups of birds on opposite sides of the clearing would suddenly fly away at the same moment, as though they had secretly coordinated their exodus. In fact, he found it too strange.

"We should get back to the camp," Ulam muttered, keeping an eye on the edge of the forest as he slowly stepped away. "Now."

"Why?" Amantius replied, his voice shaky. "What is it?"

"Hopefully nothing," Ulam grumbled, "but hope does not make for good armor."

A howl came from the woods, inhuman and deranged. Then another from a different direction, joined by dozens more. A whistling sound pierced the night as a flaming arrow cut through the darkness, embedding itself into a canvas tent. It was followed by hundreds more, together the barrage setting the entire encampment ablaze. The death-screams shortly followed as men of the warband found themselves being attacked by dark figures rushing from the edges of the forest, the bitter screech of iron on iron filling the clearing. Within minutes the entire meadow had fallen into chaos, everyone desperately fighting for survival.

Ulam fell to his knees in the tall grass, unable to move any further. He watched in horror as his comrades were being massacred before his eyes, the dark figures seeming supernatural to him. They moved with such speed and precision that Ulam's eyes could not follow, only appearing long enough to kill before vanishing into the bedlam once again. They continued to howl and shriek as they butchered the warband, no part of the camp making an organized effort to defend. Though deep inside Ulam wanted to run back to the camp, find a weapon and start cleaving these devils in

133

half, he could not find the strength to move. His limbs were heavy, numbed by fear.

"Ulam, come on, we have to join the fight!" Amantius yelled, suddenly finding either courage or a sense of duty. "Why are you sitting there? Let's go!"

Ulam sat quietly, watching as the battle was lost before it even began. Though the demons attacking the camp were nightmarish, they were not the reason he remained paralyzed with fear. In fact, he wanted to slay a few to satisfy his curiosity, as well as to quench a sudden bloodthirst running through his veins. What scared Ulam was not the murderous banshees cutting through the warband like a scythe through wheat, but the flames burning the camp to the ground.

"Amantius I cannot go," Ulam said as a cold bead of sweat dripped down his forehead, "the fire. There is fire."

"What? The fire?" Amantius turned, watched as a small group of warriors made a stand against their attackers, "You are afraid of fire? You weren't when you ran into that house!"

"I know," Ulam replied, his eyes downcast. He felt a great shame building in him, knowing his comrades were being slaughtered as he lingered in the tall grass, far enough away from the fight that the enemy had not spotted him or Amantius yet. Ulam looked at his forearm, shivering as he traced the burn scars left behind. No matter the stakes, there was no way he would be able to run headfirst into another inferno, at least no so soon after the house fire. He was powerless, his fear being his master.

"Just stay hidden," Ulam said. He was not proud of the words, he even feared that Amantius would accuse him of cowardice. But he did not care, he did not want to watch

Amantius fight a lost battle, only to die at the hands of the Mad Raven's Flock. "No need to die."

Amantius scoffed and pointed at the men making a stand. "The battle is not lost, Ulam, look! I can't stand around and watch as the men we share bread and ale with die!"

Amantius shot out of the swaying stalks of grass, sprinting towards the clash. Ulam's heart sank as he watched, a different fear now gripping him. No longer did he care about the leaping flames that swirled high into the sky, or the suffocating smoke lingering in the air, he only cared about Amantius' safety.

With a sudden burst of energy Ulam gave chase, knowing if he was going to survive, he would need to reach his tent and grab his equipment. Miraculously his hulking frame was not spotted as he crossed the open field, the combatants too engaged in trying to kill one another to notice. Although the canvas of the tent he shared with Amantius had already burned out, his weapons and armor were still lying in the open, waiting to be retrieved. Quickly he hoisted his chainmail over his head and hefted his war axe, stopping only when he noticed Amantius' equipment was still there, untouched. *Maybe he found a weapon and shield along the way.*

A maddening howl shrieked beside Ulam, drawing his attention immediately to his left. He saw a hellish creature with a goat's head and black feathers standing a dozen paces away, a large, wicked single-blade polearm raised high above. Before Ulam could observe the monster fully it charged at him, its howls echoing in the Orc's ears. It slashed at Ulam's torso when it was within range, the blade coming nowhere near striking home as Ulam jumped backward. The Orc then raised his axe and swung a counter, finding only heated air as he missed wide. His enemy shrieked again and thrust forward, catching Ulam in the hip, a minor cut that immediately began to bleed.

The shot of pain triggered something inside Ulam, a feeling that had been present since the onset of battle. There was a rage boiling within his soul, an uncontrollable fury slowly overtaking his entire being, fueling his muscles. He began to growl, his pearl-white tusks gleaming in the firelight. Ulam's grip on the axe shaft tightened as he raised the weapon high and roared a battle-cry, ready to begin his own slaughter. As he charged, Ulam saw the pure, unadulterated fear in the eyes of his enemy, his newfound madness a secret weapon even he did not know he possessed. The hellion tried blocking with its polearm as Ulam slashed sideways with his axe, but its defense was in vain as the wooden shaft shattered into pieces. The blade of the axe cut through the monster's weapon and into its neck, separating its head from its shoulders.

Ulam watched as a pool of blood stained the ground dark red, curious as to what he had slain. He walked over to the decapitated goat's head and picked it up by the horns, jumping backward as a human head fell to the ground. He then tossed the goat's head aside and grabbed the corpse by the waist and pulled, discovering that his dead enemy was wearing high-quality chainmail under a cloak of raven feathers.

Men, dressed as monsters. Ulam cackled at the revelation.

The howling suddenly stopped, the ring of iron on iron no longer filling the glade, replaced with the familiar humming of fire. A horn blast sounded as a faint cheer carried across the battleground, signaling the end of the battle. Ulam ran towards the sound, briefly searching each body along the way to make sure none of the corpses belonged to Amantius. Although he did not find his foster-brother amongst the dead, he still worried Amantius' body was out there somewhere in the tall grass.

When Ulam reached the remnants of the warband the men were no longer under duress. Instead, they were using the break in the action to patch wounds, drink from skins of water, and exchange questions with one another. Some of the men raised their weapons when they saw Ulam approaching them, but quickly lowered their blades as soon as they realized the Orc was not an enemy. As he ran across the battlefield the thought had crossed Ulam's mind that he would be mistaken for an enemy, because in the battle of man versus beast Ulam was closer to the latter in appearance. However, he was thankful that a few members of the Castle Guards survived the battle and recognized him, among them was Emmon.

He gripped the warchief's arm in the warrior's embrace as he entered their ranks, glad to see the man still lived. He did the same for the other members of the Castle Guards, all equally excited to see Ulam had survived the attack. They shared stories for a moment as his eyes jumped from man to man, scanning for Amantius. But the euphoria of the moment quickly vanished as Ulam failed to locate his foster-brother, his heart gripped by the icy hand of terror.

"Is Amantius not with you?" Ulam asked, only to be met with blank stares. He then continued running through the remainder of the camp, asking every survivor if they had seen his foster-brother. "Amantius! Has anyone seen Amantius Jeranus!?"

Silence.

Interlude

Winter is all but over here, the budding leaves and flowers have loudly announced spring's arrival. I have been unable to sleep during this time, something about the changing of seasons affects my nose and eyes in the strangest of ways. When I was younger my mother told me I was being punished by God for my lack of devotion. I can still hear her voice saying, "Rasmus, you must go to the temple and ask the Gods for forgiveness if you are to feel better." I believed her at first until I was much older and realized I contracted the same illness at the same time every year regardless of my piety.

The advantage of countless sleepless nights in the archives is that I have been able to translate much of the first book of the *Accarian Chronicles* to our language, as well as some other minor documents. The task has not been easy, as many of the words used thousands of years ago have changed meaning, or have no modern equivalent. I especially find this true when any deity is mentioned, for sometimes I cannot tell whether I have stumbled upon the name of a long-forgotten god or my translation is inaccurate. Still, I am satisfied with the progress I have made thus far. Now that spring is upon us, and the remnants of the last snowstorm begin to melt away, I believe my nights in the archives have come to an end.

I have decided to travel to Silverwater, the southernmost city on our continent of Qerus. Already I have booked passage on the TQR, or the Trans-Qerus Railroad, leaving within a ten-night. I am unaware of how long such a journey will take, but I am excited nonetheless. This will be the first time I have ridden a train, which will fulfill a lifelong dream of mine. I remember watching those metallic beasts pulling in and out of the station as a child, always daydreaming of the fantastic creatures or exotic travelers onboard. As a teen I wanted to run away from home and join a railroad company, to be at the forefront of civilization's next great industrial undertaking. However, my father, being a man of letters himself, remained ever vigilant in regards to my schooling. As an adolescent I despised him for his zeal, but now that I have reached adulthood I realize the folly of my childhood delusions. I live a far more comfortable life now than the one I would have had in the mud and grime of the railroad. Though, I must admit, sometimes I still dream of swinging a hammer along those never-ending steel rails.

I, Rasmus of Hollowcross, will be traveling to Silverwater soon, but until that time I will continue to translate and copy the text from the first volume of the *Accarian Chronicles*. With any luck, my journey will be a safe one, though I am sad to report that train robberies have been on the rise. But in case of such an event, I will not lament, because I am wholly certain that these volumes are important to only myself. And there is no greater shield against theft than to own nothing of any value.

Chapter 17
Amantius

Everything was dark.

Amantius was on his stomach, not even sure he was still alive. He wanted to open his eyes, but he did not have the strength. He wanted to move, but his limbs felt as though they were made of lead. Instead, he moaned; it was all he could manage to do.

He heard a noise, the muffled sound of voices, one high-pitched, the other low. He struggled to open his eyes again, but nothing happened. The throbbing in his head intensified with each passing second, becoming so painful he thought his skull would split in two. He felt an immense pressure on both temples, as though a giant's hand was squashing his head like a melon. He grimaced, or at least he thought he did.

Where am I? He thought, the first time he was able to string words together. *What happened?*

The voices grew louder, but they were still inaudible. Amantius was aware that whoever was speaking was near, perhaps even beside him. He tried to open his eyes again but failed once more. He let out a sigh, moaned again, and rolled over.

The ringing in his ears stopped; the voices became clearer. "He's awake."

"Struggling to be," the second person said, a woman's voice. It was gentle, as soft as velvet.

A woman? Where am I? Who are they?"

Amantius finally opened his left eye and felt a searing pain shooting through his cranium. The pain was so fierce he was forced to close his eye, waiting for some time before trying again. On his second attempt, he was able to open both eyes, moaning a thousand curses as tiny spears of light stabbed his retinas. Despite the pain, Amantius was able to keep his eyes open, although they were unable to focus on anything surrounding him.

"Easy," the woman's voice said once more, still soft. "Don't hurt yourself, you need to rest."

"Mother?" Amantius muttered. *Is that Mother speaking to me?*

The woman laughed softly. "No. Rest now, there will be time for talking later."

Amantius did as he was told, the more conscious he became the more absurd he felt about calling this stranger "Mother." His head was still pulsating with a splitting headache, one he did not think would go away for quite some time. He was fully aware now, though his eyes still struggled to see. Amantius was able to make out a few figures in the room with him, the closest being the woman speaking to him.

"Who are you?" He said as he stared at the vague shape of a person beside him.

"Who am I? Well, that is a long story," she replied, though through his blurry veil Amantius could feel a warm smile radiating from the figure, "but one thing that I am not is your mother."

Amantius felt his face flush red with embarrassment.

"My question to you, though, is who are you?"

"My name is…" Amantius stopped, forgetting who he was. *Who am I? Where am I from?* "I am sorry…I don't remember."

"Do not worry, get more rest." The woman replied. "You suffered a blow to the head, I am impressed that you are awake, to be honest. I feel like most men would have died from such an injury, let alone be conscious days after."

Days after? How long have I been here? Where was I? Where am I? Who the hell am I? So many questions...

"Can you remember anything?" A second voice asked, a man's. It was deep, though not as deep as Ulam's.

Ulam!

"I have a brother," Amantius said, a spark lighting a fire in his mind. "He's an Orc. His name is Ulam."

"An Orc?" The man repeated, the skepticism in his voice clear. "An Orc for a brother? He's still delusional, my lady."

"No, it's true," Amantius replied, though he began doubting his own words. "He's a wizard. And a monster hunter. An Orc too."

What? Why am I saying these things? He's only an Orc, not the rest!

"See, still delusional. I doubt there any monster-slaying Orcish wizards in the whole world, let alone here." The same man replied, now sounding entire convinced. "I beg your leave, my lady, I must go see to the others."

"You may go, Jaga. I will call for you when his mind is fully recovered." The woman said. Amantius noticed the authority in her voice. *Is she a princess? A queen even? This Jaga is referring to her as "my lady."*

"Apologies, my lady," Amantius blurted out, surprised by the tone in his voice, "I did not realize I was in the presence of nobility.

The woman laughed quietly. "Do not fret, I am not offended. You cannot remember your own name; I do not expect you to address me properly."

Amantius' eyes finally focused, and he saw the woman beside his bed. He felt his eyes grow larger, his mouth drop open. *She is gorgeous.*

"Are you well?" She asked, clearly surprised to see his sudden change in appearance.

Amantius failed to find any words, his mind was racing. She was slender with long, midnight black hair flowing freely over her shoulders. She wore an elegant, purple gown trimmed with white, a gold sash wrapped around her midsection. Though her eyes were dark, there was a rare lightness to them, soft and delicate. She had a gentle, amiable face with dimples on each side of her mouth, both visible as she smiled at him. Though her skin was as white as porcelain, her overall complexion was dark. At first glance, he thought she might have been Accarian, for he had not seen that combination of features in a person since he had arrived in Silverwater.

"Accaria," Amantius stuttered through his daze, more information coming to his mind. "I'm from Accaria. And I was in Silverwater."

"Accaria? You are far from home. Why were you in Silverwater?"

Amantius shrugged, surprised he could move his shoulders. There was pain to be sure, but he was encouraged that he was regaining some of his strength. "I don't remember, I was a Castle Guard, I think. With my brother."

"The Orc?"

"Yes, the Orc. His name is Ulam. And I am…Amantius! Amantius Jeranus!" He finally remembered, sitting up in excitement. A sharp, knifelike pain stabbed him in the torso and shoulders, sending him reeling back into the bed. What little energy Amantius had recovered was suddenly gone again, replaced with utter exhaustion. His sudden movement had prompted the woman to retreat as two dark figures emerged from the shadows, their hands reaching for their sword hilts. If Amantius was not already weak and in agony, he may have feared for his life.

The woman held up a hand, silently commanding the two guards to return to their posts. As they retired to the corners of the room Amantius looked around, finally taking in his surroundings. Aside from the guards and the woman, he believed he was in some kind of cottage. A fire pit was nearby, the smell of burned wood lingering in the air. The only window in the room was caked in dirt, where only a single sliver of sunlight struggled to pierce through. On a table nearby were an assortment of plants, herbs mostly, positioned beside a mortar and pestle stained green from usage. A silver goblet with a raven engraving sat on the table also, the woman's sleek fingers wrapped around the stem.

"A pleasure to meet you, Amantius Jeranus," the woman said, her words corralling his attention, "I am Morganna, the rightful Countess of Silverwater. But, I am guessing you know me better as the dreaded Mad Raven of Silverwood Forest."

Silence settled in the room; Amantius was not certain he had heard correctly. He thought the lingering fog in his mind had prevented him from understanding what he just heard.

"I see you are confused, if not a little troubled." Morganna continued. "Which part do you wish for me to explain?"

Amantius let out the breath he had been holding. "Everything. Where I am, how I came to be here. How is it possible that you are the Mad Raven when, from what I have been told, it's a deadly beast that rips out the hearts of men."

"Well, as you can see, I am not a monster looking to rip out your heart," Morganna chuckled softly as she took his hand and ran his fingertips over her forearm. Her skin was as smooth as silk and as warm as a hearth. The contact made Amantius' heart beat faster, as jolts of excitement spread throughout his body like lightning in a night's sky. "See? Proof. I am only a woman."

Morganna gently returned his hand to the edge of the bed, smiling as she did so. She then signaled to one of her bodyguards, who opened the door leading out of the cottage, allowing a blast of sunlight to flood into the room. Morganna stood and headed for the exit, flinching as soon as she stepped into the light. Before leaving she turned to Amantius and smiled once again, her dark eyes briefly flashing yellow as the sunlight kissed her. "Rest, Amantius. I will answer any questions you have when I see you next."

I will see her again! The thought shot through his mind, his excitement barely containable. *That means she doesn't want me dead, at least.*

Morganna then exited the room, her bodyguards following closely behind. One man still remained, ensuring Amantius did not try to escape. Moments later an older, frail-looking woman entered the cottage, holding a cup of something in her hand. She grinned, a dozen holes in her smile as she held the cup towards Amantius. "You need to drink this to heal. But as a fair warning, I doubt you're going to like it much."

Amantius took the cup and sniffed, wincing as a bitter aroma attacked his nose. He peered inside and saw a purplish-green liquid as he swirled the cup, wondering if he should drink the beverage. *Will I even be able to drink it? If it tastes as bad as it smells I'll probably vomit.*

"Go on, child, drink," the old woman's words whistling through the gaps in her teeth. She waited a moment before walking away mumbling, having a conversation with herself. Amantius stared into the cup once again.

Surely they aren't poisoning me. He thought, trying to convince himself to drink the concoction. *If they wanted me dead, they would have killed me already. Why bring me back if they wanted me dead?* He inhaled the vapors once more, feeling his stomach lurch. *By the Gods, the smell is enough to kill me.*

Amantius looked around the room, surprised when he could not find the old woman. He assumed she was a healer of sorts, or rather, he hoped she was a healer. But she was nowhere to be found, having disappeared almost as quickly as she had appeared. Amantius found himself alone in the room with only the lone jailor, who looked more like a statue than a living, breathing person.

Amantius raised his cup and grinned. "Cheers."

Chapter 18
Ulam

A week had passed since the skirmish in the Silverwood Forest; the remaining tatters of the warband retreating to Silverwater. As news of their failure spread the city was gripped in a panic-induced mania, propelling waves of merchants to flee northward towards the interior of the Empire. Even most of the remaining mercenaries within the city left, choosing to search for safer work elsewhere. Though the majority of Silverwater's citizenry remained, the once-bustling city had quickly transformed into a ghost town. Within days dozens of horrifying stories about the Mad Raven and her Flock had been shared so many times that each man, woman, and child in the city began believing them in their totality.

But every Orc knew the truth.

"They are not beasts or demons from a different world," Ulam said as he pounded his fist on the table, toppling a few empty tankards. "They are men."

"Men!?" One of the warriors nearly spit out the beer in his mouth. "You can't be serious! How can you say that? Did you see them? Men do not make those kinds of noises. Men do not make those infernal howls. Men do not eat out the hearts of others, and slain men do not simply *disappear*."

A cold silence settled in the room, the survivors drowning their nightmares in ale and liquor. Ulam had tried time and again to convince his comrades they did not fight against monsters, but trained warriors in deceiving outfits. He had been met with the same skepticism and ridicule each time, some even going as far as to suggest that his mind had been warped by that macabre night. But Ulam knew he was correct, he knew he was of a sound mind. He simply had no way to prove it.

There had been many arguments made against his narrative, trying to discredit what he saw. Above everything, though, he could not explain how the slain bodies of their attackers vanished after the battle. Scores of warriors on both sides of the conflict had been killed, that had been confirmed by the other survivors. But unlike the warband from Silverwater, the enemy dead had simply vanished, as though they had never existed. Even the person Ulam had struck down disappeared, the only evidence of their duel being the reddened blades of trampled grass where they had fought.

Ulam left the barracks, frustrated that not a single person believed the hell-beasts were actually Humans. He sat on a bench in the castle's courtyard, watching as the flames from a brazier danced in the night. His eyes slowly drifted to the castle walls, the stone made pale by the silvery moonlight. Ulam frowned when his eyes came across the spot where he and Amantius had often stood guard, the loneliness creating a void within him. His mind flashed back to weeks before the night of the battle, remembering how he wanted nothing more than to be alone. He had craved to be rid of Amantius' company, as well as Pelecia's promise, so he could explore the world. But with Amantius missing those dreams and aspirations were gone, replaced with guilt and self-loathing.

Ulam reigned in his thoughts as a silent shadow glided across the gray cobblestones, a sudden flash of yellow catching his eye. Though the sudden appearance of someone else surprised him, he could tell by the figure's posture they were not there as an enemy. At first, Ulam did not quite know who was standing before him, whether it was a fellow Castle Guard or a drunkard who had somehow wandered into the courtyard. But he could feel a strong presence emanating from the silhouette, and the longer he stared the more certain he became that the newcomer was not an ordinary person.

"Forgive me for interrupting your meditation," an eloquent voice called from the shadows, "Unlike many, I appreciate the importance of self-reflection."

Ulam stood and bowed slightly. "Forgive me, I did not know you were there."

"Do not trouble yourself," the person replied as he stepped from the shadows, revealing Count Aldamar. The moonlight magnified the paleness of his skin, as well as remove any color from his eyes. He wore a soft smile on his lips, almost a smirk. "Will you join me in a small discourse? There are some topics I wish to discuss with you."

Like a ghost Count Aldamar then silently crossed the courtyard, disappearing into the depths of the castle. Ulam hesitated, initially unsure if he wanted to follow. He held no ill-will towards the Count, though in his head he heard Amantius' voice telling him not to trust the man. Typically Ulam would not have paid any heed to that voice, but after two destroyed warbands, both of which were massacred in the same forest, the words seemed to carry a little more weight. Although Ulam was still not convinced of Aldamar's treachery, he trusted the man far less than before. *He could have intentionally sent us to our deaths, but what would have been the purpose? Why spend so much gold on mercenaries just to see them killed? What is the point in that?*

Ulam decided to follow Aldamar, mostly out of a sense of duty. As he entered the castle a blast of cold air swept over him, bringing a stale aroma to his nostrils. The interior of the castle had the appearance of a cellar, with every surface covered in a fine layer of dust. Cobwebs hung from every corner, with only half the torches burning in their sconces, the other half having burned out long ago. Though Ulam had spent hundreds of hours patrolling the castle, every time he stepped inside he could not help but shiver. Whether it was the cold air or the atmosphere he could not tell, but there was something about Silverwater Castle which unsettled him.

At the end of a long hallway was a large oak door, the other side of which Ulam had never seen. The door had always been locked, though that had never stopped Amantius from trying to open it. Ulam chuckled softly to himself, the sound enhanced by the narrowness of the hallway. In his mind, he saw Amantius struggling to open the door, so sure Count Aldamar performed dark deeds in the room behind. It was a bittersweet memory for Ulam, because while he found humor in the shenanigans he also found sadness in the emptiness left by Amantius' disappearance.

The specters created by Ulam's mind disappeared as soon as he reached the end of the hallway, where Count Aldamar waited by a lit brazier. Without speaking the Count pulled an iron key from a pocket and turned the handle in the lock, the metallic clicking as loud as thunder in such close quarters. With a great heave, Aldamar opened the door, revealing only a set of stairs leading into darkness.

Ulam was disappointed, not on his behalf, but for Amantius. While he did not believe he would find a sacrificial altar on the other side of the mysterious oak door, he thought there would be something of interest. Or, at the very least, something other than stairs. *Amantius would be so angry if he were here. I have to tell him when he returns...if he returns.*

Count Aldamar grabbed a torch from a nearby wall before continuing, leading Ulam downstairs into a labyrinth of rooms and hallways. Ulam was only able to get a quick glimpse of the rooms they passed, most of which were either empty or appeared to be untouched for centuries. As they delved deeper into the bowels of the castle he became more fascinated with the structure, surprised that these rooms existed within the building's frame. *I have read stories of secret tunnels allowing forbidden lovers to meet, but I did not think I would see this with my own eyes. Of course, I doubt Count Aldamar uses these rooms for that purpose.*

At last they came to the end of the maze of hallways, where a second large oak door opened into another dark room. Ulam stood in the entrance, watching the red-orange glow of Count Aldamar's torch cross the room. Even with the light, Ulam's visibility was minimal, the far reaches of the room still cloaked in darkness. It was not until Count Aldamar had ignited enough torches that Ulam discovered where they were. Excitement filled his stomach with butterflies, his eyes were wide with awe.

They were standing in the center of the largest library Ulam had ever seen, one larger than he could have ever imagined. There were shelves three times his height, filled to the edges with books, all across the room. He thought there must have been thousands of texts within the shelves, all waiting to be read. And if Ulam could have his way, he would grant their wishes immediately.

"I expected that reaction," Count Aldamar said, a soft laugh escaping. Ulam had been so enthralled by the sight of the library, he did not realize the man was standing beside him. "I have observed you reading before, engrossed in whichever book rested between your hands. I must say, I am quite fascinated with you."

Ulam returned his attention to the Count, wondering where this conversation was heading.

"Not one for small talk, are you?" Aldamar said with a smirk before taking a seat at a desk. "I suppose that is typical of your race; I have never met an Orc that enjoyed speaking in great lengths. However, I have also never met an Orc with a thirst for knowledge, for reading, such as yourself. I find that fascinating. You are not from a Sanctuary, are you? You were raised somewhere else, maybe even in a royal house. That explains why you love reading, or even why you are able to do so." His words trailed off until they were an incoherent mumbling. He was no longer speaking to Ulam, but having a private discussion with himself.

"Accaria," Ulam said, answering a question the Count had not asked him. "I was raised in Accaria. In the household of Amantius' mother." *Who was royalty in her own way,* Ulam thought, but did not add.

"Accaria you say? The small island kingdom? I suppose that makes sense." Count Aldamar appeared satisfied with the answer. "Very well. Please, Ulam, take a seat, there are matters we must discuss."

Ulam grabbed a nearby wooden chair, its dimensions just wide enough to fit his bulk. His eyes drifted back to the books as he waited, so desperately wanting to read every last title on the shelves. *The entire world's knowledge must be on these shelves. Perhaps I can find even more information about my race here.*

"You must wonder why I have brought you here, why I have singled you out from the rest," Aldamar began, drawing Ulam's attention once more. His words echoed off the walls, his face expressed the utmost sincerity. "I have questions, and I need answers."

Ulam grunted.

"Specifically, I want to know what happened in Silverwood Forest. It has come to my attention that you believe your enemy was not a host of monsters from the Otherworld, but men dressed as such. Speak freely, I wish to know everything." Count Aldamar stared, his dark eyes fixated on Ulam.

Ulam told the Count everything he could recall, from the mad howling to the unmasking of the dead goat-warrior he had slain. His pride would not allow him to tell the Count about his new fear of fire, and how the flames had all but petrified him. As he spoke he felt shame growing inside him, the embarrassment of not rushing into action sooner. With some effort he was able to push those thoughts away, choosing instead to focus on Amantius' disappearance. He told the Count of how he searched every corpse and found no signs of his foster-brother, shivering as images of those mutilated bodies with their chests ripped open flooded his mind again. The Count's expression did not change throughout the story; he showed no signs of worry or anger. He remained exactly how he always was, even-keeled and lost in thought.

A deep silence ensued after Ulam finished, the only noise coming from the low hum of burning torches. Count Aldamar stared at him for some time, before breaking his concentration to rub his face. For a moment Ulam thought he saw a crack, as though the Count's defense had been broken by his own thoughts. His always perfectly placed white hair had become disheveled, as a sort of exhaustion suddenly overwhelmed his physique.

153

"I believe you, Ulam," he said, breaking the silence, "I believe every word you have said. About the monsters being men, about the disappearance of the enemy's slain bodies."

"You do?" Ulam replied, surprised by the Count's words. There was a part of him that wondered if he spoke the truth, or if his memories were warped by recent events.

"I do." The Count fixed his hair, instantly regaining the strength that he always emitted. "I have heard reports from spies, farmers, and merchants of men wearing the pelts of wolves and bears and setting upon them. I simply assumed they were nothing more than common brigands, wearing costumes as a means of causing more intimidation. Never did I imagine a whole army, in Silverwood Forest, dressed as such." He stood and began to pace. "As for Amantius, I believe I know what happened. You say he was nowhere to be found, as well as the bodies of your ambushers?"

Ulam nodded with a grunt, a sick feeling brewing in his gut.

"They must have thought Amantius was one of them," The Count finished, his voice indicating he was completely sure of his conclusion, "Why else would he be taken away?"

Ulam thought for a moment, disappointed in himself for not having entertained that conclusion before. For weeks he had assumed either Amantius had run away and was still lost in Silverwood Forest, or he had been slain and his body had yet to be recovered. But the more he thought about Aldamar's explanation, the more apt he was to believe it. Or rather, the more he wanted to believe it. Because if true, that would mean Amantius was probably still alive.

"I need to go," Ulam said, unable to contain his words, "I need to get him. I need to rescue him."

Count Aldamar frowned. "With what army? I am sure they will not let you stroll into their camp and retrieve him. And, beg my pardon, I highly doubt stealth is an option for you. You are rather large and quite loud."

Ulam grimaced, helplessness leaving a bitter taste in his mouth. *He is right, I am completely useless.*

Chapter 19
Amantius

Damn my body hurts. Oh well, at least I can stand again.

Amantius stood from his bed and stretched, feeling his muscles burn with a thousand aches as he did so. He had been confined to the cottage for a long time, longer than he could remember. Aside from the metal cuff shackling his ankle to the bed frame, he hardly felt like a prisoner. His meals were warm and plentiful; he was given clean clothing and bedding as well. He never wanted for company, often chatting away the day with whoever was standing guard. Occasionally Countess Morganna would visit, though those visits were incredibly rare. Each time the door opened he hoped to see her slender figure enter the room, only to be disappointed when he saw the glinting armor of Jaga, her warchief.

"Standing now are you?" Jaga's voice called from the doorway as the sunlight temporarily blinded Amantius.

"Burns like a thousand fires, but I've had worse," Amantius said as he shook his leg, the chain rattling on the metal bed frame. "How much longer are you keeping me here?"

"Depends if Countess Morganna wants you here," Jaga replied with a shrug. He shut the door, "She seems to like you, though. If she didn't, I'd already have gutted you like a fish."

Amantius shivered at the comment, though he was not completely unnerved by Jaga's words. Over the past weeks, he had become somewhat fond of his captor. Jaga was a bald, grizzled warrior with a scar from a bear attack across his face, but he was an honest man who was forever loyal to Morganna. He might have been Amantius' jailor, but he was not without compassion. In a way, Jaga reminded Amantius of Ulam and was already starting to think of him as an ally.

"Think you can walk?" Jaga asked.

Amantius shook his leg again, the sound of metal on metal loud in the close quarters of the cottage. "If you removed this I would think might chances of walking would be higher."

Jaga sighed. "Doesn't matter, I suppose. You can't escape even if you wanted to." He stood up and walked over to the bed, pulling a key from a pocket as he kneeled before Amantius. With a click the pressure around Amantius' ankle was gone, the weight of iron no longer pulling down on his leg. Amantius rubbed the skin where the shackle had been and smiled.

"There," Jaga said as he returned to his seat. "Don't make me regret doing that."

Amantius walked around the room, quickly realizing his legs did not have their full strength yet. With each step, he thought his leg would buckle, as though he was standing on the deck of a rocking ship. Being released from the shackle around his ankle may not have been utter freedom, but it was a step in the right direction.

"You won't regret it," Amantius said as he stumbled towards the main door, his legs as reliable as a broken staff. He was not going to let their weakness keep him inside any longer, the desire to see the outside world once driving him forward. He smiled at Jaga and the other guard as he reached the door. "Don't worry, I don't think I can run very far."

He pushed the door open, and for the first time in weeks he felt fresh air enter his lungs as sunlight kissed his skin. He stood there for a moment, taking in the warmth of the sun's golden rays. The sensation was so overwhelming tears began to form in his eyes, surprised by how much he had yearned to be outside.

Jaga followed, the heavy thud of boots on wooden planks announcing him. The noise made Amantius open his eyes, his ocean blues now focusing on his surroundings. During his captivity he expected he was in a cottage in the middle of a small town, judging by the noise that crept through the solitary window and penetrated the walls. Instead, he was surprised to learn he was in a fort, virtually impregnable from the rear due to a sheer rock cliff that shot straight into the sky. A palisade wall surrounded the complex, fortified with a series of watchtowers. Built a couple of hundred paces away in the shadows of the bluffs was a great hall, where Amantius assumed Countess Morganna resided. Trees littered the area, great oaks, poplars, and elms soaring high above the settlement. He quickly realized that unless someone knew where they were going, they would most likely never know this place existed. It seemed to be at its own corner of the world, away from all society.

The men and women of the fort paid him no mind, carrying on with their business. Amantius heard the usual sounds of a settlement: dogs barking, people chatting, and the distinct high notes of a blacksmith's hammer crashing into an anvil. By all accounts, this place was no different than Silverwater, only much smaller and much more comely. Amantius could not quite explain it, but he already felt a connection here, as though he belonged.

"Probably not what you expected," Jaga said as he handed Amantius a large branch to use as a walking stick.

"Not at all," Amantius replied, his words barely audible above the sounds of hundreds of birds chirping in the canopy above. "Where are we?"

"Home, or at least that's what we call it." Jaga shrugged. "I guess we didn't feel the need to give it a great name when we first came here. We didn't mean to stay here for so long."

"What do you mean?" Amantius asked, relieved that the branch he was now leaning on was thick and strong.

Jaga's lips tightened until he began to scowl, "Doesn't matter. Ask the Countess if you really want to know." He took a few steps forward, "Want a tour?"

Jaga led a hobbling Amantius around the compound, explaining the different structures as they passed. Amantius was surprised by the number of people living in this forest village, the trees cloaking the actual size of the settlement. They had everything they needed; blacksmiths, bakeries, an armory, infirmary, storehouses, multiple wells, even a temple. For people who "never meant to stay long" they appeared to have been settled here for many years.

"I have to admit, I'm impressed," Amantius said as they approached the wooden palisade. His legs were numb, having been used more in the past hour than they had in the past week.

"We have a few good carpenters, and there has always been a strong supply of lumber and labor." Jaga leaned against a stout timber pillar, his expression dark. "Well, at least there had been. Now our numbers are so few."

Jaga's words trailed away, but Amantius knew what he meant. The two warbands from Silverwater had inflicted a significant amount of casualties, the graves still covered in fresh dirt from the most recent battle. He wondered if the survivors from Silverwater had created a cemetery in the middle of the forest as well, burying their dead in a mass ceremony. *What if Ulam was one of them, if he is buried out there somewhere? What about me? Does everyone think I'm dead?*

"Look alive, kid," Jaga said as he stood, straightening his tunic, "Countess Morganna is coming."

Amantius' heart leaped at the mere mention of her name, goosebumps forming on his arms and neck. The energy shot through his veins, willing him to stand even though his legs felt as though they were being stabbed a thousand times over. He placed almost all of his weight on the branch he used as a staff, hoping it was sturdy enough to support him.

Then he saw her, approaching from across the fortress with a few bodyguards flanking her. She wore a modest raven black gown, the same color as the flowing locks of hair that gently poured over her shoulders. The dress was trimmed in white and purple, the fabric hugging her curves perfectly. Amantius thought he was in the presence of a goddess, come down from the heavens to grace the unworthy with her divine beauty. Though she might not have been a deity, she wielded an almost supernatural power over him. To Amantius, it was as though there was nothing else in the world; no trees, no sunshine, no people, just her.

"Close your mouth, boy," Jaga growled behind him. "And keep it closed."

"Feeling better, I see," Morganna said, dimples forming from her radiant smile. "But please, relax. I can see you are placing a great strain upon yourself by standing for me."

160

Amantius scolded himself for appearing weak in Morganna's presence. Though he wanted to impress her with his toughness, he was somewhat relieved that he was allowed to sit down again. His lower limbs were screaming in pain, the muscles having already stiffened during the stroll he took with Jaga.

"Showing him around Home around you?" Morganna asked. Jaga nodded silently, his usual grimace plastered on his face. "So Amantius, what do you think of our little community?"

"I've never seen anything like it," Amantius replied. There were many aspects of Home that impressed him; the sheer vastness of the place, its hidden location underneath a thick canopy, even its efficiency as a proper city was notable. There was a natural beauty to the forest stronghold, and the wafting aroma of wildflowers and fruit made Home the best smelling settlement he believed he would ever see. That is if he was ever allowed to leave. After all, he was still Countess Morganna's prisoner.

"There's much worse places for me to be held captive," Amantius continued with a faint smile. He winced at the last two words. *I shouldn't have said that, hopefully she wasn't offended. I don't feel like a prisoner, and she doesn't make me feel like one either.*

Countess Morganna smiled, though there was no warmth in it. "Held captive? But Amantius, you are not being held captive here. We are simply healing you, and when you feel you have recovered entirely, you may leave if you wish." She took a few steps closer and laid a hand on his shoulder. "Although, I hope you would stay here, with me. I would be ecstatic if you became one of us."

Amantius' heart thundered so loud he feared it would rip from his chest. Countess Morganna's eyes slowly drifted to where his heart was, as though she could hear it too. *No, that's nonsense. She can't hear my heartbeat. Maybe she can feel it, though? Who cares, she wants me to stay here! With her! How can I say no?*

"You do not have to answer now," Morganna said as she pulled away, the smile on her face indicating she already knew what he would choose. "Take a fortnight, rest a while longer. Come to my hold when you have decided," she began to walk away, her bodyguards following. A few steps later she abruptly stopped, turning to face him again. "Or come to my hold just to see me."

"I will!" Amantius blurted out, instantly regretting his eagerness. *You can't let a woman know what you want, Amantius. Gods, you are a fool.*

Countess Morganna walked away, disappearing behind a row of buildings. Amantius sat still for a moment, his heart thumping so hard it began to hurt. His stomach felt as though he had swallowed a family of butterflies, his arms and legs suddenly felt light. He began to giggle quietly to himself, unaware of anything else in the world.

Then he felt a pain in the back of his head.

"I told you to keep your mouth shut," Jaga muttered, his expression forever unchanged.

Chapter 20
Ulam

Ulam spent countless hours in the depths of Count Aldamar's personal library, stacking dozens of books all around the desk where he read. Scouring each text for anything regarding the Orcs and their disappearance was how he kept his mind off Amantius, plunging himself into a world of yellowed pages to escape his current reality. Initially, it had been difficult to fight the urge to return to the Silverwood, but with each passing day he accepted the helplessness of his situation even more. Though his pride wanted him to believe he could rescue Amantius by himself, he knew Count Aldamar had spoken the truth. *If I were to go, it would be a suicide mission. The enemy knows the lay of the land far better than I, and no matter how strong I may be, I am still just one person against many.*

When he was not reading, Ulam continued his weapons training. Initially, it was difficult to find a sparring partner, however, as Ulam was so much bigger and stronger than the others. Even though he was not trained for combat, he was able to overpower many of his comrades, inflicting punishment even with wooden weapons. One by one people began refusing training with Ulam, until eventually Captain Karraman himself picked up the mantle. By that time the Captain had fully recovered from his injuries, having resumed the full responsibilities of his post.

The first few weeks of training were rough for Ulam, because while his brute strength would defeat a less experienced duelist, it did not work well against Captain Karraman's speed and finesse. Time after time the Aldamar's captain defeated Ulam, expertly parrying heavy blows from the Orc while also landing counterattacks. Despite the constant beating he received from Karraman's wooden sword, Ulam never gave up. Each day he returned to the practice yard, and each day he left with new bruises. As time went on, the bruises became fewer and less severe, until one day the roles were switched and he struck Captain Karraman first.

"By the Gods," Karraman said as he retreated, rubbing his shoulder where the wooden practice axe had crashed into him. "I'm going to have to start wearing armor just to protect myself against wood."

Ulam smiled, unable to contain the pride swelling inside him. Captain Karraman was a tough old veteran, having fought more battles than he could count. He had scars on his arms, walked with a limp, and could drink more ale than the rest of the Guards combined. He was a warrior at heart who lived for the rush of battle and the stories that inevitably followed. And although he never complimented someone directly, Ulam took the Captain's groans of pain as the highest form of praise.

After the sun slipped behind the city walls, Captain Karraman and Ulam headed for the Bride's Oasis to quench the thirsts and lick their wounds. As usual, the tavern was full of women, most of which paid them no attention. Although as Ulam scanned the room, a few smiled at him and even called out greetings. Finding himself in unfamiliar territory and unsure how to react, he grunted and headed straight for the bar, like an arrow seeking its target. *Their friendliness is strange. Why are they being so friendly? No one is friendly to me, except for the barkeep, Captain Karraman, and Count Aldamar.* Ulam chuckled to himself. *Strange company I keep these days.*

"Hello, my good Guards," the barkeep shouted as he hurried to the end of the bar, where Ulam and Karraman were sitting. He was as cheerful as ever. "What can I do you for this evening?"

"Same as usual, Korso," Captain Karraman said. It was the first time Ulam had heard the barkeep's name used.

The barkeep returned with two mugs of ale, giving them to Ulam and Karraman. The Captain tossed a few copper coins on the counter, which Korso swept into his pockets in a single motion. He held up a hand as Ulam reached for payment of his own. "No need for that, lad, the first one in on the house. Business has picked up since word got out that you drink in here. It seems the women-folk feel safer here than in their own homes. Since you jumped into that fire and pulled out that woman and her kid, you're kind of a folk-hero now."

Ulam grimaced as memories of the hungry flames biting his skin resurfaced. He looked at the scar running the length of his forearm where had been severely burned, tracing it with his other hand. He then thought of the fire in the camp and how he had been paralyzed in fear; his grimace quickly became a snarl. *How could I have been so weak? Now Amantius is gone, possibly dead because of my failure to join the fight. Not to mention, will I always be afraid of fire?*

"Cheer up," Captain Karraman said with a jab to Ulam's bruised ribs. "The man just told you that you're a hero and you're sitting there sulking into your beer."

"I am not a hero," Ulam replied before drinking half his beer in one gulp. *I am a coward.*

Captain Karraman finished his beer and then smiled. "That's what a hero would say. Cheer up, lad, be thankful

165

you're one of the few who returned alive. The Gods know I am."

Ulam grunted. *How can I be thankful for anything? I dreamed of being free of Mother's promise from the moment I made it, and now that Amantius is gone, all I feel is emptiness and shame.*

"Not much for conversation tonight, are you? It's all the same, I suppose. I've noticed you've garnered some favor with Count Aldamar recently." Captain Karraman said with a satisfactory nod, changing the subject. "Good. He needs people he can rely on in times like these, and I fear that list isn't as long as it once was."

Ulam grunted. *He is a very private man; I can understand that.*

"Don't drink too much," Karraman said as he finished his beer and stood from the bar. "I'm going to need you to be sober tonight. I have an…errand…I must run tonight and I need someone to help me. You don't have to come, but if you want to, meet me in a few hours on the training grounds. Also, try not to wear anything too expensive."

Captain Karraman then headed for the exit, Ulam staring at his back all the way. He meandered for a few moments after finishing his beer, wondering about the Captain's orders. He was curious why Karraman wanted to meet at such a late hour, especially since they had already spent the better part of the day together. Ulam grunted, shrugged his shoulders, and made for the exit as well.

The night's air was crisp, the constant wind a refreshing change from the musty, ale soaked walls of the Bride's Oasis. Aside from a few guards escorting women home from various places, the streets were abandoned. Ulam heard laughter and screams of delight coming from the direction of a brothel, and for a moment thought of Amantius. *No doubt if he were here he would be in there tonight.*

Before he realized it Ulam was standing in the castle's gateway, staring across the city. Tall plumes of peaceful smoke danced in the wind, born from the hundreds of fires burning in the hearths of Silverwater's homes. Bats occasionally darted overhead, squeaking in delight as they roamed the skies. They held Ulam's attention only for a moment before he returned to scanning the city. He was not looking for anything in particular; he was simply staring.

"Where are you, Amantius?" Ulam heard himself mutter, his words dripped in worry. He had spent many nights with his foster-brother standing vigil over the castle's entryway, listening to him ramble on about anything and everything. Though he had hated it, at that moment he would have given anything to hear Amantius' pointless ramblings once again. *Gods, it was annoying. Never thought I would miss it, though.*

Ulam spent the following hours in the library, the aroma of stagnant air and melted wax comforting to him. He usually poured over texts regarding his race, but his mind was focused on a different topic this time. Instead of researching Orcish history, he carefully studied a pristine map of the region, attempting to memorize every geographic marking. He grunted when he realized Accaria was not on the map, wondered if the omission was due to a lack of space on the parchment.

Ulam reached into one of the nearby drawers, rummaging through old documents and other clutter until he found what he was looking for. He wrapped a hand around a cold, glass bottle filled with a dark liquid, placing the object on the desk before him. He then grabbed the goose's feather that was in the same drawer, its tip stained black from use. Ulam proceeded to open the bottle, dipping the tip of the feather into the black liquid settled at the bottom. He then aimed the darkened quill's point into the ocean southeast of Silverwater and drew a peculiar shape, labeling it "Accaria."

"There," he muttered to himself after he finished, a grin splitting his face. Though he realized it was highly unlikely anyone would ever see this map, let alone use it to find Accaria, he was satisfied with his addition.

His eyes scanned the rest of the map, a highly detailed work by an incredibly gifted cartographer. The handwriting was superb as well, Ulam guessing the author had been a scribe. By comparison, he felt embarrassed by his sloppy letters, vowing to practice his penmanship in the future. *Perhaps my hands are just too big for this quill? Which bird has such large feathers that my hands will not dwarf a quill made from one? I will grab a book on the subject, after I finish with the map, of course.*

Ulam was surprised to see how large Silverwood Forest was, not realizing its magnitude as they had marched with the warband. He noticed a bare spot a few leagues into the forest, unmistakably the meadow where the ambush had taken place. He grimaced as the image of Amantius running towards the battle resurfaced in his mind, the shame of watching helplessly washing over him again. He closed his eyes and willed the guilt away, the void filled with anger instead. Anger at the Mad Raven, anger at Count Aldamar, and anger at what started everything: King Roderic's death. But most of all he was angry at himself for having been so afraid, for having been so weak in the presence of fire.

He opened his eyes, allowing himself to relax. He focused on the map once again, the orange glow of the candle illuminating the far side of the parchment. He saw a small "X" deep in Silverwood Forest with a description written above it in a different hand. *It appears I am not the only one who has updated this map.*

"Home?" He muttered. "What does that mean?"

Ulam heard voices echoing off the halls outside the library and knew it was time to meet Captain Karraman. Before standing he placed a heavy book on each side of the parchment to prevent the edges from recoiling and smudging the fresh ink he added. He then grabbed a lantern and exited the library, immediately coming face to face with both Captain Karraman and Count Aldamar.

"As you see, I am correct," Count Aldamar said with a smirk as he stepped around Ulam and entered the library, "I knew he would be here, surrounded by my life's work. We share a common thirst for knowledge, a thirst that is sadly lost upon men of your caliber, Jalkett."

Captain Karraman rolled his eyes, mocking the Count with a slow clap. "Yes, yes, congratulations, you found the only Orc in Silverwater. You must feel so accomplished."

Count Aldamar chuckled, a sound Ulam could not recall ever hearing. Though he could not explain why, somehow it was unsettling. It was high pitched, even shrill, the notes feeling like barbed arrows piercing his eardrums. *I should aim never to make him laugh.*

"I see you have been studying your surroundings," Count Aldamar stated as a finger tapped parchment. The laughter was gone from his voice, as though the prior moment had never happened. "Not thinking of mounting a rescue attempt for Amantius, are you? I thought we had come to an understanding that such an errand would be suicide. Besides, you do not even know if he is alive."

Ulam grimaced, his lips bending into a semi-snarl. "I know these things. I just wanted to be more familiar with the geographical area."

"Of course you were," Count Aldamar replied, no change in voice. His eyes were fixated on Ulam, an intensity that the Orc felt was burning a hole in him. *What is he hiding?*

Silence settled in the room, the only sound being Captain Karraman's tapping foot. "Are you two done talking maps? Who cares about that, we've work to do. Come on, Ulam. And here, take this."

Captain Karraman tossed a dusty, old burlap sack at Ulam, as well as a black hood. The smell of cow dung immediately filled his nostrils, causing him to cough. Upon further inspection, Ulam realized the bag was about as large as him, with three large holes cut out of the fabric. He grunted. *I do not know what we are doing, but I know this is not going to be a pleasant night.*

"I know I said you had a choice," Karraman continued, "but even if you said no, I was still going to order you to come. Come on, let's get going."

Ulam grunted and then turned to bid farewell to Count Aldamar, but when he turned around Aldamar was gone. Every candle was extinguished, the smell of burned wick lingering in the pitch-black room. Even though Ulam could not see the man, deep inside he somehow knew Aldamar was watching. He could feel the man's eyes locked onto him, the thought causing the hair on the back of his neck to stand. *Maybe you were right, Amantius. Maybe he is hiding something.*

Ulam followed Captain Karraman through the castle's corridors until they were outside once again, the moon coloring the entire city silver. In silence they left the castle behind them, taking the main avenue through Silverwater as they headed towards the south gate. Aside from the occasional patrolmen or drunkards, the city felt entirely abandoned. Ulam assumed the brisk night's air was the main culprit, its sharpness convincing denizens to remain indoors. With tales of the Mad Raven quickly spreading, though, he knew only the brave and foolish dared the streets at night.

They passed through the south gate unobstructed, the sentries dutifully removing the heavy plank that kept the gate shut. After passing under the archway, Ulam found himself in the vineyards south of the city, along the road he had taken with Amantius upon their arrival in Silverwater. The landscape was a far cry from how it appeared on that day. Grapevines still aligned both sides of the stone-gray road, but now many were no more than a tangle of skeletons. With each gust of wind, a medley of brown and yellow leaves shifted across the ground, the smell of rotting foliage new to Ulam's nose.

Ulam felt his moss-colored skin begin to prickle with goosebumps, his body shivering from time to time. Both were new sensations. *By Kevea's grace, I miss Accaria's weather. Is this what it feels like to be cold? I cannot say I much like this feeling. Should have worn more than a linen tunic and breeches, something warmer. Like cotton. Oh well.*

Ulam quickened his pace, hoping the extra energy would generate enough heat to keep his teeth from clattering. His mind wandered to Accaria, the tropical island kingdom with its lazy palm trees swaying in the wind. The hot days and warm nights, with a sweet summer sea breeze blowing off the waves. He would be firmly entrenched in a chair, a book appearing miniature in his big, Orcish hands. He would be wholly engrossed by the words on the pages, whether he was

171

reading a history book or an anthology of fairy tales made no matter. Amantius would be nearby complaining about the heat, using anything to wipe the sweat from his brow. Pelecia working a thread and needle, her concentration unfazed by her child's moaning.

Something strange happened as he reminisced; Ulam felt a fist clenching around his heart, a pit of emptiness in his stomach. It was not a feeling he expected by any means, in fact, he had worked hard to convince himself that he was invulnerable to such emotion. But as he trudged through the countryside with a silent Captain Karraman, Ulam was overcome with homesickness, a longing to be back in Accaria with Amantius and Pelecia.

I should have cherished those moments, Ulam thought as he continued following his comrade up a hill. *But how were we to know? I suppose that is one of the cruelties of the world. We do not recognize the best of times until they are over.*

An owl ended Ulam's reminiscing, returning him to the present. He found himself on a grass laden knoll, Silverwater's silhouette decorating the horizon behind him. When he squinted he could see the outline of the castle, a series of black shapes jutting into the indigo sky, tiny beams of orange and yellow dotting the city walls where the guards kept their fires. In front of him was a shadowed vale, the tall trees on the other side preventing the moon from illuminating the landscape. A gentle breeze blew, Ulam's nose crinkling as the smell of dung filled his nostrils once again. He did not need to see anything to know where he was or what was in the valley before him. *Why have we come to a farm?*

"What's wrong? Don't like the fresh air?" Captain Karraman said with a smirk. "Come on, put the sack over your body. We don't have all night."

"Why?" Ulam said, hesitating. "Why are we here? Why do we need these?"

Captain Karraman looked away, staring into the vale as well. "Does it matter why we are here? Now put it on, we're about to get messy."

Ulam quietly slipped the burlap sack over himself, the armholes almost too small while the hole for the head and neck was comically large. The coarse fabric and remnants of grain irritated his mossy green skin, as the sack had not been cleaned before being repurposed. Meanwhile, Captain Karraman's clung tightly at the torso, like a flimsy chainmail shirt. *Hopefully, there is not any fighting tonight. I cannot imagine this material being able to stop a thrown acorn, let alone a javelin.*

Although the sack was irritating him to no ends, Ulam was far more uncomfortable not knowing the nature of their midnight excursion. Or specifically, why he had been chosen to accompany Captain Karraman on this mission. It was obvious to him that the Captain had been here before, the farm's location so remote that even finding it in daylight would have been quite difficult. *Not sure why I have been chosen, but I am flattered to be trusted with this secret. Is it a secret though? It certainly feels like one.*

"Whatever happens tonight, you can't tell anyone. Just so we're clear," Karraman said with a nod; Ulam thought the man had read his mind. "Hopefully nothing happens. But, you never know with farm folk. Stay here, keep watch."

Captain Karraman disappeared down the embankment, his silhouette becoming one with the shadows. Clouds had passed over the moon; the world pitch black except for a hearth burning in a nearby building, the smoke a welcomed break from the dung. The Orc stood alone on the hilltop now, not entirely sure what he was supposed to be doing. *Be a guard,* he thought, *but what does that mean? What if someone comes? Do I yell? Or do I remain still, hoping they pass by without noticing?*

Ulam crouched down, hoping the stalks of grass were long enough to sufficiently hide him. His eyes flickered back and forth, searching his entire field of vision for any signs of movement. As time passed he began to become bored, the icy wind being the only reason he was still awake. On occasion fear would strike him in the gut, worried Captain Karraman had been discovered or captured. But the feeling was easily suppressed. *I have heard no shouting, no screams. Surely that is a sign of luck.*

Suddenly a woman screamed, her terror echoing in the night.

There goes our good luck.

The collective glow of a half dozen lanterns filled the valley floor; Ulam now aware of the size of the farming community below. Two homes on the left, another on the right, no more than simple shacks built by the best craftspeople the small community could offer. At the far end of the compound was a large barn, dozens of pens filled with various farm animals. Ulam heard horses and cattle call out in alarm as well, a clear indication that everyone and everything knew Karraman was skulking amongst them.

Ulam remained crouched on the hill, his eyes searching for any sign of his comrade. Figures emerged from the homes holding cleavers and pitchforks, gesticulating wildly at one another. Within moments a dozen lanterns were spreading in every direction, like a colony of ants evacuating an anthill. Though Ulam's heart rate had increased tenfold, he was still in complete control of himself. Instead of worrying about being discovered or captured, he was excited.

"Ulam, you brute, get down here." Captain Karraman's voice called from the base of the hill. "These bags are too damned heavy."

Ulam sprung to life and ran downhill, intercepting Karraman halfway down. The Captain was covered in a dark liquid; his burlap sack stained black. In each hand he carried a bag, shapes bulging from below, the same liquid dripping out of one.

"Here, grab these." He yelled as he thrust both bags into Ulam's hands. *Wet and slippery, what is this?*

At that moment the moon reappeared, shining its light, revealing the answers to Ulam's questions.

"Blood?" Ulam heard himself say, surprise mingled with horror. He stared at the Captain.

"Aye," Karraman said as he limped up the hill, "And there'll be more if you don't get your legs moving too."

Without another word Ulam ran up the hill, overtaking his comrade at the crest. As they descended the other side, the shouts of the farmers behind them became fainter, until they were all but gone. A new sound replaced the yelling, though, indistinguishable at first but slowly becoming louder. When Ulam realized what they were he stopped and turned around, watching as the first few shapes poured over the hill. *Hounds. Lots of them.*

"Keep running, you oaf," Karraman said in between breaths as he passed by.

"They have hounds," Ulam replied matter-of-factly. Even he was surprised by how emotionless his voice was.

Karraman stopped in his tracks and began rummaging through his bag, cursing loudly as he did so. Ulam watched impatiently, the barking echoing in the night, growing louder with each heartbeat. He was beyond anxious, his legs involuntarily moving again. He saw Karraman pull something from his bag, the object dark and oozing liquid.

"Grab something from your bag and drop it," Karraman said as he tossed the thing on the ground. "That'll buy us enough time to get away."

Ulam reached down and felt a dozen slimy items inside, his stomach churning as he failed to grasp any of them. Everything inside was too squishy, the texture slick and nearly impossible to grip. Eventually, his big Orcish fingers wrapped around something firm, like finding a stone in a puddle of water. He pulled his hand out of the bag and held up the object, his eyes growing wide as he realized what he was holding.

"It's a heart." Ulam heard himself mutter, though he had attempted to remain silent.

"Who cares what it is," Karraman yelled a dozen paces ahead of him, "just drop the damn thing and keep running."

Ulam was as still as a statue, watching as the blood twirled down his arm and dripped into the grass. Sickeningly, he almost believed the heart he was holding was still beating, but he knew the thumping he felt was his own banging inside his chest.

"Drop. The. Damn. Thing. And. Run!" Karraman screamed from somewhere in the darkness.

Ulam turned his gaze towards the hounds and saw they were in full sprint, no more than thirty paces away. He pulled his arm back and tossed the heart, watching as it nearly smacked one of the beasts in the face. To his surprise the hound stopped, sniffed the heart, and begin to feast upon the organ, no longer caring that Ulam was standing close nearby. Ulam then reached inside the bag and tossed another object in their direction, a kidney or liver perhaps, and then a few more until a dozen fights broke out amongst the greedy curs. When the charge of hounds had been completely broken, Ulam turned and chased after Karraman.

After running for what felt like an eternity, Ulam finally caught up to his leader, who was sitting on a large stone along the main road back to Silverwater. Karraman smiled as the Orc approached, a laughter of relief coming in between ragged breaths. "I'll be damned; you're still alive."

Ulam sat down beside the rock, gasping for air as well. He had not stopped running since he gifted a dozen organs to the hounds, fearing one would wonder what Orc-flesh would taste like. Dawn began to break in the east, the black sky slowly transitioning to gray. For the first time Ulam noticed that both he and Captain Karraman were covered in blood, the burlap sacks they wore soaked stiff. Though they were a gruesome duo, he was thankful that none of the blood was their own.

"Alright," Karraman stood up, "there's a stream nearby. The water will be cold, but we need to wash up before returning to Silverwater. The townsfolk may think we murdered an entire village together if they saw us like this."

Ulam grunted. *Did we?*

Chapter 21
Amantius

Amantius stood along the riverbank directly outside the timber palisade, skipping stones into the gentle stream. An earlier attempt had skipped six times, a new personal record, and he had tried for hours to push it to seven. He threw until the nerves in his arm started to tingle, an obvious sign that he should quit for the day. *A few more,* he thought, *and then I'll go back inside.*

He threw another, only two skips. Then another: two again. He threw his last rock, counted as it got to five and disappeared. *Oh well, six will have to do for now.*

He turned and looked at the fortress, known simply as "Home" to its residents. The wooden wall surrounding the compound was double his height with several gaps between the individual pikes. The men and women who were loyal to Morganna seemingly cared little for the state of their defenses, instead putting their faith in the remoteness of their fortress. Amantius realized the truth in their confidence, for even though he was standing near the entrance he could barely see the front gate.

He walked back inside, seeking out Jaga. For the past week the old warchief had been Amantius' sparring partner, teaching him how to better wield both spear and sword. Every session ended in bruises and curses, sore muscles and hurt pride, but Amantius could tell he was getting better. He still had not landed a successful hit on Jaga, but with each day he came closer and close. *Someday.*

Amantius strolled across the compound, the sound of his legs shuffling through piles of leaves filling the air. Each day the canopy above became weaker, allowing sunlight to bathe the compound more and more. Great swathes of brown and yellow leaves had fallen from the massive oaks and poplars, creating mountains of plant decay along the ground. Amantius had been part of the cleanup crew, along with a dozen new recruits, removing the debris and dumping it outside the palisade wall. Amantius reasoned every few days they had to resume their work, because if they did not, Home would drown in a sea of brown, yellow, and red. And such an ocean was extremely flammable as well.

His destination was the weapons court, a small makeshift arena located in the shadow of the Great Hall. Since the Great Hall had so many windows overlooking the court, Amantius often wondered if Morganna watched him spar with Jaga. He had seen little of her lately, occasionally catching a brief glimpse from a distance. He was forever hopeful she would call upon him soon, his patience threatening to turn into desperation. Many times he considered going to the Great Hall to see her, something she implied would be acceptable, even wanted, during their last interaction. But no matter how much he analyzed that moment in his mind, he could still not bring himself to approach her. After all, he was still her prisoner, and still constantly watched by guards at all times.

Prisoner? Amantius thought, an eyebrow arching, *I don't feel like a prisoner. If anything, I feel like part of this commune now. I'm even in charge of cleaning the leaves. Sure, it's minor, but it's a responsibility. A duty.*

Amantius saw Jaga marching across the fortress, a dozen people behind him. They all were heading in his

179

direction. *I even think of Jaga as a friend, a mentor. If I were truly a prisoner, why would he teach me how to fight? If I were a prisoner, why do they let me outside the walls whenever I please? I could probably just walk outside and never come back, go straight to Silverwater, find...*

Amantius' thoughts died, a lump in his throat. *Ulam. Still no news. Even the foraging parties and scouts claim they have not seen him. I need to get out of here, just for a while, just to see find out if Ulam lives or not.*

"Want to come with us?" Jaga said, grabbing Amantius' attention.

"Where?"

"To get food. We need to feed everyone." Jaga said as the others walked past him towards the armory. Amantius noticed the group was a mix of veterans and the new recruits, the "initiates" as they were called, some of which were part of his cleaning team. *Strange, I have been here longer than most of them.*

"Not enough in the gardens?" Amantius said, knowing there was not. The weather was getting colder, what little crops they grew were either barren or dead. His reply was automatic more than anything.

"There is if you only plan on living another week or so," Jaga replied, "Me? I'd like to see at least another twenty years if I can."

"So where are we going?"

"There's a busy highway to the south of us, farmers and merchants litter it at this time of the year. Plenty of food there. We'll go down, harass them, and take what they have. Should go smoothly, always does."

Robbing honest folks, how very noble. "I don't want to take part in killing anyone. Sorry, Jaga, I think I'll remain here."

Jaga grimaced. "Who said killing? If no one pulls a weapon on us, then no one will die. Think of it as a toll for using the road."

Amantius still did not like the idea of stealing from honest people, depriving them of their livelihoods. But Jaga had a valid point, they did not have enough food to feed everyone. *If the gardens are dying, then we'll need to "forage" plenty of food. Maybe I should go back to Silverwater instead and not be part of this. But if Ulam is not there, then what do I have there? Aldamar?* He shivered.

"Come on, lad, I need an answer," Jaga said impatiently. "Time is wasting, and the longer we stay here, the less food we get to eat."

"Couldn't we just pay them for their goods? Like a market?" Amantius said.

Jaga sighed, which turned into a laugh. "With what coin? Amantius, I understand you don't want to hurt anyone, especially people you have no quarrel with. But lad, if we don't get anything to eat, we will all starve to death. Me, you, everyone."

"Even I will," a heavenly voice said behind Amantius, sending his heart aflutter. He did not need to turn around to know who was speaking "Go arm yourself, Jaga, I will speak with him."

"Very well, my lady," Jaga said with a half-bow and followed the others to the armory.

Amantius turned and saw Morganna standing only a few steps away. The butterflies that had been sleeping in his stomach had suddenly awakened, filling Amantius with a child-like nervousness. She smiled at him, the dimples appearing on both sides of her face, reducing the world to just the two of them and no one else. In the back of his mind,

Amantius knew others were nearby, specifically her bodyguards, but he did not care.

"M-m-my, my lady," Amantius stuttered while awkwardly bowing too far, too fast.

"Relax, Amantius," she said, gently grabbing his arm, the same smile on her crimson lips. "I am only human."

You're a goddess. Amantius thought. He focused on her hand, her thumb gently caressing his skin, leaving a trail of goosebumps in its wake. He felt himself blush, red swelling his cheeks. *Keep it together, man! You're making yourself look like a fool in front of her.*

"Walk with me, will you?" Morganna said, wrapping her arm around his, pulling herself closer. Amantius could smell strawberries on her breath, the aroma sapping his legs of their strength.

Amantius walked with Morganna through the fortress, arms interlocked, as though he was escorting her to a royal banquet. As they walked in silence he focused his eyes on the Great Hall, not wanting to give the appearance of a love-struck fool. But at one point his will faded, and when he turned to her he saw she had been staring at him the whole time.

"You have been here for quite some time now," Morganna said as she looked up at him, her beautiful dark eyes melting his heart. "Are you enjoying your stay?"

"Now I am," Amantius blurted out, embarrassment quickly settling in.

Morganna giggled. It was soft, angelic. "Oh?"

"What I, what I mean is," Amantius began to stutter again. *Keep it together, Amantius. You look like a dolt.* "Now that I have my mobility back and my muscles don't scream at me, I am enjoying this place more. I don't like being inactive." *Good recovery.*

"I understand that," Morganna replied, "I have noticed you have been more active lately. Helping clear the leaves, helping with other chores. My followers have spoken highly of you."

"They have?" Amantius felt good knowing that he was impressing people close to Morganna. More important to him, though, was that she admitted noticing his actions lately. Her sudden admission overwhelmed him with excitement. *So she is watching me.*

"But of course. We are a small community, in many ways we are simply one large family." Her smile disappeared for a second, replaced with a quick flash of pure hatred, before her countenance returned to an angelic glow. Amantius saw the sudden change and recoiled, but not enough for Morganna to notice. Though he had never been more attracted to any woman he had ever laid eyes upon, there was something about that moment that unsettled him deeply. Just now, she reminded him of someone he had met before.

"But family cannot always be trusted," Morganna said, sadness filling her words. "For some, they are everything. You stand by them against the world, would do anything for them."

Pale skin.

"However, that is not the case for everyone. Take my family for instance. When I was still a girl, my family was strong. Nothing could hurt us, tear us apart." Morganna stopped, stared at the entrance to the Great Hall before them. "But all that ended when Mother died. Father grew delirious, violent even."

183

Dark eyes. They're so dark, almost black even. It could just be the lighting.

"But he was still a good man. He did not deserve to be killed. Murdered." Morganna's words were heavy with longing, though there was an element of anger lurking in them as well. "Especially by his own son. My own brother."

Brother? An image floated in his mind, a man's face. The answer to his question was so obvious now, hitting him like a kick to the gut. *No, it cannot be!*

"You know him." Morganna continued, her grip strengthening around Amantius' arm. He flinched as her nails dug into his skin. "He is your employer, the man you fought for. The man whose claim so many have died defending."

"Count Aldamar!" Amantius spat the words from his mouth as though they were poison resting on his tongue. A thousand thoughts shot this his mind, like a barrage of arrows, each with a different question attached. *Morganna is Aldamar's sister? He murdered their father? How can this be?*

"Yes, Aldamar," Morganna replied, her voice surprisingly calm. "I refuse to give him the title, though. I am sure you can understand."

"I never liked him, I knew there was something evil about him," Amantius replied, the words flowing like water from behind a broken dam. "I could tell the moment I met him." *What of Ulam? If he is still alive, he would still be in Silverwater. By the Gods! How could we have been so blind!? I need to go back, I need to rescue him.*

"Well, unfortunately not everyone is as astute as you." Morganna continued, tracing his bicep with a finger. "He has fooled many throughout the years, no more so than the people of Silverwater. That is why I fight, Amantius." She

184

broke away, walked to the steps of the Great Hall, and turned.

"I fight so that someday I can liberate those poor souls under his rule." Morganna began, her voice louder, as though the world was her audience. "When he has been defeated, and defeated he shall be, I will welcome an era of peace and prosperity for Silverwater County. Something this land has not seen in many years."

A couple of the veterans milling about echoed her sentiments before returning to their tasks. Amantius turned and saw Jaga coming towards him, wearing a full set of armor, looking the part of a warchief. His cloak was long, reaching the ground, a mix of gray and black fibers. It had been made from the pelt of a great wolf, one large enough to cover Jaga's frame. Under his arm was his helmet, decorated with the wolf's snarling head. *If this turns into a fight, he'll look like a demon-wolf.*

"You should come," Jaga said, the same grim expression on his face, "going out there will do you some good. If you stay in here too much longer you might go mad with boredom. And boredom may get you into trouble; if you get what I mean."

Amantius chuckled, though it sounded more nervous than he intended. "Well, when you put it that way." He began to follow Jaga when he remembered Morganna on the steps, but when he turned to say goodbye she had vanished. Though he could not spot her or her bodyguards, he could still feel her eyes on him. *Just like her brother, only infinitely more beautiful and less terrifying.*

"Check the armory," Jaga said as they strolled across the fortress, "Wear whatever you can find. Also, find a helmet. We should have a few spares in there. Generic, some

185

don't even look like real animals. It doesn't matter, people go blind when they see the fangs." Jaga stroked the polished teeth of his wolf's head.

"Do you trust me to carry a blade?" Amantius said as he split off, walking towards the armory. "After all, I am technically your prisoner."

Jaga's face tightened, and for the first time in weeks, Amantius felt as though he was being judged. "Should I not trust you?"

Amantius hesitated. *You should be able to trust me, but I don't know. This would be much easier if Ulam was here, or at least not possibly still fighting for Aldamar.*

"Suit up, Amantius," Jaga continued, his frame relaxing. "You're one of us, now, even if you don't know it."

Jaga walked away, disappearing into the group of people gathered at the gate. Amantius watched for a second, Jaga's words echoing in his mind. *You're one of us, now, even if you don't know it.*

"Yeah, maybe I am," he muttered, "but Ulam isn't."

Chapter 22
Ulam

Days passed without Ulam seeing Captain Karraman or Count Aldamar. He found it quite strange, considering their midnight mission had been conducted in secret. But he did not mind the lack of contact, though. He wanted to be alone, to give himself time to reflect on that night; the scenes of which played a million times over in his mind.

Ulam's memory was impeccable; he could still see and feel every detail of that night. He remembered waiting on a hilltop, a brisk wind nipping at his neck. The silence was then broken by a series of screams and a thunder of barking dogs. He remembered the fear that struck him at the sound of the alarm, which only intensified when Captain Karraman sprinted by him. He remembered the stomach-churning stench from inside the bag, the squish of the organs as he tossed them at the pursuing hounds. He remembered the sound of the stream as they splashed around, washing the blood from their bodies. By the time they returned to Silverwater the sun had risen, forcing them to use back alleys to avoid the eyes of any early risers. When back at the castle Karraman had taken all the sacks of organs and disappeared in the castle, promising he would explain later.

But when will "later" be?

Ulam was in The Bride's Oasis, working on his fourth mug of ale. He began frequenting the establishment more after that night, choosing to drown his thoughts in alcohol and friendly conversation. Korso the barkeep was always quick to provide either.

"Have you heard the latest news?" Korso said as he polished a mug, "Rumors from the south, apparently a farm was attacked by wraiths the other night...or something like that."

Ulam grunted. "Wraiths?"

"Aye, wraiths," he put down the mug and grabbed the next. "Don't know if I believe it or not. Never seen one. Now, that doesn't mean I don't believe it. Hell, after all, we have the Mad Raven running amok out there. So why not a wraith?"

Ulam grunted again. *Was that us?* His heart began to beat a little faster, a cold sweat forming on his brow. "How many died?"

Korso shrugged. "Who can say? One person says twenty, another says zero. That's the best part about rumors, they're almost always complete horseshit. Probably wasn't anything supernatural about the attack, either. Most likely a couple of jackass kids raising a little mayhem, scaring some farm folk." He started to chuckle. "The Gods know I did my fair share back in the day."

Ulam did not like that Korso had news regarding a night attack on a farm community to the south of Silverwater. Not because he did not like or trust the barkeep, but he knew that such an isolated man would only know such information if someone had told him. If Korso, a barkeep in a predominately female tavern in the far corner of Silverwater, knew about Ulam and Captain Karraman's night raid, then everyone else in the city knew as well. *Hopefully, no one learns the truth. It took saving a family in a burning building just to get people to stop glaring at me with hate in their eyes.*

"Well there's someone I haven't seen in a while," Korso shouted, breaking Ulam's concentration. A blast of chilly air pushed through the front door, sweeping brown leaves onto the wood floorboards. "Been wondering if you were still alive, Jalkett."

"I go a few days without seeing your face and you wonder if I've been killed?" Karraman replied, his tone light. "I'm hurt."

"Well you never know," Korso replied as he placed a full mug of ale in front of Karraman, "these are weird times, my friend. First, we have the Mad Raven, and now we have wraith sightings. Hell, not to mention an Orc is my most loyal patron!"

"Wraith sightings?" Karraman sounded confused, but there was something about his reaction that seemed forced. Or at least, Ulam thought he was pretending to be surprised.

"Just told your comrade here about a farm down south that was attacked by wraiths a few nights ago. Probably just superstitious folk being superstitious. You know how farmers are."

Captain Karraman and Korso continued their small-talk for a bit longer while Ulam waited impatiently. He needed to have a private conversation with Karraman; he needed answers to the questions that had been keeping him awake at night. *I need to know the truth, dammit.*

Korso eventually disappeared into the far reaches of the tavern, leaving Karraman to his drink. Ulam knew this was not the time or place to ask his questions, but he was being driven mad with curiosity. He felt his lips moving before his brain was able to stop himself from speaking. "What did we…"

Karraman held up a hand. "Not here."

189

"Then where?" The Orc's voice was an irritated grumble of pent-up frustration mixing with the embarrassment of broaching the subject in public.

Captain Karraman sighed. He swirled the remnants of his beer before putting the mug to his lips for the last sip. "Meet me in the castle after the sun goes down. I suppose you should know the truth."

Ulam watched as the Captain slung a cloak over his body and left the tavern, letting another flurry of leaves sweep inside once again. He waited a few moments and then followed, shivering as the wind brushed against his skin. Ulam had never experienced such bitter weather before; the coldest of nights in Accaria was usually a thing to celebrate, a respite from the oppressive heat and humidity of the island. Silverwater was different though, which surprised Ulam, because the palm trees and sand dunes in the area suggested a much warmer locale. And for the most part this was true, but in recent days the weather had become downright unbearable to him. However he was not the only one who felt this way, most of the townspeople openly complained about the icy blasts of wind and lack of sunny skies. Even they seemed surprised by the sudden change as well.

Ulam headed straight for the armory upon returning to the castle, hoping to find anything to help check the bitter wind. Although none of the clothing was large enough for his body, he opened a chest and found a silver and purple Castle Guard cloak that was clearly too large for any human. He pulled it out, slung it over his shoulders, and clasped the top. It was a little short, the bottom touching his upper legs, but he was content with his discovery. After all, he did not have the money to have a tailor make clothes to fit his broad shoulders and chest. *Free and short is better than nothing at all.*

The sun had completely disappeared over the horizon as Ulam exited the armory. Silverwater was now an ocean of lanterns, yellow and orange glowing across the whole city. Along the surrounding walls he could see the small bonfires lit by shivering sentries, their silhouettes contrasted by the bright flames. Although Ulam had a newfound fear of fire, even he dreamed of being near one, basking in its heat.

He entered the castle, his boots echoing off the cold stone walls of the entrance hall. The interior was characteristically dimly lit, only a few torches burned in their sconces. Ulam followed them, partially because of the heat they provided, but also because he assumed Captain Karraman had left the trail for him to follow. Within moments he found himself in the grand hall, a wide, mostly empty room with a dais at the far end. On top of the platform was a rather plain velvet chair, a large, purple cloth bearing a silvery crescent moon draped over its back. Above him was a massive iron chandelier, the candles of which were aglow. From their light he was able to distinguish a row of paintings aligning the walls of the Great Hall. Upon further inspection, he discovered the paintings were actually portraits, each depicting a different former Count of Silverwater. Ulam noticed the last three looked very similar, as though they were the same man each time.

"The resemblance is uncanny, I know," a soft, yet stern, voice said from behind Ulam, causing him to jump. "I never believed I looked so much like my uncle, the former count. However, the artist clearly disagreed."

Ulam turned and saw the cold, black eyes of Count Aldamar staring at him, a whimsical smile creasing his lips. He did not hear the Count come into the grand hall, nor did he hear the man approach him. *How did I not hear him? Was he there the whole time?*

Count Aldamar's smile was empty and void of any warmth, much like the grand hall itself. Ulam shifted his weight, with every second of silence he grew more uncomfortable. Though Aldamar was staring at him, Ulam's eyes flickered around the hall, looking for Captain Karraman, hoping the man was also present. He was nowhere to be found.

"No doubt you are searching for your captain, seeing how he arranged this meeting," Count Aldamar began pacing the room, his footsteps were as light as a feather. Ulam closely followed each of the Count's steps, his eyes honed in on the man's highly embroidered shoes. *Does he float? How does he walk so silently?*

"Jalkett trusts you," Count Aldamar said. Although his back was turned to Ulam, his voice still echoed off the walls of the grand hall. "You should feel honored, he is not one to blindly place faith in others."

The Count walked further into the darkness that engulfed the room, becoming nothing more than a silhouette with snow-white hair at the edge of Ulam's vision. There was a sudden pop, followed by the sound of liquid being poured. A moment later Aldamar returned with two crescent-engraved chalices in his hands. Even from a distance Ulam could see inside the cups, where dark red wine threatened to spill over the brim. The Count extended an arm and nodded, a rueful smile creasing his lips. "I stash wine underneath my chair. I find it much more preferable to have wine nearby at all times, instead of rummaging through the cellar or kitchen at all times of the night. I have scared more servants and guards than I care to remember." He tasted the wine and smacked his lips. "Perhaps that is why no one lasts longer than a month, or why I rarely have visitors from the other counties of the Empire. Not that I care, mind you, the less the better."

Count Aldamar disappeared into the dark once again, the pouring of more wine once again filling the room. Ulam sniffed the wine in his cup and wrinkled his nose, the smell too acidic for his liking. Even though wine was the favored drink of most Accarians, Ulam had always preferred ale. *I would like nothing more than to be still in the Bride's Oasis, a beer in my hand, not giving a damn about anything. I better drink this, though, I do not want to offend the Count, especially when no one else is around.*

He tipped the cup to his lips and drank, grimacing as the first notes touched his tongue. He stomached a few more gulps before he stopped to wipe his mouth. *Halfway there. I just have to do that one more time.*

"It is a local wine, made with local grapes." Count Aldamar said as he reappeared, his chalice filled to the brim once more. "A little fuller-bodied, but with a nice touch of blackberries. Wouldn't you agree?"

Ulam grunted. *Tastes like wine.*

"Anyway, to discuss wine is not why we are here," Count Aldamar said as he walked towards the dais, gesturing Ulam over. "Come. We have some time until Jalkett arrives. Tell me about yourself, from whence you came. I would be pleased to know more about this mysterious Orc who showed up in my city almost a year ago, with the least stereotypical Orcish qualities I have ever seen."

Ulam recounted most of his story, carefully omitting details here and there, specifically Amantius' lineage. He spoke of his childhood, reading every book he could get his hands on, and how he was forever thankful that Pelecia had taught him how to read. He described Accaria and the forests surrounding its white walls, the smell of the ocean infused into every structure in the city. He spoke of the rebellion that capsized their idyllic life, forcing them to flee across the ocean. As his monologue continued he delved into his bond with Amantius, forged as infants and tempered by adversity.

"Accaria is a tolerant island. It has to be with the merchants that sail in and out of the Whaleport," Ulam said as he wiped droplets of wine from his lips, "But as I grew, and as my muscles became stronger, and my tusks began to extend from my jaw, I could see the fear growing in their hearts. My own neighbors, who I had known my whole life, shared bread at the dinner table many times over, no longer wanted my company. Mothers and fathers would herd their children into their homes and stand guard, watching my every movement. No one was openly hostile, but I heard the rumors, the voices in the dark. They called me Savage. Greenskin. Beast. Monster. Child-eater."

Ulam tipped the goblet back and sucked down the rest of the wine, extending his arm for a refill. He could not remember how many cups he had consumed already, but he did not care. Something strange had happened during his discourse; he began to trust Count Aldamar. The man said very little, but he listened to every last word. There was a look of empathy emanating from the Count's wrinkled face that Ulam had only ever seen from Pelecia. In some mystifying manner, the Orc believed that Count Aldamar found his life story relatable.

"Amantius never acknowledged this, that people were whispering foul things behind our backs. He forever remained optimistic that we would grow old in Accaria; that we would both find brides and have many children together."

Ulam chuckled. "I do not know who he thought I was going to marry."

Count Aldamar laughed, a genuine joy lighting up his dark features. "Naïve, of course, but we believe many absurdities when we are youths. You cannot fault his optimism though, I suppose."

Ulam grunted in agreement, nodding his head. "Aye. You can fault him for many things, but never his optimism, or his loyalty." Ulam felt a lump in his throat and his heart clench, he had stumbled into uncomfortable territory. "He stood by me all those years. Even when sailors from the mainland would come to port and get violent, or try to start a fight, he was the first to defend me. He even found a place at the base of Mount Meganthus where I could hide from the world; a safe place only we knew how to find. Truth be told, I would have died years ago, murdered in an alleyway, if not for Amantius."

Ulam closed his eyes and hung his head, a wave of shame coursing through this body. Tears began to well in his eyes, but they did not fall. *He gets captured or killed, and I have not even attempted to find him. Here I am, crying about my misfortunes to the Count of Silverwater, while he is still missing. If the roles were switched, he would have come looking for me, even if it meant his death. Why am I such a coward? Why would he risk his life for such an unworthy being, one that even calls him "brother?"*

Count Aldamar stood and stretched his old limbs. In the firelight, Ulam could see the outlines of muscles coiling in his milky white skin, where a deceiving strength hid in an otherwise small frame. He slowly walked over, his steps producing no sound, and gently laid a hand on Ulam's shoulder. His hand was cold and heavy, like an ancient glacier

195

had encased his entire right side, yet it was surprisingly comforting.

"I know your pain," Count Aldamar's voice was haunting, as though spoken by a ghost, "I was raised in a hold to the west of here, deep in the heart of Silverwood Forest, surrounded by giant trees that blanketed the sky above. My childhood home was nestled in between a giant, stone cliff and a gentle, crystalline river. Even now, many years later, in my mind's eye, I still see the rays of light reflecting off the water; I can still taste its coolness on my lips."

Count Aldamar was looking into the darkness, his eyes seemingly captivated by something Ulam could not see. "Our father was lord of that small village, a dozen or so families worked the surrounding land. We all worked together, in unison, for the betterment of all. My lot was hunting. I learned to track all types of animals: deer, bears, rabbits, so on. Pardon my boasting, but I must admit, I was quite good. Hardly did I venture into the woods without returning with something slung across my back."

The image reminded Ulam to unclasp his cloak and sling it over his body; a stale chill was beginning to pierce his torso and legs. The sound garnered Count Aldamar's attention, his dark eyes taking in the sight before him. Ulam saw a flash of curiosity on the Count's face, though the emotion disappeared just as quickly.

"In truth, I had a little help," Count Aldamar continued as he returned to his velvet chair, filling both of their goblets with more wine before sitting again. "My sister joined me on many hunts. Like me, she enjoyed the challenge of finding a trail in the underbrush and the thrill that came when we found our prey. We were inseparable in those days, as though we were attached at the hip. Wherever I went, she followed, and wherever she went, I followed. But then…"

Count Aldamar stopped, his face cold and blank, though Ulam could see a thousand years of pain behind his eyes. Aside from the occasional creaking coming from the far depths of an old castle, and the air escaping through Ulam's nose, there was no sound in the room. Only absolute silence.

Just as Ulam began to wonder if the silence was going to last for all eternity, Count Aldamar took another sip of wine to wet his throat. "One day, after a steady rainfall, my sister and I were out looking for game when we came across a set of footprints. Not imprints made by iron boots, mind you, but actual feet. So naturally, we followed them, wondering who was lurking barefoot this deep in the forest. We knew it was not one of our own, one of our neighbors, because we were too deep into the Silverwood. We must have followed those tracks for hours, going forever further and further into the forest."

"The footprints led to a cave beneath a pair of oaks with trunks as wide as the towers of this castle. The sun was fading, and I wanted to return to the hold so we could bring more people the next day. My sister, though, was adamant about finding this mystery person we had followed for leagues in the Silverwood. 'We did not come all this way to just turn around' she told me. So we explored."

Count Aldamar drank from his cup, his face expressing no emotion. "We went inside, without the help of fire or any other aid to our vision. The odor was overwhelming. Foul. There was death in the air. I wanted to turn back, but she did not. She kept going, deeper and deeper, until I lost sight of her. And then…she screamed."

"Without a second thought I sprinted into the darkness, tripping over Gods know what until I came to her. She was in a large chamber, a crack in the roof letting in just enough light for my eyes to see the horror that was before me. She was slumped over, a dark figure with bright eyes standing above her, blood dripping from fangs. In my rage I charged into the creature, hurtling it into a rock. Even to this day, to this moment, I can still hear the crack its head made. I grabbed my sister, slung her over my shoulder, and ran out of there."

Count Aldamar's left hand was clenched in a fist, shaking on the armrest of his velvet chair. Ulam began to fear an explosion of anger, once again hoping Captain Karraman would walk into the room. *If the Captain comes, though, perhaps the Count will not keep telling this story.*

"I ran back to our home, screaming, crying the whole way. I was met by a few of our neighbors, who took her the rest of the distance." Aldamar released his fist, stretching his long, boney fingers. His muscles had loosened as well, slipping into his normal posture. "I went back to the cave with a dozen men and women, armed with torches, knives, swords, whatever we had available. But it was gone, there was no sign of the creature I attacked, the one that had almost killed my sister. It had simply vanished."

"Vanished? How could that be?" Ulam said, the words falling from his mouth. "You even said you heard the crack and saw the blood."

Count Aldamar shook his head quietly, clearly still in disbelief after all this time. "I know. What we found, though, was far worse. Mountains of bones, organs, rotting carcasses stretched throughout the entire cave. Men, women, children, deer, horses, everything. We went back to our little village, and over the next few days, my sister recovered miraculously. She lost so much blood we all thought she would perish, but alas, she did not. But she did not only heal quicker than anyone could have imagined, she also grew stronger. Even wrathful. So violent, she…"

Count Aldamar looked away, his eyes focused on the chandelier. Ulam was completely engrossed by the story, so much so that he did not realize he had sat down at some point, or that he abandoned his chalice long ago and was drinking directly from a bottle.

"One day I went hunting, and when I came back the whole village was gone. Slaughtered. Our mother, our father, our neighbors and their children. Dead." Count Aldamar continued, a solitary teardrop sliding down his pale cheeks. "All except for my sister. She had become a feral monster in my absence. She looked the same, still as beautiful and graceful as always, but there was a savageness in heart, in her eyes. She feasted on our parents, and she would have done so to me as well, except…"

"Except what?"

Count Aldamar sighed. "Except I buried a sword deep in her heart."

The Count stared wide-eyed at his hands, as though he could still see blood on them. As Ulam watched a lifetime of pain escape the Count's soul, a terrible thought entered his mind. *Amantius is out there somewhere. Has he become food for that monster too? Dammit, Ulam! You need to go find him!*

"It was the Mad Raven, it had to have been," Count Aldamar said as his eyes remained focused on his hands. Though his voice was no more than a whisper, intense loathing dripped from every word. "The Mad Raven killed

199

my sweet, darling sister, and our whole village. Its poison changed her, turned her."

Ulam stood suddenly, the mere mention of the Mad Raven's name was enough to put worry into his heart. The motion caught Count Aldamar's eyes, and instantly all the emotion on his face vanished into the dark room.

"Enough storytelling tonight," the Count said as he rose from his seat, "I have quite enjoyed your company, Ulam. I thank you for it. You should go rest, which is where I assume our faithful Captain Karraman is at this moment."

Ulam grunted and bowed, then turned to walk away. He did not think he could rest on this night, too many thoughts were borrowing a hole in his mind, most of which concerned Amantius. As he approached the exit he stopped and turned to ask Count Aldamar one more question, something he had meant to ask throughout the Count's story.

"What was her name? You only referred to her as your sister."

Count Aldamar stared from across the grand hall, a white shape cloaked in purple upon a dais. Though he was far away, Ulam could still see the pain on the Count's face. "Her name was Morganna."

Chapter 23
Amantius

Amantius shivered as a bone-chilling wind cut through the forest, the coldest he had ever experienced. The sudden gust filled his heart with nostalgia for Accaria, a longing he had not felt in quite some time. He found it quite strange, if not a little shameful, that his homeland had escaped his thoughts recently. Prior to his capture, nary a day passed without Amantius seeking out news of Accaria or crafting some scheme to return at the first opportunity. But so much had happened to him in the past months that he now felt a world away from the soft sands and salty air he loved, with no hope of ever returning.

Silverwater seemed so far away, and now I am even further. Amantius sat on a log near a campfire, his eyes blankly staring at the flames jumping from the pit. Occasionally the smell of stew would swim up his nostrils, reminding him he was hungry. *I don't even know how to get back to the city from here. I could be a day away, two days, or a week. Do I even want to go back, though? There I'm a guard, dying of boredom while protecting an evil man with some dark secret. Here I have freedom, though I'm not fond of these "toll collections."*

Amantius had participated in the "toll collections," as some of the others had taken to naming their misdeeds. While he never felt particularly proud of what he was doing, Jaga kept reminding him they were only doing this so that everyone could be fed. Even though Amantius realized this was for the greater good of everyone from Home, he still felt ashamed of robbing innocent merchants and farmers.

"Here," one of the veterans gave him a bowl of stew, "starving to death isn't going to help you any."

Amantius took a spoonful and swallowed what he hoped was a chunk of meat, cringing at the taste. *All these folks have been robbed, yet our food is still just terrible. Apparently, no one knows how to cook. Maybe instead of stealing food, we should start stealing recipes. Maybe we can even hold a cook hostage, at least until they teach a thing or two about seasoning.*

The veteran snorted. "If you don't like it, cook your own."

Even he knows this stew is garbage. Amantius did not return his gaze, instead choosing to stare into the distance, watching as lonely leaves fell from their trees to join their brethren on the ground. The thinned canopy revealed yet another gray sky, the hazy clouds perpetually hiding the sun. According to the people around him, the weather had been unusual, many claiming they had never experienced such temperatures before. Unlike Amantius they welcomed the gray skies and colder weather because it made wearing their heavy animal skins much more bearable. *The whole lot of them are insane. I would give anything to see the sun again.*

Amantius turned his attention to a veteran polishing her armor, clearing any rust that might have gathered since the last time it was used. Behind her was a man sharpening a stack of swords, and even further away a duo collected brush and tree branches to keep the fires fed. At the very edge of his vision, Amantius saw a fletcher crafting arrows, while a partner tested their flight path on a straw target. There was so much activity in the camp, yet Amantius sat idly, uncertain what to do, unsure if he could even do anything.

Have I no skills? Am I completely worthless? He wondered as his eyes flickered from person to person, all occupied with some task that benefited the camp. He remembered back to his childhood, never realizing how pampered he had been. He never had to find his own food, dinner was always provided for by his mother. He never learned how to stitch or plant a garden. He did not know how to cook; he could not discern which berries would kill him and which ones would not. Where many his age were taught how to use a weapon, sharpen a blade or repair armor, Amantius had instead learned how to make maidens swoon with a couple of steamy poems and an immodest amount of charm. *I have so much to learn.*

Grunts and thuds from the other side of a row of tents reached his ears, the sounds of people practicing their swordcraft. Amantius meandered over to the arena and observed for a few moments, seeing if he could learn anything from watching. He noticed many of the veterans sparred with one another; their movements polished and precise from a lifetime of training and combat. The battles among the initiates were no more than a brawl, neither side knowing how to swing a sword with any real skill or technique. Amantius laughed to himself as he watched, thankful for the little bit of training he had already received.

"Think you're better, do you?" Jaga said as he approached.

"I know I'm better," Amantius replied, confident in his stance. "I'm not a master swordsman by any stretch of the imagination, but I'm definitely better than they are."

"Alright then," Jaga tossed him a sword, the blade covered in sheep's wool, "let's see what you can do."

A pit opened in Amantius' stomach, his confidence washed away in an instant. "I said I'm better than them, not you. You know this; you've beaten me a hundred times over."

Jaga snorted. "Tip of advice for you, you can't get better unless you spar with someone better than you. You don't learn anything from winning every time. Now raise your damn sword and prepare to get knocked around."

Amantius stepped into a clearing with Jaga and raised his sword, the wool at the end making the blade heavier than he would have preferred. He took a few practice swings to loosen his muscles, the cold air having caused them to contract. As he did so he kept whispering words of encouragement to himself, remembering one of the Castle Guards in Silverwater telling him that fighting was just as much mental as it was physical. He did not know if the advice would help him or not, but it was surely worth a try.

Amantius stepped in close and nodded at Jaga. He raised his sword, the heavy blade cumbersome in his hands. *Alright Amantius, let's just see how good you are. Maybe you can even…*

Before he knew it, he was on the ground, pain throbbing across his back. Though Jaga was using a similarly wool-cloaked sword, Amantius thought his back had been cracked in half by a giant's warhammer. He heard some snickering around the circle, and immediately realized everyone was watching him. As the pain dulled he returned to his feet and held out the sword again, nodding once more.

Though the result was much the same, Amantius was marginally pleased that he was able to dodge a few swipes before once again being thrown to the ground. This time his chest felt as though it was caving in on his heart, but he was not going to let the pain incapacitate him. Amid a few mock cheers, Amantius slowly regained his footing and stood, leveling his sword once again.

The corner of Jaga's mouth curved as he nodded, something akin to respect passing over his face. "You might not be the best, but no one can question your toughness."

Or stupidity, Amantius thought. Though both his chest and back felt like they had been crushed by a rockslide, he still had enough strength to hold his sword with some sense of stability. He could tell by the looks on the faces of the bystanders that they too were impressed, although some pleaded for him to take a knee to end the madness. *Maybe if I am lucky he'll kill me this time, surely death can't be as painful.*

While Amantius laughed at his own joke Jaga lunged at him, initiating combat once again. Although slightly off guard, Amantius was able to block a flurry of strikes from the old warchief, surprising everyone watching the duel. After parrying so many attempts in quick succession, Amantius began feeling good about himself, so good that he decided to go on the offensive, which he quickly learned was a mistake. In one swift move Jaga once again knocked him to the ground, this time by sweeping his legs from underneath him.

Amantius hit the frozen earth, staring straight into the evening sky. As a dual set of aches filled his legs, he relived the past few seconds in his mind, trying to understand where he had committed his error. *I need to learn how to counterattack like that. I wonder if he'll teach me, assuming I'm not crippled.*

"That's probably enough for today, eh?" Jaga said as he walked over, his boots crunching on the fine layer of frost. "It's getting late. Besides, next time around I might take off your head."

Amantius wanted to laugh, but his lungs burned too much. Instead, he opened his mouth and watched the steam come out, escaping towards the sky. "Tomorrow."

Jaga smiled. "I have a feeling you're not going to be feeling too pretty tomorrow. But if you can stand up and if we have the time, then we will continue."

"Someone's coming, Chief," someone nearby said, "looks like one of our scouts."

"There's a caravan!" The scout's words called out across the camp, her words quickly spreading across the camp. "Two wagons, maybe more. Lots of loot!"

The scout's words injected a jolt of energy and excitement into the camp. Their previous targets had been smaller, usually only a few people carrying all they could in backpacks or on a single mule. The items they had stolen to this point where barely enough to keep their small crew fed, and definitely not the big score they had been waiting for. Before the scout had time to fully explain all the details, the entire camp had mobilized. Men and women began arming themselves, helping each other equip their helmets and chainmail. Within seconds the party had transformed from a band of thieves into a host of hell-beasts.

Amantius was by far the least enthusiastic of the group, the idea of petty highway robbery still disgraceful to him. He was also the least mobile at that moment, his body no more than a mass of throbbing pain. While the others galloped through the mountains of dead leaves, Amantius massaged his legs, hoping to regain some strength. There was no way he could miss the biggest holdup of their expedition without angering the others, so he willed his way to his feet, using the sword as a makeshift staff.

He armed himself as best he could, forgoing his armor aside from the hellish helmet given to him. He then chased after the others, jogging at the only pace his aching body would allow. He caught up with the rest of the group at the very edge of the forest, where everyone cautiously waited behind the last wall of brush. Jaga issued orders silently by using hand signals, sending people in various directions. When he had finished, Jaga motioned for Amantius to join him behind a tangle of briars.

Amantius kneeled down and followed Jaga's eyes to the road, where a couple of ox-drawn wagons covered in animal hides slowly rolled down the stone-paved highway. A dozen men and women accompanied the convoy, only one of which appeared to be armed. Amantius could see the man's armor was old and rusted, and assumed the man's sword was most likely dull as well. *Probably just to give the illusion of comfort. Those poor men and women have no idea what's about to happen.*

The wooden wheels of the wagons creaked as they rolled over the individual stones on the ancient highway. Aside from the occasional snort of an ox, it was the only sound coming from the caravan. No one spoke, and as they drew nearer, Amantius saw that their eyes were all focused on the forest, though it was evident they did not know exactly where amongst the trees the threat would be coming from. His heart thundered in his chest, his forehead dripped with cold sweat. He was conflicted; part of him was afraid they had been discovered, while the other part was hopeful. *If this goes well, we will have all we need and we can stop robbing people. Just one more robbery, Amantius. You can do this.*

"Now."

Chapter 24
Ulam

The candle was nearing its end, its wax pooled at the bottom of the stick. Very little light penetrated the library deep within the castle, but there was still enough left for Ulam to read. Dozens of books were stacked all around him, piles upon piles resting on the floor. Unlike previous times, however, there was a common theme among the texts.

Ulam had been fascinated with Count Aldamar's tale, insomuch that he did little else other than research. He had been so absorbed by the Count's past that he had completely forgotten about his midnight excursion with Captain Karraman or the fact that the man did not show for their meeting with the Count.

Ulam fulfilled his duty as a guard every day, patrolling the castle with a few of the others. The shifts were long, seeming as though they would never end. Though his body was in present-day Silverwater, Ulam's mind was always in a different time and place. He did not leave the castle for weeks, instead electing to take his meals in the confines of the library. At one point he even set up a makeshift sleeping area for himself, his desire for knowledge burning white-hot in his mind. He was on a quest, one given to himself by himself, to discover what kind of monster had devastated the Count's life. He searched for any eyewitness accounts to such attacks, hoping someone in the past had the diligence to record such events. Unfortunately, his search had been fruitless.

Ulam used the flickering flame of his dying candle to light one more wick, knowing he did not have much time before the library would be plunged into total darkness. He then picked up the last book he had pulled from the shelf, debating whether or not he should give up on his mission. After finding no new information in the first dozen books, he was not overly confident he would discover anything of value in the last one. But regardless of his lowered expectations, Ulam pressed on and opened the last book.

His stone gray eyes scanned the pages; his mind absorbing little of what had been written. Like many of the previous books, this one was full of myths from all across the continent. There were some passages regarding monsters and creatures of the night, but none of their descriptions matched what had attacked Count Aldamar's sister. *It is of no use, there is nothing in his book either.* Ulam was about to close and clasp the covers when a phrase caught his eye in the next chapter, something that immediately grasped his attention.

"As we have seen many times among the different races of our world, many ancient texts are a retelling of the history of a kingdom and how they have been blessed by a divine. There are some historical accuracies, no doubt, but we must be careful to not assume everything we read is true. After all, are we really to believe an alliance of Elves and Humans was directly responsible for the disappearance of every Orc in our world? While only a fool would doubt the capabilities of Elven magic, could they truly possess the skill and knowledge to eliminate an entire race forever? Does such magic even exist?

Much further into the chapter, there was a map with a note wedged in the crease of the book. Though the penmanship was awful, it was just legible enough for Ulam to read. *"I was told there were a few Sanctuaries near here. The closest is a two or three-day walk north of the city. Hopefully, I find Orcs there; I am starting to become road-weary."*

"Only a few days north of Silverwater?" Ulam said aloud. Though his voice was just above a whisper, it echoed in the silent library. Without hesitation, Ulam removed the map and note, latched the book shut, and exited the library. He did not bother putting away the books, feeling as though there was no time to do so.

He made his way out of the castle and to the barracks, where he ignored the curious looks of his comrades as he rummaged through a trunk of his belongings. He packed a bag full of provisions, slung his cloak over his shoulder, and grabbed a one-handed axe. Though no one asked what he was doing or where he planned to go, he felt like he should give the men in the barracks some information.

"I will be gone a few days," Ulam grunted. He reached into his pockets and pulled out a few copper coins, tossing them onto a nearby bed. "Take these as compensation for covering my patrols while I am gone."

"What will we tell the Captain or Count Aldamar? It's not like you blend in with the rest of us." One of the men asked as the others collected the coins.

Ulam had not thought about that. In truth, he was not sure if Captain Karraman or Count Aldamar would even notice he was gone. So many days had passed since he had seen either man that he wondered if they were even in Silverwater.

"If they ask, tell them I am searching for Amantius," Ulam replied and turned his back, not waiting to field any more questions. He did not like lying, but this time a lie was easier than the truth.

Ulam left the castle grounds and descended the hill towards the northwestern gate. After passing through the arch into the fields surrounding the city he proceeded northward, following a road leading towards the Silverwood. Memories of the march came back to him, as well as the night

Amantius disappeared. He could still feel the heat of the roaring flames in his face and the fear that had paralyzed him, rooting him to the ground. His heart clenched tight when he thought of Amantius; his mind delving too deeply into what may or may not be happening to his brother at that very instant. Though Ulam knew he had to put those thoughts out of his mind, he failed to do so; the quiet countryside provided scant distractions.

The open, flat fields surrounding Silverwater disappeared a few miles north of the city, being consumed by rolling hills thick with briars and other prickly bushes. A stone-paved roadway winded through the hills and vegetation, many of the gray blocks worn down with extensive usage. Connecting Silverwater County with the rest of the Empire fated the road to be heavily traveled, much to Ulam's chagrin. He passed scores of people, most of whom stared at him with a mixture of fear and hate, even a little curiosity. Their gazes reminded him of how spoiled he had become in the castle, its stone walls sheltering him from the pervasive ignorance of the Human race.

Ulam was thankful no one attacked him on the road, though the men and women who passed him shot arrows with their eyes. He realized the further he was from Silverwater the more vulnerable he became, that no one would come to his aid in a fight. As the sun began to hang low in the sky doubts about his quest crept into his mind. *Should I turn around? There may be bandits about, though I have nothing of value aside from this cloak. What of the Mad Raven, or her Flock? Are they out there, setting traps for fools like me who travel alone?*

Ulam stopped at a fork in the road, the main highway continuing north while a smaller path hugged the base of a hill before disappearing. He reached into a pocket and removed the map he had found, remembering the artist had drawn a fork in the road miles north of Silverwater. Ulam assumed he was at the spot, estimating the smaller path led to the Orc Sanctuary.

What if it is not even there? What are the chances this Sanctuary still stands? Judging by the reactions I receive I assume it is abandoned. Gods, is this a fool's errand? Ulam walked further on, his mind swarmed with hundreds of thoughts. The road he traveled suddenly disappeared; the smooth, gray stones of the main highway were replaced with a dirt path covered in crunchy, brown leaves. It was clear to Ulam that this passage was rarely used, though there were signs that someone, or something, used this path at some point. The vegetation that normally envelopes a forgotten area had been stunted, preventing vines and branches from reclaiming what was originally theirs.

What if the Sanctuary is still there, hidden by this sea of trees? Perhaps the Orcs there have carved out their own society, away from the malevolent eyes of Humans. I cannot blame them if they have.

Ulam pushed through, his heart full of excitement. After a hundred paces he came across a column on the side of the path with words etched deep into the stone. It was in a different language, one Ulam could not speak and did not believe he had ever seen before. He traced the letters with a finger, brushing dirt and plant decay from the column's face. *Bexataar Khag? Is that Orcish?*

Beside the column was another dirt road, though it was much more concealed by overgrowth than the others. Ulam followed the road with his eyes as far as he could, though he lost the trail as it ascended a heavily wooded hill. He pulled out the map and looked for any indication that he had not gone astray, but there were no more landmarks drawn on the parchment. He returned the map to his pocket, picked up an elm branch on the ground to fashion as a walking stick, and began his trek up the hill.

Though he was thankful for the warmth and protection his cloak provided, the fabric kept getting ensnared on briars. Halfway up the hill, he came across a clearing where he removed the cloak and placed it in his backpack. He looked to the sky, cursing the gray shroud once again covering the sun. Because of its disappearance the world was a frigid place, where even the smallest of winds sliced to the bone. For a moment he contemplated building a fire and making camp, hoping the next day would be warmer. But Ulam knew he had to keep pushing through, at least until he came across a more suitable campsite.

He winced as he plodded through the storm of briars, each sharp point galvanizing his resolve even more. His mind was so focused on his destination that he did not pay attention to the dozens of cuts his arms and legs. After he reached the top of the hill Ulam immediately slung his cloak over his shoulders again, rubbing his arms and legs in hopes of bringing warmth back to them. It was in that moment he realized he had been sliced by hundreds of little knives, the wool cloak stinging like salt in an open wound.

Ulam looked up and saw the remains of a timber wall, camouflaged by a brown labyrinth of chestnut, elm, and maple. He followed the perimeter with his eyes, realizing the years of neglect had not been kind to the defenses. Though he stood on the outside of the Sanctuary, he could tell it had been abandoned long ago. He sighed as he surveyed the state of the fortifications, while what little hope he had harbored floated away in the wind. He slung his bag over his shoulder once more and proceeded, determined to use the last few hours of sunlight to explore as much as he could.

Ulam passed underneath the rotting gate and into a large courtyard, with rows of weather-worn buildings spreading in every direction. Directly in front of him was the largest building in the complex, which he assumed had once been occupied by the chief of the Sanctuary. All around him stood homes and workshops, most of which with minimal damage. He searched inside the structures, only to find tools still hanging on the walls of a forge, while coin purses littered the floors of homes. Outside a shop Ulam spotted a fully functional wagon, finding piles of neatly folded clothes resting in the trunks. Despite not having been inhabited in decades, centuries perhaps, the Sanctuary showed no signs of strife or battle. There were no markings of fire, nor were there arrowheads embedded in posts or walls. *It is as though they simply vanished.*

Ulam then entered the great hall, passing through the remains of an oak door that had fallen from its hinges. Holes in the roof allowed the day's weak sunlight to filter into the hall, providing Ulam with enough light to see. He immediately noticed the hall was much different from Silverwater's castle, not just in architectural style but also in design. Instead of a series of multiple rooms with specific functions like Count Aldamar's home, this hall was wide open with a long, central hearth running the length of the room. At the head was an ornate chair, much larger than the rest, with all the appearances of a throne. Ulam investigated the throne first, quickly noticing an empty socket where a particularly large jewel had once been. *I am not surprised. Probably treasure hunters, but could have also been the Orcs that lived here taking their valuables as they left. But where did they go?*

From a hole in the roof Ulam noticed the day was
fading fast, so he decided to spend the night in the Sanctuary
because there was no way he was going to brave the thicket
of briars in complete darkness. He went about collecting
firewood from the abandoned buildings, feeling fortunate
that he had a large supply of timber as well as a hearth to
build a fire to keep himself warm throughout the night.
Though he felt some degree of anxiety about sleeping so
close to the fire, he was comforted in knowing that the hearth
was surrounded by stone.

While rummaging through the homes earlier he had
found deerskin blankets, as well as feather-stuffed pillows
that he intended to use to make a bed. Within minutes of
returning to the hearth he had the flames roaring, and for the
first time in weeks, he felt warm. Ulam held his fingers
towards the flames, their stiffness being worked out by the
heat. He laughed at the sensation, finding humor in the idea
that someone from Accaria could forget what warmth felt
like.

*If I had known what autumn and winter were going to be like,
I would have been less anxious to leave Accaria.* Ulam chuckled,
remembering how eager he had been to explore the
world. Though homesickness affected him from time to time,
ultimately he did not regret coming to this land. After all, if
he had never left he would not have found himself in the hall
of an Orc Sanctuary. In a way, he was living his dream,
although in those dreams were scores of Orcs welcoming him
into the community with open arms.

Ulam leaned back on his makeshift bed of fur and
feather, impressed with his ability to scavenge and improvise.
It was not as comfortable as a real bed by any means, but it
was by far better than sleeping in a chair or on the cold, stone

215

floor. He spread out and stretched his limbs, which were still irritated by the dozens of cuts from the briars. If he had not been so exhausted the nicks might have bothered him, but at that moment, beside a warm fire and surrounded by the echoes of his people, Ulam simply could not care.

What was that? Is someone else here?
Ulam opened his eyes, waiting for his vision to completely return. He did not know when he had fallen asleep, only that someone or something had just awoken him. He heard very little, only the hoot of an owl and the quiet hum of the wind. Within the hearth, the fire still burned, though the flames had rescinded greatly while he slept. He waited patiently, fearful of moving, not wanting whoever or whatever had woken him to know he was there. He did not move his head, only searching with his eyes, watching the collapsed door at the entrance for any sign of movement. He even opened his mouth to breathe quieter. *If someone is there I cannot let them know where I am. Thank the Gods my axe is right beside me.*

He felt his fingers wrap around the weapon's handle, feeling slightly more secure now that he would be ready to strike in a moment's notice. He waited for what felt like a thousand years, watching the entrance, praying there was no other way into the hall. He could hear his heart beating, feel it pounding against his ribcage, but as time went on the thundering slowed. So much time had passed that he began to believe nothing was there, that an owl or the occasional crackle of the fire had startled him awake. Ulam stretched back out on the bed and slowly closed his eyes, relaxing as he listened to the fire's low rumbling.

Then he heard another noise, one much closer to him. With a panicked jerk, Ulam opened his eyes to see a mangy rat digging through his backpack, undoubtedly aware of the bread and fruit packed deep inside. Ulam swatted at the backpack, scaring the rodent out of its wits, and watched as the furry creature zigzagged across the hall and into the darkness once again.

Ulam was wide awake now, the sudden rush of adrenaline pumping through his veins. He rubbed his face and began to cackle, relieved that his intruder was only a hungry little rodent. After some time the excitement began to wear off, and he crawled back under the blankets, closing his eyes once again. Before doing so, though, he stashed his backpack under the blankets with him to protect his furry friend from running off with any of the provisions.

"Just a damn rat," Ulam muttered with a chuckle.

He rolled on his side and shifted under the blankets, hoping to find that sweet spot that was so comfortable earlier. He yawned and scanned the room one last time, just in case there were any other opportunistic critters waiting for him to doze off to sleep.

And then he saw it, at the entrance, perched on top of the decayed oak door. A dark silhouette with two bright, yellow eyes staring right at him.

I am not alone!

In an instant Ulam jumped to his feet, his axe whistling in the air as he raised it. All the panic and fear that had disappeared moments ago now returned tenfold. A cold sweat poured down his forehead as his heart clenched in terror. As quiet as a shadow the silhouette entered the hall and bolted straight for Ulam, seemingly gliding over the stone floor. For all of its grace, though, Ulam knew there was menace behind its yellow eyes.

His legs began to sway, as though he were on the ship from Accaria once again, while the iron axe in his hands only grew heavier. Instinctively he entered one of the fighting stances Captain Karraman had taught him, though he was not sure how effective the stance would be against a beast or phantom.

At last, his enemy entered the waning light, suddenly stopping and shielding its eyes from the glow coming from the hearth. Ulam stepped back, completely numb with shock as he looked over his attacker. It was a man, or what was left of one, his very being corrupted by some wicked affliction. The man was a full head shorter than Ulam with a wild strength coursing through his body. His skin looked decayed in many places, as though his flesh was made of melted wax, while his eyes burned a bright yellow. His mouth was covered in blood, red ooze dripping from his chin as he snarled. Every time the fiend opened his mouth Ulam could see razor-sharp teeth, also dripping from a fresh kill.

Ulam did not know what to do, unsure if what stood before him was a Human or a monster. He wanted to try to communicate with the man, to learn what had happened, to perhaps find a solution. But Ulam knew there was no hope as he looked deep into those yellow eyes and saw soulless hatred staring back at him. Ulam knew what he had to do; he knew he had to kill the deranged man standing before him.

The flames appeared to have a paralyzing effect, keeping his enemy at bay. It stood at the edge of the light, gnarling at Ulam with an unsettling pair of voices, as though it had two mouths speaking at the same time. Its words were incoherent, a jumbled mess of syllables that Ulam did not think belonged to any language.

Ulam gathered his courage and approached the fiend, cautious not to step within range of its arms. He held his axe high and estimated from that angle he would bury it deep within the corrupted man's head, killing him instantly. Though he felt uneasy about killing this person standing in front of him, he knew it was the right thing to do.

"Be still," Ulam muttered, "and I hope you find peace in the next world."

Ulam swung down with all his might, closing his eyes as he did so. He did not want the memory of blood and gore shooting from the man's head to be etched in his mind forever. He pushed down until the blade would go no further, assuming the axe had split the man's skull into two. But when Ulam opened his eyes, he discovered the axe had not even reached its target's head. Instead, the fiend was holding the weapon by the top of the handle, the blade inches away from its flesh. In one effortless action the man yanked hard, sending the axe into the endless shadows that filled the room.

Pure terror poured through every inch of Ulam's body as he had watched the malevolent creature toss the iron axe aside as though it were a child's plaything. It snarled again as the axe clanged in the darkness somewhere, the dual-voices more pronounced and vicious than before. It looked more confident now, content to wait out the fire before feasting on Orc flesh. Ulam knew he had to devise a plan quickly, because much like the glow in the hearth, with every passing second his chances of survival waned.

Ulam reached into his boot and pulled out an iron dagger, a weapon he was not overly skilled with wielding. He thought that perhaps instead of splitting open the fiend's skull, he would gouge a dozen holes in its body to make it bleed out. He had to be cautious, though, because if he came too close then he ran the risk of being caught in its tenacious embrace, and he was not sure if he could break free if that happened.

Ulam stepped to the edge of the light once more, his fingers wound tightly around the dagger's hilt, but the fiend was out of range for a thrust. Though the corrupted man's yellow eyes burned with rage, it still had the presence of mind to stay deep in the shadows, content to wait for the flames to dwindle. Ulam cursed as he realized this.

I have two options. I can stand here and wait for the fire to die out completely and let him charge me, or I can try to take him by surprise. If I wait, I might be able to use his aggression to stab a dozen holes in him before I am overwhelmed. If I charge, I might be able to bury the dagger in his heart before he has time to react. He looked at the hearth; the last few logs struggling to stay aflame. *Regardless, it is time.*

Ulam charged at the yellow-eyed fiend, his hand gripping the dagger tightly. Within an instant he crashed into his target and began jabbing, hoping one of his thrusts would strike true. The hall echoed in a chorus of screams, most of which belonged to the corrupted man's dual-voiced shrieks. Ulam was shouting too, not realizing he was bellowing an incoherent battle-cry. They tumbled around on the hall's stone floor, a tangle of arms and legs as they fought for dominance. To Ulam's surprise, he still held the dagger in his hand, but the fiend had wrapped its polluted hand around Ulam's wrist, pinning his entire arm to the ground.

Ulam was now on his back, desperately punching the fiend's face with his free arm. He kicked a couple of times too, but his blows only unbalanced his enemy. His wrist felt like it was about to be crushed into powder as the grip tightened, the pain so excruciating that Ulam's whole arm had gone numb. His eyes opened wide as he saw the fiend open its mouth and extend its fangs, fetid saliva dripping down onto Ulam's neck.

Is this the end? Is this how I die, feasted upon by some abomination?

As Ulam lay there with the fiend snapping its jaws at him, he felt a white-hot fury boiling deep within himself. The same that reared its head the day in the market, the same the night Amantius disappeared. It felt natural, wonderful even. His muscles grew stronger, any aches or pains left his body, and time began to slow. Flames fueled by pure, unadulterated anger spread throughout his body, consuming all his thoughts and replacing them with rage.

"No."

Ulam punched a few more times, knocking the fiend off-balance as it lunged for a bite. With each successive strike Ulam's strength and anger swelled until the fiend began to struggle to remain astride. Eventually one of Ulam's punches dislocated the creature's jaw, the crunch of snapping bones filled the great hall as unhinged teeth flew from its mouth. It jumped off, held both hands to its face, and shrieked in pain.

Ulam wasted no time; he recovered the dagger and jumped to his feet, leaping at the fiend's heart. Though wounded, the creature was able to dash aside, the knife sinking into its shoulder instead. It let out a terrible scream, and a putrid stench filled the room as black blood poured from the gash. Without hesitation Ulam buried the blade deep into the creature's heart, immediately stepping away as it slumped over.

The hall became deathly quiet as Ulam waited for the fiend to die, taking the moment to check himself for any wounds. Although the pain began to return to his wrist, he was certain none of the bones were broken. He touched his neck, feeling a wave of relief wash over him as he discovered the fiend's fangs had never touched his skin. Moments later the smell from the monster's rotting black blood began to reach Ulam's nose, causing the Orc's stomach to turn. The odor was so overwhelming he retreated a few steps and vomited, the convulsions forcing him to ignore his vanquished foe for a few seconds.

When he stopped retching his eyes focused on something in the shadows, an object with edges that glistened in the otherwise dark hall. An unknown presence called to him as he reached for the object, his actions being driven by a mystical magnetism he had never experience before. Upon first contact Ulam's fingers wrapped around a handle, the grip fitting perfectly in his palm, as though the item had been crafted specifically for him. A mysterious power surged through his body, a sensation that was both foreign and familiar to him. *What is this that I am feeling? I feel like a God.*

Ulam pulled the object into the moonlight, revealing an ancient axe, one unlike any he had ever seen. It was not like the iron weapons forged by Silverwater's smithies, or the bright, highly impractical blades used for ceremonies in Accaria. This axe was dark green, jade even, with wicked curves and mysterious symbols etched into the blade. Though both handle and blade were made of some unknown metal, the axe was as light as a feather and whistled in the air with each practice swing. Ulam grunted in approval.

As his initial excitement began to settle, Ulam towards his defeated enemy, assuming to find it dead in a pool of its foul blood. But when he turned around the creature was missing, leaving a trail of black ooze leading out the main doors. The sudden disappearance caused fear to pierce his heart once again, but he was able to suppress it with a concentrated effort. Cautiously Ulam followed the blood trail, his new axe ready to strike if needed.

As he neared the doors a cold breeze blew through the doorway, overwhelming his senses with the fetid stench of death. He looked outside and saw the fiend hunched over an object, the silhouette obscured by the lack of moonlight. It was feasting on something, the sloppy sounds of teeth tearing into flesh enough to unnerve even the bravest warrior. Ulam knew he had to strike while the fiend was distracted, otherwise he ran the risk of being overpowered by the monstrosity once again. Quietly he tried to step over the fallen doors, but the wood shifting under his weight was loud. Too loud.

The noise alerted the foul creature to Ulam's presence, causing it to spring to its feet and begin howling. Much to Ulam's surprise, there was no indication of a dislocated jaw or any other injury, even the stab wounds to the shoulder and heart had completely healed. *What the hell is this thing and how do I kill it!?*

The fiend charged once more, its dual-voices filling the night sky. Though its wounds had disappeared, Ulam noticed it was slower. There was little doubt the fiend was sluggish due to their first bout, but it was still far from weak. It tried to tackle Ulam, but the Orc's stance was stalwart enough that the creature bounced off and landed in the dirt at his feet. Ulam then raised his newfound axe high and swung downward, keeping his eye on the fiend's exposed neck, and watched as its head harmlessly rolled away.

223

He kicked the lifeless body a couple of times, still not trusting the abomination had truly died. As he watched he saw the yellow in the fiend's eyes disappear, while its fangs retracted back into the gums. The body began to rapidly decay before his eyes, the stench magnifying tenfold. With the battle won, and to prevent any further retching, Ulam decided to return to the hall for the rest of the night. But as he turned around he heard a noise, one that stopped him dead in his tracks. It was not the maddened howl or shriek of a dying monster, nor the call of nocturnal scavengers waiting for dinner, but instead the pained cry of someone gravely injured.

Suddenly the clouds parted, allowing the moon to bask the area in silver light. The silhouette that Ulam could not make out in the dark was no longer a shadow, but a woman in a nightgown, her dress soaked in blood. He ran over to her as a new type of panic overcoming him, his heart thundering with each step. Her eyes were shut tight as she desperately clung to life, the occasional whimper escaping her lips. Ulam saw the bite marks in her neck, large chunks of flesh missing where the fiend had feasted on her. His heart sank as he looked at the wounds, realizing there was nothing he could do to save her. Quickly Ulam shot a glance at the fiend, still headless and immobile behind him, which was only a small comfort. *I hope you rot in the Otherworld, you bastard.*

While he cursed the fiend's very soul, Ulam was not completely without pity for the creature. After all, that corrupted person had once been a man, perhaps even with a family. He could not fathom what kind of torture the dead man must have experienced while the curse polluted his soul and destroyed any remnants of humanity within him. A soft whimper beside Ulam pulled him away from his endless

224

speculation, drawing attention to the woman suffering beside him. She was ghostly pale and shivering from the frigid air, with an expression of abject terror etched across her face. Ulam had seen the same look before in many times before, usually in sheep and cattle the moment they understood they were doomed to be killed by a butcher or sacrificed by a priest. He had never seen that primal fear expressed by a person before, and now that he saw it on the tender face of the woman beside him, it threatened to shatter his heart.

I must end this for you before you become an abomination as well. No one should have to live the life that thing did, feeding on the innocent. I wish there was some way to save you, but you are in agony. I will make it quick; that is the right thing to do. Quick and painless.

"I am sorry," he whispered in her ear, unsure if his words would even register in her mind. Ulam brushed back her hair gently to expose her neck, a steady stream of tears pouring from his sad gray eyes as he did so. "Rest easy. Soon you will have peace."

Ulam raised his axe.

Chapter 25
Amantius

Everything was a blur.

Amantius was kneeling in the center of the road, the old stones scraping his knees. His hand trembled violently, his sword clattering off the hard ground. Someone's blood was splattered across his face; he did not think it was his. The blood dripped from his chin, forming a puddle on the ground, the sight of which caused his gut to churn.

They said no one would get hurt. They said we didn't even need our weapons.

Faintly Amantius heard screams, heard the death cries of those around. His vision was fading, his heartbeat echoing in his head. Shapes shot past him as he tried to focus; he assumed they were allies. Had they not been, he would have been slain in that spot.

He felt a mailed hand heavy on his shoulder and looked up to see Jaga standing above him, his customary somber expression unchanged by the events. Blood matted the fur on his wolf's head helmet. "Are you hurt?"

No. At least not physically.

"Amantius, are you hurt? He didn't put a knife in your belly did he?" Jaga used the end of his bloodied falchion to point towards a nearby body.

"No, I'm fine." Amantius muttered. The words felt distant, as though someone far off had spoken them.

Jaga nodded his head. "Good."

"They ran this way!" Someone shouted. Who and from where Amantius could not tell.

"Stay here. Compose yourself, lad." Jaga said with a pat on the shoulder and then ran off, quickly disappearing behind a line of wagons.

Amantius sat there, in the middle of the road, reliving the sequence of events in his mind a dozen times over. The plan had been simple: pop out of woods, scare the travelers, and then steal their goods when they had run away. Quick, easy, nonviolent But everything had spun out of control so quickly. No one had expected the merchants to be armed, to put up any kind of resistance, especially to a host of hell-beasts from the Otherworld. They resisted, though, and now the road was littered with their corpses.

What have we done? What have I done? Amantius felt numb. His eyes shifted to the man he had killed, motionless and bloodied. A fresh wave of guilt pulsated through his soul; his gut began to retch. Luckily he was able to remove his helmet before he vomited.

After his stomach had been emptied, Amantius marveled at how quiet the world had become. Moments ago there had been a skirmish, a bloodbath, with the screams of the dying echoing off the nearby wooded hills. Now, though, the only sound came from fallen leaves rustled by a gentle wind. He sat up, using a nearby wagon wheel as a backrest. He fumbled around his belt for a skin of water, hoping to wash away the foul taste in his mouth. As he did so he heard something new: weeping.

Amantius immediately grabbed for his sword, and with a shaky arm aimed its point at a pile of moving blue and green blankets. "Who…who is there? Show yourselves!" *I guess they know I'm not a demon now.*

A head popped out, a woman's, followed by a golden-haired girl's. Both wore terrified expressions, though

Amantius could see the fierceness in the woman's eyes. It was the same look that transcended all species: the look of a mother protecting her child. He knew from chasing woodland creatures through the forests of Accaria that she was equal parts afraid and dangerous, and any wrong move would be the last he would ever make. That was not all, though, for there was something about this pair that seemed strangely familiar.

"I know you," he heard himself say, his words hardly more than a whisper. "Where have I seen you before?"

Neither offered a reply, the golden hair child continued whimpering while the mother scowled. A glint of sunlight flashed off something metal from within the wagon, the glare blinding Amantius for a brief second. He shielded his eyes and instantly saw the woman clutching a dagger at her side. *No! There's already been too much killing!*

Amantius stepped back and lowered his sword. "I don't want to hurt you. I didn't want any of this." He gestured with his free hand. "I don't even know why I'm here."

He stood in silence for a while, keeping his eye on the fingers wrapped around the hilt of the woman's dagger. He was not sure what to do. Part of him was afraid that if he let these two survivors leave one of his comrades would see them and slay both the mother and her child. The other part of him was terrified of having to kill them himself, whether out of self-defense or because of duty to Morganna's cause. *How could I kill a child?*

The golden-haired child suddenly stopped sobbing and wiped her eyes, focusing them on Amantius. Her stare made his skin crawl, as though he had already committed the terrible atrocity. Within a blink of an eye, though, everything had changed. Her wide-eyed terror disappeared, transformed into a softer, even comfortable expression. The little girl seemed to be no longer afraid of Amantius, but rather the exact opposite.

"I remember you," she said, her eyes red from her sobbing, "I remember you! You're the Orc's brother!"

Amantius dropped his sword, suddenly remembering everything. The golden-haired girl in the wagon was the same that gave Ulam the lavender flower in the market square when they first arrived in Silverwater. The woman beside her was her mother, the foul woman who had incited a riot that nearly got both Ulam and Amantius killed that same day. *Seems like forever ago.*

"And I remember you," Amantius said, a dash of hope in his words, "you were the little girl who was nice to us." He had to use every fiber of his being not to glower at her mother, remembering full well everything that had happened that day. *This bitch might yet still try to put a hole in me. Should've held onto my sword.*

"Yep! That's me!" The little girl nodded fiercely, her smile brightening an otherwise dark atmosphere. She tried to crawl towards Amantius, but her mother's free hand snagged her by the ankle and dragged her back to her bottom.

A hundred thoughts shot through Amantius' head, tangling in his mind like vines on a trellis. Of them all, though, there was only one he absolutely needed to ask. "Ulam. His name is Ulam. Is he still…" He almost could not finish the question from fear of the answer. "Is he still there? Is he still alive?"

"I saw him." The woman finally spoke, her voice as vitriolic as Amantius remembered. Her muscles loosened, though she still kept a tight grasp on the hilt of the dagger. "A couple of weeks ago, with the Count"

"Thank the Gods!" Amantius fell to his knees again, a wave of relief washing over him. *He's alive! I need to let him know I am too, let him know how to find me. He needs to escape Aldamar before he too is betrayed.*

Somewhere down the road, there was an inhumane howling, the high pitched notes riding on the wind. Amantius knew it was the victory cry of his allies and realized they would be returning soon. The howl caused both mother and child to begin trembling again, the little girl burying her face into her mother's bosom. He saw the woman's eyes dart in the same direction, her fingers grasping the dagger's hilt. The horrible image of a butchered golden-haired child came to Amantius' mind, driving a spike of fear through his heart. He knew the tandem had to run now if they were going to have any chance of surviving. *Or any chance of contacting Ulam.*

"Do you know the way to Silverwater?" Amantius asked, capturing the woman's attention.

"Aye," she replied, her expression still grave.

"Then run, before they get here. I'll stall them, somehow." Amantius jumped to his feet and grabbed his sword, sliding the blade into its sheath. Without hesitation the woman leaped from the wagon, dragging the little girl behind her. She slung a satchel filled with provisions over her shoulder and then swept her child into her arms, the little girl's face all the while still hidden by the woman's body. The woman took a few steps and then turned, the scowl on her face now gone, replaced with gratitude.

"Thank you," she said, tears welling. "I'll never forget this."

"Just do one thing for me," Amantius replied, his eyes still focused on the road ahead of him. "When you get to Silverwater find Ulam, the Orc. Tell him his brother lives."

"What if he won't see me? What if he doesn't believe me? I haven't been the nicest person to him." The woman yelled back.

"Just say the name 'Pelecia,' to him. It's our mother's name. That should be enough to convince him." Amantius saw figures wearing animal furs appearing around a bend in the road, "Now go!"

He staggered down the road towards the others, his legs still heavy with dread. He did not risk a glance behind him, fearing the attention would expose the mother and child's escape. His veins turned to ice as the returning warriors approached him, his heart pounded in his ears. A few of the more bloodthirsty members of their party came first, their helmets tucked under their armpits. Both were covered in gore, the red ooze matting not only their cloaks but their faces as well. Upon first sight Amantius would have believed the pair had feasted on the blood of the slaughtered, but he dismissed the thought as being far too deranged.

"You don't have to worry," the first man said, "we're on your side. So you can go ahead and close your mouth now."

"Aye, you might swallow a fly if you're not careful." The second chimed in while both of them chuckled.

As they brushed past Amantius the rest of their small group came into view, the glint of moonlight on Jaga's armor announcing his arrival. The sight of the old warchief was somehow comforting, his presence being one of the few aspects of this mission that Amantius did not dislike. Behind him were the initiates, many of which were as gore-laden as the veterans, a sight that unsettled Amantius even further. Together the whole squad laughed and sang, each member taking a turn to celebrate their prowess in combat.

"You should have been there," one of the initiates said as they drew near, "they would have gotten away if Skitch didn't catch them. That damned guy is the fastest runner I've ever seen!"

"Oh please," the one named Skitch said. He was short and lean, looking more like a thief than a warrior. "It wasn't nothing more than an afternoon jog. Get some grub in m'belly and I'll show you what speed really looks like."

Amantius forced a smile for the sake of appearances. The banter between the initiates barely registered in his mind; all he could think about were the mother and daughter running desperately to their salvation. He took heart that no one had sounded an alarm yet, that no one suspected anything. With the sun having long set, they would also be aided by the cover of darkness, which Amantius hoped would be enough to save them.

Jaga approached next and gripped Amantius by the forearm in a display of respect that the latter did not think was warranted. "You better now? Find your legs?"

Amantius nodded, forgetting momentarily that he had killed a man. Suddenly an image of the dead man's horror-struck eyes flooded his mind, creating an avalanche of self-loathing that swept across his whole body. His knees began to buckle, and his stomach turned rotten once again.

"Easy," Jaga's grip was all that kept Amantius from crashing to the ground, "you're fine, lad, just take it easy."

Amantius fought back the tears. That little rush of excitement or fear he had felt had completely vanished, leaving him feeling hollow inside. He was embarrassed, confused, hurt, and angry at the same time. He was so ashamed he could not look Jaga in the eye, shaking from a combination of humiliation and the ice-cold wind. *I want to go home. I want to be on Mount Meganthus with Ulam again.*

"The first time is never the easiest," Jaga muttered, just above a whisper. Though his voice was gruff, there was a touch of empathy behind his words. "I remember the first man I killed, too."

"Really?" Amantius said, now looking the old warchief in the eye.

"Oh yes," Jaga replied, nodding, "you never forget the first time. But just because there have been many more, so many more, since then, that doesn't mean it gets any easier. Your mind just processes it differently." He slapped Amantius on the back. "Take it easy on yourself, lad. You'd have to be psychotic not to feel some remorse."

Jaga's words were encouraging, and although they did not remove the feeling of anguish gnawing at Amantius' soul, he took heart in knowing that what he felt was natural. He was happy to know there was not something wrong with him, that he was not a freak. *But if I'm not the abnormal one, then what does that say about the others?*

"Remember, lad, psychopaths."

Chapter 26
Ulam

It had been a nightmare; the unfortunate woman's anguished face still seared into Ulam's memory. He had spent the morning after burying her, giving her as proper of a grave as the hard soil would allow. As for the fiend that had kidnapped and fed on her, Ulam set fire to his corpse. He figured he could never be too cautious with curses or diseases.

Poor weather forced Ulam to stay an extra two days in the Sanctuary, causing his already limited provisions to run thin. Realizing he would not be able to survive much longer in the frozen wilderness he hurried back to Silverwater, relieved when his eyes spotted the familiar outline of the castle. He was famished, his legs begged for a reprieve, but he knew resting would mean certain death. The wind was too cold, too unforgiving, and a layer of frost blanketed the land. The thought of a fire and a warm bowl of stew kept him going, giving his aching body the strength necessary to stay the course. *Just a little further, I am almost there.*

Silverwater's city guards were huddled around a fire as Ulam neared the northwest gate. He could see four on duty, all of which wore enough fur to be mistaken for a family of bears. Upon seeing the approaching Orc, one of the guards broke away to offer him a cup of a steaming liquid.

"It's just water, no one thought to bring food with them," the guard shrugged, "but the heat should warm you up a little."

"My thanks," Ulam muttered while taking the mug. He wrapped his big, Orcish hands around the outside, absorbing as much heat as he could. "How do you stand living here?"

The guard shrugged. "I've never seen anything like it, even the old folks don't remember ever seeing frost. There's something unusual about this year, and the sun hiding behind the clouds for this long doesn't help." He looked at the axe slung across Ulam's back, an inquisitive expression passing over his face. "Where did you come from?"

"Up the road," Ulam grunted, then drained the cup of warm water. He did not want to speak of his trip to the Sanctuary, especially to someone he did not know. "I must go; I need to see the Count."

Silverwater's streets were largely abandoned, the frigid weather preventing anyone from being outside for too long. There were a handful of community fires blazing about, acting as unofficial checkpoints for people traveling from one side of the city to the other. Ulam used these to his advantage, standing near the blaze whenever he could, though he involuntarily flinched every time a flame jumped high. He still did not like fire, the terror of black smoke filling his lungs and the searing pain on his skin still fresh in his memory. But on this day he assumed freezing to death was not only much more likely, but also much worse.

Ulam crashed through the castle doors like a battering ram, eager to be out of the elements. A few of the Castle Guards nearby came rushing over, relieved to find the nearly frozen Orc standing before them. They hurried him to the fireplace in the antechamber while another poured a bowl of soup for him, the scent of fish reawakening the ravenous hunger in his stomach.

"Care to explain your absence?" Captain Karraman's voice echoed from somewhere behind him. Ulam did not care to turn around, he simply grunted while slurping the soup.

"We're already missing many men, and a few more have died because of this weather. We need everyone we can muster at the moment, and I can't have my guards disappearing."

And where have you been? Ulam wanted to shout the words at him, the frustration only tempered by a full mouth of burning hot soup and the desire to consume more. He still had dozens of questions about the night they terrorized the farm community, specifically why they filled sacks full of hearts and livers.

"Well?" Captain Karraman came into view, "Are you going to tell me or not? As your captain, I demand…"

"Leave him be, Jalkett," Count Aldamar's measured, yet commanding voice called from deeper within the castle, "I gave him leave to pursue an inquiry for my personal gain. Ulam, proceed to the library, I will accompany you after I have a brief discourse with Captain Karraman."

Ulam quickly finished the rest of his bowl, pleased with the warmth spreading through his limbs but lamenting the lost chance at seconds. Though he wholeheartedly expected the inner depths of the castle to be inhospitable with a frigid staleness, he was pleasantly surprised to find each room was of a tolerable warmth, especially the library.

Ulam stood in the middle of the room, surrounded by dozens of shelves overpopulated with dust-covered texts. Fires burned in the dual fireplaces located on each side of the room, providing enough light and warmth to make the library a cozy place. On the table nearby was the book that revealed the location of the Orc Sanctuary, exactly where he had left it. Beside the book, though, was an ornate chalice engraved with a crescent moon, which he knew he did not leave behind. *So Aldamar found the book too.*

"Shall I pour you a drink as well?" The Count's voice sounded from behind Ulam. Had his joints not been stiff from hiking through rough terrain, the Count's voice would have caused him to jump.

"Wine warms the soul just as much as the body," he continued. Count Aldamar silently glided across the room and filled an empty cup with wine. "Besides, I feel we have a great deal to discuss."

Ulam grunted. *That we do.* He followed the Count's movements, noticing the man's eyes were focused on the book resting on the table.

"Have you found it?" Aldamar said without removing his eyes from the text. "Have you found the Sanctuary?"

Ulam nodded. *I found more than the Sanctuary.* The dying woman's pleading eyes flashed in his mind: dark green and filled with fear, pain, and gratitude. A shiver ran down his spine as he remembered her weeping, a river of sorrow ran straight through his heart. The smell of the cold, hard ground from her grave was still fresh in his mind, as well as the odor of burning flesh that had lingered in the air. Even then, standing in front of Count Aldamar, Ulam had trouble wrapping his mind around everything that had occurred during his excursion. *Did all of that really happen, or was it all just a dream?*

"Abandoned, I assume?" Count Aldamar continued. "Much time has passed since any news reached Silverwater. Though that is not unusual considering the Orcs are a fairly private people. A pity, really, I have always had a particular affinity for your race. Of course, you already know that."

The Count raised his chalice in the form of a salute and drank, Ulam mimicking the motion. The man wore a thoughtful expression on his face, his eyes forever looking into the darkness. As they stood quietly in the library, Ulam even believed he witnessed sadness spread across the Count's face, an unusual display of emotion from an otherwise stoic man.

"Yes, abandoned," Ulam broke the silence. "Mostly, abandoned."

Curiosity flashed in Aldamar's eyes. "Mostly? Did you find other Orcs?"

Ulam slowly shook his head, the hair on the back of his neck stood as he remembered the bright yellow eyes of hatred and corruption staring at him in the darkness. "No. There was something else there. Something evil."

Count Aldamar arched an eyebrow. "Evil you say?"

"A man, twisted by some malevolent force," Ulam replied. *Was it a disease? A curse? Dark magic?*

Count Aldamar smirked. "Most men are born twisted, Ulam. But please, continue."

Ulam recounted his encounter with the fiend, sparing no details. Count Aldamar listened, interrupting rarely to interject his musings. When Ulam had finished, the Count released a deep sigh, clearly troubled by what he had heard.

"Do you think it was the same creature that…" Ulam's words trailed off, he did not want to offend the Count by mentioning his sister.

"The same that changed my sister?" Aldamar finished for him. "I appreciate your concern and hesitation, but my days of grieving are long past. No, I highly doubt this fiend

238

was one and the same. Could this man have been afflicted with the same condition? Perhaps, though your experience sounds different than my own."

At that moment the library door opened, Captain Karraman stood at the entrance. Behind him were a pair of figures, obscured by the poor lighting, though one was much smaller than the other. As they entered behind the Captain, a jolt of familiarity shot through Ulam's mind; he somehow knew this woman.

"Jalkett, what is the meaning of this?" Aldamar said, his face stiff and voice stern.

Captain Karraman was unfazed, dismissing the Count's tone with a lazy shrug. "This can't wait."

"Forgive us, my Count, but this is urgent." The woman said, her voice trembling. Her gaze alternated between the three people in the room, while a child whimpered behind her skirt. "We were attacked on the Western Pass. It was the Mad Raven's Flock."

Ulam shifted his eyes to Count Aldamar, who looked more impatient than concerned. *If they were attacked on the Western Pass, then the Mad Raven is growing bolder, getting closer to the city. Does the Count even care? He looks bored.*

"We're merchants, we come to Silverwater a few times a year to sell our wares. But…" the woman broke down into tears, the child behind her finally emerging to embrace her mother. The flash of golden hair in the otherwise dark room caught Ulam's eye, and then he saw a glimpse of the child's face and knew exactly who they were. Though he felt incredibly sad for the child, spite suffocated any sympathy he may have had for the woman.

"They came from the forest, swarming us before we had a chance to defend. And they had these claws, long and sharp like a bear's, that they used to rip apart our friends and family." The woman began wailing, squeezing her daughter tightly. "Some ran away, some were butchered where they stood. My daughter and I hid under the blankets and prayed for the Gods to protect us. And that's when he saw us."

"Who did you see?" Aldamar asked, impatient, yet intrigued.

The woman pointed at Ulam. "His brother."

Chapter 27

Amantius

For days Amantius kept to himself, going out of his way to avoid any interaction with the men and women who had participated in their highway banditry. He had overheard the story of their attack a dozen times over, the initiates bragging about their exploits to others over a pint of ale, each telling less truthful than the previous. Amantius wanted no credit for his role in the affair, cringing if anyone spoke of his involvement, especially if someone mentioned the man he had slain. His dreams were still haunted by the dead man's face, the blood-soaked blade shaking in his hand. He had grown fearful of sleep, knowing only nightmares and guilt awaited him.

He kept busy around Home, the wintry weather guaranteeing no shortage of tasks to be completed. He often found himself in the middle of the forest, a hatchet in hand, hacking away at the trunks of trees. He liked gathering firewood, each swing and proceeding thud easing the anxiety that permanently lived in the pit of his stomach. Mostly he enjoyed being surrounded by the giant oaks and pines, finding peace in the solitude it provided. It was just like his childhood in Accaria, save for the snow and ice.

"Never seen snow before," Jaga said. His approach had been announced by the crunching of snow underneath his boots. "Doesn't snow where you're from either, does it?"

"No," Amantius spoke, watching the steam escape his mount and disappear in the air. "They say the last time it snowed in Accaria was hundreds of years ago, something about a God who had been displeased with an impious priest. I don't remember. It was just an old wives' tale."

"Probably. That's what old wives do."

They stood together in the clearing, a dozen small logs loaded on a sled nearby. In the distance a branch heavy with snow snapped, the sound scaring away a few cawing crows. Amantius rotated his shoulders and stretched his neck, then hoisted the hatchet once again. *Don't want my muscles getting tight.*

"Some of the others have noticed you haven't been around," Jaga said as splinters of wood fell near him. "They've been whispering."

Amantius shrugged. "Let them."

Jaga sighed. "You're already considered an outsider, lad. No need to make things harder on yourself than you need to."

Amantius dropped the hatchet, the blade disappearing in the snow. "Or what? You'll have them chop me up like those poor folks we met on the highway?"

Jaga narrowed his eyes. "Don't give me that lip, boy. They pulled their weapons; it was self-defense. Hell, you even killed a man."

Like I don't remember! Amantius picked up the hatchet and continued chopping at the trunk of a tree. Anger and shame fueled his arms as each progressive swing became more vicious. "It didn't need to happen. You told me there wouldn't be any killing…"

"Unless it was necessary!" Jaga shouted at him, his patience disappearing quicker than the breath from his words. "What would you have me do? Let any rabble of merchants and has-been mercenaries dictate who gets robbed and who doesn't? What good are our disguises if no one fears us? Stop being a child; sometimes there are no good endings to the stories we are writing."

Amantius returned to hacking the tree, refusing to turn to face Jaga. *I am not a child! I've had to go through so much in the past year! First I lost my home and my mother! Then I lost Ulam! Hell, I don't even know if he still lives! And now I am just here, and I do not know why!*

Jaga sighed. "This fight against Aldamar has gone on for too long. It feels like a hundred years, to be honest. But it feels like it's coming to an end, soon. The Countess is growing restless; she's been telling us the time to strike Silverwater is now, while Aldamar is still weak."

"Then why doesn't she?"

"There's a lot of emotions and personal feelings involved in this business, lad." Jaga frowned. "People don't think straight when they can't look at something objectively. Plus, we're being cautious. We've all lost a lot, some of us our entire families, and all we have left is each other. I think there's a fear that if we attack now we'll lose even more, possibly too much."

"So if the time to strike is now," Amantius replied, finally turning to face the old warchief, "then why are you here, in the middle of the forest, talking to me?"

"The Countess wanted me to find you, to talk to you." Jaga's face was stone cold, revealing nothing. "She has taken an interest in you and wants you to stay here, be one of us. Those whispers I mentioned? She's heard them too."

Amantius felt his heartbeat thunder in his chest, the flow of fresh blood warming his stiff limbs. *She wants me to stay? It's a shame she sends Jaga instead of telling me herself.*

"If you stay," Jaga continued, "I am to train you to be a warrior. To help with your swordplay, though I feel like you

243

are better suited for a spear instead. That is if you don't mind getting knocked on your ass multiple times a day."

Amantius snorted at the jab. The insult did not affect him much, though, because his mind had already moved on. *If I stay, will I ever know the truth about Ulam? What if we assault Silverwater, slay Aldamar, and Ulam is not there? Will I just be at Morganna's side, much like Jaga has been, for the rest of my life?*

"Regardless, the Countess wants to see you." Jaga continued. He walked over to the sled loaded with timber and grabbed a handle. "That is if I wasn't successful convincing you to stay. And judging by the dumb look on your face every time I mention her, we can just pretend I wasn't successful. Now help me drag this damn wood back."

Together they returned to the compound, toting the wood-filled sled behind them. Jaga helped unload the firewood into a storage shed before disappearing into the frozen landscape, leaving Amantius alone in the abandoned street. A part of him wanted to go back to the healer's hut, which still served as his quarters, and warm his hands and feet. However, a more convincing voice in his head told him to go to the Great Hall and seek out Morganna. *She'll have a fire blazing in there, as well. Plus, she's much easier to look at then that old hag that calls herself a healer.*

Amantius' nose was filled with the smell of roasting spruce as he approached the Great Hall. After two knocks the door was opened, a wave of warmth greeting him, as well as the stares of Morganna's personal guard. In the center of the hall, the hearth was being fed by a servant, while the few children in Home were scrubbing at red stains on the tables. Amantius guessed dinner had ended only moments ago, the main course being some kind of meat.

It was the first time he had been in the Great Hall, never having the courage to call on Morganna. Though she had clearly taken an interest in him, and Jaga had directly told him as much, Amantius still could not work up the courage to request a meeting with her. After all, she was a Countess and he was no one.

"State your business," one of the guards spoke, stepping out of the shadows.

"I have come to speak to, with," Amantius stuttered, "with the, with the Countess."

"Amantius, is that you?" A honeyed voice spoke from the back of the hall, "Why this is a pleasant surprise, I was beginning to fear I would never have you as my guest."

Morganna emerged from behind a beautiful, exotic tapestry that obscured a doorway, wearing a fire-red gown with a silver brooch just above her left breast. Her hair cascaded over her shoulders like a waterfall, breaking over each side of her face to frame the smile on her ruby lips. Amantius could not tell what burned hotter; the flames in the hearth or those in his heart.

"Speak when you are spoken to," a dead-eyed guard muttered, a stark coldness contrasting the warmth emerging from Morganna at the end of the hall.

Amantius nodded nervously. "Y-y-yes, it is me. It is I." *Which one is right? Dammit, man, pull yourself together!*

"Don't forget who you're addressing," the same guard growled.

Gods, Amantius, you are such a nitwit. "Yes, my lady."

Morganna descended the dais at the end of the hall and motioned for the guards to stand down. She sat at a table along the hearth and beckoned Amantius by quietly patting the open space beside her with the palm of her hand. All around the scrubbing children disappeared, vacating the hall for Amantius, Morganna, and a couple of loyal bodyguards to share. The last person to leave was the servant resuscitating the flames in the hearth, and even he left before the job was completely finished.

Amantius noticed little of what was happening around him, his vision clouded by the desire burning in his soul. He could feel Morganna's eyes on him as he crossed the hall, trying his best to find some degree of composure. His breathing shortened, and time felt as though it stood still.

He took a seat near Morganna, although not the one she had indicated with her hand. He attempted to straighten his posture, an aspect of polite society that had always eluded him. As he did so he could hear his mother chastising him, telling him he would someday regret not learning the basics of high society. *I should have listened to her. Maybe I wouldn't look and feel so stupid right now, especially with Morganna watching me. You're such a moron, Amantius.*

Morganna watched the awkward display, a playful smile on her lips. She poured two cups of wine, sliding one across the table to Amantius. She then leaned on one elbow, calmly sipping the wine in her goblet. She said nothing, choosing to observe instead. When she was not drinking she was tracing the top of the goblet with her index finger, her skin glowing from the light from the hearth.

Surely she isn't waiting for me to speak. I don't even know what to say. With only a few gulps Amantius drained the wine in front of him. He had originally planned to ration, to take small sips, but he was too nervous for such restraint. So nervous, he unintentionally consumed two entire cups before Morganna finished her first. *You're already a fool, Amantius, and if you don't slow down you're going to be a drunken fool instead.*

"I do not know about the customs in Accaria," Morganna began, a smirk forming on her lips, "but in this part of the world, when a guest visits, they at least attempt to converse while drinking their host's wine. Perhaps you are exhausted from the day's labors. After all, if you did not continue to cut firewood for us, I am afraid my hall would be quite chilly."

Amantius nodded, grinning sheepishly. He could not tell if she was praising or chiding him. Maybe a little bit of both. "Apologies, my lady. My mother always said I wasn't the best type of guest."

"On the contrary, you have been a most pleasant guest." Morganna smiled, dimples forming on her cheeks. "You must remember, when you arrived here you were my enemy. Sworn to slay me and everyone who fights for me, or rather, against my brother. And now? We are in my home, sharing wine together, basking in the glow of the hearth. I would say you have been the best kind of guest."

"And you have been the best kind of captor," Amantius replied, adding extra emphasis to the word "captor."

Morganna chuckled at his jest, the joy filling the room and Amantius' heart. She had politely laughed at his silly jokes before, but for the first time he thought she was genuinely laughing. She raised her goblet in a mock salute to him. "To the best prisoner I could have. May your sentence be long."

He returned the gesture. "And to the best captor, may the key to my invisible cell never be found."

They continued to drink, creating nonsensical chit-chat to fill the conversation. As time passed the butterflies in Amantius' stomach disappeared, and eventually he grew bold enough to sit next to the Countess. They swapped stories of their childhoods, joked about how serious Jaga always was, and even played a few card games. After everything that had happened in the past year, Amantius needed a night like this, one where he could just relax and be himself. Ever since he was exiled from Accaria he felt trapped, as though all the gaiety of life disappeared as soon as he stepped foot on that ship bound for Silverwater. But in this moment with Morganna, Amantius felt the warmth of happiness return to his soul, a feeling he thought had long abandoned him.

Time slipped away from them as they enjoyed each other's company, the fun only ending when Morganna emptied the last bottle of wine. Amantius felt a pang of disappointment at seeing the last red droplet fall from the bottle into her cup. He had hoped that whichever entity had slowed down time earlier would perform the same action now, only so that the night would not have to end.

"It appears we have exhausted our supply of wine," Morganna said as she placed the empty bottle aside. "At least for this room, anyway. I have my own personal stash of wine in my chambers, we can continue playing cards there. That is if you want to join me."

Of course! Amantius screamed internally, and he would have spoken the words aloud had it not been for the sudden emergence of one of Morganna's bodyguards from a dimly lit corner. It was the same person from before, with the same dead eyes that made Amantius feel uneasy. In truth, everyone else had been so quiet and out of sight that he had completely forgotten they were not alone in the Great Hall.

"Beg my pardon, my lady, but I am not sure if that is a good decision." The guard said, his voice as steady as stone.

"Not a good decision?" Morganna repeated, her tone instantly changing from warm and inviting to cold and commanding. "Why is that? Please, humor me."

Amantius shifted in his seat as the guard shifted his gaze to him. He watched as the man sized him up, examining every last inch of his body. The lifelessness behind the man's eyes unsettled Amantius, much like Count Aldamar had the first time they had met. The longer the man's attention remained focused on him, the more Amantius thought his mind and heart were being exposed. In response he forced himself to think of anything other than what he was truly thinking, which had been his defense against Aldamar as well.

"Because, my lady," the guard said, his stare intensifying as the words left his mouth, "this man is our enemy. He fought against you, and even now may be plotting an assassination. I would prefer him to be within my eyesight at all times because we do not know his true motives."

I thought my motives were pretty obvious. It's late, she's beautiful, and there is wine involved. It doesn't get too much more obvious than that. Amantius would have laughed, but the guard's piercing gaze still burned hotter than a thousand suns. He was afraid to laugh, fearful of hurting the man's pride in front of Morganna, knowing he would forever have an enemy here. Amantius sat still, fixing his eyes on the Countess instead, taking solace in one aspect of this exchange. *One thing is for certain, though, I know he can't read my mind. Otherwise, we would be talking about sheep. Big, fluffy, sheep.*

"I appreciate your loyalty, Movan, but I can assure you he does not wish me harm," Morganna replied, measured and with grace. "He has been given every opportunity to leave Home, and every day he chooses to stay. I can say with the utmost certainty that Amantius is one of us now."

Movan's lips curled like he was holding back vomit, as though an intense disgust was building inside him. "I accept my lady's judgment, but he will never be one of us."

I need to stay away from him. Amantius thought as he watched Movan return to the shadowed corner from whence he came. There was something else bothering him, though, something about the way the guard had said those last words. *He will never be one of us.*

"Do not mind him, Amantius," Morganna said as she stood, "he is fiercely loyal to me and only has my safety in his mind. So long as you do not intend me any harm, you should have nothing to worry. Now come, bring the cards, more wine awaits us."

Amantius gathered the deck and quickly followed the Countess, wanting nothing more than to be out of Movan's sight. Even as he followed Morganna across the hall and behind the elaborate tapestry, he could feel the guard's daggered eyes piercing his back. The stalking only ended when they entered Morganna's private chambers, deep within the Great Hall.

Amantius was immediately struck by the design of the room, the stone face of the giant cliff behind the Great Hall served as the back wall of Morganna's chambers. Crystal clear water ran gently down a small ravine cut into the rock, green moss growing on each side. A large bed draped with fine, silk curtains sat on one side of the room, a sofa with a large table on the other. Dozens of candles were littered across the room; one by one Morganna lit them until the whole room was engulfed in a golden glow.

"You have the cards, yes?" The Countess nodded towards Amantius, who did the same. "Good. Now get comfortable as I find the correct bottle of wine; if there is one. I am quite happy that you have helped me cull my wine stock this evening."

"Happy to be of service, my lady," Amantius replied with a wink. He did not mean to wink, blaming the action on the alcohol pouring through his veins. *Yep. You're a drunk fool.*

"So tell me of your home," Morganna said as she selected an unmarked bottle from a wine rack. "Tell me of Accaria. What is it like? I have always wished to travel, but unfortunately my situation prevents me from doing so."

Amantius took a deep breath and closed his eyes. He could smell the ocean in the air, and feel the sun's warmth on his skin. In his mind, he heard the swaying of palm trees in the breeze, the songs of hundreds of birds filling the sky. When he reopened his eyes he saw Morganna was sitting across from him, quietly waiting for him to speak.

"It's warm, always." Amantius started, his voice soft, like a distant echo. "No one ever wears a coat, really. In truth, I had only seen them on trade ships before arriving here. It's an island, as I'm sure I've mentioned before, where everyone knows everyone else."

"Is it small?" Morganna asked, reclining in her seat with her goblet of wine near her lips.

"The city? It's bigger than Silverwater, possibly twice as big. I've heard stories of cities on this continent that are much bigger than Accaria, though. Outside the city are some fields with farms; cows, chickens, sheep, the usual. A few villages dot the island, mostly no more than a dozen fishing huts in each. Trees of all types form a dense forest that surrounds the mountain at the heart of the island. Mount Meganthus." Amantius stopped, imagining the little nook he had found with Ulam years ago. He felt his heart tighten, remembering all the evenings spent together there. "I used to go there a lot, with my brother."

"The Orc?" Morganna said. "I do not remember his name. To be honest, I thought you feverish when we spoke for the first time in the healer's hut. I was not even aware Orcs were still around; I cannot remember the last time I saw one."

"His name is Ulam. I've only seen one Orc in my life, and it's him." Amantius said with a shrug. The more he thought about Ulam the tighter fear gripped him. He worried about the Orc, forever afraid that he was no longer alive, that he had died in the meadow during the ambush or in the Silverwood afterward. Even if he received word that Ulam was still living, the news would only bring him a modicum of relief. After all, if Ulam was alive and well in Silverwater, he would still be a pawn in Aldamar's nefarious schemes.

"I can see the worry on your face," Morganna said, herself appearing concerned. "There was a time when I would have felt the same about my brother."

"Aldamar," The words tasted like poison on Amantius' tongue. "He sent us to die."

Morganna nodded, a sad smile passing over her lips. "Men of his type will always do this. They send others to fight in their stead, to die for their cause, offering them gold in return. Unfortunately for many of those poor souls, they never see their payment. Instead, they die in a foreign land fighting someone else's war. You know this more than anyone, Amantius. Fortunately enough for you, you are here now."

"Will you make me fight too?" Amantius asked, afraid that his voice would somehow reveal cowardice. Images of the man he had killed flooded his mind, as though they broke from a dam he constructed in his mind.

Morganna sat up and took in a deep breath, smiling warmly as she exhaled. "I do not require anyone to fight. Everyone here does so because they want to, because they want to exact revenge on Aldamar for the pain he has caused all of us throughout the years. You are not the only one that used to be part of his ranks, there are a few others here that defected to our side. So no, you do not have to fight if you do not want to fight. Not everyone is a warrior at heart, despite what the tales of great heroics would have us believe. All I ask is that you do not hinder our operations, and ultimately, you do not betray us."

A silence set on the room, the only noise coming from the gentle pouring of the stream along the rock wall. Amantius held Morganna's stare for a few moments, until she focused her attention on her goblet of wine. While she drank his thoughts turned to the mother and daughter he had let escape, wondering if they safely reached Silverwater. *What if I have already betrayed you?*

"What is on your mind?" Morganna asked.

I cannot tell her. What if she has me killed?

"Amantius. Dear. What ails you?" Morganna asked again. Her voice was as sweet as honey, yet there was a stern undertone to her words.

"Forgive me," Amantius said as he broke eye contact, looking at the wine cup in his hands. "I'm afraid I might have already betrayed you."

"How so?" Morganna leaned forward, setting her goblet on the table between them.

Amantius sighed. "When we were gone, we ambushed a passing caravan. You know the story." He

253

stopped, debating whether or not to proceed with the story. *This is going to be your death.*

"Yes, I know. They pulled their weapons and a skirmish commenced. Jaga told me."

A massacre, more like. "Everyone ran off after the survivors, those who fled. Everyone but me. I stayed behind, to guard the wagons." *Not entirely true.* "And I heard some whimpering. There were two people hidden in the blankets. A mother and a daughter, both scared out of their minds." He stopped speaking, taking a deep breath, trying to gather the strength to say the next few words waiting to jump from his tongue.

"Go on," Morganna said.

"I let them go." Amantius finished, saying the words so quickly they almost sounded as one whole word. "I set them free. I covered for them so they could get away. I am, I am so sorry, my lady."

Amantius continued to stare straight into his wine cup, not daring to look at Morganna from fear that she was boiling with rage. With each passing second he waited for her to call the guards, for Movan to come in and strike him dead with a blow to the head. He almost welcomed the cold bite of a blade, for he was infinitely ashamed of betraying Morganna and her hospitality by giving aid to those that opposed her.

Suddenly Amantius felt something warm grip his forearm gently. He looked up, saw Morganna staring at him with a smile on her face, the dimples on each cheek forming. The fear in his heart, the anxiety, all melted away at that moment. *She's not angry?*

"Good, Amantius," Morganna said as she began to caress his arm. "You did me, us, all a great service."

"I did?" He replied, unsure of how that could be true, "You're not angry? You don't want my head on a stake?"

"I would, but I am afraid that would ruin our conversation." Morganna laughed, her humor as dark as her hair. "That is exactly the kind of thinking our outfit has been missing for so long. We have been missing a sense of humanity. We have been so focused on defeating warbands and overthrowing my brother that we have not stopped to consider what comes afterward."

"And what comes afterward?" Amantius asked, though he was not sure if he should have. After all, most people still viewed him as an outsider and probably would not be comfortable if they ever discovered he knew what their plan was going forward.

"Ah, yes, afterward," Morganna said as she sipped her wine. "It is all a ruse, smoke and mirrors, if you will. We have caused a great deal of havoc here for some time; you undoubtedly heard the stories about the Mad Raven when you arrived in Silverwater. We need the populace to fear something, to need someone to be their savior."

"What if the people in Silverwater do not accept you, though?" Amantius interrupted. "What if their loyalty to Count Aldamar is strong enough that they are willing to fight against you? After all, we dress as hell-beasts from a different plane."

Morganna nearly choked on her wine as the words left Amantius' mouth. "The common man does not care about coups, they only want to be left alone and not taxed too much. The real threat is whomever my brother has under his payroll when we strike, and those who are closest to him."

Like Ulam. The idea that Ulam may be in the castle defending the Count when Morganna launches her assault stirred mixed emotions within Amantius. On one hand he wanted Morganna to succeed, to usurp Aldamar and bring peace to Silverwater County. On the other hand, he did not want to run the risk of him and Ulam being on different sides.

"But I digress," Morganna continued, "our tactics are fairly straightforward, however, timing will be of the essence. We need to sneak into Silverwater, preferably in darkness, and penetrate the castle before anyone sounds the alarm. Once inside we will only have a matter of minutes to locate Aldamar and defeat him. After that is accomplished we will announce my brother's assassination along with news that his sister will take his place as Countess of Silverwater. In the following days, I will officially arrive, send out a warband of our own, and 'slay the Mad Raven.' Thus making my brother's rule appear weak and ineffective while demonstrating my value to the city."

Amantius mulled over the plan in his wine-soaked mind, thinking it sounded plausible. The lies and deceit needed for the scheme to succeed did not settle well with him, however not much had been agreeable with him lately. Whatever little hope he had nurtured about living an adventurous life void of hardships had been crushed out of his soul by a metaphysical mortar and pestle. Now all he could do was weigh his options, and choose the one that was easiest to stomach.

"Timing will be critical," he said finally. "And I guess this also explains the costumes."

Morganna smiled proudly. "That was precisely what I had in mind the first time we wore the outfits. The small warband will return with the 'heads' of the Mad Raven and her Flock. Essentially, they will gather a bunch of our helmets and parade them through the streets. The people will love us, they will love me. They will have forgotten my brother by the end of the week."

Amantius nodded, though there was still one more aspect of Morganna's strategy that irked him. *Aldamar's defeat, what does that even mean? Kill him I assume, but maybe she doesn't want to since he is family. Even if Ulam was evil I don't know if I could do it. Probably not.* "What are you going to say when you see him?"

"Say? I do not know." Morganna said as she began to slide her dress off her left shoulder, "But I will repay him for this."

Just above her left breast, near her heart, was a scar silvered with time. With her free hand she stroked the blemish, a pain washing over her face as she did so. The glow from the candles magnified the contrast between the scar and her perfect, smooth skin, which captured Amantius' entire attention.

"He gave that to you?" Amantius whispered.

"Oh yes," Morganna replied. "He tried to kill me after he murdered our father. Luckily he missed my heart; the blade only cutting deep enough to wound me. When I touch it I can still feel the ice-cold blade piercing my skin. I can see the maniacal look on his face. I can still feel the betrayal." She looked at Amantius and reached out for his hand. "Here, feel for yourself."

Amantius wanted to reach out and touch her, to have his hand make contact with her skin. He could not tell if his heart had stopped or if it was beating so quickly that it had gone numb. He was not a fool; he knew what would happen if he sat by her on the sofa and felt the area above her breasts. He knew his hands, and hers, would drift to different parts of each other's bodies. The entire night had been leading to this moment, this was only the next step. The debate was not whether he wanted to touch Morganna, to use this as an avenue for a more romantic, or passionate, evening. He had been dreaming of this moment ever since he laid eyes on her. The question was whether or not he was ready for the consequences from the next day onward.

"Let me get closer," Amantius said as he moved next to her, "and I can let you touch some of my scars as well."

Chapter 28
Ulam

Amantius is alive.

For days Ulam repeated those words, the shock of the
statement never truly subsiding. He spent many hours staring
westward from the top of the castle's gateway, his eyes fixed
upon the distant Silverwood Forest. He wanted to pack
rations and leave the city, the desire to rescue Amantius
burning in his heart. He would have left already, if only
Count Aldamar had not convinced him of the folly of his
plan.

"You do not know where he is," Aldamar had said to
Ulam the previous day. "The most likely result of such an
adventure would be death. I would wager you would get lost
within a day or two and wander until either you succumbed
to the elements or a pack of hungry wolves. When the ground
thaws and this bitter weather disappears we will revisit this
subject. To take action now, however, would be disastrous."

Ulam knew the Count was right; he knew his chances
of finding and rescuing Amantius were nearly zero percent. It
killed him inside, to know his foster-brother was out there,
and there was nothing he could do. Pelecia's promise
replayed a hundred times over in his mind, filling him with
great shame. He blamed himself for the situation, for not
being able to conquer his fear of fire and charge into battle.
He believed if only he had been able to summon the courage,
Amantius would not have become the Mad Raven's prisoner.

Is he a prisoner though? More unsettling than the
realization that he could do nothing to help Amantius was the

idea that perhaps his foster-brother had defected to the other side. *That woman said he was dressed as one of them, had even killed a man.* Ulam could not believe Amantius would do such a thing, to slay an innocent man defending a mother and child. He often questioned the validity of the woman's story. *Perhaps she was so distraught that she thought it was Amantius, but someone else had been the one to strike down the man. Yes, that has to be true.*

But why has he joined the Mad Raven? Has he done so out of necessity, or because he still believes Count Aldamar is truly evil? He stared at the castle, focusing on a window halfway up one of the towers. He thought he glimpsed a set of yellow eyes staring back at him, like two beacons on a midnight coast. It had lasted for only a few seconds, the eyes disappearing as quickly as they had appeared. Frozen in shock Ulam watched for a little while longer, waiting for some sort of affirmation to what he believed he had just seen. But when nothing reappeared in the window, he started wondering if his mind was tricking him into seeing things that were not there.

I am going insane. He had been seeing yellow eyes everywhere, from dark windows to kittens roaming Silverwater's alleyways. His sleep cycle had been disrupted lately as well; he felt as though someone was always watching him. Even when he had managed to doze off, his dreams had been so intense and twisted that he often found himself drenched in cold sweat when he awoke. Ulam kept quiet about what he was experiencing, petrified that if he confided in anyone he would be thrown in a cell on the grounds of lunacy. He missed having Amantius around, knowing he was the only person in the world Ulam could have told without fear of judgment.

I need to take my mind off things, keep myself busy. Ulam went to the arms court, hoping someone would want to spar with him. But no one was there, he assumed everyone was still avoiding the sunless sky and bitter cold. Part of him wanted to go to the Bride's Oasis, to have a pint or two, but he knew the alcohol could loosen his tongue, and speaking was currently his greatest enemy. Having nowhere to go and afraid of Human interaction, Ulam chose to find refuge in the library, hoping a book would entertain his mind.

For the first time he lit every lantern in the room, wanting to flood the library with light. Though he told himself it was so he could see the words on the page easier, deep inside he knew he wanted the light to shield him from any yellow eyes potentially lurking in the darkness. He then sat at the desk, a pile of books stacked on one end, and began to read. He flipped page after page, but after a while his mind was no longer comprehending the words. He could only think about Amantius, and what it would take to find him.

Ulam retrieved the map he had found months prior, the one he had updated by drawing a brief outline of where he thought Accaria was located. He found the Western Pass and traced it with his finger as it twisted through the Silverwood Forest, noticing there were no towns or villages along the route, only a solitary marking indicating a lumber camp. He wondered how far down the highway the mother and daughter had been when they were attacked, and made a mental note to ask the mother if he saw her again. However, Ulam had not seen either victim since the night they brought word of Amantius, nor had he heard any news of them. *Are they still in the city? If not, I suppose I cannot blame them.*

His eyes shifted to the clearing where his warband had been destroyed by the Mad Raven's Flock, the last time he had seen his foster-brother. Images of that night flashed in his mind: searing flames, a cacophony of screams, and a dead

261

man at his feet. Shame once again spread through his soul like a plague, followed by a fresh wave of fury deep in his heart. He wanted to rip the map apart, to cause some degree of destruction as a release, but he knew that would solve nothing. Only through an immense amount of discipline was Ulam able to check his emotions, preventing himself from causing irreversible damage to the parchment on the table.

"Home." He heard himself say, his voice an angry grumble. Ulam noticed the only other marking close to the Western Pass was located at the top of an imaginary triangle composed by the highway and the clearing. "Is that where they could be?"

"Where who could be?" Count Aldamar said as he entered the library, his crescent-engraved wine chalice in hand, the red liquid staining the area around his lips. As he looked around the room he grimaced, as though the collection of light produced by the lanterns personally offended him in some way. "I must say, for someone who prizes books and reading as much as you, the welfare of those same texts seems to not be a high priority. There are too many lanterns in here; if one tips the whole castle will be set ablaze."

Ulam grunted. *Better than seeing yellow eyes in the dark.*

As Count Aldamar approached the desk his eyes drifted to the map on the table. Something crossed his face, some emotion Ulam did not expect. *Is he concerned? His eyes have been lingering on the map for quite some time. Does he see what I see?*

"I assume you were speaking of Amantius," the Count's tone sounded strange to Ulam's ears, as though there was a bitterness that had not existed before. "Where do you believe him to be, precisely?"

Ulam shrugged. "I do not know exactly. There is a place on this map called 'Home.' It is deep in the Silverwood, just slightly north…"

"Ah, yes, I know the place." Aldamar sipped from his chalice once more. "My childhood home; the land has been owned by my family for generations. I have not set foot there in decades. I doubt your brother is there; I would have known if the Mad Raven was using the remains of my family estate as a base of operations."

"How?" Ulam asked. "You have not been there in decades."

"A fair question," Count Aldamar said as he licked his fingers and placed them on a burning wick, dimming the light in the library. "Our family's groundskeeper survived the attack orchestrated by the corrupted body of my sister. He was away, tending to his dying father in a village on the opposite side of the county when chaos ensued. He returned the day I buried the bodies and helped me dig a mass grave. Afterward, I gifted him a sizeable plot of land and asked him to inform me if anything noteworthy were to happen to my family's estate." Count Aldamar nodded his head, pleased with his story. "Jaga was his name. A good man. He would have told me if the Mad Raven had occupied the area, assuming he still lives. Mind you, Jaga was old the last time I saw him, and living in solitude in the Silverwood is not the easiest life."

"So there is still a chance he is there." Ulam realized the likelihood Amantius was at Aldamar's childhood home was very small, but he still clung to the hope that he could find and rescue him. "You say this Jaga has not contacted you in quite some time?"

Count Aldamar fixed his gaze on Ulam, a sliver of barely noticeable anger behind his eyes. "As I have told you time and again, if you attempt to go there by yourself then you are a complete fool. You would be dead within days. The terrain is harsh, this unusual weather is brutal, and the Silverwood is teeming with creatures waiting to feast on your body. You must be patient and wait for the correct opportunity."

"I must go!" Ulam thumped a clenched fist on the table, unable to control the fury building inside him. He had grown tired of Count Aldamar's insistence to wait for spring, when the roads would be less hazardous. "Because if I do not go, no one else will. I am tired of waiting for the right timing. If I wait any longer he will be dead, and all because we were waiting for the frost to thaw, or for more soldiers, or any other excuse. No, I will not wait! I have waited long enough!"

Ulam stormed out of the library and headed straight for the barracks. He was not sure if Aldamar protested as he left the room, his frustration and determination dulling most of his vision and hearing. He gathered the same equipment he used when he searched for the Orc Sanctuary, only this time he had his new axe as well. *If anything attacks me, I will be prepared.*

It was almost midday when Ulam left Silverwater, weaving his way through the daily throng of people trying to enter the city to sell their wares. On the other side of the traffic the road emptied, nothing but cobblestone, remains of dead crops, and leafless trees as far as he could see. The weather was marginally better than in months past; the air not too cold, just chilly enough Ulam did not sweat under his cloak. He felt hopeful about the journey he was undertaking, whether because he was no longer confined to the castle or because he was truly enthusiastic he could not tell. But with each passing step the pit of hopelessness inside him dwindled, replaced with optimism for the future.

By sunset, he had come to the lumber camp on the edge of the Silverwood, the one that had been marked on the map. With the memories of his last solo trip still fresh in his mind, he did not want to be outside in the middle of the night. Near the lumber camp was a makeshift inn, a resting spot for travelers voyaging to and from Silverwater, where Ulam decided to seek shelter until morning. As he neared the front door he passed a stable, where the smell of horse dung wafted in the air. Inside were a couple of steeds gnawing on their dinner, neither troubled by the Orc's presence. *Strange, I assumed they would be afraid of me. Perhaps someday I will learn how to ride one.*

As soon as Ulam entered the inn he drew the attention of everyone inside, many patrons eyeing him with a mix of surprise and fear. It was a reaction Ulam came to expect, the daily exposure in Silverwater numbing him to their stares. Over time he learned to look past the gawking of strangers, instead placing emphasis on locating concealed weapons. After Ulam assessed the level of danger he stepped towards the counter, where an old man with wispy strands of white hair was counting small stacks of money.

"It's two coins a night if you want a room," the old man said in a raspy voice without looking at Ulam. "Or if you want to chop trees for a day that's worth one night also."

Ulam placed a couple of coins on the desk, the metallic ringing gathering the old man's attention. He swiped the coins off the table and finally looked up, squinting as his eyes scaled the towering Orc.

"I haven't seen one of your types in a long time," the old man said, "I didn't know any of you still existed."

That was another sentiment that no longer affected Ulam; if people were not treating him with fear and hate, they were paralyzed with awe and wonder. *No one has seen many of us in a long time, it seems.*

"You guard types hardly ever come out this far," the old man continued, his bony fingers pulling on Ulam's cloak. "Ah yes, the crescent moon of Silverwater. Thought I saw that."

Ulam could not help himself from laughing. *Does he only see me as a guard?*

The innkeeper looked at him with a strange expression on his face. "Nothing funny about what's going on out here. Surprised Aldamar only sent one person to check into the attacks on the Western Pass. But Aldamar always was selfish and interested in protecting his own hide. Can't blame him I guess, I'd be the same way if I were him. That's why you're here, right? Not too long ago we had a mother and daughter come through here, had my sons escort them to Silverwater. They were all kinds of distraught, those two."

Ulam nodded. "Yes, I am checking into the incidents on the Western Pass, but not on Count Aldamar's behalf. I am doing it on my own."

"On your own, eh? Well, I wish you luck." The innkeeper yawned. "Tell me before you leave in the morning. Also empty out your chamber pot before you go, if you don't mind. You can use the stables, the horses don't care."

The next morning Ulam did exactly as he had been asked, checking out with the innkeeper before leaving. He left right before dawn, determined to use every minute of the

266

sun's struggling light to his advantage. He covered a lot of ground before midday, jogging at a steady pace while keeping a watchful eye on the edges of the Silverwood Forest. He knew from the account of the survivors, as well as his own experience, that the Mad Raven's Flock preferred to emerge from the forest's depths to waylay unsuspecting travelers. He did not think anyone was waiting for him, but he knew it was always better to be safe and alive than reckless and dead.

Shortly after midday Ulam came across the markings of an ambush site, the ghostly remains an unsettling scene. Dark red stains painted entire sections of the cobblestone while rotting bodies littered the highway. The foul stench of death and decay lingered in the air like an invisible beacon for crows and ravens, which they gladly followed. The scavengers barely noticed Ulam as he explored the carnage, continuing to gorge themselves on their magnificent buffet of necrosis. Ulam had to use every last ounce of strength not to vomit, and even then he was not sure if he would be able to withstand the urge.

This must be where the mother and child came from. He looked further up the road and saw more corpses strewn about, while two blackbirds fought over the same dead body. *If the Flock left after this attack then they should have gone north from here.* Ulam looked to the northern side of the road and immediately spotted a clue: a pair of rivets worked into the hard mud where a wagon had been taken into the forest.

This must be the way to their lair! Excitement poured through his body, and before long he was sprinting on a manmade route through the forest. At first, he tried to temper his emotions from fear of false hope, but as he cut through the Silverwood he became more and more convinced he was on the right path. Not just the path to the Mad Raven's mysterious lair, but to Amantius as well.

Eventually Ulam came across a deserted wagon, rendered defective by a broken wheel. The insides had been emptied of anything valuable, all that remained was a wool blanket covered in holes. In that moment Ulam realized he had lost track of time, cursing when he discovered the day was much later than he had anticipated. He knew soon he would have to decide where to camp for the night, though he did not like any of his options. Either he would have to trek all the way back to the inn in darkness, or spend the night in the abandoned wagon.

At least it still has the canvas on top, Ulam thought as he inspected the wagon, *but if I am correct, I will be very close to the Mad Raven's lair. Luckily they did not leave anything behind in here, so the chance they come back for the wagon is slim.* He looked down the path towards the highway, remembering the stench from the rotting bodies in the road as though the smell was trapped in his mind. *I also do not want to smell that again today. If ever.*

Though some daylight still lingered Ulam did not want to be seen crossing the Silverwood, especially with night quickly approaching. Having made his decision, he climbed inside the wagon and unpacked his blankets to form a makeshift bed. He then tied the wagon's curtains together with a needle and thread, leaving a slit large enough for only a sliver of sunlight so he could read. When comfortable he pulled out a book about Gnomish culture and customs, and waited for morning.

Chapter 29
Amantius

Jaga and Amantius stood in the courtyard, their hands over an open flame. Nearby were sets of wooden weapons, heavy with nicks from brute force collisions. They had been sparring all afternoon, the weather having warmed enough for the snow to melt, leaving their makeshift arena cold and muddy. Jaga had personally taken it upon himself to see to Amantius' weapons training; the two of them practicing every day. The first few days had been painful for Amantius, every round ended with him on his backside with a new bruise as a temporary souvenir. But recently their matches lasted longer than a couple maneuvers, sometimes Amantius was even able to land a successful blow on the old warchief.

"You're getting stronger," Jaga said as he rubbed his forearm where Amantius' wooden blade had made contact. "Your swordsmanship needs some work, though. You've been slower than usual; you seem tired."

Amantius smiled. *Morganna makes sure I don't get too much rest at night.* He had spent every night with the Countess, a whirlwind of romance and passion that left him on the brink of exhaustion. She was completely insatiable, demanding his company whenever he was free. He had obliged every time, partially because he feared disappointing her, but also because he lusted for her just as much. He felt as though she had cast a spell over him, one he was not sure he could break, or ever wanted to break.

"I'd be careful if I were you," Jaga interrupted Amantius' thoughts, "the Countess may be fond of you, but there are plenty of people here who are not."

"Oh, she's more than fond of me," Amantius mumbled, followed by a smile. He felt good about his situation for the first time since he arrived in Home, perhaps even since he had left Accaria. *Now if Ulam was here, too, everything would be perfect.*

Jaga shook his head. "This is a tight-knit group you stumbled upon. Most have fought together, and lost together, for a very long time. We're all loyal to her, so if something were to happen, and things go sour, just know no one will stand beside you."

The thought that his relationship with Morganna would deteriorate was so preposterous to Amantius that he almost laughed aloud, but there was something in Jaga's voice that checked his reaction. *No one will stand beside me. Is that his way of telling me that I'm still an outsider? Even though I have more than pulled my weight in chores and have even killed a man for these people, they still don't consider me as one of them? What more do they need?*

"Alright, lad," Jaga picked up a wooden sword with his right hand, tossing a second towards Amantius with his left, "a few more rounds and we'll be done for the day. Show me what you've got."

They parted after sparring, Amantius covered in more bruises than he could count. *I have more bruises than the time I fell out of the tree in Old Man Casius' yard.* He started laughing at the memory. *By the Gods, I thought he was going to kill me. How was I supposed to know the tree was dead and the branches were rotten? Ulam laughing also didn't help any.*

Amantius touched a bruise on his leg, wincing at the pain. *That one is going to take some time to heal.* The sky above was starting to lose its color, indicating that night was quickly approaching. He knew Morganna would be expecting him soon, as she had every night, but his muscles were so sore and drained of energy he was not sure if he would be able to satisfy her demands. *I wish I could rest, but would she understand? What if she doesn't, what if she gets offended, and I have to run for my life? Is that what Jaga meant by his warning?*

Amantius had mindlessly wandered outside of the palisade wall, standing a dozen paces away from the entrance to the compound. His eyes rested on an old dirt path that cut through the vegetation, the same path they had used to reach the highway. As he stared down the pathway he relived every step of his journey through the woodland, recalling the stone highway at the very end where he had slain his first man. Shame started to fill his stomach again, but he quickly forced himself to think about something else, particularly the mother and daughter. In his heart he prayed they found Ulam, hoping the Gods had delivered them safely to Silverwater. *To Silverwater.*

"I know how to get to Silverwater," Amantius whispered to himself, the realization burning away a fog in his mind. "I could go to Ulam myself."

He glanced at the fortifications, feeling a spark of excitement grow in his belly as he realized they were deserted. *No one knows I'm here.* He then turned his attention towards the Great Hall, the structure nestled in the shadows of the towering cliff behind it. *Morganna is expecting me though. Dammit! But if I'm going to go, this is my chance. I could be halfway to the highway before anyone notices I'm gone.*

Fear and indecision paralyzed him, as well as a sense of loyalty to Morganna and Jaga. After all, they could have killed him a thousand times over if they truly thought of him as a prisoner and enemy. By trekking to Silverwater alone, he ran the risk of being branded a traitor, of not being welcomed when he returned. At the same time, though, he needed to go to the city, to find out for himself if Ulam still lived, and if he did, to convince his foster-brother to return with him.

"I'm sorry," Amantius said, his eyes fixed on the silhouette of the Great Hall, "I'll come back as soon as I can. Please understand."

Amantius sprinted down the path, wanting to use the day's fading light to cover as much ground as possible. Bright red lines appeared on his exposed arms as he shielded his face from countless briars and twigs, their razor-sharp stings galvanizing his resolve. After some distance he began to suck in great volumes of air, his lungs burning as though they had caught fire in his chest. Because of this he suffered a lack of vision, causing him to trip over a stone he did not see. If not for quick reflexes he would have crashed into the frozen ground, but instead he was able to save himself by wrapping his arm around the trunk of a small tree.

"Dammit Amantius, what are you thinking?" He sputtered in between gasps. "You can't see. You don't have any food or water. And you don't know where you're going. Or even how to get back." A brisk gust of wind prickled his skin, causing him to shiver. "And now you're cold, with no way of even making a fire. Great plan."

He sat down on a log to regain himself, to plan his next move. A little bit further down the path, he spotted the tilted shape of the wagon they abandoned, the one with the broken wheel. They had loaded it with too many spoils and the front wheel gave out, breaking into three or four pieces. A small amount of anger sparked inside of him as he thought about that, remembering how they had to act as pack mules and haul the goods back to Home. *The idiots should have known the wagon wasn't going to make it through the forest.*

He used a sleeve of the bearskin cloak gifted to him by Morganna to wipe the sweat beading on his forehead, fearful if it froze to his skin he would succumb to the elements. He knew if he had any chance of finding the highway he would have to do so before nightfall, otherwise, he was doomed to wander the Silverwood all night without provisions of any kind. His only other option was to turn back, follow the path back to Home, and hope Morganna and the others had not noticed he was missing yet.

Amantius kept his head on a swivel, taking turns looking at both directions, weighing his options. *One direction is Ulam, possibly, and a cold night without blankets or a bed. The other is hot food in my belly, a warm bed, and a beautiful woman to fill it. Hopefully.* No matter how hard he tried to justify continuing towards the highway, in the back of his mind he knew to do so at this time of night, in this weather, with all sorts of creatures roaming about was practically suicidal.

"Forgive me, Brother," Amantius said as he stood, his eyes transfixed on the silhouette of the crippled wagon, "I'll come for you some other time. I just hope you'll still be in Silverwater when I do." *And I hope we'll be on the same side.*

Amantius turned his back and began hobbling towards Home, eventually breaking into a leisurely jog. He had covered a lot of ground during his dead sprint earlier, and his legs were screaming for rest, but he wanted to be back before the last ray of sunlight disappeared. He prayed his absence had gone unnoticed and that he had enough time to clean up before seeking out Morganna.

How am I going to explain the cuts? Amantius was worried about the myriad of red slashes across his arms and face from the briars, thinking their presence would betray him. It was one more reason why he wanted to hide from everyone until he could wash himself, hoping some basic salves would camouflage the smaller scratches. *I have to clean them out first, the sweat in the cuts makes my arms feel like they're on fire.*

As he strolled up to the main gate Amantius was relieved to find the palisade wall was still unguarded. Immediately he went to the nearby stream and plunged his arms into the icy water, only stopping when they were completely submerged. His arms instantly stopped itching, the burning extinguished by the freezing temperature. For a moment Amantius enjoyed the sensation, until the brisk current began to numb his limbs. He pulled his arms out, using the dripping water to wash away some of the sweat on his face, tasting the saltiness trickling onto his lips. He then used his cloak to wipe his face and arms before the water could refreeze to his skin. *Don't want to get frostbite.*

"There you are," Jaga's gruff voice said from behind him. "Been looking for you."

Seems like someone noticed I was gone. "Well, I'm right where you last saw me."

Jaga grunted, arched an eyebrow. "Yeah. But you didn't have those on your arms and face. Where did you go?"

Of course he sees those, but to be fair, they do stand out on my skin. "Oh, yeah. I chased a rabbit through the woods. Briars cut me to pieces."

"A rabbit, eh? What made you think you could catch a rabbit?" Jaga said, the look in his eyes suggesting he did not believe the lie.

Seems like he's not buying it. "It was a fat rabbit, and I've done it before. It got away though, maybe next time."

Jaga grunted, though his expression was unchanged. "You're more likely to sprain an ankle. Anyway, we're having a meeting and the Countess wants you there. If you need to keep washing yourself then do it quick."

Amantius wiped as much dirt and sweat from his skin as he could and then hurried inside the walls, following Jaga's trail to the Great Hall. Even though he seemingly convinced the old warchief that he was only chasing a rabbit, he knew he would also have to repeat the same lie to Morganna too. Deep inside, he did not like the idea of lying to her, feeling like she did not deserve such deception. She had never done anything to warrant it, at least to the best of Amantius' knowledge. She had always treated him with respect and honesty, and even shared a bed with him. A little flare of guilt sparked inside of him as he thought about lying to her, but he quickly banished the feeling from his heart. *It's for the best that she doesn't know the truth. How could I possibly explain that I was going to Silverwater without her permission?*

Amantius followed Jaga into the Great Hall, sneaking in quietly as a few men argued over something. Their voices died away the moment they saw Amantius, both wearing the same unsure expression on their faces. Amantius noticed everyone was sitting around the hearth, Morganna at the head. She sat with her back straight, hands folded over her lap, a serious expression on her face.

"Thank you for joining us." Morganna's voice was cordial, neutral. Amantius could not tell whether or not she was pleased to see him. *At the very least, she's not angry with me.* He turned his attention to the other faces in the crowd, receiving a mixture of responses. Some faces were friendly, some not. Then there was Movan, lingering in the shadows behind Morganna, his cold dead eyes fixed on Amantius. *By the Gods he makes my skin crawl.*

"It's my pleasure." Amantius felt a quick jab to the ribs from Jaga. "My lady."

Morganna bowed her head and then immediately turned her attention to the assembly.

"Friends, it is time," Morganna started, provoking murmuring. "Our wait here is over. Soon we will assault Silverwater."

The murmurs grew into open conversations, some elated by the news, others not. Amantius had mixed feelings about Morganna's statement. In some ways he wanted to leave tomorrow, to go with her and overthrow Aldamar and be reunited with Ulam in the process. But in other ways he was scared, petrified that convincing Ulam to switch camps would prove impossible, that they would be on opposite sides of the battle. He wanted a little more time, just enough to go to Silverwater, find Ulam, and persuade him to fight for Morganna as well.

"When will we leave?" One of the men said over the commotion.

"If the past few years are any indication, Aldamar will begin hiring mercenaries as soon as the New Year arrives," Morganna said as the individual conversations faded away. "My brother is a creature of habit, and I fully expect him to do the same thing this year as well. I propose we strike now before men and women from all over the continent come seeking fortune. If I am to be honest, I am not sure if we can

276

hold out much longer here. Each successive warband seems to penetrate the Silverwood a little further. It is only a matter of time until they find us."

Morganna looked at every single person in the room, saving Amantius for last. When her dark eyes made contact with his ocean blues, he felt his heart leap to his throat. He had to use all his remaining energy not to smile or wink, instead focusing entirely on holding her gaze. She eventually looked away, her complete lack of emotion irking Amantius a little. Even though he knew it was absurd to think she would show him any affection at a time like this, he still felt slighted by the lack of recognition.

Morganna held up a hand, nonverbally demanding the assembly's attention once more. "Over the next few days we will discuss the logistics, but as of right now I suggest you all return to your homes and get some rest. If the weather permits, we will leave in five days. You are all dismissed."

One by one the members of the assembly exited the Great Hall, until only a few people remained. As Morganna continued issuing orders on the other side of the room, Amantius turned his attention to Jaga and noticed a small frown creasing his lips. From a distance, it would have been imperceptible, but at close range, Amantius could see the displeasure written on the man's face.

"You don't like the plan, do you?" He asked the old warchief in a voice barely above a whisper.

Jaga shrugged. "The plan is fine enough. I don't like the timing. We barely have enough people for an ambush, let alone a coup. But she is right, we're running out of time. In a month Aldamar will begin buying a new warband, and within two we'll have an enemy at our doorstep. And with the flow of recruits coming to a trickle, we won't have the numbers to repel them." Jaga turned away, heading for the exit. He stopped as he put his hand on the door, opening it just enough for a chilly breeze to filter into the Great Hall. "She also probably wants to go while you're still with us."

Amantius' face turned as red as a rose; he could feel the blood rushing to his cheeks. "W-w-what do you mean?"

Jaga shook his head slowly. "I might be old, lad, but I'm not stupid. You weren't chasing a damn rabbit."

Jaga stepped outside, leaving Amantius alone in the Great Hall.

Chapter 30
Ulam

"I found it. I found the Mad Raven's lair."

Ulam had spent an entire day scouting the enemy's base, being careful to stay far enough away that a sentry could not spot him. He took heart in the state of the defenses, believing in the event of a siege the fortifications would be easy to overrun since sections of the palisade wall had fallen into disrepair. He spent two more nights in the abandoned wagon, hoping with each following day Amantius would come close enough to rescue. But as time went on Ulam ran out of provisions, and after two long days of waiting, he began the trek back to Silverwater, even spending a night in the same inn at the edge of the Silverwood. Upon returning to the city he first sought out Captain Karraman, and together they went to the castle to inform Count Aldamar.

Ulam had been functioning on pure emotion for days, reinvigorated by his discovery and all its potential. Despite his excitement the Orc knew he had to resist the desire to push the Count too hard on sending an expeditionary force to attack. He realized there was something about the topic that made Aldamar uncomfortable, whether it was nostalgia or something else Ulam could not tell. In the event that the Count would dodge the subject again, Ulam was already planning the logistics of a covert operation to find Amantius. He decided if he must save his foster-brother alone, he would have to bring enough provisions to last a week or more. Ulam figured the abandoned wagon would suffice as his base of operations since it was close enough to reach the Mad

Raven's lair within a few hours of walking, but far enough away that no one would accidentally discover him.

Count Aldamar had been sitting on his high chair at the end of the grand hall, his crescent-engraved wine chalice attached to his lips. The news did not affect his disposition at all, if anything the Count looked annoyed.

"And pray tell, where is it?" Aldamar said with a wave of his hand.

"Where I thought it might be," Ulam replied, "it's your childhood home."

Count Aldamar sighed. "Do not waste my time, Ulam. There is no way you traversed the Silverwood by yourself, with no map, and returned safely. In less than a week, nonetheless."

Ulam felt a little offended by the Count's lack of trust. He did not think the distrust was justified, for he had succeeded in everything that had been asked of him. A surge of pride swelled in his heart, causing him to stand taller and puff out chest. "I do not lie. I have found the Mad Raven's lair." He said again, louder and with more conviction. "It is where I told you. If you do not believe me, I will take you there."

Before Aldamar could reply, Ulam recounted his trip to the Silverwood and back. He spoke of the inn along the Western Pass, where the proprietor openly lamented the lack of protection. He then told the Count about discovering the ambush site, as well as the hidden trail through the forest north of the road. He spared no detail of what he saw, including giving an accurate account of the unguarded palisade with its decrepit defenses. Ulam then speculated the neglect was because the Flock believed their remoteness was more than adequate protection against intruders.

"Makes sense," Captain Karraman chimed in, "it sounds like they are so deep in the forest they don't expect us to ever find them." He grinned. "But we found the bastards anyway, it's just a matter of time until we can muster the strength to attack. Good work."

"Yes, excellent work," Count Aldamar echoed, though the tone of his voice seemed hollow to Ulam. "As Jalkett says, though, there is nothing we can do until we raise a warband. And I have told you on various occasions, this will not happen until after the beginning of the year. Perhaps in a few months."

Ulam felt the wind in his sails leave; he still had hoped Aldamar would agree to attack sooner rather than later. His only solace was knowing that he knew the way to the Mad Raven's lair, and by extension, Amantius as well.

"And I forbid you from seeking out your brother," Aldamar said as he stood from his chair. He crossed the room, as quiet as a ghost. "If you get caught, then they will know we know their location. It is more tactical to be patient and strike when ready."

Ulam grunted. *Waiting is more tactical, but he is mad to think I will wait. I'm leaving at the first opportunity. I just need to buy some more food and refill my skins of water.*

"Do you understand?" Aldamar's voice was stern, so much so Ulam shuddered a little.

"Yes." *I understand, but I will not abide.*

"Excellent." Aldamar walked away, eventually vanishing into the shadows of the castle.

"Come on, Ulam," Captain Karraman said with a jab to the shoulder. "Let's celebrate at the Bride's Oasis. You're probably starving. I'll even pay."

Every fiber of Ulam's being wanted to collapse into a bed and not wake for a week, but the mere mention of food caused his stomach to growl. He had rationed nuts and dry fruits for days, his limited provisions having dwindled quicker than he expected. The idea of freshly smoked herring or a slab of mutton sounded like a godsend to him.

Ulam followed Captain Karraman to the Bride's Oasis, where he devoured two plates of smoked fish that Korso had brought him. He had never been so hungry in his life, eating so quickly he choked a few times. He washed it down with two or three ales, the alcohol relaxing his muscles as it spread throughout his body. *I needed this.*

The meal had sapped the rest of Ulam's energy, his levels so low he questioned whether or not he had the strength to return to the barracks for the night. As he sat on the stool he remembered the tavern had lodging in the attic and thought maybe he would spend the night there. He reached into his pocket, pulled out a couple of copper coins, and tossed them on the counter.

"Will that cover a bed for the night?" He asked, too tired to care about manners.

Korso swept the coins off the bar and nodded. "Sure will."

Captain Karraman gave Ulam a sidelong glance. "Too tired to walk back up the hill to the barracks, are you? Surely you're not drunk already; you've only had three beers so far."

Ulam did not respond, he was too tired to care about forming sentences. His eyes were so heavy that his vision became blurred; he was no longer able to make out individual faces in the tavern. After Karraman departed for the castle, Ulam climbed the loft, each step feeling as though his legs were made of lead. When he reached his bed he fell face first onto the straw mattress, his body quickly fusing with the blankets. Within minutes Ulam slipped into the dream realm, so exhausted was he that he did not even take off his boots first.

That did not last long. At least not long enough.
Ulam stretched, his muscles warm but tired. He rubbed his eyes, picking at the gunk that had collected in the corners. A lazy yawn escaped as he rolled out of the bed and continued stretching. Afterward, he turned to the bed and frowned, discovering he had stained the sheets with mud and grime. He grunted. *Probably should throw Korso a couple more coins, just to be courteous.*
The Bride's Oasis was eerily quiet, the only sound a scratching noise from a mouse chewing on a table leg. Ulam approached the counter, left a few extra coins for the barkeep, and then exited the tavern. The air was chilly but not as frigid as it had been in recent months, something else for which he was thankful. He looked to the sky and smiled, for it was the first day in a long time that the sun was not cloaked in ash gray clouds. Though the sun's presence was brilliant and spiritually uplifting, Ulam could not enjoy the moment for long. *I need to return to Home and find Amantius. But how many more times can I disobey Count Aldamar?*
By the time Ulam reached the castle the sun had risen enough to bathe Silverwater in a golden aura, a heavenly sight for anyone awake to witness. In a way he felt special, as he seemed to be the only person in the entire city, the only one allowed to enjoy such a beautiful morning. He crossed the courtyard and entered the barracks, expecting to find people still sleeping. But much to his surprise the building was empty, even though a freshly built fire was crackling in the

fireplace. *I am not going to complain about a warm room, but where is everyone? Is there an assembly somewhere?*

Ulam tossed his backpack on his bed, not bothering to unpack its contents just yet. Aside from a dagger and a handful of nuts, there was not much inside. He took off the leather vest he had been wearing the last few days and slipped on some armor, the standard-issue made by the castle's quartermaster. He then grabbed the jade green axe he found in the Orc Sanctuary, taking a moment to marvel at the craftsmanship once again. Though he did not understand why he felt such a strong spiritual connection to the weapon, he could not deny that such an enchanting magnetism existed.

Ulam returned to the courtyard and immediately felt something was amiss. Like the barracks, the courtyard was empty as well. No one stood guard over the gatehouse, no one sparred in the training grounds. He climbed a watchtower and looked over the city, the hum of civilization reaching his ears as the locals began their day. But behind him, there was only quiet, as though the castle had been abandoned overnight.

Where is everyone? Ulam thought as he looked around. *Perhaps the Count will know.*

Ulam pushed open the double doors of the castle, the sound of the creaking hinges amplified by the silence within. Inside the hall was darker than normal, the only beacon being a solitary glow of a gleaming lantern near the entrance. As he entered he grabbed the lantern, using its light to illuminate a path through the darkness. Though he wanted to move cautiously through the halls, the jitters he had from the stale air and dreadful silence compelled him to walk faster.

Somewhere behind him, Ulam heard a sound. Quickly he turned around, pointing the lantern in the direction of the noise. He saw nothing as he waited, searching the edge of the lantern's light for any sign of movement. Deep inside he expected to see yellow eyes, and was quite surprised his mind had not played that trick yet. But he saw nothing, and a minute later he began walking again, backpedaling as he kept the lantern aimed behind him.

Suddenly Ulam tripped over something heavy on the floor, sending the big Orc crashing to the ground. Helplessly he watched as the lantern bounced across the hard tile floor, eventually stopping when it reached a wall. He let out a sigh of relief when he saw the flame burning inside, realizing without the lantern's light he would be lost in a maze of never-ending darkness. *Thank the Gods.*

Ulam crawled across the floor and gathered the lantern before climbing to his feet. As he stood he turned around, shining the light in the direction from whence he came. But he was too far away to see what tripped him, the object was still cloaked in darkness. Slowly he retraced his steps, searching the edge of the light for the culprit. *What the hell did I trip over?*

Suddenly he saw something in the middle of the hall, the flame from his lantern reflecting on iron. As Ulam drew near his eyes grew huge, while the arm holding the lantern began to shake. It was the body of a Castle Guard.

Ulam's breathing shortened, his heart threatened to break free from his chest. The cold fist of fear gripped his spine, paralyzing him from doing anything else other than standing still. He needed all his willpower to break free of the trance that shackled him, eventually willing himself to move. Immediately he placed the lantern on the ground and retreated into the shadows, hoping whoever or whatever killed the man had not seen or heard him. As he watched and listened he tried organizing his thoughts, as well as plan his next course of action.

What should I do? What can I do? Run to the town, get the City Guard and return? What of Count Aldamar? Is he still alive? In danger? By the time I rally enough people, the Count could be dead. No, there is no time. I must defend this castle, even if I must do so alone.

Ulam grabbed the axe hanging from his side, giving the green blade a few practice swings in the dark. Newfound courage spread through his body as he listened to the blade whistle in the air, its sweet melody remedying any remaining fears. In his mind's eye, he saw himself slay the Sanctuary fiend once again, and felt a swell of confidence invigorate his soul. *I have defeated evil before, I shall defeat it once again.*

Ulam emerged from the shadows, axe in hand, prepared to fight whatever came his way. Realizing he would need light to see his enemy, he methodically sought out lanterns and lit them, basking every room in a soft yellow glow. As he did so he saw the bodies on the floor, all of whom wore the purple and silver of the Castle Guard. Their corpses were covered in blood, many of the bodies mutilated beyond recognition. Judging by the puncture wounds in the armor the men had been killed with blades, even though their throats had been ripped out as well. While anyone else may have run away from this grisly sight, Ulam felt a small degree of relief sweep over him. These same deathblows were widespread the night they were ambushed in Silverwood Forest, and also at the site of the massacre along the Western Pass. Ulam knew who his enemy was, but more importantly, he knew he could kill them. *No monster or crazed lunatic did this, this was the work of the Mad Raven's Flock.*

He pushed onwards, checking for survivors in each room of the castle on his way to the grand hall. But

everywhere he searched he only found more death as the
blood-soaked bodies of the Castle Guards littered each room.
Though he would not allow the bloodshed to discourage him,
as he neared the entrance to the grand hall Ulam had a
moment of uncertainty. He was unsure if he alone would be
enough to defeat the Mad Raven's Flock, especially since
their numbers were a complete mystery to him. Once again
he debated whether or not he should leave the castle and
return with the City Guard, but he feared doing so would not
only lose valuable time but also leave the city unprotected. As
he stalled he heard the sound of iron striking iron coming
from inside the grand hall, followed by a death cry. Ulam
tightened his grip on the axe handle and pushed open the
doors, his decision made. *To battle.*

    The grand hall was in chaos. On one side of the room
was Captain Karraman and four Castle Guards, all protecting
Count Aldamar. Across from them were ten of the enemy,
wearing an assortment of helmets designed from the heads of
wild beasts. Corpses from both sides littered the area in
between, with a pool of blood staining the tiled floors red.
Without any hesitation Ulam ran across the room to Captain
Karraman, who stood in front of the Count with his sword
held high.

    "It seems we've evened the odds a little more, you
bastards!" Captain Karraman yelled across the hall before
turning to Ulam. "Damn, I'm happy you're here."

    There was a twinkle in his eye, a genuine enjoyment
of what was happening. Initially, Ulam thought Captain
Karraman had lost his mind, but as he stared across the hall
at his enemy he felt a flicker of excitement in his heart as well.
"I am too."

One of the enemies stepped forward. "Surrender Aldamar and we will spare you. This does not have to get bloody."

"Get bloody?" Captain Karraman almost choked on the words. "Get bloody! Look around you, we're already swimming in a lake of blood, and there's only one way this ends. With your heads separated from your shoulders! Follow me, lads!"

Captain Karraman charged the enemy, screaming a battle-cry as he crossed the room. Instinctively Ulam followed, raising his axe high as he roared like a lion. Before he could swing his weapon Karraman had already decapitated someone, the Captain moving with such power and grace that Ulam was sure victory would be theirs. The Orc barreled into a man wearing a helmet shaped like a stag's head, with antlers protruding from the top. He used his disproportionate bulk to send the man flying, bringing his axe down before his enemy could recover. Ulam then felt something heavy scrape against his back and was thankful the chain links of his mail turned away a blade. With almost no effort he swung his axe and shattered his new enemy's sword, the metallic rasp of iron filling their corner of the grand hall. Ulam then unleashed a flurry of blows until he had completely overwhelmed his foe, the jade green of his axe painted red with gore. He stopped for a breath and saw the man was on the ground, his neck exposed. Without any hesitation, Ulam swung his axe and watched as another head rolled across the floor.

Having been engaged in combat Ulam lost track of friend and foe alike, becoming completely unaware of what was happening around him. As he looked for his next victim he saw Captain Karraman fighting the last of the enemy, with a trail of headless corpses behind him. Of the four Castle Guards, three were dead from puncture wounds, while the fourth desperately clung to life. Count Aldamar was in a corner, his expression unreadable. Their eyes met and Ulam approached, feeling some degree of duty to stand guard now that no one else could. By the time he navigated the carnage the last of the enemy had been slain, one more bodiless head a gruesome decoration for the grand hall.

"Is that all of them?" Captain Karraman called from across the room in between breaths.

"Not quite."

Three more entered the room. One person wore a helmet with a wolf's head, one wore one with a cougar's, and the last wore a raven's.

Is that the Mad Raven?

"Three more, eh?" Captain Karraman said as he raised his sword once again. "Very well. Come on, Ulam. Looks like we got more fools with a death wish."

Ulam returned to Captain Karraman and stood in an attacking posture, watching as the three newcomers entered the room. They stopped when they saw Ulam and immediately began whispering amongst themselves. The person dressed as a raven then stepped forward and took off their helmet, revealing a young, beautiful woman with pale skin and jet black hair.

"Impossible…" A weak voice said from the back of the grand hall. "Do my eyes deceive me? This cannot be…"

Ulam did not want to take his eyes off the woman in front of him, though she appeared to be unarmed. He could not believe the voice behind him came from Count Aldamar, a man who was the epitome of self-control. He risked turning around, only to discover Aldamar was directly behind him, with disbelief and shock written across his face.

"No, Brother, your eyes do not deceive you," the woman replied. Her voice was as sweet as honey, her dark eyes shining bright in the flames from the lanterns. "I see you still do not understand how to properly entertain guests."

Brother? Is that Morganna? Thousands of thoughts shot through Ulam's mind, mostly pertaining to how this was possible. *Does this mean the Mad Raven is Aldamar's sister? I thought Count Aldamar killed her. Did he lie?*

"Morganna?" Aldamar said, his voice trembling. "But you are dead! I killed you myself! I stabbed you in the heart! How can this be?"

"Please, Brother," Morganna said with a sigh. "Always the dramatic one. I am sure you know how."

"No…"

"Ulam!?" A new voice interrupted from outside the grand hall. "By the Gods, Ulam, is that you?"

A fourth person walked in wearing a cloak made from a bear, a hideous helmet in one hand and a sword in the other. He had midnight black hair tied into a small ponytail at the nape of his neck and a full beard desperately in need of grooming. Dark circles had formed under his eyes, his mouth hung open. Though he was on the opposite side of the room, Ulam knew who had just called his name. He knew from the voice, the same voice he had heard his whole life.

"Amantius!" Ulam said and took an involuntary step forward, only stopping when he saw the wolf and cougar draw their swords.

"I've found you," Amantius said and began to run forward, "I finally found you."

290

"Stop." The man in the cougar helmet said, one arm holding a sword towards Ulam while the other grabbed Amantius by his cloak's collar. "He is your enemy."

"Let go of me, Movan," Amantius said as he struggled to break free. "Or I'll kill you myself, you son of a bitch."

"Amantius, calm down," Morganna said as she stepped back, placing a hand on his chest. "Movan is not your enemy, and Ulam is not ours. Everything will be fine, I promise."

Ulam stood perfectly still, seconds feeling like years. He waited for an opportunity to strike, to rescue Amantius. But as he watched his worst fears came to fruition, Amantius had clearly chosen the other side. Not only did his foster-brother not want to be saved, he did not feel as though he had to be. He saw Morganna's hand gripping Amantius' arm and noticed the way he reacted to her touch. He knew she had his heart and there was no chance he would choose the dry cordiality of Count Aldamar over her grace and charm.

"Which side are you on, lad?" Captain Karraman said, interrupting both reunions unfolding in the grand hall. "Are you with us, or with them?"

Amantius straightened, looking as though he was trying to say words that had not formed in his mind yet. Ulam could see the pleading in his eyes, begging him to join the Mad Raven. The thought disgusted him because switching sides would condemn both Captain Karraman and Count Aldamar to certain death. *How could I betray them after all they have done for me? They accepted me for who, and what I am, and even trusted me with some of their secrets.*

"Is it not clear, Jalkett," Count Aldamar said calmly, the previous panic completely gone from his voice,

"Amantius has chosen to think with a different part of his body. My question is, can we trust, Ulam?"

Ulam felt a flash of anger at Aldamar's words, though he realized they were not entirely inappropriate. It was only right to question whether he would still protect the Count now that he knew Amantius was fighting for the Mad Raven. Ulam did not have an immediate answer because he could not organize his thoughts to properly make one. Before he could make a decision, he needed to know the answer to one simple question.

"Why did you join them?" Ulam said. "Is the Count correct? Was it her beauty?"

"No," Amantius blurted out, "well, not originally. Sure, they captured me, but they also healed my wounds and so much more. They gave me shelter, they gave me food, and they gave me friendships. Just because the Countess and I are...it doesn't matter!" He stepped forward and pointed a finger at the Count. "He's the monster, Ulam! He murdered their entire family! You must believe me!"

"The Count told me she murdered their whole family," Ulam replied, surprised by the defiance in his voice, "Long ago she was attacked by some wicked creature in a cave and was corrupted by its bite. And then she slaughtered their whole village and feasted on the dead bodies of their neighbors." *That sounds insane spoken aloud. Maybe Amantius is right.*

Morganna began to laugh, each chuckle more vicious than the previous. "Is that what he has told you? That I killed our family and ate them? Brother, you always had quite the habit of exaggerating. No, my dear Ulam, he has simply fed you lies. He murdered everyone before trying to kill me, but his blade missed my heart. I even have proof." Morganna slid her dress far enough down to show the silvery scar just above her left breast. "And I would have died as well if it was not for Jaga, always faithful Jaga."

"Jaga?" Count Aldamar said, "Jaga saved you?"

Jaga. I know this name. He was the groundskeeper?

"Yes, I did." The wolf said as he removed his helmet. Though he was an older man, Ulam could sense the immense strength hiding behind the wrinkles.

"You have betrayed me too, have you?" Count Aldamar said, a small hint of anger in his otherwise restrained voice. He bent over and picked up a sword, testing it for balance. "Very well, if I am to be surrounded by traitors at least I will not die without a fight."

"Excellent," Morganna said as she stepped away, Amantius' arm entangled in hers. "This is why we have come. Ulam, I extend upon you the protection I have given Amantius. If you wish to join me then I will not have you harmed in any way. Your brother has spoken highly of you ever since he woke up in our village, and I would very much like to keep him happy as well." She signaled to her two other companions. "Jaga, Movan. Bring me my brother's head."

In a flash, the room erupted in chaos once again, Captain Karramar fighting the one called Jaga to a standstill. Ulam was pushed aside as Count Aldamar locked into combat with the person named Movan. He was surprised by the ferocity the Count displayed, his attacks as graceful as a butterfly's wings. Within moments Movan was cut down, Aldamar having used a combination of sword and dagger to slash him a dozen times over. In the other duel Captain Karraman was badly wounded by a vicious swing, blood streamed from a wound in his already hobbled leg.

Without thinking Ulam rushed to his friend's aide, determined to defend him at all costs. But before he could reach Karraman's side he felt Jaga's blade skid off the chain links of his mail. He countered with a strike of his own, one that was easily dodged. He was astounded by how fast Jaga was, especially for an old man in chainmail. Ulam swung wide again, connecting with a stone pillar in the middle of the room, sending an eruption of sparks shooting in every direction. Before he could recover from his swing he felt a blow to the back of his head, causing his legs to buckle and sending him crashing to the floor.

Ulam's world was spinning, his hearing hindered by a high-pitched ringing. He struggled to keep his eyes open, and when he could they would not focus. He was aware of Jaga's presence beside him, ready to strike, but Ulam was not worried about his impending doom. He had systematically failed everything he had attempted since leaving Accaria. He did not find any more Orcs, nor did he discover any of the world's ancient ruins. He failed to rescue Amantius, failed to defend Count Aldamar, and failed to protect a defenseless Captain Karraman as well. Worst of all, however, he was breaking his oath to Pelecia, and that broke his heart. *Forgive me, Mother. I do not deserve to live.*

Suddenly there was a scream beside him, followed by the heavy sound of metal hitting the ground. The presence that had been there was gone, replaced with a familiar shadow of purple and silver. A chorus of laments sounded, and then Ulam heard nothing. The world turned black.

Amantius...

Chapter 31
Amantius

How has this happened?

Everything had gone according to plan. They entered Silverwater before the gates closed in the evening, dressed in everyday clothes. When night had fallen Jaga and Movan had taken all but a few people to the castle, while Amantius remained behind with Morganna and a few of her personal guards. After a few hours, Jaga returned to say the castle was all but taken, only Aldamar and a small group of those loyal still held out in the grand hall.

"Was an Orc with them?" Amantius had asked.

"Not that I have seen," Jaga had replied, "Perhaps your brother is not here?"

Jaga had then escorted them to the castle, while Amantius split away so he could search for Ulam. He had checked every room thoroughly, including the bodies that were strewn about the floors. He had felt his heart stop every time he had spotted a new figure motionless on the floor, praying silently that it was not Ulam. He had been in the foyer when he had heard the sounds of battle coming from the grand hall, and had immediately rushed inside with hope and panic swirling in his heart.

And then he had seen him.

A whirlwind of emotions had stirred upon seeing Ulam, specifically relief, hope, and fear. He had been supremely confident Ulam would switch sides, that he would lay down his axe and allow Jaga and Movan to capture Count Aldamar. All he had to do in order to convince him was to tell him the truth, to tell him that Aldamar was a murderer and have Morganna validate his story. Ever since they were children Ulam had been the more logical of the duo, always making decisions based on facts instead of impulses. When presented with evidence from a firsthand source, he knew the Orc would see the error of his ways and join Morganna's cause.

But then everything had spiraled out of control.

Aldamar had flown into a fit of rage, striking down Movan like a farmer reaping wheat. He could not believe the strength, speed, and grace in which the Count had moved. Movan stood no chance, falling before he could pose any real threat to Count Aldamar. Amantius was a little ashamed that he had felt a small degree of relief and elation watching Movan die, but those feelings had been quickly subdued when his eyes had turned to the duel between Jaga and Ulam.

Amantius had tried to run to them both, to try to separate them, but he had been held in place by Morganna. Her strength had surprised him, because he could not imagine her lithe frame concealing such power. He attributed her sudden brawn to fear since Count Aldamar lingered nearby with blood-stained weapons, knowing firsthand the kind of superhuman power that fortifies the muscles when someone is in danger. A loud crunch had stolen Amantius' focus from the Count, followed by a cold dread that had instantly filled his heart. Ulam was on the ground, motionless.

"No! Stop!" Amantius had yelled until his voice became hoarse. "Don't hurt him! He's my brother! Jaga, please!"

He had watched the old warchief go from a hand's width of executing Ulam, to standing idle. Amantius had then let out a breath he did not know he had been holding, and felt relief wash over him like rain. His thoughts had then turned to Morganna, who was still standing beside him, her dark eyes frantically searching the room.

"Where did he go?" She had said, a touch of panic in her words. "Where is Aldamar?"

And then there had been a cry of pain, and Jaga had crashed to the floor beside Ulam. Count Aldamar then emerged from the darkness, a dagger dripping in blood.

How has this happened?

"Traitor," Aldamar muttered as he wiped the blade on a fallen man's cloak.

A sudden burst of rage filled Amantius. He wanted to rush forward, grab a sword, and place the blade deep into Count Aldamar's heart. He struggled for his freedom though, Morganna's grip seemingly made of the strongest iron. No matter how hard he tried, he could not escape.

"Let go of me!" Amantius demanded as he squirmed. "How are you *this* strong!?"

"Yes, Sister," Count Aldamar said, a smirk on his face, "Please enlighten us. Amantius may not be the strongest man in the world, but surely he should be able to break free from your grasp."

Aldamar's expression, and Morganna's hesitation, alarmed Amantius. He struggled a little more, not putting any real effort into escaping while alternating his eyes from brother to sister. *Wait. Something is not right. Does Aldamar know something I don't?*

"For all the reasons you are, Brother," Morganna replied. "I have the same gift you have, but you know this already. You knew this the second I appeared, did you not?"

Same gift? What the hell are they talking about? What kind of gift makes you a thousand times stronger, especially when you are as old as Aldamar or as small as Morganna?

"Gift." Aldamar spat the word. His face twisted; he was utterly repulsed by the notion. "It is not a gift. It is a curse, a prison sentence. Tell me what is so romantic about being confined to the shadows of a musty, old castle? To forever live in fear of being discovered by the common folk and hunted like a monster? What is so wonderful about forever battling these cravings, these wretched desires to feast on blood? Tell me, Sister, how is being a vampire a gift?"

"A vampire!" Amantius watched as Count Aldamar's eyes turned from their usual deep black to bright yellow. Two fangs protruded from his upper gums, saliva dripping from them. Amantius saw the muscles in Aldamar's forearm swell, slowly expanding until he could see the veins bulging under the skin. It was a terrifying sight, to watch someone who looked so frail transform into a bloodthirsty monster before his eyes. Amantius stood perfectly still, mouth wide open, in absolute terror.

"Yes, a vampire." Count Aldamar said, his voice as calm and collected as always. "I must say I am impressed; when we first met you suspected I carried some dark secret. As a sort of entertainment, I watched you search for clues around the castle, as well as eavesdropped on some of your conversations with your fellow Guards. Of course, I would never be so sloppy to be discovered by such an amateur sleuth, but I do applaud your tenacity. I have met thousands of people who had no idea, who so easily believed my ruse as an eccentric old man. I must ask though, how did you not realize she was a vampire as well?"

Somehow Amantius finally broke away from Morganna's grasp, either because she had loosened her grip or he finally found the strength to break free. He stood in between them, his eyes fixed on Morganna, hoping she would refute Aldamar's accusation. As he waited he felt a sickness growing inside, a rotten air taking hold of his lungs. *Please say you're not a vampire, too! Please don't let it be so!*

"I suppose I owe you an apology, Amantius," Morganna said as her eyes changed from pitch black to a shining yellow, while fangs slowly dropped from her gums. "I should have told you sooner. Alas, I was caught up in the throes of passion and could never find the right time. You must believe me, I never wanted to lie to you, to hide such a huge part of who I am from you."

Amantius nearly fell over backward, his legs turned to mush. His eyes flickered between brother and sister, both equally terrifying in their own right. Where Aldamar inspired fear through size and strength Morganna took on a more sinister look, her raven black hair highlighting the unnatural tint of her eyes. He looked across the floor at Ulam, his foster-brother still motionless on his back, and felt a wave of regret wash over him. *How did we get involved in this, Brother? How?*

"Darling," Morganna said, her tone as soft as velvet, though her appearance was ghastly, "I hope this does not divide us. I want you to be with me after this is all over, to help rule over this city and beyond."

He refused to look at her, focusing on her honeyed words, pretending she was still the beautiful woman he had known and not the nefarious creature before him. He thought about what she had said about the future, living a life with her in Silverwater. It sounded insane at first, but the longer he mulled over her proposition the more likely he would accept it. After all, he would be close to Accaria and could sail across the sea when the turmoil had ended. He would be with a beautiful woman and have strong children with her, assuming she was able to reproduce. Although he was not sure if a vampire could conceive, especially with a non-vampire, his lack of knowledge would not prevent him from trying. As her husband, he would have both wealth and power, two things most men desired above all else. Overall the idea had its merits, but there was still one unresolved issue that impeded his final decision. Ulam.

"What about my brother?" Amantius said, pointing to the Orc. "He just defended the Count and raised his axe against you. Will you forgive him?"

Morganna's face softened, though her fangs were still terrifying. "I forgave you, did I not?"

A sudden optimism shot into his heart. *That's right. I had fought against her, and now I am fighting for her. Very well. If Ulam is forgiven and allowed to live here, assuming he wants to, then I will be the next Count of Silverwater.*

"She is manipulating you, you fool," Aldamar said with a bitter sigh, like a disappointed mentor watching their pupil fail. "How can you be so blind? She is just using you to get what she wants, and then when my head is on a pike she will do the same to you. Although, she might feast on your blood first."

"Stop lying," Amantius replied, finding the courage to stand up to Aldamar, "You turned into a vampire first and then killed everyone, you even tried killing her!"

"And I did not succeed because she was a vampire before me," Aldamar replied. "This is pointless; you have already decided who to believe in this matter. It is a shame you have chosen her, Amantius Jeranus, your brother always spoke highly of you." He raised his weapon into a striking position. "Well, Sister, it looks like we must settle this once and for all."

Aldamar jumped across the room, his dagger flying at Morganna's throat. She sidestepped with grace, the thrust harmlessly slicing the air. She then grappled with Aldamar, the two of them rolling on the ground throwing punches and kicks. While on her back Morganna kicked up with her legs, sending Aldamar straight to the ceiling, crashing with enough impact to create a fissure. Somehow on his descent, he landed on his feet, looking completely unaffected by the blow. Calmly he wiped dirt from his arms and straightened his clothes, and then lunged at Morganna's throat once again.

As the two became locked in combat Amantius crawled across the floor to Ulam, cradling the Orc's head in his lap. Upon first glance he feared his foster-brother was dead, afraid Jaga had crushed his skull with the blow to his head. Amantius tried to place a hand inside Ulam's chainmail shirt to find his heartbeat, but the armor was too heavy for him to wiggle his hand under. Instead, he held his hand underneath Ulam's nostrils, releasing a sigh of relief when he felt long breaths grazing his knuckles.

"Thank the Gods," Amantius said as he gently stroked Ulam's hair. Warm tears slid down his face and onto Ulam's forehead; he had never been so worried about anything else before. Being so distracted with an unresponsive Ulam, the familial duel happening behind him did not even register in Amantius' mind. At that moment he only cared about Ulam, and how he was going to save them both.

Amantius heard a crashing of stone, followed by a cry, and turned to see Morganna had all but defeated Aldamar. Sections of the ceiling directly above them had broken apart, with two giant stone slabs having fallen on Aldamar's legs. It was a testament of the force both siblings possessed, the true ferocity with which they fought. Morganna was on top of Aldamar, a blade hovering inches above his throat, as he desperately tried to keep the iron from biting his flesh. Amantius noticed they both had a dozen cuts on their bodies, none of which bled, just silver scars adorning their pale complexions.

"I have waited so long for this moment," Morganna said through gritted teeth, trying to summon the strength to finish him off. "So many years of waiting, planning. I dreamed of this moment so many times, at least when I still could dream."

Aldamar's face turned purple as he struggled to keep his head attached to his shoulders. He opened his mouth to speak from time to time, but the words only came out as a vicious screeching. He was able to free a hand, punching wildly at Morganna, missing with almost every strike. As her sword slowly descended towards his throat, Aldamar began to squirm in hopes of avoiding the inevitable. As he did so his cloak unfastened, exposing even more of his pale flesh. Amantius knew it was only a matter of time until Aldamar met his demise.

Morganna shifted her weight, giving Amantius a better view of the impending deathblow. From his new vantage point, he was able to see exactly where the iron blade would cut through Aldamar's neck, a spot where the Count had two bright red dots. It was an unusual blemish on the Count's skin, their appearance further highlighted by his ghostly complexion. Amantius assumed they were bite marks, given to him by the vampire that had passed the gift onto him. His mind then turned to Morganna's body, finding it odd that she did not have the same markings on her neck. And he would know if she did, too, because he had seen her unclothed many times before.

Perhaps those aren't bite marks on Aldamar's neck. After all, I am far from an expert on vampires, Amantius thought as he saw the blade make contact with Aldamar's skin, but not deep enough to truly wound him. *Ulam would know why, probably. He has read so many books about vampires that he would know the truth.*

Amantius' thoughts drifted to Accaria, specifically to the last time Ulam had mentioned anything about vampires. They had been sitting in their secret spot on the side of Mount Meganthus on a lazy summer day. Although over a year had passed since that moment, his mind was able to piece together the memory.

What was it he said to me? Something about the red marks. Was it that they were passed on from vampire to vampire, like some families have round noses? Is it the mark of a new vampire? Or do the red marks stay on a vampire until…no…

Until a vampire turns someone else.

He had stumbled upon the words, not knowing how to react. He tried to deny it at first, tried to blame a faulty memory for the realization. But no matter how hard he tried, he knew that was what Ulam had told him. He could even hear the phrase coming from Ulam's deep, grumbling voice. There was no doubt in his mind.

Amantius removed the cloak from his back and folded it, creating a makeshift pillow. He kissed Ulam's forehead and then gently placed it on the cloak, the Orc's eyes still shut tight. He then crossed the grand hall, navigating the chaos of broken pillars and destroyed furniture, until he reached where Aldamar and Morganna were. Without thinking he approached Morganna from behind and pulled on the collar of her shirt, invoking her wrath as he did so. She snarled at him while displaying her fangs, a truly terrifying sight to behold. He felt his courage wane as he stared into her yellow eyes; a part of him fully expecting her to toss him aside as easily as she had Aldamar.

"What are you doing?" She snapped. "I have almost killed him!"

Amantius took a deep breath in hopes of fortifying his resolve. "Where are your red marks?"

"My what?"

"Your bite marks, from when you were turned." Amantius insisted. He knew he was walking a very dangerous line. To an extent, the questioning even seemed a little absurd to him, especially at that particular moment. "You have them, right?"

"They disappear with time," Morganna replied curtly. Her fangs retracted, her eyes returned to their usual color, and the rage that she had shown at first was all but gone. She was still irritated, though, with Amantius' questions being the culprit. "Sometimes, darling, you ask too many questions. Help me end this and we will talk about it. I promise."

Amantius nodded and grabbed a nearby sword, keeping his eyes on the Count. The man made little effort against Morganna now, his strength having been almost completely sapped from the slab of stone crushing his legs. There was still a defiance in the Count's eyes, the last bastion of emotion fueling his will to live. As Amantius approached he noticed something else, though, a more powerful emotion lurking in the depths. It was one Amantius had not expected, one that had caught him completely off-guard. It was the look of soul-crushing sadness, a look the Count reserved for Morganna. There was something in his eyes which struck a chord with Amantius, a recognition of unconditional love, in this case, for a sibling. Amantius knew the emotion well and realized if he were in Aldemar's position with Ulam on top of him, he would have been overwhelmed with sadness as well.

"That works," Morganna said while her fangs descended from her gums again. "I will hold him still. Just make sure to line up your strike. One clean blow and it will all be over, we can live together forever. Just me and you, my darling, the Count and Countess of Silverwater. It is so close I can taste it."

One clean blow.

Chapter 32
Ulam

Where am I? What is this?

Ulam was in a world of darkness; he did not know where or who he was. His body was falling, slowly twisting and turning. He felt like he was in the ocean, at the mercy of the waves, being pushed and pulled by the tide. Eventually, his descent began to slow as a legion of white streaks appeared from the blackness, circling him. They began to cling to his skin, holding him upright, until he had finally stopped. More streaks of white created a solid foundation beneath his feet, painting in the darkness like an artisan with a black canvas. Then the streaks began to create a bridge, stone after stone laid across an invisible gap, leading to a towering gate.

The white streaks disappeared, their work finished. Suddenly there was a burst of color, the entire fabricated world lit by some unknown source. The bridge was a rustic reddish-brown, the sky a soft shade of blue, and the ground a vibrant green with swaying grass. He did not know what to do, nor where to go. With the rush of chromaticity, he could see a radiant light shining above the gate, like a beacon directing a ship to shore. Without any deliberation, he began walking towards the gate, driven by the beauty he saw like a moth to a flame. But with every step, he felt an emptiness growing within him. At first, the feeling was negligible, but by the end the void inside had all but consumed him. He felt soulless, as though his body was a vase without any flowers.

Ulam was close enough to touch the gate; he could sense a powerful aura dwelling from the other side. He gently placed a hand on the bars before him and watched as gold wisps entwined themselves around his wrist. He pulled away, the wisps disappearing like smoke. He placed his hand back on the door and the wisps returned, circling him once more. He pushed the gate open, and stood in a room filled with rays of golden light.

There was a pearl silhouette in the middle of the room, as tall as Ulam and with a feminine form. It floated across the room as he entered, the golden wisps around his arms and legs melting away as she approached. Though Ulam had no idea what was happening he felt no fear, his capacity to feel having vanished. Without any hesitation the silhouette entered his body, filling the emptiness inside him. He could feel her in his mind, searching his memories, causing him to relive his life. He watched in chronological order his childhood and adolescence. spent mostly on the slopes of Mount Meganthus or with a book at home. He then watched his departure from Accaria, aboard a ship heading for the mainland, which eventually landed south of a city named Silverwater. He remembered the fight in the marketplace, followed by the house fire. He watched the ambush, as well as the night he spent in the Orc Sanctuary. He finally saw the battle in Silverwater, where the Mad Raven and her Flock had infiltrated the castle. His last memory being a fight with a man dressed as a wolf, and then finding himself here.

Sometime during this he remembered who he was, remembered that he was an Orc named Ulam. He remembered Amantius, Pelecia, Count Aldamar, Captain Karraman, and the little girl with the flower. He recalled the smell of lavender, the taste of ale, and the joy of laughing. A warm glow began to spread through his body again, causing him to feel alive once more. The craving to travel and adventure around the world had been rekindled, the desire to experience everything the world had to offer burned in his soul.

Then suddenly the pearled silhouette exited, leaving Ulam feeling empty once again. Whatever light she had provided abruptly drained from the fabric of his being, his memories and aspirations going as well. She looked at him with two golden eyes; a saddened expression formed on her face. Then she turned away, heading for the opposite side of the room, where a new door suddenly appeared.

"Wait," Ulam shouted as he watched, "where are you going?"

The silhouette turned back to him. "It is not your time quite yet." Her voice was celestial, unlike anything Ulam had ever heard before. "You have made your decision. Now go back to the world of the living."

Thump. Thump. Thump.

Ulam thought someone was playing a drum inside his skull, every beat vibrating through his cranium like a thousand thunderclaps. He struggled to open his eyes, his eyelids were as heavy as stone, locked in their place. In between the poundings, he thought he heard a chair scrape on the floor nearby, his ears hypersensitive to any noise. He had no thoughts, at least none that were complete; his mind entirely fixated on the crushing pain in his head.

He heard voices, distant and echoing. He wanted to turn his head to see who was speaking but he could not move, even his arms and legs refused to budge. He felt frustration building inside him, an anger burning with the fire of a thousand suns. He tried to open his mouth to shout, to scream, but little happened. All he could feel other than the throbbing in his brain was the vibration in his throat, where his yells had been stifled by immobility.

Ulam tried again, and again and again. To him, it seemed as though he attempted to move or scream a hundred times, all of which ending the same way. Then suddenly he felt a foot move, then his arm. Then he stretched both his arms, wildly punching the air before gripping the sides of whatever he was laying upon. He tried to move his neck, but a great pain ached in his muscles, keeping his head in position. Last his eyes opened, a surge of light burning his pupils all the way to his skull. The sensation amplified the constant pummeling in his brain, but at least he could see again.

With time his eyes started focusing, the bright light slowly retreating until it was relegated to the hearth burning in the corner of the room. Ulam immediately realized he was in the barracks, the surface he was laying upon being a bed. He tried sitting up but the immense weight in his head kept him shackled to the bed. He opened his mouth but no words came out, his throat too dry to do anything other than wheeze. Ulam tried time and again to speak, hoping whomever was nearby would hear him, but his efforts were in vain. He struggled so much that he began to cough, a horrible, burning sensation setting his already dry throat further aflame.

Then he was aware of a presence nearby, an unknown entity hovering beside his bed. It had been quiet on its approach, as silent as a ghost. having given away no indication of even being in the same room. For a moment fear passed through Ulam's heart, but it quickly subsided, being defeated with logic. *If they wanted to kill me, I would already be dead.*

"How nice of you to return to us." An eloquent voice said beside him. "Your brother will be pleased."

"Amantius?" Ulam managed through the burning coughs. "Where is he?"

"He should arrive shortly. I sent word when I saw you were beginning to stir."

Ulam heard the door crash open, the noise sending a new shudder through his brain.

"Is he awake!? Ulam!"

Ulam heard footsteps running across the floor and saw Amantius suddenly appear. He could see tears forming in his foster-brother's ocean blue eyes as their hands interlocked, the big Orc even struggling to keep his own dry. He felt a smile spread across his face like the sun spreading light at dawn, his world no longer cloaked in darkness. They were finally together again. *At last.*

"How do you feel?" Amantius said as he kneeled beside Ulam's bed.

"Like death," Ulam replied through a grunt. No matter how much joy their reunion was bringing, Ulam could not escape the hammering in his head.

"Well, you look the same too," Amantius replied with a grin, "don't smell any better either."

Ulam grunted and squeezed Amantius' hand until he began to whelp, the sound causing both to laugh. Meanwhile, the shadowy presence beside him passed a chalice to him, the smell of red wine drifting to Ulam's nose.

"Drink," the voice said, "you must be parched."

Ulam chugged the contents of his chalice without stopping to feel the burn of wine in his throat. The cup was refilled a few more times, each time Ulam finished before he actually tasted the wine.

"My thanks," Ulam muttered, "Not just for the wine, but for saving my brother as well."

"It is not I who saved your brother," the shadow said, "but rather he who saved me."

Count Aldamar moved into Ulam's vision then, a series of silver cuts and gashes adorning his skin. Of all the wounds, he saw a small outline spreading across the Count's neck, something he had never seen before. *Must have been from the fight. But who would have given it to him?*

"Where is the Mad Raven?" Ulam turned his attention to Amantius, who was looking away. There was pain in his eyes, a grief he was trying to hide. With one look he understood what had happened, or at least he thought he did. He might not know the means, but the end was evident.

"She is gone," Aldamar replied, a touch of sadness in his voice. The emotion surprised Ulam, but he understood. *After everything, ultimately she was still his sister.*

Ulam grunted and decided not to ask any more questions related to the Mad Raven. "How long was I unconscious for?"

"A few days," Amantius replied, returning to the conversation. "I thought you were going to die too. Everyone else did." The last words he whispered. He then let go of Ulam's hand and stood up, shaking off the dust on his clothes. "I'm going to get food for us, I'll be back in an hour or so. Rest, Brother."

Amantius then exited the room, leaving Aldamar and Ulam alone in the barracks. A silence settled over them, the Count sipping wine while pouring a little for Ulam. With every taste the alcohol quieted the drum march in Ulam's mind, providing him with enough relief to organize his thoughts. There was one that prevailed over the others, though. *How is Amantius still alive?*

"I can see you are not satisfied with Amantius' recounting," Count Aldamar said, his voice steady. "You wish to know what happened, yes?"

Ulam grunted. Aldamar proceeded to tell Ulam of how he struck down Jaga and then became interlocked in combat with his sister while Amantius stayed away. Ulam felt tears form in his eyes as Aldamar explained how Amantius held his head while he was unconscious, even amidst the melee. Finally, he explained how Morganna held a blade to his throat after he had been crushed by a broken slab of stone, only inches away from beheading him.

"I thought my life had finally come to an end," Count Aldamar continued, "Morganna was on top of me, pushing a blade down to my neck. You can see the scar she left as it cut into my flesh. Then Amantius appeared and began to argue with her."

"Argue?" Ulam repeated, not sure if he heard correctly. "About what?"

"Yes, argue." Count Aldamar leaned over the bed into Ulam's sight and pulled his collar down, exposing two red marks on the side of his neck. "Over these."

Ulam looked but did not know what he was seeing. *Freckles? That is a strange place, and allocation, for freckles. What are those?*

"That is peculiar," Aldamar said as he returned to his seat, "Those are what saved my life. Those are what caused Amantius to…"

"Kill her." Amantius' voice called from the entrance. "I killed Morganna, the Mad Raven. I cut off her head." He entered the room, bread and smoked fish in his hands. "She had tricked me. Led me to believe she was something she wasn't."

Ulam's eyes grew wide as he shifted them towards Aldamar. Everything began to make sense to him, like a thousand puzzles pieces finally fitting together. He remembered the vague conversation the Count and the Mad Raven had before the clash of arms in the grand hall, the story of how Morganna turned into a savage monster that had killed his family. He then focused on the red marks on Aldamar's neck, suddenly realizing what they were. *The mark of a vampire!*

Count Aldamar's eyes began to shine yellow, reminding Ulam of the fiend he had killed in the Sanctuary. A coldness shot through his veins, turning his blood to a river of ice. He began to shake and he reached for his axe, but it was not there.

"Easy," Amantius said, laying a hand on Ulam's shoulder, "you need rest."

"He is a vampire!" Ulam said, gripping Amantius' tunic with his free hand.

"Yes, you are correct." Count Aldamar replied, his voice balanced. "I am, in fact, a vampire, and so was my sister. Before you accuse me of leading you astray, or of betraying your trust, I have done no such thing. I told you the truth, many moons ago. My sister was bitten in that cave, deep within the Silverwood, by a vampire. She turned into one, growing ever more violent as time passed until she feasted upon our entire village. Myself included."

Count Aldamar stood, retreating into the darkness. His eyes turned back to their normal color, no longer reflecting the flames leaping in the hearth.

"In our struggle, she had bitten me, and with time, I too turned into a vampire. Of course, at the time, I was unaware of what had befallen me. With every day I felt a new strength in my body. I was able to run further, jump higher, and lift heavier objects. I no longer grew hungry for traditional foods, but I forever had an unquenchable thirst. I drank copious amounts of water, perhaps even enough to fill an ocean, but nothing would whet my palate. I traveled far and wide looking for answers, all the while drinking different concoctions, hoping anything would satisfy me, but nothing did."

"My uncle was the Count of Silverwater at that time. He was a fat man, as you can gather by the size of the castle's kitchen. He was quite old when I arrived, never having married or siring any children of his own. He was a drunkard as well, a glutton in every sense of the word. He received me when I arrived, and we spent days, weeks, months gorging ourselves over lamb, beef, fish, whatever he wanted. We emptied the cellars of every last bottle of wine, then imported more, and drank those as well. He liked me because I could drink from sunrise to sunset and not feel anything. I could eat all day, and never be full. When he grew ill he passed the title of Count to me, officially making me Count Aldamar the First."

"Aldamar the First?" Amantius said. "I thought you were the Third?"

Count Aldamar smiled, an empty, lifeless gesture. "Oh yes, I am that as well. I was Count Aldamar the First, Count Aldamar the Second, and now I am Count Aldamar the Third. Soon I shall become Count Aldamar the Fourth. This curse has given me an unnaturally long life, I am afraid. I am 172 years old."

314

172 years? And to think, Amantius was sleeping with his sister.

"172 years!" Amantius shouted, "That means…"

"Yes, Morganna was 168 years old." Count Aldamar replied as Amantius vomited.

Apparently, he just had the same thought. Though initially trying to suppress his humor, Ulam could not help but break out into a fit of laughter. He flicked his eyes towards Count Aldamar, who also had a mischievous smile on his face. Amantius gave them both a sour look.

"Every so many years I have Jalkett start spreading rumors about a child that I have had, who then becomes my heir. It is a ruse, of course, there has never been any child. In fact, I do not believe vampires can have children, at least that is what the consensus is amongst scholars on the matter. Eventually, my subjects accept they have a new Count with the same name, just with a different regnal number. In fact, it is almost time for Jalkett to spread rumors once again."

So Captain Karraman is alive. Ulam felt a swell of pride inside, realizing he had successfully prevented Karraman from being killed by Jaga. *But if the Count has used him before, does that mean Captain Karraman is a vampire too?*

"What if someone visits you, wouldn't they realize you are the same count as before?" Amantius asked. "Or what if they wish to see the child, your heir?"

Aldamar shrugged. "There are enough bastard children running around this city to fill that need if it should ever arise. As for not knowing I am the same man, it is not difficult to hide that secret since I rarely have visitors. Most people do not care, nor do they live long enough to suspect anything. This system has been working for quite some time, and I do not expect it to fail anytime soon."

"How long are you going to live?" Ulam muttered.

"Unfortunately, I do not know." Count Aldamar said with a sigh. "Perhaps I am immortal, assuming I do not have my head removed from my shoulders. That seems to be the most effective way to kill a vampire, though I have discovered an enchanted blade to the heart of a vampire will kill one as well. That is why both Jaga and the other one died without having their heads removed. The dagger I always carry with me," Aldamar retrieved an unassuming weapon from his sleeve, "is one such blade. I bought it from a vampire hunter turned caravan master a century ago. To test it Jalkett and I caught a vampire and stabbed it in the heart. The man did not lie."

"Captain Karraman is a vampire too, then?" Ulam asked.

"Yes, sorry, that particular detail slipped my mind." Count Aldamar said. "In the process of capturing the vampire, Jalkett was bitten. Together we share in this curse, which makes this ordeal a little easier on us both. If you look at his neck he still has the red marks as well."

Ulam nodded, feeling his neck hurt from the stiffness. He finally found the strength to sit up in the bed, leaning on the wall for support. All his muscles screamed for him to stop and the pounding in his skull returned, but he was happy his body was erect. It was easier to see both Count Aldamar and Amantius since they were sitting on opposite sides of the bed from each other.

"Those red marks are what saved my life," Count Aldamar said. "They only disappear if you spread the curse further. Jalkett discovered we can eat cow hearts and livers to keep away the thirst and hunger for blood, and that is why you went on that midnight excursion with him some time ago. Our cupboards were bare and we were hungry. You must believe that we do not wish to spread this curse to anyone. If anything, we would aim to eradicate it from this world."

Ulam grunted. *If he has suffered for over 150 years with vampirism and has not given into his unholy cravings, I believe him.* He turned his attention to Amantius, who listened with a stone-cold face but with interest in his eyes. "How did you know about the markings?"

Amantius' features softened as he gripped Ulam's massive, green forearm. "You told me, of course. You were reading that book right before we left Accaria."

Ulam smiled, his tusks shining in the firelight. "You were listening?"

"I do from time to time," Amantius replied with a matching smile.

"What do we do now?" Ulam said, turning his attention to Count Aldamar.

"The Mad Raven is gone, the people will rejoice with a feast. The weather is almost warm enough to travel again. I will raise a warband to go to my childhood home and demolish it. Amantius, if you wish, you can lead the expedition. The decision is yours, I will not hold a refusal against you. The two of you are free to do as you wish, I absolve you of any oaths to me you may have made, as well as any grievances I may have held. You will receive boarding for as long as you wish, and are always welcome in my castle. Jalkett and I are forever in your debts, gentlemen. If there is anything you need, please do not hesitate to ask."

Count Aldamar stood and walked to the exit, forever as quiet as a shadow. He turned and faced Ulam, his bright yellow eyes glowing in the darkness.

"One last thing," he said, his voice grave, "my condition must remain a secret between us. If I learn you have told anyone my story, I will hunt you down, even if you are my friends."

Ulam felt a shudder go down his spine; he looked at Amantius.

"At least he called us his friends."

Epilogue

I have made the journey south to Silverwater, situated at the bottom of our continent of Qerus. It is an ancient place, known around the world for its wine. The trip was an uneventful one, aside from the occasional traveler becoming motion sick while we crossed through the heartland's hilly terrain. I, on the other hand, loved the entire experience, often spending hours on the back deck of the caboose, taking in the world around me. I have never seen a more beautiful sunset than those which set in the bluffs of Redgate, nor had I seen fields of deer grazing happily on the lush vegetation beneath them. Though Hollowcross will always be my home, I cannot help but wonder if I have wasted too much of my life in dark rooms filed with musty books, instead of experiencing the world's vibrant riches. A man at the railroad junction in Eastlock even told me that he heard rumors of a set of twins working on a device that would allow people to fly. To fly! What an exciting era in which we live!

Back to the task at hand, I am not sure how different Silverwater is now compared to the time of the *Mad Raven's Tale*, though I can see the city is much larger. The northwestern gate mentioned many times over is no longer in use, in fact, the city walls barely exist. I have found some pieces of the wall, ruins covered in grass and vines, echoes of a bygone era. The only semblance of an operational wall and gate system is on top of the hill where the castle is located, just as it was in the *Mad Raven's Tale*.

As I walk through the streets I notice the homes here are mostly made of brick with tiled roofs. I see children

319

playing in the streets as merchants align the avenues to sell their goods. All in all, Silverwater seems to be a place of great joy, unlike the perpetual cloud of gloom that was written in *The Mad Raven's Tale*. I cannot blame the locals for their joviality, the weather here is as close to perfection as it can be. I have asked a couple of people if they have ever seen snow, none of which ever have, even the older denizens have no memory of fluffy flakes falling from the sky. This leads me to believe that whoever is responsible for writing the story of Count Aldamar and Countess Morganna had never visited this wonderful locale, otherwise, they would have known winter has never touched this land. I am also starting to believe that Amantius and Ulam, and all the events that took place in *The Mad Raven's Tale*, are a complete work of fiction. It is possible the story was rooted in some actual event, as many legends are, but had taken on fictional elements through time. Perhaps a rebellion had taken place centuries ago between siblings, familial power struggles are nothing new, but I doubt that an Orc and his foster-brother forever changed history due to their actions. I just find such a thing impossible to believe, not to mention there have not been any reported cases of vampirism in the past five or six centuries, and even those accusations were most likely made to further personal agendas. Regardless, I have come here for a reason, and that is to potentially locate volumes three and four of the *Accarian Chronicles*. And, maybe I will enjoy some local cuisine and drink.

As I climbed the hill to the castle the guards spotted me and asked my name and my purpose. I was able to secure entry by presenting my badge to them, which bore the insignia of the Academy. However, I must admit, for a moment I was truly worried I had just traveled the length of the continent only to be denied access. After all, how much sway could one of the Academy's apprentice mages possibly have on the other side of the continent?

Once through the gates, I began to take in the architecture of the castle, guessing by the style and materials it had been built only a few hundred years ago. This discovery disappointed me, of course, because I had hoped to find the castle to be the same as the one in *The Mad Raven's Tale*. Of course, that was nothing more than a delusion, because only a master architect could have built a castle to have lasted over a thousand years and still be habitable.

Upon entering the castle I asked the first person I saw to point me to the library, once again having to display my badge. An accommodating attendant led me through a corridor until we came to a large hall, all the while a guard hovered directly behind me. They were nuisances, what with their boots thudding on the tiled floor behind me, however, I understood the necessity. I suppose from their perspective espionage could be in order, though I find that is beyond absurd. I am here to uncover long-lost books, not secret plans.

I passed through an elaborate doorway into the library where I was shocked by what I saw. Rows and rows of shelves, as far as I could see, like a field of crops stretching to the horizon. I was overwhelmed by the sheer magnitude of the library, books upon books, scrolls and maps as well. A man could spend his entire life in this library and still only read a quarter of the books here. How was I to find a specific book amongst this ocean of literature?

"I can see from your expression this is your first time here," a scholar said to me, an elderly man with a serious face and dark eyes. His skin was pale like mine, clearly, he did not see the sun much either. "Tell me, what has brought you here?"

"I am looking for a book series," I said to him, "I do not know its proper name, I have just been referring to it as *The Accarian Chronicles*. They are multiple volumes, at least five that I know, and I only possess books one, two, and five."

"*The Accarian Chronicles* you say?" The old man said, his voice surprisingly strong for his age. "Unfortunately I can only be of minimal help," he led me to one side of the library, down a long aisle. "If I have such a work here, it is most likely in this aisle. This section is dedicated to myths, legends, and history, both local and distant. Perhaps there? Best of luck to you."

"My thanks." I turned to face the man, but he was gone. He seemed to disappear into the shadows of the library without a sound.

I set off, scanning the shelves for anything that looked relevant. At about the halfway point of the aisle, I noticed portraits were hung on the wall behind me, paintings of the Counts and Countesses of Silverwater. Centuries worth of rulers who governed this southern city, stewards of the single largest wine exporter in the world, as well as one of the main ports connecting the other continents of the world with Qerus. The first portrait I saw was of Countess Zerana, the first countess. After her was her son, Count Ferran, then her grandson, Count Lorient. Before long I found myself examining the portraits, no longer paying any heed to the books. I was surprised that there was a painting for each count and countess, a long tradition that seemed to go unbroken.

Countless names passed through my mind until I saw one I noticed, one that took me by surprise. At first, I could not believe what I saw, but as I investigated the portrait I came to accept it. Towards the back of the library was a portrait of an old man, with milky white skin and dark eyes. He wore a purple robe with a silver crescent moon emblazoned on the shoulder. Although I had never seen this man in my life, and he had been dead for a very long time, I knew exactly who was in the portrait. It was Count Aldamar.

Count Aldamar had been real. I moved to the next portrait, the man looked exactly the same, only in a different setting. I used the sleeve of my tunic to wipe the plaque at the bottom of the frame, where the name "Count Aldamar II" had been engraved. I moved to the next, and then the one after it. Every successive count was the same man with the same expression and features, except for Count Aldamar IV. The fourth Aldamar had a silver scar across his neck, looking like he had been cut at some point between Aldamar III and Aldamar IV. I could not believe what I had just discovered, the excitement giving me such a jolt of energy. I practically started running through the library, my eyes fixated on the portraits. I ran until the picture finally changed, no longer of Count Aldamar, but instead to a woman named Countess Mercet.

I caught my breath and returned to the last portrait of Aldamar, which looked very much like all the others. He still had the silver scar across his neck, and he still wore the same purple robe. Using my sleeve again I revealed the name at the bottom and gasped when I read the words. *Count Aldamar XXVII*

"Count Aldamar the Twenty-Seventh," I whispered. "But how?"

That was not the only question in my mind. If this was, indeed, the same man twenty-seven times over, then was the story of his vampirism true? I was inclined to believe Morganna was not the invention of some creative mind, now that I saw the scar across Count Aldamar IV through XXVII's necks. And if all this was true, then how did Count Aldamar die? What killed him?

"I guess I will never know," I muttered as I stared at the last portrait.

I turned my attention to one of the windows in the library and watched as a puffy white cloud slowly moved across the blue sky. I had come so far to see this library, to find answers to some of the questions I had been asking since I discovered *The Accarian Chronicles*. But this journey has only raised more questions, most of which will probably forever go unanswered. But there is one answer that, above all others, I desire to know:

Were Amantius and Ulam real?

ACKNOWLEDGMENTS

I grew up in West Virginia in a place called Point Pleasant, a small town nestled against the Ohio River a few hours away from everything. I could not be happier with where I was born and raised, because one of the greatest advantages of growing up in Appalachia was that I was surrounded by some of the best storytellers in the world. While kids in other parts of the country were at malls or at amusement parks, I grew up surrounded by people with vivid imaginations, armed with story-telling techniques passed down to them from their Scottish/Irish/Hungarian/German immigrant parents and grandparents. I grew up in the shadow of the Mothman, a legendary creature that terrorized the Point Pleasant area in the 1960s. There was also Cornstalk's Curse, named after the Shawnee warrior who allegedly cursed Point Pleasant with his dying breath while he was being murdered by European settlers at Fort Randolph. With every misfortunate event that strikes the area, Cornstalk's Curse gets another chapter.

There are hundreds of other local legends and ghost stories that can be found in other books, many of which have roots in the Old World. I only give these two as examples of the rich storytelling environment I was born into and molded by, as a way of explaining where my love for fiction originated. In this way I want to acknowledge the State of West Virginia, and Appalachia as a whole, for nurturing me in this way.

If I were to list everyone who has helped me along the way, I would have to add an additional 300 pages to the book. Chief among them is April Stevens, my girlfriend of many years, who has spent countless hours giving feedback and listening to me whine about having to do actual work. My close friend Joe Messmer, who was one of the first people to read the original draft of *the Mad Raven's Tale*, and has helped me navigate the waters of this whole process. Kit Dennis, who gave me food and shelter during the most vulnerable point of my life, and told me every day not to give up on my dreams. Cristina Tănase, the brilliant artist who designed the cover of this book, whose enthusiasm for this series is utterly contagious. Todd Gavin, an artist in New York City who, as a complete stranger, gave me his laptop after I told him that my computer was destroyed in a flood, with the caveat that I get published someday (I did it!).

And most importantly, Curtis "CC" McConihay. My best friend and brother, who tragically lost his life a few months before publishing. While Ulam is not based on CC in any way, the love Amantius and Ulam have for one another is definitely influenced by the brotherly love CC and I shared.

I love you, Bub.

About the Author

Andrew Walbrown is a guy who hates writing about himself, because Orcs, Dwarves, Trolls, Gnomes, and everything else is so much cooler. But if you want to know about him, he grew up in West Virginia and started college in his homestate, before finishing his education in Massachusetts. He earned a degree in history, and proceeded to use it to become a bartender, because unfortunately the Gods did not give him the gift of foresight. When he's not making the best Manhattans and Cosmos that you've ever had, he spends time over-salting everything he cooks, watching his favorite sports teams lose, and wishing that he could find a portal to an alternate universe where he could eat ice cream all day without gaining a single pound.

Also his cat is suuuuuper cute.

Made in the USA
Middletown, DE
04 July 2020